Anonymous

Talks and Tales

Anonymous

Talks and Tales

ISBN/EAN: 9783337119959

Printed in Europe, USA, Canada, Australia, Japan

Cover: Foto ©Andreas Hilbeck / pixelio.de

More available books at **www.hansebooks.com**

TALKS AND TALES.

A MAGAZINE

——PUBLISHED BY——

The Conn. Institute and Industrial Home for the Blind,

Nos. 334 and 336 Wethersfield Ave.,

HARTFORD, CONN.

F. E. CLEAVELAND, President.

Edited by Mrs. ELLA B. KENDRICK.

One Dollar a Year,   -   -   Ten Cents a Copy

PRESS OF
THE CONN. INSTITUTE AND INDUSTRIAL HOME
FOR THE BLIND.

Table of Contents.

BUST OF A LADY.

By permission of the American Bronze Co.

TALKS AND TALES.

VOL. II.   HARTFORD, CONN., FEBRUARY 1899.   NO. 5.

ALEXANDER CAMERON.

(A blind student at Yale Divinity School.)

I SHALL in this article attempt to give a description of the village of St. George and the country surrounding it. The town itself is about fourteen miles from Eastport, Maine. Eastport however must be reached by water. The village is situated on the Maguagadavic river about four miles from its mouth. The river empties into Passamaquaddy Bay, or St. Andrews Bay, as the people who dwell along its shore call it. At St. George there is a fall in the river of about fifty feet.

The chief industries of the village are granite polishing and milling. At present there are several quarries in operation within a mile or two of the village. There are three granite sheds running where the granite is polished. Granite of rather an excellent quality is produced from these quarries. At present there is only one saw mill in operation. The country all through New Brunswick like that in Maine is covered with dense forests except where the hand of man has cleared it away.

Owing to the timidity of the people in speculation lumbering interests are not carried on as successfully as they were formerly. During the Civil War in the United States lumbering was at its height in St. George. The village being so near the American line it furnished a favorite rendezvous for skedaddlers. After the War the Americans left and since that time the work in lumbering has declined. Several attempts have been made to establish a pulp mill in the village but thus far they have proven fruitless. Every time the matter is discussed, disputes arise in connection with the rights of water power. There is a sufficient volume of water pouring over the falls to run a mill of considerable magnitude but this power is at present utilized only for the granite sheds. The work in these sheds is exceedingly unhealthy. The average life of a polisher is only about seven years. The granite dust is breathed into the lungs and cuts the blood vessels thus causing death by bleeding. Several young men die in this way every year.

We have now mentioned the main points of interest in the village itself and so are prepared to glance at the country about the villages.

My knowledge of the country about St. George is based chiefly on what I gained in preaching tours which I made about the country last summer. My work was chiefly at four points, namely, Mascarene, which is at the mouth of the Magnagadavic river where it empties into the Passamaquaddy Bay; La Tite, which is on La Tite passage where the Passamaquaddy Bay empties into the Bay of Fundy; Back Bay, which is on a branch of the Bay of Funday, and Le Tang, at the mouth of the river of the same name and on Le Tang harbor which is a branch of the Bay of Fundy. This is one of the largest and finest harbors in America but it is little used. There is nothing to draw ships into it and probably never will be. It is about fifty miles across the Bay from Le Tang to the Nova Scotia shore. These places which I have mentioned are within ten miles of St. George. These places would all make excellent summer resorts if it were not for the fog which seems to hang about the salt water almost incessantly. There is scarcely a single day in summer when it it is at all uncomfortably warm anywhere along this shore, but the place is not sought out as fog seems to be very injurious to the lungs. In Passamaquaddy Bay there are many small islands, the largest of which are Deer Island, which is seventeen mile in length with an average width of two and a half miles, and Grandmanan, an island considerably larger than Deer Island.

A few miles from Eastport just where the Passamaquaddy Bay enters from the ocean Lubeck is situated, which is the place where the great mining swindle was practiced last summer. There are very extensive works built at this place and many more works which were just begun. The swindlers made a very fair show of being in earnest in their cheat.

The Bay and the rivers which empty into it abound in great quantities of fish. Herring is the principal fish, but polluck, haddock and cod are also abundant. The herring are caught in wiers which are around in all the rivers. These wiers are made of brush right in the river. They are usually from fifty to ninety feet in width and are arranged like cattle pens. There is an opening towards the mouth of the river. The herring enter the river with the tide and enter the opening. On each side of the opening there are wings built to gather the herring into the weir. When the herring are once in they do not understand how to get out again. When the tide is low the fishermen go out to the wiers and take the herring out with seines.

A good wier at its best will fish seventy-five hogsheads at one catch. This does not very often happen however even in the best of conditions. In the rivers the great fishing season begins about the first of August and lasts until the first of November. Along the shore of the islands the fishing season begins in April or May and lasts till the wiers in the rivers begin to fish. A good wier sometimes brings as high as four thousand dollars in a season to its owner. For the last two years the fish have not been as plentiful as formerly in the bay. In September last summer however the fish became so plentiful that the price was reduced to a dollar a hogshead and the fishermen refused to sell them for that price. They sold to the farmers instead who used the fish as land fertilizers. The fishermen are very improvident, and when they have had a good fishing season they squander the money so that they have as little left at the end of the season when they have taken in four thousand dollars as when they have only taken a few hundred. There are about fifty wiers in the Maguagadavic river and an equal number in the Le Tang river. The work of attending to these is very tedious and uncertain. A fisherman does not know what tide will bring him two or three hundred dollars.

In the middle of the summer the herring sell for from five to ten dollars a hogshead and any tide may bring fifty to seventy-five hogsheads into the wiers. It is very probable however that there will only be one or two hogsheads in the catch and possibly none. The faithful fisherman tends to his business however, every tide and meets repeated disappointments in a very unconcerned way. The wiers must be looked after once in the night and once in the day so that the fisherman never has a regular night's sleep.

Next to fishing, the sailor's life is the most important work which these dwellers along the coast follow. I am personally acquainted with eight retired sea captains. These men have all spent long lives on the water sailing to almost every port in the world. Many a pleasant evening have I spent listening to them tell of their voyages to Cuba, India, South America, Australia, as well as many ports in Europe. One sea captain told me of a voyage from Calcutta to New York which lasted fourteen months, several stops being made along the way.

We are liable to think now that the days of the sailing vessel have passed and been superseded by the steamboat, but there are still many sailing vessels afloat on the ocean. There are certain cheap freights, as lumber and fish, which it does not pay to have carried in steamboats. A large steamer would burn more coal in a trip from the United States to India than her cargo of fish or lumber would be worth. Sailing vessels are used to carry these cheap kinds of freight. A sailing vessel can go about trading from port to port which a steamer can not afford to do. Every family along the shore has its lists of the drowned, in some families the list is very large. These men have been lost either on the ocean or in the bay.

There are other occupants of the salt water besides herring that are found in the waters of Passamaquaddy Bay. Several seal made their permanent home in the Magnagadavic river. Occasionally one is shot. The regular inhabitants of the shore never attempt to shoot the seal and they are only molested by the sports who come to spend their summers along the river. These sports also have an opportunity to test their marksmanship shooting at the loon which are seen sailing on the surface of the water. It is very seldom however that a shot finds the bird waiting for it.

These birds are so skillful and so quick in their movements that they dive beneath the surface of the water after they hear the report of the gun and before the bullet reaches them. Three sharks have in time past entered the river and been immediately killed. A few years ago a whale found its way into the quiet waters of the Magnagadavic river but did not long survive in its quiet retreat.

As we ascend the Magnagadavic river above the falls, we meet with fresh water scenes. The falls in the river stops the flow of the tide and keeps the water above the falls fresh. The people up the river are engaged in occupations very similar to those which you find in any New England farming region. There are some very beautiful spots along the river. The principal of these is Lake Eutopia which is located five miles above St. George. I have heard people, who have seen the grandest scenes of the Rocky Mountains, say that they never saw a place which for quiet simple beauty could surpass Lake Eutopia. The lake is three miles in length and a mile in width. All about the lake are mountains from one to three hundred feet in height.

The country all about St. George is exceedingly hilly. In whatever direction you drive you may be sure your journey will consist of a continuous series of hills and valleys. The hilliest country is that lying between St. George and St. Andrew, the region known as Bokabec. On either side of the road are mountains rising to a height of three or four hundred feet while the road lies in a gulch between the mountains.

The country around St. George is more and more attracting people from the American cities during the summer months. There is a club house on Lake Eutopia which is in constant demand in summer. There is also a summer hotel at Bonny River, which is six miles up the Magnagadavic River from St. George. The chief summer resort in this region is the Algonquin hotel, at St. Andrew. This hotel draws large numbers of the wealthy classes from American cities every summer. The islands in Passamaquaddy Bay are also being occupied by summer hotels, and are attracting the interest of pleasure seekers. Campa Bella, Deer Island and Grandmanan are the chief resorts.

In this sketch I have attempted to give some idea of the country in the neighborhood of St. George. I am sure any one tired of the hot close cities would find this country a most refreshing spot in summer.

JIM'S BOQUET.

ADELIA M. HOYT.

THEY stood on either side of the orchard fence, Kittie and Jim. He was a tall, broad-shouldered country lad, she a typical country maiden. Behind her lay the orchard of Grandpa Williams, and just beyond stood the old-fashioned farm-house that had been Kittie's home ever since her parents died and left her, a wee bit of a girl, to the care of her grandparents. On the other side stretched the green meadows belonging to Jim's bachelor uncle, for whom Jim's widowed mother kept house. As to the fence, it simply marked the boundary line separating the two farms, and had never been a barrier to the two young people, although in the present instance it was between them; for Kittie Williams and Jim Harvison had been constant companions ever since they could remember.

By the same path they had gone to the little white schoolhouse in the valley, where they had learned the same lessons, often from the same book. As they grew older, he became her escort to singing schools, church socials, and all the festivities of their rural neighborhood, and their elders, looking on, nodded as if to say—why not? So free and constant had been their intercourse that scarcely an event or association of either life was not somehow interwoven with the other. Like two clear mountain streams, they were flowing side by side, so near that the same lights and shadows were reflected in them both. But just as these two streams seemed about to unite to form a single current, one took a sudden turn, leaving the old familiar channel for a new and broader one.

The snag that caused the turning was just a letter from Willis Williams, Kittie's uncle in the city. The rich banker, having married off his only daughter, and finding his home rather lonely, bethought him of his orphan niece. He promised, if she would come and live with him, to give her every educational advantage. And Kittie suddenly realized that it was for this she had been living these seventeen years; this had been fore-shadowed in all her day-dreams, and without it her life would have been incomplete.

After much talk, her grandparents reluctantly consented, and the day was set early in September. Her trunk was packed, and on this last evening before her departure Kittie and Jim met by appointment at the old meeting place down in the orchard.

There were so many things the girl wanted to say. She meant to thank

Jim for all his kindness to her, and to urge him to become a good and useful man, besides much other sisterly advice. Jim, too, had something on his mind, but like all last interviews the time passed and neither said what he or she intended.

The light faded out of the west, and the September twilight deepened. Long shadows crept in among the trees, while a timid new moon, low down on the horizon, cast sidelong glances at the couple from underneath the maple boughs. They talked of the last picnic, the apple crop, how soon the corn would be beyond the reach of frost, the need of rain for the fall pastures, and many like subjects, and then there was a pause. Kittie was just thinking how best to begin, when Jim broke the silence with a deep sigh followed by the remark, "So you're really goin' away to-morrow?" "Yes," Kittie answered. Another sigh from Jim. Then the girl laid a little brown hand on the top beard of the fence, and said, looking up half beseechingly, "Oh, Jim, don't look so blue. You make me 'most wish I wasn't going, and you know it's such a splendid chance. I mean to learn so much, and some day when I come back maybe you'll all be proud of me"

"Oh, I s'pose so," was the rather unsympathetic response, "but 'pears to me you know a plenty now for a girl, and as to your comin' back, t'aint at all likely you ever will, and if you do you'll be changed, much changed." And the young fellow sighed dolefully.

"Oh, Jim," Kittie's voice was full of real distress. "You know I'll never change that way, at least. not—not—" she hesitated, dropped her eyes, and poked the fence post vigorously with the toe of one shoe as she concluded primly, "I am sure I shall always remember you, Jim." A big, rough hand came down upon the little one lying on the fence, got all around it, and held it tight, while Jim leaned farther over, and asked earnestly, "I say, Kittie, we've known each other a good while, ha'nt we?" "Yes, Jim." "We've quarrelled, but we've always made it up," he went on, "and we've had lots of good times together," "Yes, Jim," came the faint response.

He continued, "But I ha'nt never said nothin'. special, now, have I?— though we've been good friends always—and you ha'nt neither."

"Oh, no, of course not, Jim; how very silly to think of such a thing," and Kittie laughed a little hysterical laugh, and tried to draw away her hand. But she did not succeed, and Jim continued, soberly, "I dun know 'bout it's bein' silly. Maybe 'tis and maybe 'tisn't. If you'd stayed here right along, maybe—but—well, as I's guin' to say, I ha'nt never said nothin' special, and I ha'nt goin' to now. If you ever come back there'll be lots of changes, I reckon, and I want you to go away as free—as—" he cast all around him for a fitting simile, but finding none, ended with another doleful sigh.

The girl's heart was beating very fast. She had always known that she liked Jim, now she knew that it was something more.

Just then, if he had said that "something special" of which he hinted, Kittie would, without doubt, have willingly renounced all her dreams of the future and been content to stay with Jim on the farm.

But fortunately for them both, he said no more, and she, lifting up her head, said half tearfully, "Thank you, Jim; you are very good to me, you have always been, and I shall never, never forget you." Their eyes met, and somehow they read each other's hearts.

Was it the soft September twilight that cast such a halo about their faces? or was it something from within?

***   ***   ***   ***   ***   ***   ***

It was the class day at one of our Western colleges. The exercises of the afternoon were over, and the students scattered in groups about the campus were discussing the programme.

The senior flag floated proudly from the flag staff on top of the main college building, despite the efforts of malicious juniors to drag it down. Noble forest trees, that had been spared when their companions were cleared away to make room for this temple of Minerva, cast a welcome shade across the deep green of the velvety grass. To and fro trooped gay young people in their holiday attire, with here and there a grave professor unbending to join in the mirth. And over and around all were the blue sky, balmy air, and bright sunshine of a perfect June day.

One group seemed more enthusiastic than the rest. The tall, graceful young woman in their midst had been the star of the afternoon, and was now very modestly, but with evident appreciation, receiving the many compliments paid her.

As she stood there in her dress of snowy white, her abundant black hair waving back from a face full of intellectual strength, and womanly sweetness, Kate Williams made a pleasing picture.

So thought a stranger as he came slowly up the street, and pausing at the college entrance, addressed a group of freshmen standing near. His manner and appearance plainly bespoke the uncultured countryman, and the students eyed him critically, while one asked in a rather incredulous tone, "Did you say you wanted to find Miss Williams, Miss Kate Williams? There must be some mistake." But on being assured that was the name, he pointed out the young lady, and curious glances followed the stranger as he moved up the walk.

"Miss Kate, some one wishes to speak with you."

The crowd parted, and Kittie and Jim looked into each other's faces after five years of separation. She knew him at once. That honest face and those blue laughing eyes could belong to no one else.

There was the same awkward, half defiant manner that Jim always assumed in the presence of strangers. Kittie told herself that he had not changed in the least, yet she was glad to see him.

She told him so, as she held out her hand, and her dark eyes spoke even more eloquently than her words. Then turning to those immediately around her, she presented him as an old friend.

"You will come home with me," she said. The crowd parted, and few dared even to stare, or look surprised, as the two passed out of the grounds together.

"I was in the city, and just thought I'd hunt yu up, and see if yu'd remembered a feller like me," Jim said as they walked along. Kate answered that she was very glad he did so.

"My, but this is a perty place," he said, looking round him. Then turning to his companion he remarked, "Seems to me you've grown to match it. Sort of looked as if yu belonged here. Dun know as I'd huv known yu, but you did me," he concluded with a queer sort of smile. "Yes, I think I should have known you anywhere," was her reply. Jim had well expressed it, when he said that Kittie had grown to match her surroundings. These five years had revealed wonderful possibilities to the simple country girl.

The atmosphere into which she had been transplanted had been like dew and sunshine, and in it the flower of her nature had expanded, strong, pure and beautiful. She had drawn nourishment not only from books but also from life. In her uncle's home she had every social advantage, and whether from early training, or something inherent in herself, society had not spoiled her.

Within a year after coming to the city, both her grandparents died, so that Kittie never returned to the farm. She and Jim had never corresponded. Kittie heard that Jim's uncle married, and that Jim and his mother had moved away. That was all she knew.

But the memory of that night in the orchard had remained, sweet and fragrant, like some flower pressed between the pages of a book.

Many were the leaves of life she had turned since then, but somehow it had perfumed them all. She had thought little about their ever meeting again. Indeed, he had become more of an ideal than a real personage. But now the meeting had actually occurred. Here was Jim in flesh and blood; Jim, rough, uncultured, but as good as ever—what should she do with him?

They sat in her uncle's parlor, and talked of old times and of people they both knew. He asked her to sing, and she did so, choosing a simple song that seemed to please him.

Once she caught him looking at her in a way that brought the color to her cheeks, but in a moment she was herself again, cool and composed. "Well, Miss Kittie," Jim began presently—he used the old familiar name, prefixing the "Miss" with a tone of great respect—"I s'pose yu've got a heap of edycation; now I'd like to know what you mean to do with it? that is, if yu don't mind tellin'."

"Certainly not," Kittie answered. "I have just finished the college course, but that is only beginning, you know. I have chosen a profession, and expect to spend two years in the study of law, and then enter on my life's work."

Jim whistled softly. "Well, now," he said, "that sounds like business; sure yu ha'nt no notion goin' into partnership with any of these fine lookin' chaps round here?" "None whatever," she answered. "Look here, Miss Kittie," Jim said, growing very earnest, "I alwas felt somehow as if you and me wuz jest made for each other. You liked me once, I know, and I—well, I thought a sight of you, and I ha't changed my mind one bit; but I reckon there ain't no show fur the likes of me long side of law and them things; now say, is there, Miss Kittie?"

Some girls might have laughed at his blunt way of putting it, but not Kate Williams. She saw the wistful look in his eyes, and knew that he was in earnest. Besides, his words touched a responsive chord in her own heart. The love that had lain silent so long found voice and pleaded Jim's cause.

After all, was there anything better in life than love? There were so few true hearts—ought she to refuse this one?

But only for a moment did she hesitate, then another voice whispered, "No, you would not be true to him, nor to yourself. Even though you love him, for love alone never made lasting happiness; there must be sympathy and congeniality." And Kittie answered with gentle firmness, "Yes, I did like you once, and I have never found any man I liked better, but I couldn't marry you now, it wouldn't be right.

"Education does make a difference. It is not that I am better than you, but so much has come into my life of which you know nothing. We could not enjoy the same things, and might soon tire of each other. I believe many married people are unhappy just for this reason, they have little in common and must live most of their lives apart. Oh, my friend, how often I have wished for you to have the same advantages that I have enjoyed; you would have improved them so well. Perhaps it is not too late even now. Many young men of my acquaintance have worked their way through college, who hadn't half your energy and ability. Will you not try it?"

The girl had spoken rapidly and with much earnestness, and when she finished, James Harvison was standing in front of her, looking eagerly into her face. "And if I should, what then?" he asked, "would there be any chance for me then, Miss Kittie?"

"Oh, I didn't mean, I—I wasn't urging you for that," stammered Kittie in confusion. "I know that," replied the young man, "but I want your answer." "Why, as to that," said Kittie, "you know you might change your mind by that time, but your education would be its own reward, and I wish you would try."

"Thank you, Miss Kittie," Jim said, "I shall take your advice. Who knows but I shall turn out a lawyer, too? At any rate you will hear from me again. Good-by." And before Kittie realized it, Jim was gone.

The next morning dawned warm and close, as all commencement days are sure to be. The college auditorium was crowded to its utmost capacity. The speaker was a man of considerable eminence, but his scholarly address received little more than passive attention. At its close he was heartily applauded, and then a flutter of genuine interest swept over the audience, as the heads of the various departments brought forward their graduates and presented them to the president to receive their diplomas.

Then from all parts of the room came numerous floral offerings, besides books and other tokens of friendship. Many of these found their way to where Kate Williams sat, and among them was one that attracted special attention. It was a large boquet.

Most of those who saw it only thought it beautiful and striking without knowing why. A few, with more artistic sense, perceived that it was a rare combination of the old and the new. There were the old-fashioned flowers such as grew in Grandma Williams' garden, side by side with the rarest products of the florist art. There were bright hollyhocks and geraniums and costly roses, wood violets and German pansies, feathery larkspur, golden marigolds, and rich carnations, delicate wild blossoms of all kinds, and sweet strange flowers. The effect of the whole was charming beyond description. A card attached bore the name of James Harvison, written in a bold, clear hand. "Dear old Jim," Kittle said to herself. "How nice of him to remind me thus of my old home while not forgetting the new."

"I wonder if he really thought of that?"

She meant to express her appreciation, but when the audience dispersed, Jim was nowhere to be seen, and Kittie walked home a little perplexed. On the table in her room she found a large envelope lying addressed to herself in the same bold handwriting.

She tore it open hastily; but was again disappointed. What she saw was a programme of commencement exercises, the following week, at a college some fifty miles distant. "Who could have sent me this?" she said as she turned it over and glanced at the list of graduates. Then she sank speechless into the nearest chair, for the first name on the list was that of James Harvison.

Could there be another by that name? No, she was sure there was not. Presently she picked up the envelope that had fallen to the floor, and a letter fell out. She opened it and read:

My Dear Miss Kittie:

I hope you will forgive the part that I have played for the sake of old times, and the purpose I had in view.

I, too, have been in college for the past four years and next week shall graduate with honors. I have kept watch of you all the time. Some times it has been hard to keep silence, but I had determined to do it. I came to you yesterday, to learn whether or not my old time friend had been entirely supplanted by the brilliant college graduate. To serve my purpose better I assumed as nearly as possible the manner and appearance of the country Jim you left five years ago. I thought if you had forgotten me, or were ashamed to take me by the hand in the presence of your associates. just because you thought me less cultured than they, then I should know that you had wholly changed, and I would go away and treasure the memory of my little schoolmate as of some one dead and gone.

Well, you know the result. I found you changed, yes; but only as flowers change from bud to blossom.

In the boquet that I sent you this morning I have tried to symbolize this change. The girl has grown into a woman, retaining all the simple, natural graces of mind and heart; while adding to them those that come from culture, study and experience.

I do not think we ever change radically, we only grow.

Your cordial welcome gave me courage. Perhaps I risked a good deal in saying what I did to you, but your answer showed your common sense, and I admire you for it; however, I shall not accept it as final.

But for the present I only ask to meet you on equal ground and let you see what changes time has wrought in me.

Strange as it may seem, I too had already chosen the law for my profession. I am obliged to leave the city by an early train, but shall see you soon. Till then I am, *yours truly*,   J. H.

The rest of our story is quickly told. Kate and James were classmates for two years in the law school, and when admitted to the bar and ready for business decided to form a partnership, and the firm goes by the name of "Harvison & Harvison."

For James Harvison has grown broad-minded in many ways, and no longer thinks that a girl needs less education than a boy, for as he said to his wife the other day, "The world needs just such women as you, with courage, heart, and brain to defend the right and plead for justice without losing one jot of their womanliness—women who will not change their sphere but only broaden it."

Among Kittie's choicest treasures, kept sacredly apart from law documents and the like, is a picture made by an artist friend. It is in natural colors, and faithfully represents Jim's boquet.—[Woman's Journal.

A POST-GRADUATE HONOR.

GRACE BLANCHARD.

THE minister was giving out the notices.

They seemed to Helen Graham a trifle provincial. The sermon, too, had not given her the mental gymnastics she craved. She missed having a note-book in her hand; for she was just out of college, and her attitude towards the world was still that of receiving. She did not yet realize that the intellectual bow is the one of all others which must not be kept continually bent. She was neither well nor happy,—not well, because, she had overstudied getting her degree of A. B., and not happy, because she wanted the post-graduate honor of attaining to the degree of A. M.

As the minister read the calls to attend benevolent society, Alliance association, and parish fund sociable, Helen pondered how she could coax her father to let her go abroad to study. But she was the only one left to Dr. Graham of a family of wife and children, and to have her in the lonesome house after four years was a great comfort to him, and it seemed as if he could not let her go again. He was a famous old physician, but he did not understand the case of his little girl. He fitted up a large room, opening from the side entrance, as a library for her sole use; and laughingly called it her office, as it was remote, like his own consulting-room, from the rest of the house. And there he expected Helen could finish her education and grow as wise as she pleased—when he was out on his rounds; when he came in, he must have her to pet and tease. And Helen, who had ranked at college so high as to be talked of for the European fellowship, which, after all, *must* be kept for poor girls, wailed, "Why was I born rich?"

She knew just what she should make the subject of her post-graduate work. All her father's love for the theory of medicine and for prolonged laboratory work, which had been unindulged because of his hourly rush of calls, had been made over by inheritance to Helen, his baby. She was particularly fascinated with a certain germ; and, if she could only go to study it in its native country, and prove it to be the cause of the appearance of bloody sweat in the old miracles, she would be made master of arts as soon as the ink on a diploma could dry. Dear, dear! If Anna had not married and left her father, *she* could; and she was quite cross with this big sister by the time the minister closed his notice with:

"Those young ladies of the congregation who are interested in forming a band of King's Daughters are asked to meet with Miss Eva Perrine, next Wednesday afternoon, at four o'clock."

"Do you not like E. E. Hale's work, Miss Graham?" inquired the pastor, as he overtook her on the way home from church.

"Hale's works?" she echoed, misunderstanding, and never thinking there could be any but a literary aspect to the question. "Indeed I do; his 'Man without a Country is—is'"—etc. And she went on criticising so cleverly that her door was shut behind her before the minister recollected his intention to ask her to consider herself one of the young ladies alluded to in the last notice.

And on Wednesday afternoon, at four o'clock, Helen was lost to all outside claims, as she browsed in the reference room at the public library, and tried to find if Mrs. Jameson, in her "Sacred and Legendary Art," alluded to the miracle she was studying.

There were, therefore, seven instead of eight who met at Eva Perrine's. Their platform was already made, and perfect with its four planks:

> "Look up and not down,
> Look forward and not back,
> Look out and not in,
> And lend a hand."

There was, then, nothing to do but elect the three other members to make the "Senior Ten," which they proposed to be.

Helen could have helped them much by her knowledge of parliamentary rules, learned the year she was president of her class at college; but as it was, they said, if they wanted to, "I move this vote," and had a "real good time."

The minister's pretty young wife was first suggested as a member.

"She is in everything: let's be different, and not ask her," mutinied Ella Clark.

"I think we would better have her," said Frances Upton. "My mother says people and clubs ought not to try to be odd, that everybody has angles enough without trying."

That settled it, for Mrs. Upton was the one woman the girls united in admiring; and it was voted to extend a call to Mrs. Atwood, the pastor's wife.

"Helen Graham ought to belong," suggested Ella.

"Of course she ought," assented Eva. "She ought to be here this minute, telling me how to conduct this meeting."

"Helen feels above us since she went to college," Ella ventured. "She knew this meeting was called, and I saw her in the library as I came by."

"Yes," snapped the spoiled wit of the circle, "Helen's brain is on the search like an electric light, but her heart penetrates about like a tallow-dip."

"She isn't very well," put in the peace-maker.

"Well, this Ten is to be nothing if not practical," summed up Frances. "And last Sunday, when we were asking to whom the pulpit flowers would better be sent, Helen was fussing to know whether they were staminate, or pistillate, or something; and Nina Smith knew that old Grandsir White's senses had all left him, except eyesight, and that he doted on flowers. So I move that we have Nina for our tenth. Helen could tell us what elements a right-minded soup ought to have; but Nina could make it anywhere that oats, peas, beans, and barley grow."

And Helen Graham was blackballed. That did not trouble Helen. She was not likely to pay much heed to the mental processes of girls to whom she had written frequently in Freshman year, but to whom she had sent only a Commencement invitation in Senior year. She could hardly tell Susy Perrine from Eva now.

Dr. Graham would have stoutly maintained that it was a joy to have Helen around the house, and a relief to feel she was not able to fly away again just yet; but that was the father in him speaking. As a physician, he noted her drooping, and bought a lovely new carriage for her daily airing. He hardly realized that the house was not cheerful, though it now backed a bakery and overlooked a bargain store. The block it was in had been known as Brides' Row when he brought Helen's mother there, and it still held its charm for him. What ailed the child, now that she had gotten over her longing to take a degree abroad? She had simply buried the wish deeper when she saw how its expression hurt him, and we all know how an intangible disappointment, shut up in the heart, makes that organ tangibly weaker.

As Helen drove listlessly about, she often passed groups of bright-faced girls; and, if she had noticed, they often were carrying something which she could have offered to carry for them,—an umbrella-stand for ferns at the Home Mission dance, a huge flag for the Harry Wadsworth fair, a banquet lamp for a fancy table at the Lend-a-hand's sale.

But Helen only bowed; and thought: "How can they find that interesting?" And the girls bowed, and thought, "Selfish thing!" One was mentally reviewing a term's study of comparative religions; the others were practising the only kind they knew anything about.

And yet Helen was so pretty, and so sweet, and so dismal, and, at last, so sick!

It was not many hours after she could not get down to breakfast, one morning, before her heart seemed failing her; and a cool, strange doctor, not the anguish-stricken father, was keeping up its faint flutter by every known device, and Sister Anna had telegraphed that the instant she could leave the new baby she should start.

The King's Daughters, seeing the Graham's horses exercised daily without an occupant in the carriage, grumbled healthily a little, at first, over such a waste of opportunity, and then said perhaps Helen was ill,—they had seen a strange buggy there.

So the officers of the Ten went, as was their duty, to inquire, and, learning that Helen was sicker than their worst case in a back alley, and much more forlorn than there, where the neighbors dropped in, they began, as was their custom, to think what they could do for her.

The president took her samples of all the spring goods she had received from New York and Boston. The vice-president sent her a book of happy pictures. The treasurer loaned two kittens; and the secretary painted a different letter prettily on six fresh eggs, made a birch-bark nest full of sweet-grass, and Helen rearranged the eggs till she saw that they spelled "H-e-a-l-t-h." The musical member played her violin softly in the hall below, and the jolly one hunted up the paper dolls with which she and Helen used to play; there was one with a home-made face and a ball dress which had been fondly named "Helen Graham," and which made her laugh and .augh now. Frances made a dozen powders, with very professional directions as to taking; and inside the different ones she put a bright conundrum, or a loving word, or an item of local interest from the paper. And Frances' mother sent a growing plant.

Every day the gifts kept coming, fulfilling their mission of making Helen feel herself a centre of loving interest, so that she could wait more patiently and happily for Sister Anna's coming. And Helen, who could not think with her head—for her brain could not now stand anything stronger than a Prudy book—thought with her heart—and that is possible—about the different givers, till each stood out with an interesting personality, and Eva did not seem like Ella, or Frances like Nina, any longer.

As soon as Helen was able to sit up, she looked for the girls from her windows; and now, when her own back ached, she noticed that they were tugging great parcels in their philanthropic zeal, and she resolved that, when she got well, she would ask if she could not do errands for them. It was not many days before another layer of self-absorption peeled off; and she realized that she need not wait till she was well, but could that very day put the carriage at the service of the Ten.

There was a Convalescents' Home to which they often went: and Helen's bright wits, no longer tangled in Greek roots, had a funny time planning how she could make an old doll of hers, that needed a new head, to be even convalescent itself, a life member of that little Home, and pay the $35 for its becoming such. Dolly made a ripple of amusement that spread and spread; and shortly a wealthy woman furnished a room finely at the Home for the accommodation of Miss Dolly and another member.

Helen regretted, now, that notifications of clubs and meetings had stopped coming to her. Dr. Graham felt a little worried about her sanity when she asked to have him read aloud the town topics from his evening paper. But it became a pleasant evening custom, for in the first reading was the intelligence that the King's Daughters were to give a box luncheon to the newsboys. Whereupon Helen had Martha, the cook, come up beside her sick chair, and told her to take as much hearty fine food as she had exchanged for gruels the past months, and make it into lunches, exactly alike for the box party. And Martha, the cook, sniffed, "Lor, Miss Helen, yon never et nothin' noway," and went down and cooked a ham and a tongue and a turkey.

And the next day after the boys ate even the crumbs that fell, the Ten threw kisses up to Helen's window; and her eyes filled at this, which looked very much like being loved. Then the miserable little thought crept in: "They like what I can do for them; but, oh! I want them to care for me! But I never walked for them when I was tired, or sewed for them when I wanted to read. And to think I thought it was awful that Eva had not read 'Social Evolution!' There they go now—the dear things! I wish they had asked me to join." But, after many days, this cry came to be the exceeding humble one, "I wish I were unselfish enough to join."

Sister Anna arrived by this time, and was a great tonic; for she had always known the lessons which Helen was just learning.

"Of course, Helen," said Anna, "I always said your head was up in the clouds,—that so much of you never left heaven to come to this family. And you have been fretting yourself sick to study abroad, dear? Well, let me be the one to think about that. Here's the last *St. Nicholas* I have bought to send the children."

By fall Helen was still delicate; and there came on a very rainy season, so that she became one of the shut-ins, and it occurred to her new perceptions that the Senior Ten must have had hard times splashing around to one another's houses. There was her own den down stairs, sequestered, unoccupied, and right on the line of electrics. Why not offer it to the Ten for their meetings? She straightway had Sister Anna tender the use of it; and on the next Wednesday had the satisfaction of hearing the girls tiptoe in, and then laugh delightedly after they were in. It seemed to her all ten must have turned out. If she only could have seen them enjoying her quarters—two in the hammock, three on the couch, one in the steamer-chair, one at her desk, tall Ella Clark, with her funny propensity for liking what did not suit her style, draped over a little rocker, and President Perrine using Helen's own Morris chair as a rostrum. She rapped the meeting to order with what first came handy, and it looked like a nice white sausage. It was a magnified bacillus, and, had it presented its visiting card, it would have turned into a shriek Eva's impressive—

"Ladies, as members of the Senior Ten of the King's Daughters connected with the First Unitarian Church of this city, it becomes us to extend a vote of thanks to the owner of this room. Isn't it the loveliest place; girls? And don't you think it would be nice to make Helen our tenth, now that Alice Gray has moved out of town? Do you suppose she would care to belong? Now that I see her resources, I do not wonder that she did not simply flock to us. There is her sick bell now," as it sounded twice. "Give me a nurse's cap and apron from that bundle we finished last week for the hospital." And the President, tying her strings, departed to drop a courtesy on Helen's threshold.

"Does that mean you want two kisses, dear?" And the girls held each other close a moment, before Martha toiled up with what two bells really meant—a cup of hot, salted milk.

The president slipped back again, and found business progressing briskly, with the vice-president in the chair, or, rather, behind it; for they scrupulously felt it should be kept for Helen herself.

"And, furthermore," the voice of authority was saying, "that Miss Helen Graham be notified of her election this afternoon, and that the member who likes to costume herself go out in the rain and purchase a King's Daughter badge to accompany our notification. Eva, change your apron for a waterproof, and go to Birk's for their very best silver cross."

The errand was done in a trice; and the afternoon was rounded off by sending note and pin up-stairs by Sister Anna, who had knocked to see if the heat of the room was agreeable, and had been retained to help the cutting committee over some baby-clothes for a poverty-ridden woman who requested that they be pink in color.

Helen's pleasure, as she read the note, was so great that the elder sister feared it would overtire her—good Anna, who only that stormy morning had been "building castles in Germ-any" to divert Helen, and promising to use her influence to have Dr. Graham plan a trip to Europe for himself and Helen which might result in his leaving her there for study, provided he saw her comfortably fixed.

But the restful gloaming followed the note; and Helen lay happily quiet through it, so as to be ready to call the instant the doctor came in from his day's labors—

"Oh, papa, papa, come up here as soon as you are rested, and see what those dear girls have done! Made me a member of their Ten! I'm a 'K. D.'" And then she nestled up to him, with a pretty lovingness and added, with a sweet shyness: "I shall not need to go abroad now. I've got my post-graduate honor!"—[Christian Register.

STITCHES.

MARGERY SWAIN REYNOLDS.

THE girls were seated in the Bryans' pretty sitting-room—six of them—sewing. The subject under discussion was the failure of married life, in many instances, to bring happiness. Being perfectly free from prejudices formed by personal experience, they deemed themselves all the more capable of an intelligent consideration of the subject.

It had come up very naturally in connection with the particular kind of sewing in hand. Mrs. Johnson was so unfortunate as to have a dissipated husband, and the girls, being philanthropically inclined, were making some much-needed garments for the little Johnsons.

Grandma Bryan sat by the window with her knitting, a dear old lady whose little lace cap sat on the gray hair with an air of having found its proper place, while the placid face below it showed that her life had at least been one of quiet content. The girls always liked to have grandma in the room, for she was one of the people whose sympathies do not grow old, and the girls had long since found it out.

"Mrs. Johnson made a comfortable living for herself as a dressmaker before her marriage. What a pity she didn't stay single!" said Mabel Grey.

"How did she know that her husband was going to drink?" said Carrie Bryan. "The thing I should like to know is, how a girl is to avoid such an entanglement as that? There will, undoubtedly, continue to be marrying and giving in marriage to the world's end, but there ought to be some way to put a stop to unhappy unions."

"There will be unhappy marriages as long as a man can get whiskey," said Ethel Brown, who worked faithfully in the "Y," and always displayed her white ribbon.

"Oh, a man wouldn't find whiskey such a temptation," spoke up pretty Marian Evans, "if his wife always had his slippers warming for him when he came home, and wore pretty gowns herself."

"There, Marian! that's just like you," cried Edith Miller; "but I fancy you'll find that your John will want something more substantial than warm slippers and pretty gowns to live on. Now, I believe the old adage, that the way to a man's heart is through his stomach. If you'll give a man plenty of good things to eat, he'll be amiable."

"Yes, Edith," said Ethel, "you would ruin his digestion, and then he would be sure to take to drink. I heard some men talking down at the market one morning, and one of them advocated the use of liquor on the ground that it cured indigestion."

"Well, if a girl contemplating marriage were to come to me for advice, I should tell her to beware of the man who talks about a 'woman's sphere,'" said Jennie Raymond. Jennie was a tall, slender girl, with features which bespoke decision of character. She was secretary of the local woman's suffrage association, and never omitted to wear her little yellow ribbon. "I visited a college friend last winter whose brother was always talking that sort of nonsense. Said women were too fine to go out and battle with the world; that they were made for something better. I told him a woman didn't want anything finer and better than to be able to work and to get a just remuneration for her labor. You may depend upon it that the women who marries a man who believes in woman's sphere will find her sphere limited by the four walls of the kitchen. It may extend to the parlor on the weekly sweeping day, but she'll seldom have a chance to find out whether her best chairs are comfortable or not."

"Behold, the oracle hath spoken!" cried Marian. "Jen, why don't you wear a yellow necktie instead of that tiny bow?"

"Well, to tell the truth, I should like to; but, unfortunately, yellow doesn't suit my complexion."

"Why, Jennie, to think that with all of your wisdom, you should have one weak point! 'Vanity of vanities, saith the preacher;' but who would have dreamed he was talking to you!" said Mabel. "But I believe you opened the way to a solution of the problem, when you said a woman wants nothing better than to be able to work, and to receive just pay for her labor. Most married women don't have enough money at their disposal, and to women who have been self-supporting, or have had allowances previous to marriage, it is intolerable to ask for money. I once heard my aunt tell a nice little story of a woman who asked her fianceé to give her an allowance after their marriage. He said that he would give her no allowance, but half of his salary would be hers."

"That is ideal!" cried Edith. "I wonder if there are any more cut by that pattern?"

"You'd never get one, if there were," said Carrie. "You're too generous. I shall expect to hear of your taking in washing when you are married, and giving two-thirds of the proceeds to your husband to buy kid gloves and neckties."

"How absurd!" cried matter-of-fact Jennie. "I believe a woman should stipulate before marriage that she shall have a certain proportion of the family income. I once heard a couple of physicians discussing why it was that more farmers' wives became insane than any other class of people. They accounted for it by the uninteresting in-door drudgery. They said the farmer's work is quite as much drudgery, perhaps, but it is out of doors. There was a bright little woman by at the time, and she said that, besides differing by being in instead of out of doors, the woman's work differs from her husband's in that she gets almost no return for it. The farmer finds his work interesting, no matter how hard, because it brings money, which goes into his own pocket. His wife sees no income from her never-ceasing labor, and so the drudgery becomes more than she can bear. A man, or woman either, will do the hardest kind of work, and with some enjoyment, if there is money in it. I am morally certain that Paul's stenographer made one mistake. Paul undoubtedly said the *lack* of money is the root of all evil."

A general laugh followed this outburst from Jennie, in which grandma, whose face had shown much amusement throughout the discussion, joined as heartily as the rest. As quiet returned, the girls, with one accord, turned to ask what she thought about it.

"Well, girls," said grandma, "in my day we didn't think much about the money we should need after we were married. Our clothes were the product of our own labor, and there didn't seem to be so many ways of spending money as there are now. Life was not so complicated. The thing I seemed to need the most of all was a large supply of patience. There are times in the married life of every two people, I imagine, when things do not go smoothly. Just such times as the day baby Ruth screamed with the colic, and, while I was trying to comfort her, Annie broke two panes of glass, trying to see how hard she could strike without breaking them. They were little panes, but they were expensive in those days. At the same time, little Ned—your father, Carrie—got into a keg of tar, and almost covered himself with the sticky black stuff. Grandpa came in, in the midst of the confusion, and mildly suggested that I ought to have watched the children better. I heatedly told him that my duty was to the screaming baby, no matter how much damage the other children did. I oughtn't to have said it, but there were times, you know, when even Job lost his patience. Grandpa didn't say a word, but led the children off, one to be rebuked, and the other to be washed, while I sat down and cried over my now sleeping baby. Such times are sure to come, and so I advise every girl to take a large supply of patience with her into her new home."

"It might be well for her husband to do the same, mightn't it, grandma?" slyly suggested Mabel.—[Woman's Journal.

A PIECE OF PASTURE.

HARRIET PRESCOTT SPOFFORD.

"YES," said Mr. Dexter, "honest poverty is nothing to be ashamed of."

"Nothing to be proud of, either," said his son John.

"And very disagreeable, anyway," said Sylvia, his pretty daughter.

"Well, I don't know why we need to talk about it. It's something of which we have no experience," said his wife, "honest or otherwise."

"Yes," said Mr. Dexter again—looking round at the breakfast-room, whose walls were lined with Sylvia's vines and flowering plants that made it a bower of greenery, at his shining table, and the pretty, petulant woman with her pink ribbons at its head—"We have every comfort, and some luxury—"

"Papa means mamma for the luxury."

"No; he means her for the comfort," said John, who was her especial care.

"Thanks, thanks," said mamma, bridling a little. "Comfort is quite relative."

"A very dear relative, sometimes," said John.

"John," cried Sylvia; "you really must go into politics!"

"Heaven forbid!" said his father.

"He has such a capacity for pretty speeches he would be invaluable in diplomacy," urged Sylvia.

"It is all he has a capacity for," his father thought. But he did not say so. "No, no," he said; "the less politics the better. His desk in the book-store is the place for John."

"I should be well enough content with that if I owned the shop," said John. "But this spending the best of your days for others isn't what it might be."

"It is a great deal better than running into debt for your beginning," said his father, as he left them.

"Yes," said Sylvia; "save your salary and wait till I can help you."

"You!" was the contemptuous reply.

"I do think," said Mrs. Dexter, "that a little dose of poverty wouldn't be amiss for Sylvia. She always feels such immense capabilities that it might bring her—"

"To a realizing sense of her inefficiency," said Sylvia. "Well mamma," she added, presently, sipping her coffee—John having gone up-stairs again to change his tie—"you speak as if that would give you pleasure."

"No, I don't; not at all. But you are always opposing John—"

"Why, mamma!"

"Yes, you are. The moment John comes anywhere near proposing to your father to give him the money to buy out the stock of that place, you come in with your influence against it."

"My influence, mamma! As if there were such a thing!"

"Well, there is! You are so exactly like your father that he hears all you say. And he feels you behind him and laughs the whole thing off. Saving his salary, indeed! He might as well think of buying the crown jewels with his salary! A salary is a dreadful thing; it binds you down in chains. Yes; there is no doubt about it, a salary is a dreadful thing."

"But, mamma, do you think it is right when papa has you and the little children on his hands—I don't speak of myself, because I suppose I can see to myself."

"There it is again! Your immeasurable conceit of yourself."

"But, mamma, there are quantities of young girls who do take care of themselves."

"Their name is not Sylvia Dexter, then."

"Well, if I can't see to myself, it seems to me there is all the more reason for papa's not crippling himself by giving his money to John and risking everything."

"There is no risk about it. You are a selfish and unnatural girl, Sylvia! You would let your poor brother toil and moil all his life rather than make a little sacrifice yourself. And he has always been so good, so kind; he was such a beautiful child—I remember when his curls were cut off that Mrs. Dares said—"

"Mamma, dear, you sent Julia on an errand, and said you would make John's lunch—"

"Sylvia! And it's almost train time! Why didn't you see to it? So full of the good of the family theoretically—and poor John all day in town with nothing to eat—"

"And not a restaurant handy," said Sylvia. "Well, I have seen to it. And there's an egg sandwich, and a breast of duck, and some celery, and some salt, and a buttered muffin, and a little tart, and a doughnut, and a flask of coffee. John has a better luncheon than we shall have. He has it every day."

"I should think you grudged it to your brother!"

"No, indeed! John likes good things, and I like to put them up for him; so we are even. John doesn't think so badly of me as you do, mamma."

"I don't know what you mean, Sylvia. I never said I thought badly of you. You annoy me with your jealousy of John—poor, dear John; he was meant for a prince—and you uphold your father in his severity."

"Here, John—excuse me, mamma—here John;" cried Sylvia, hurrying to the door as he went by, "don't forget your luncheon."

"Oh, hang the luncheon!" cried John, as he took the parcel. My father's economies will be the ruin of this family yet. If there's any one thing that has a cheap and detestable look, it's this pulling a luncheon out of your desk instead of going out like a man with any independence."

"I'm sure you needn't take it, John, if you don't wish," remonstrated his mother.

"Yes; take it, John," interpolated Sylvia. "A penny saved is a penny earned. It means more than a half dollar toward your capital."

"Come, now, that's interesting! Work it out for me while I'm gone, and see if I will have enough at that rate to put out at interest before I die."

"There," said Sylvia to herself, "I shall say no more about it. If papa chooses to take the risk—poor papa! Well, it's fortunate that Aunt Jeannette has invited me to visit her just now." And she put on her jacket to go and call upon the neighbor whose cow pastured in her lot, and see if it would not be as convenient to pay the rent now as later, so that she need not ask her father to open his purse for her. And she came back with so bright a face that her mother declared she thought that cow-right was worth more to Sylvia than the whole place to them.

"Perhaps it is," said Sylvia; "for it's mine, mamma. And it isn't going to be absorbed and lost in John's business, if the rest of the place is."

For the little three-acre lot was Sylvia's. She had bought it and paid for it from her small savings, together with the two hundred dollars her grand-mother had left her when there was rumor of its purchase for some unpleas-ant purpose, it being just at the foot of the garden. Her mother had never given her any peace concerning it, so to say. She ought to have lent the money to John, was the tenor of Mrs. Dexter's frequent remarks; and doubt-less she would have done so but for Harley Melton's influence, and for her part she wished Sylvia had never set eyes on Harley, undesirable and unsuit-able as he was! But Sylvia, for all that, had been a proud and happy land-holder and taxpayer ever since, and had enjoyed the sight of the neighbor's cow under the great trees, and drinking from the little brook formed by the spring that bubbled there as cold as if it had come all the way from Spitz-bergen; and she had enjoyed quite as much the ten dollars a summer that the neig:bor paid her.

She had had another pleasure in it, too; for often had she and Harley Melton laid out those three acres in their strolls across them; and here should be the house, and here the little lawn, and here the orchard; and it would be so pleasant, being near papa; and if Harley did not think it would be so pleasant being near mamma, he kept the thought to himself. Sylvia, with her great blue eyes, her lovely fairness, her sweet and sparkling brown-haired beauty, was so precious, that if the mother who bore her was not perfect, too, he was not sure that the fault was not in himself. He loved Sylvia beyond any words, the bright and busy little creature, alive to the tips of her hair with interest in all things and all people, feeling all things alive as well to her, the bird on the bough, the blossom there, too, the child playing beneath it. They had no idea of marrying, except far in the indefinite future; they had nothing to marry on; it was enough to love each other now; by and by they would build the little house, perhaps in the piece of pasture.

They used to wander over the bit of land as if it were an estate, with a joy of possession; and where the spring bubbled out of the ledge that cropped up beneath the group of great trees, they would sit and watch the water as if every bubble were a miracle.

Just look down in it, Harley—how clear! Look at the jewels on the bottom; they are rubies, sapphires, emeralds. opals, topazes, beryls—oh, what a glitter! What color, what splendor! It seems as if I could put down my arm and scoop up a handful of the gorgeous things."

"The pebbles down there? It is the wonderful clearness of the water that makes them seem so near; and I suppose it is the vertical sunbeam that makes them seem so beautiful. They are really a dozen feet beyond your reach," said the young chemist.

"They can't be, Harley!"

"Yes, I sounded the spring last week; it is eighteen feet deep; and I don't dare to say how many gallons it pours out a minute that all go to waste through the Telassee River."

"To think that our brook makes part of a big river!"

"And I analyzed it, too. The river that went out of Eden could not be purer. One drinking this might think he was drinking of the water of life."

"Well, it will be Eden when we have our littte house up there on the knoll, What a beautiful earth it is, Harley, when such freshness and purity pour out of its dark places! What a dear earth, to let us call this little piece of her, ours!"

"I really should think," said Mrs. Dexter, when Silvia came in, "that that spring was full of diamonds by the way you and Harley Melton hang over it."

"It is, mamma—it is!" and Sylvia danced away with no idea of the truth in her words.

It was lonesome at Aunt Jeannette's, in the big town, twenty miles away. Her father and John and Harley came in every day to their business, and for five minutes she saw Harley, who made occasion to go by the gate. Her father and John found time for few visits. Her first letter from her mother informed her that she would be glad to hear that her father had at last sold his bonds and given John the proceeds to buy out the business where he had slaved so long as a clerk. Silvia knew, however, under what unbearable pressure her poor father had been brought to yield; and her indignation and pity for him made her feel at first as if she never wanted to go into the house again. Succeeding letters were very jubilant and happy; it gave his mother so much pleasure to see John taking his place as became him, a man among men. She thought his business must be flourishing, for John had a little naphtha launch on the river, in which he went to town now, instead of traveling, with all the dust and jar of the railway. Of course there had been opposition, the letter said, for his father was one of those men who never liked innovation; but probably he would soon be going into town on it himself. He was always prognosticating evil; any one would think John was committing an unpardonable extravagance in having devised a healthier way of going to business than they had ever known before. Mr. Dexter did not approve of John's new horse either; and yet any one could see that the horse was as gentle as a woolly lamb, and he ate apples and sugar from the children's hands, and when he traveled he simply flew.

When Sylvia made an errand to her father's office, she found him as anxious as she had expected. But it would do no good for her to go home with him just now; she would show her disapprobation of the state of affairs too plainly; and she couldn't if she would, for Aunt Jeannette was ill with typhoid fever, and, of course, it was out of the question to leave her. There was really a pestilence of typhoid in town. All the drinking water was drawn from a river that passed large polluted towns and tanneries, and every day a new case appeared, till there was almost a panic in the place.

Fortunately for Sylvia she was one of those creatures so full of vital strength and fire that fear was unknown to her; and so well had she nursed Aunt Jeannette that, when she was a little rested, the hard-pressed physician begged her to help him on another case. And so it chanced that she went from one sick bed to another, and presently came to be offered large payments for her services; and in view of her apprehensions concerning John and her father's unsecured loan to him, it seemed best for her to continue both earning money and carrying relief. Harley protested that she would wear herself out; and she protested in return that she was well and young and strong, and liked it; and that even if the duty had not been set so plainly before her in relation to the sick and her ability to help them, it would be a wanton waste for her to refuse to earn the money thus offered her. "Oh, Harley!" she cried, "I must do all I can for them. For when I think of the poor creatures dying for want of good water, murdered by bad water, and remember our spring in the pasture bubbling up fresh and pure every second,

I feel like a criminal; as if I kept health and strength all to myself; as if I, and not the spring, were wasting what would be life to them."

"Such a morbid feeling shows that you are tired and in no condition to be nursing the sick," said Harley. But suddenly, as they went along together —for he appointed to meet her almost every day now in the hour's walk allowed the nurse by custom—his face flushed and flashed with a sudden thought like the passing of a sunbeam. "Will you give me permission to do what I please, to take all I want of the spring water, and in the way I think best?" he said.

"The idea!" cried Sylvia. "Permission, indeed! Isn't what is mine yours, I should like to know?" And they passed to more purely personal matters.

"I don't know if you are aware'" wrote her mother, some weeks afterward, "that Harley Melton is meddling with the spring in your piece of pasture, as you call it, meddling, in my opinion, most unwarrantably. He has had men there scooping it out and curbing it; and he has rigged an unsightly derrick there, and men are filling great glass demijohns by the wagonful. And at this rate there'll be no spring there at all presently. I suppose it is to save himself the trouble of distilling water for his prescriptions—that is so pure. I'm sure if he has money enough to hire men and rig derricks and all that, and cares as much as he pretends about you, he had better lend it to John, who can't sleep nights for worrying about his notes."

Sylvia was too busy with her sick and dying people to wonder much about the burden of her mother's letter. She knew that whatever Harley did was likely to be right. She could not spare the time to go and see her father again; she could not get the time; but she felt oppresssed with fear for him, and she laughed a little bitterly at herself to think she had supposed she could help him with her earnings, when a whole year of them would not amount to $1,000. But at any rate she was glad that she was lifting any portion of expense from him, be it ever so small.

It was some weeks afterward that, when she went out for her morning walk in a new direction, and saw great posters on all the fences and telegraph poles, "Drink water from the Sylvan spring and prevent typhoid," she understood with a double thrill of joy, for themselves, and joy for the sick, what Harley was doing. And when she met him driving in with a load of the glass carboys filled with Sylvian spring water, which he left from house to house, before going to his headquarters for fresh orders, she felt as if he were really an angel of the Lord in mortal guise. And he held out his hand for her to mount to his side, and she rode back into town with him, feeling as a devotee might do who carried holy water to the perishing and penitent.

Sylvia had gone back to her Aunt Jeannette's for a short rest after the hard and cruel winter, when, one bright May day, her father came to see her.

John had failed; and all that Mr. Dexter had saved and spared in the long years had gone into the gulf with the money of the other creditors. There were no assets to speak of—a few notes, the remnants of an ill-chosen stock, the horse that had gone lame, the disabled naphtha launch. Sylvia felt as though her heart would break when she saw her father's despondency. "I don't blame your poor mother," he said. "Love is a good fault. It was her love for John, and her 'belief' in me. She thought I was equal to any trouble that might come, superior to it; but even I supposed John had some capacity. It's hard, my child, to begin life over again at sixty."

"I don't think you will have to do that, Mr. Dexter," said Harley, who, coming in just then, had heard the last words. "I am just making a return to my chief; and I am sure it will be a joy to Sylvia to replace a good portion of your losses by indorsing this check to you."

"Harley!"

"I have deducted all the expenses and my own commission," said Harley. "You will see by the schedules that we supply in this town and others along the route and on the further side—for the typhoid scare is widespread now—more than a thousand families with the Sylvan spring water, at fifty cents a week. Of course the expenses are heavy; but then the net profit is heavy, too. It gives Sylvia and me enough to build our house in another spot at some distance from the water-work, a pasture of mine. And if you, Mr. Dexter, will take the management of the business in town—I think it need not interfere with your present arrangements; and John will oversee the teams—that is quite within his power; I can attend to the spring house until the time, that is, when the towns take the works off our hands and pay us fifty or a hundred thousand for our plant, with permanent positions in the business."

"There is no more honest poverty in ours, papa," cried Sylvia.

"Harley!" said Mr. Dexter; "you are my salvation."

"Well, sir, you can reverse the thing and be mine by giving your daughter a command to become my wife here and now."

"Without her mother?"

"Well, papa," said Sylvia, blushing rosy-red, but feeling obliged to come to Harley's help, "Aunt Jeannette would do. And you know that mamma has a great—great faculty for obstruction. I think she will be so relieved about John that she will forgive us. And we will make her a wedding present of a paid-up mortgage of the house."

"You are a *nouveau riche*, Sylvia. Harley must not allow you to be too free with your money."

"Oh, it isn't ours, it is a trust the dear old Mother Earth gives us. We are to be happy. And, oh, what happiness it is to bring health to whole towns full of people! Don't you remember, I told you the spring was full of saphires and rubies and emeralds, Harley! And real ones, you see, papa!" for Harley had slipped a ring on her finger some little time before. "Papa, you are quite another person already," she cried, pinning on her hat and going out to the minister's with them and her Aunt Jeannette.

"Oh, you dear, sweet, confiding old Mother Earth," Sylvia exclaimed, kneeling at her window that night, and looking out on the dark, slumbering, champaign country behind the town, "I love you so!"

"I think," said Harley, "you had better be saying how you love me!"

"That goes without saying," she replied, leaning back her head on his arm. "But this dear earth—she makes us so happy while she rolls with us about the sun that it seems to me now only a happiness to think of the time when we shall be a part of her—just brown dust together in her bosom?"

"Oh, but a long way off!" he cried, folding her still more closely in his arms.

It was about the same hour that Mrs. Dexter, having inspected the released mortgage and the gratifying check, had coquettishly picked out the pink ribbons of her cap and was remarking to her husband:

"Well, it was the most thoughtful thing Sylvia ever did—to save me the fuss of a wedding. That piece of pasture! Is John to have a salary—or a commission? A salary is so comfortable. You always know where you are with a salary—it has to be paid. Oh, yes, a salary is the best thing. I have always said so. Harley Melton is turning out better than I thought. I never said there was any harm in him; only that he was so inefficient. Still, with the money coming in, Sylvia could have done better. She could have married almost any one. It is vexatious, say what you will, to have an outsider like Harley directing family affairs—it is just the thing for John himself to do; and it is my private opinion that John suggested the whole businses in the first place. He always said that water was pure. John is so full of ideas!"— Independent.

AN OLD LADY'S HOME.

VICTOR GAGE KIMBERT.

MRS. BRIGHAM was in a state of utter disgust. She had come home the week before and remarked with great complacency that she did hope Mrs. Warner would appreciate the extra efforts made in her behalf, for it had taken a good bit of diplomacy and no small amount of labor to induce the managers to accept her without the usual fee, but that finally they had been successful, and the way to the Old Ladies' Home was at last opened for Mrs. Warner.

It had been impossible to raise money sufficient to pay the amount required, but, after much deliberation, the trustees had decided to accept Mrs. Brigham's protegee, and use the rental of a small house, of which Mrs. Warner had a life lease, as part payment.

There had been many who had said with emphasis that it was a shameful thing that the widow of Rafe Warner should be compelled to want for anything, so generous, so liberal, had he been during his life, and the whole of his comfortable provision for her was lost in one of the too common bank failures, in which human sharks remorselessly swallow the means of their victims. Although much sympathy was felt and expressed, the fact remained that Mrs. Warner had not been far from starvation during the preceding winter. She had made no complaint, but kindly disposed persons had made the matter known to Mrs. Brigham, who, in her capacity as director of a half dozen charitable enterprises, and contributor to a dozen others, for she was nothing if not charitable, had seemed the one to take the matter in hand. She had done her best and relieved many of her wants, without discovering that starvation would have been only a little harder to the poor woman.

Mrs. Brigham felt indignant, and no wonder, for after all her efforts to get her admitted to the Home, Mrs. Warner had cried like a child and begged to remain where she was. To do Mrs. Brigham justice, it was not alone for praise and gratitude she worked for others, but she did like to have her work appreciated, and enjoyed managing other people's affairs. If, sometimes, she overlooked individuality; and classed her poor people together as a man would a flock of sheep, it is but due to her to remember that she attempted and accomplished a great deal for others, and, being human, it follows that even her good works should have a flavor of herself.

"I'll go over and get Miss Vincent to take her in hand," she said, after a little reflection. "She'll make her listen to reason if any one can, and after all that's been said and done I'm ashamed to have the matter end like this."

Little Miss Vincent was a valuable adjunct to Mrs. Brigham, though the latter had looked askance two years before when Miss Vincent's father had sent his annual check to her with a note saying that his daughter would hereafter take his wife's place on the board and asking that any deficiency in finances be referred to him, as he was desirous of continuing his support to the work in which his dead wife had been so interested. The check was altogether too large to admit of any objection being made to his suggestion, though the maturer woman felt that "that slip of a girl" was really too young to be of much value in their councils, but they soon learned that Agnes Vincent brought a devoted heart and life to the service, and, in her pleasant, winning way, accomplished much that they would not attempt.

"Of course I will go," she answered Mrs. Brigham, "and I think I can put the matter in such a light that she will be glad to consent;" but within a half hour after going over to Mrs. Warner's she had gone entirely over to the enemy, and was doing her utmost to contrive in some way so that the old lady need not leave her home.

Mrs. Warner was taking up a few late dahlia toes and tying up some geranium roots when Miss Vincent came, and the look upon her face, as she learned her errand, went to the girl's heart.

"Oh, if they would only let me alone, I would die before I would ask for anything," she sobbed. "I didn't ask for anything last winter; some one told them I was suffering, but oh, Miss Vincent, if you'd lived here as long as I have, and loved every stick and stone in the yard, every bit of wood in the old house, you wouldn't want to leave it either. It takes so little to keep me, and I would rather have only half enough to eat here than everything over there. I hate a prison and that's all them institutions be," she finished, forgetting grammar in her earnestness.

Miss Vincent talked long and kindly to the poor old soul, who finally sobbed out that she wished she could die and be out of people's way; adding, "If only my boys had lived, I could make a home here for them and be a burden to no one."

Her visitor looked up quickly, a thought flashing across her mind. She put out her hand: "Just a moment, Mrs. Warner. I almost believe that I can help you in your own way instead of in ours. I know that when strong men walk the streets in search of work and fail to find it, that it seems almost impossible that you can have work brought to you, but I think we can accomplish it. Your remark about making a home for your boys was the electric spark I needed. There are many boys in whom I am interested who have no home. They have a place to eat and sleep for which they pay more than they can afford. Now I think you and I will give them a home. You have this house, which is very fortunate. How many boys do you think you are able to cook for and attend to generally, except the washing? Four? I do not wish you to overdo, but the boys whom I shall get will be glad to give you $2.50 a week, apiece, which will give you $10 in all. Should you find it impossible to get fuel with that amount I will help you out, but you will find it ample, I think, for everything, as many families are brought up nicely on $10 a week, when rent has to be paid besides. This will not leave you much for your own work, but it will supply you with good food, a warm home, and I think a little extra. Each boy must give you a quarter a week for washing, and then you can have some woman come in and do the washing and ironing for you, and any little odd jobs you may wish done. There are plenty of women who will be glad to come and work for you an entire day for a dollar. What do you think of it?"

Think of it! Never so long as she lives will Miss Vincent forget the utter abandon of joy with which the woman received her proposition. She went down on her knees, clung to her skirts and cried out that she was an angel. The transition from almost a pauper to one who could work for others, even hire another to help her, was too much for her over-wrought nerves, and Miss Vincent feared an attack of hysteria, but she gradually calmed her, as she went on with her calculation of items and their probable cost, which would be required to make the experiment a success. "Give them plenty of plain food," she said, "it will be cheaper than keeping them half starved; besides, they are going to pay for it, and I wish them to have all the liberties you can give them and still keep within proper bounds. Give each of them a key, for boys like to be trusted, yet have it understood that you do not wish the house open, ordinarily, after a certain hour, and I think they will respect your wishes. I know, of course, what boys I shall send you, and I shall trust you to make it as homelike as possible for them, for they have no homes of their own. I will see that they have good reading matter. They are inclined to be a little musical, and I believe we can so interest them that they will be better men than they would otherwise have been."

All the mother in Mrs. Warner was aroused and she began preparing for the boys as if they were really her own, and mentally decided that they should have some genuine homemade bread and doughnuts, to say nothing of mince pie, and a chicken at Christmas. She knew even better than Miss Vincent that ten dollars a week would run the house with a fair margin, for she was a careful buyer and excellent cook. The furniture was there in plenty, and she was glad that she could again be of use.

That evening Miss Vincent went to the evening school where she expected to meet the boys. She told them of the plan she had made for them, saying,

"You know the college boys gather in a house and hire a woman to cook for them, finding they can live much cheaper in a club than when each pays for separate board. This will be very much the same, only this lady does not expect to charge you for her work. You will have no wages to pay, but she will of course board with you, and you will each be at liberty to bring home fruit or anything extra you may wish, if you have friends come to visit you. We have made the price low, and expect you not only to appreciate that, but also the fact that you will really be at home, for this is what I expect my manly boys to do; go to this old lady's home and help make one for her and yourselves at the same time."

"We're going to found an old lady's home rather early in life I think, don't you, Miss Vincent?" laughed one of the boys who was thoroughly delighted with the proposed plan.

She selected four of the boys whom she had found the most trustworthy in her dealing with them, and the next week found them snugly settled in their new home. The plan was a success in every way, and at the expiration of three months the boys begged that another bed might be set up so that two more of their friends could have the same advantages. Mrs. Warner consulted with Miss Vincent and they concluded that by hiring a little extra work done it could be managed.

Mrs. Brigham was good enough and unselfish enough to be really pleased; though she said, "No one but you, Agnes, would ever have thought of such a thing. I am sure you deserve a great deal of credit."

"Oh, no," laughed Miss Vincent, "I just knew there were those boys without any home, and here this woman without any boys, so I simply brought them together. and, presto! the thing was done, and my old lady's home complete."—[Northern Christian Advocate.

GROWTH OF HUMANE SENTIMENT.

RODNEY DENNIS.

HOW slowly the years have dragged their weary length heretofore, while the early champions of some righteous but unpopular cause have toiled on through discouragements and delays, arising from ignorance, indifference or active opposition! It is one of the mysteries of the human mind and heart that they awake so tardily and unwillingly and move so slothfully in matters of righteousness and humanity. A notable instance is before our eyes, in our time and in our own commonwealth.

While the Perkins Institute in Boston has furnished home and education for a favored few, no provision has been made until recently for the afflicted poor, or for children at an age when succor and education can be most profitably extended.

During the past two years a few zealous, self-denying people, principally women, pioneered by the able and indomitable "Blind Lawyer," F. E. Cleaveland, Esq., who was deprived of sight when a young man just entering upon a brilliant career as attorney—these people, with unexampled assiduity and personal expenditure of energy and means, have illustrated by actual experiment, the possibility of educating the blind and furnishing them with appropriate and remunerative employment; so that they become useful, contented and self-supporting men and women. They have gathered the children into a school and kindergarten, where they are taught to use their existing faculties and senses in the same ways that seeing children use theirs, thus sweetening and making useful, self-reliant and cheerful, lives that otherwise would linger in discontented helplessness, a burden to their friends and to the community.

Seeing people would be willing to make sacrifices to help the blind, did they fully realize the gravity of the calamity borne by the latter—an impenetrable veil that excludes the light of day, the grand pageant of earth and sky in all their multiform ongoing change and beauty—and, most trying of all, the longed for faces of family and friends.

While individuals should count it a privilege to contribute towards the alleviation of this life-long great calamity—one which they are mercifully spared—it would seem that the state whose record is unsurpassed for its care of the disadvantaged and unfortunate, should be prompt and generous in its aid to these most helpless and deserving children and wards.

The feeling has too commonly obtained, both among individuals and legislators, that the blind are a hopeless and helpless class and their care and education a too great and expensive task. The success that is attending the experiment and the efforts hereinbefore mentioned, it is hoped, will go far towards removing this impression.

The humane determination to make place and standing room for the blind, is not the first or only tardy and difficult evolution on record. Humane sentiment has had hard and prolonged struggles in other fields. *Prison Reform*, espoused and personally advocated through all the Capitals of Europe by John Howard, who died a victim to the pestilence he strove to prevent and abate, was finally adopted and measurably effected when at last the sympathies and consciences of the public were reached. The Slave-Trade was abolished in Great Britain only after a long struggle and vigorous warfare waged for the rights of man by Wilberforce and his associates in the English Parliament. And later in our own country; the way was prepared for the same reform by the courage and devotion of Garrison, Hale, Phillips and their associates, until, by persistent agitation and the final tragedy of a great war, American soil no longer bears the imprint of the bondman.

The evolution of a humane sentiment is also strikingly shown in the rise and progress of the interest aroused in England, relative to the prevention and punishment of "Cruelty to Domestic Animals." This reform was instituted by the same man who labored for the rights of man and the liberty of the slave. Year after year, for fifteen years, Lord Erskine advocated the passage of a bill in the English Parliament, called "The Cruelty to Animals' Act." It passed the House of Lords but was defeated in the Commons, where the bill was met by jeers and was denied a respectful hearing. Lord Erskine patiently persisted in his attempt from time to time, until, one day in 1824, a little red-headed Irishman from Galway, known to be a man of muscle and one to be reckoned with—a lover of animals, with a heart as tender, as brave—arose in the Commons and began earnestly to contend for the consideration of Lord Erskine's bill. He was met by the accustomed derision, and some member uttered a cat-call which goaded him to exasperation, whereupon "Fighting Tom Martin" inquired for the name of his adversary, and with cuffs turned up invited him to stand out then and there to settle the matter. This turned the tide; cheers followed, and the bill— after the fearless and magnetic advocacy of Martin, supported by Wilberforce —passed overwhelmingly. Immediately upon the passage of the bill, the subject enlisted the sympathies of a number of the most eminent men of that day. A society was formed; early support was given to it by Queen Victoria, who placed her name at the head of its patrons and conferred the right to call it the Royal Victoria Society—donating to its funds one hundred guineas. The most renowned men in Church and State became the friends and patrons of this society, albeit it took fifteen years for the sentiment it represented to arrest the attention of the English public and Parliament, though advocated by one of the ablest and most accomplished men of his time.

The long struggle on behalf of personal libery in this country—a contest which shook the foundations of our government—ending in a war the most tragic and the most expensive in history, furnishes a notable example of the slow evolution of a sentiment. During the struggle the press was partially subsidized and measurably stifled. Individuals were ostracised, families and communities divided and estranged.

A striking instance of this occurred under my own observation more than fifty years ago, in this city, when Wendell Phillips and Abby Kelly came from Boston—both of the "Garrison Abolitionists"—to deliver their unwelcome protests against human bondage. Mr. Phillips was then in his prime. He had family, wealth, a commanding and graceful presence, a voice finely modulated, musical, penetrating and wonderfully persuasive, a courage undaunted, and he was as aggressive as fearless. Upon their arrival in Hartford, they met with no friendly reception, and the speakers could find no hall in which to address inhospitable and inimical hearers. No owner of real estate would risk the safety of his premises for this purpose for fear of a possible riot. The two shelterless people passed down the sidewalk on the west side of Main street, finally turning in at the alley-way between the Center church and the crockery-store of S. P. Kendall & Co.—in the building now occupied by Eckhardt & Co.—which was under the Center church lecture room. Mr. Phillips mounted a box which was taken from the front of Mr. Kendall's store (I remember the mark S. P. K. & Co.) while Abby Kelly stood upon the pavement beside him. There assembled a noisy mob of men and boys in front of him, reaching across the walk and down into the street. In the rear, and where the Center church parlor now is, was the engine house of No. 4 (those were the days of the old hand machine) filled with firemen and half-grown boys. Amid the jeers of the crowd in front of him, and the shouts and trumpeting of the firemen and boys in the rear, Mr. Phillips patiently wrestled with the attempt to drown his voice and defeat his purpose, until, by that masterly and magnetic power which carried him through many a similar encounter, he succeeded in hushing every hostile voice and gaining a quiet and sympathetic hearing.

Dr. Joel Hawes was then in his vigorous manhood, the conservative pastor of the Center church—conservative upon the subject of slavery, as the majority of his parishioners were—which Mr. Phillips well knew.

In the course of Mr. Phillips' remarks, or rather invective, he bitterly denounced the indifference of the clergy to the woes of the enslaved. Pointing up to Dr. Hawes' pulpit, he declared that "the slimy serpent had crawled up yonder pulpit and was gently bestowed and protected between the lids of the preacher's Bible." At this declaration there was a momentary outburst of indignation, but straightway the crowd was again subdued by the marvelous power and sweetness of the speaker's tones, and he held his audience thereafter until he completed his whole message, when he was allowed to depart in peace, and with much more friendly feeling than was evident when he came.

To show the change wrought in public opinion by the power of Truth and by the logic of events, in less than twenty years after, when this hunted and persecuted champion of a once hated cause had reached his later prime—having impatiently waited for the Salvation of the Lord, anon it came—the slaves were freed, the confederacy had fallen; and now Mr. Phillips was invited to address the citizens of Hartford, at a meeting called to celebrate a victory wrought through the smoke and carnage of battle—the triumph of a cause he had once almost alone and at his peril espoused and defended. The people of Hartford flocked into and overflowed the largest hall in the city to hear him, and the great audience was charmed with his glowing and triumphant sentences, full of hopeful and grateful acknowledgement and prophecy. The scene had completely changed. Instead of riot and insult, the speaker received a grand ovation—a notable instance of the power of Truth to work its way against heavy odds.

Let us hope that the earnest and persistent efforts of the friends of the blind will succeed in winning a place for them alongside of the seeing and more fortunate people of the commonwealth.

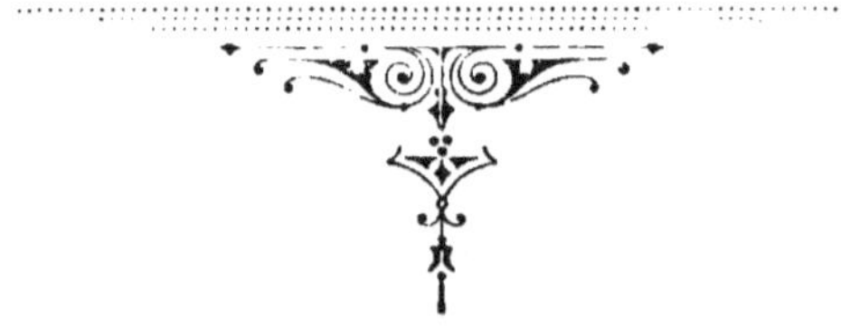

THE LAND OF LIGHT.

H. STENNETT ROGERS.

"What wilt thou that I shall do unto thee? And he said, Lord, that I
may receive my sight."

I'm out and in rout for a glorious land,
  Where I shall see, where I shall see;
With rapture I'll gaze on the radiant strand,
  When I shall see, ever see.
I'm told it's a land of superlative light;
A country in region transplendently bright;
A kingdom eternal, with never a night,
  What a sight to my soul it will be !

The wonderful words of my guide-book declare
  That I shall see, that I shall see,
The ransomed of earth and the glories they share,
  When I shall see, ever see.
Their city, it says, has a street of pure gold;
A fruit-bordered river of depths yet untold;
Great walls and foundations immense to behold,
  What a sight to my soul it will be !

Perhaps I will hear some harmonious strain,
  Ere I shall see, ere I shall see;
The breezes may waft from that vernal domain,
  Ere I shall see, ere I'll see.
It tells on Mount Zion a royal throne stands,
Encompassed by numberless song-singing bands,
Proceeding with heads crowned and harps in their hands,
  What a sight to my soul that will be !

To many I've said, on the journey along,
  Soon I shall see, soon I shall see.
I fain would be one of the triumphant throng,
  Watching and bec'ning for thee.

I there shall see Jesus, the giver of sight;
My Saviour, deliverer from evil and blight;
He'll call me by name, and will robe me in white,
  Sight supreme to my soul that will be !

It cannot be far to the Jordon divide,
  Siloam for me, Siloam for me;
I'm seemingly close to that tortuous tide,
  The upper Siloam for me.
I'm told at its verge there are beings of might,
  With pinions of pattern for supernal flight,
Who'll bear me from thence to this Eden of right,
  There and then I shall satisfied be.

I ventured this prayer: "Jesus, hear Thou my plea;
  How shall I see? When shall I see?"
The Spirit responded, my Book telleth thee,
  Believe, and follow thou Me.
In my Father's house many mansions there are;
  For you I am going a place to prepare;
Again I will come and receive you, that where
  I am, with me ye also may be.

I'm waiting Thy coming, abiding in thee,
Thy words in my heart set free;
Believing Thou dost, and Thou wilt do for me
Better and more than my plea.
On earth I have Jesus, a heaven right nigh;
In Heaven I'll have Jesus, a Heaven on high;
On earth or in heaven, all my needs He'll supply,
All in all to my soul He shall be.

JUST BETWEEN OURSELVES.

There is a new proverb to the effect that the truly intelligent man knows everything about something and something about everything. Surely, that is a high standard whereby to judge of one's intelligence in these days, when "everything" embraces a wide range. Particularly is this true in the field of literature. "Of making of many books there is no end; and much study is a weariness to the flesh." That is an ancient saying, and we cannot but wonder what its author would say had he been confronted with a list of the publications issued before the recent holidays. Of this we may be certain, that there is no possibility of any mortal man keeping abreast of the flood of modern literature. We have to pick and choose, and far too often have to regret that we did not choose something else. Resplendant bindings and good printing and abundant illustrations, too frequently lure us to our temporary financial ruin. Fine feathers no more make a fine bird in the book-mart than at the poultry stall, and more than once have we appreciated the feelings of Moses Primrose, when he traded his father's horse for the green spectacles.

* * *

"And the end is not yet." If the rivulet of literature bids fair to become a roaring, devastating torrent, we may look to the periodical tributary as a source of great danger. My occupation is such that I may be supposed to know something of the magazine business, especially of its extent. Hurrying to the Northern Station not many days ago, I arrived in time to see my train moving out at the farther end of the train shed. I beguiled the tedious half-hour's wait by studying the ornate display on the counter of the news-stand, and saw not less than three magazines—new-born to be sure—of whose existence I did not know. They were pretty and they were cheap, with a cheapness that extended to everything within the covers, but I doubt not they found purchasers. The very novelty of the thing will sell the first number of a magazine; the critical time will come later on. The flowers of January do not always bear fruit in April.

* * *

Speaking of magazines, what a nonsensical performance it is to begin to issue "Christmas numbers" six weeks before the holidays. Each year some ambitious publishers try to get their "Christmas numbers" on sale before their competitors, with the result that this year we were reading our Christmas stories before we purchased our Thanksgiving turkey. It makes us wonder where the race will end. Are we finally to have Christmas mixed with the Ever Glorious?

* * *

But to return to the matter of keeping abreast of the swift tide of literature. In the opinion of some good people we ought not to try to do it at all. And beyond all question it is better to know a few books then to know about a great many books. It is better to study Bunyan's "Pilgrim's Progress" and Defoe's "Robinson Crusoe" than to try to read a dozen of the modern novelists' productions. But it is a narrow kind of culture that comes from this sort of limited reading. One does not like to live in these days and know nothing of a literature later than the age of Queen Anne. Nor is it necessary that one should become superficial because of knowing much or little about books. To know something about a good book is more likely to make one desirous of knowing the book itself than never to have heard of it at all.

* * *

Discrimination is the watch word in reading. And one needs something more than the title page and the publisher's announcement to base his judgment upon. The busy men and women of this world who want to know what the pen and printing press are doing, who want to read something of more permanent worth than the newspaper with its conglomeration of fact and fiction, turn to the book review. To know what a book is about, to get an unbiased opinion of its style, to get an idea of whether it is worth the buying, is worthy information to furnish, as it is is sometimes valuable information to receive. And just as the very atmosphere of a library has the charm of cultivation, so it is not possible for any one to learn something of good books, be the knowledge never so superficial, without that knowledge tending toward culture.

* * *

"We have plenty of 'tales' but precious few 'talks' in our magazine," said Mr. Cleaveland to an over-busy man some weeks ago; "and if you could see your way clear to doing a little for us after the style of what you do for ——, it would be a great favor." And the over-busy man, full of interest in a noble work, consented to the proposition. If in so small a way he can contribute to the success of an undertaking which ought to appeal to the sympathy of all, he will not be sorry that he so rashly promised his assistance. And he is confident that the kind of people who will give their loyal support to this beneficent work will likewise be of those who want to get at "The Heart of Things."

ELLIS WORTH.

THE HEART OF THINGS.

FAR BELOW ZERO.—Through the newspapers we have all learned something of Lieut. Peary and his Arctic explorations. One of his company was a young Norwegian, Eivind Astrup by name, who accompanied Peary on both voyages. Now he has written a book, detailing his experiences in the far North. And a rough time they had of it, as Arctic explorers ever do. Profiting by the experiences of others, they went prepared to meet the rigors of the sunless winter. They carried with them, and erected, a portable house, twenty-two feet long, twelve feet wide, and divided into a larger and a smaller room. Then they built a stone wall about the house, three feet high. The whole was then covered with canvass, and their quarters were thus made snug and warm. The house of the second expedition was somewhat larger, as provision had to be made for Mrs. Peary and the nurse, who came to care for the baby that was born during the winter.

Mr. Astrup does not enter into the details of the expeditions so much as into a study of life among those curious natives who were their neighbors. And excellent neighbors they were. Gentle folk, appreciative of every kindness shown them, ready to do their best to help in the work their visitors came to carry on. Filthy in their personal habits they may be, but we gather the distinct idea that they are more civilized, and more nearly Christianized than some people who live in brown stone fronts, with the advantages of a bath room. We are told of one amusing incident, wherein a native went out to shoot a reindeer. Now, like all the deer family, these animals are keen of scent. The little Eskimo, well aware that he was not a savory object, divested himself of every vestige of clothing, stole upon the deer, mortally wounded one and then hastily returned to his clothes. When we learn that the thermometer was ranging about thirty below zero, we gather an idea of the haste with which Kaschu jumped into his bird-skin shirt and deer-skin trowsers.

Probably contact with their whiter brethren will not be an unmixed blessing to these little people. The use of fire-arms has driven out the bow and arrow, with the result that the game is being slaughtered, not for food alone, but with the civilized idea of "sport." The consequence of this will be devastating famine, sooner or later. Probably the use of alcohol, among people to whom stimulants of all sorts are unknown, will work its customary ruin. It is not a pleasant spectacle to contemplate, and is a sad commentary on the civilization of a highly civilized age.

[With Peary near the Pole. By Eivind Astrup. J. B. Lippincott Co. $3.50.]

AMONG CANNIBALS.—Down on the west coast of Africa, extending far into the interior, is the Congo state, a Belgian colony, or more properly speaking a Belgian dependency. Here is being carried on the great work of building railways and creating trade and in all known ways "developing" the country. One of the men who has served as an administrative officer there for three years is Capt. Guy Burrows, a retired officer of the English army. I suppose there must always be a fascination in reading of an unknown country, and that fascination inheres in Capt. Burrows' book. We learn of the customs of the people from an eye-witness and, for the most part, decide that New England is preferable to the Congo state as a place of residence. The author says that contrary to the general supposition, cannibalism is still rampant among certain tribes in the interior, and he believes that the white man has a difficult task in stamping it out. The custom is a curious one, and most singular of all is the fact that the cannibals are not the lowest tribes. They are, on the contrary, comparatively intelligent and generally monogamous. It is not at all reassuring to learn that they never eat blood relatives, since that does not interfere with a brisk demand for travelers and missionaries. Nor does it prevent the killing of aged and useless relatives and selling them to others. Capt. Burrows facetiously remarks that it is quite a common thing for a thrifty cannibal to inform his neighbors that "we have just killed old uncle this morning. He was in prime condition. Which joint do you prefer?"

It is consoling to think that this revolting custom must go before the onslaught of civilization. Rum may enter, but cannibalism must go out.

That will be some gain. There can be no doubt of the rapid opening up of the country. Its productions are immensely valuable and its trade profitable. Give the white man time and the two chief evils, fever and cannibalism, will be vanquished.

[Among the Pigmies. Capt. Guy Burrows. T. Y. Crowell & Co. $3.00.]

THE LITERATURE OF POWER.—There is a kind of secular congregation which gathers in the Broadway Theatre out in Denver, to whom from week to week the Rev. Myron W. Reed delivers an address. Some of these addresses are gathered into a little book recently published by The Bowen-Merrill Co., of Indianapolis. Mr. Reed has a quaint and wonderfully interesting way of putting things, as witness this passage which should be read and remembered:

"There is a literature of power and a literature of knowledge. A patent office report sent by a congressman to his beloved constituents belongs to the literature of knowledge. The parable of the prodigal son belongs to the literature of power. One puffs up, the other warms, kindles. For some purposes in life I get more out of a ballad than out of a sermon, more out of a violin than out of an argument. I know more about flowers than my mother. I do not feel them as she did.

"I try the literature of knowledge on a boy. I impress upon him the chemistry of sedlitz powders. If an alkali meets an acid there will be a sizzle; that is an important fact. But one night I read to him the speech of Judah to Joseph that he might remain hostage in Egypt and that Benjamin might go back to his father. 'If the lad go not back my father will die.' I noticed his chin quivered. That is the literature of power.

"Read the best that has been thought and said. One face we inherit, the other we make. The face we make and die with is made out of thoughts."

[Temple Talks. By Myron W. Reed. The Bowen-Merrill Co.]

A NEW STORY BOOK.—Every mother with young children will welcome a beautiful book, "chock full" of rhymed stories for the little people, to which the author, Mrs. Mary Whitney Morrison, has given the melodious title of "Stories True and Fancies New." We suspect we can discern the truth from the fiction, but both are equally pleasing. Mrs. Morrison is evidently a close observer of child life, and a ready pen turns the common-place incident into attractive form. As in "The Echoed Song:"

"Said Bridget to our little Sue,
    Now sing this pretty song;
'Tis all about Susanna, dear,
    And is not very long.

"The words are these, my pretty pet,
    They're easy words, you see:
'Susanna, oh, Susanna,
    Oh, do not cry for me.'"

"'Twas thus she echoed back the song,
    The dainty little midget,
'Susanna, oh, Susanna,
    Peas do not ky for Bidget.'"

Then there are stories of boys and girls, and cats and dogs, some of them possibly true, some of them surely created by a clever brain. And then the pen and ink artist, Louis J. Bridgman, has put some of his best work into sympathetic illustration. When the little feet and legs grow tired, and blocks and dolls lose their power to charm, here is the means ready at hand to while away an hour in mother's arms.

[Stories True and Fancies New. By Mary Whitney Morrison. Dana Estes & Co. $1.25.]

"THE ASSOCIATE HERMITS."—Everybody has an opinion about Mr. Frank R. Stockton. Almost everybody enjoys his quaint humor, but now and then some one finds him insufferably dull. I suppose this is the case with any popular author, but Mr. Stockton's admirers find it difficult to understand how any one can fail to delight in the oddities of "Rudder Grange." And they will feel a like enthusiasm, we suspect, for the author's latest work. Its beginning is quite equal to the originality of which Mr. Stockton is so prolific. Mr. and Mrs. Hector Archibald have an only daughter who is about to be married. With that perversity so common to American young women of to-day, Miss Archibald does not incline favorably to the idea of a wedding trip. With that conservatism so frequently met with in contented middle-aged folk, her parents do not approve of her iconoclastic notions. "During the honeymoon a young couple should live for each other, with each other, apart from the rest of the world. It is a beautiful custom, which should not be rudely trampled upon," said Mrs. Archibald. But Kate Archibald is not to be turned from her purpose. She will spend the honey-moon at home. She has no objection to spending it alone with her husband, but as to the wedding journey, if any is taken her father and mother must take it. And despite Mrs. Archibald's objections, that is exactly what was done. And this is the start of an interesting and amusing series of adventures.

They decided to go to the Adirondacks and they took with them the young and charming daughter of a friend, Margery Dearborn by name. First proceeding to Peter Sadler's hotel, they engaged from Peter a log camp in the woods, surrounded by trees and solitude, and cared for by two accomplished guides. Things begin to get complicated at the very start. First, there come two young men and establish themselves in a tent near at hand, not to woo nature in her most charming mood, but to pay court to Miss Margery. As two admirers are not enough, one of the guides, an educated but poverty-stricken youth, is added to the list. By this time things are as mixed as might seem necessary, but at this juncture comes a clerical looking tramp who answers to the appelation of "the Bishop." He does not seem inclined to fall in love with anyone, but he gets into plenty of trouble none the less. Still the *dramatis personae* is not complete. One of the above-mentioned admirers of Margery brings his sister and establishes her on the ground, being possessed of an insane notion that his love making is to be facilitated thereby. Alas for the futility of human hopes and plans, Miss Corona Raybold's hosiery is of the azure tint, and assistance in any love affair is quite apart from her line of thought or action. She cannot be expected to give her attention to such trivial affairs while more important subjects throng her capacious thinking apparatus. Schemes for the amelioration of the condition of the human race must be put into action, even in the Adirondack wilderness. For a starter she proposes that they shall drop the hampering conventionalities and allow their individualities to assert themselves. Having agreed to this proposition, in order to quiet this preaching prophetess, the inhabitants of the camp find themselves ushered into a state of most awful chaos. Just one day of unrepressed and rampant individualism suffices to dissolve the Associated Hermits combine. In fact, Mrs. Archibald gets frightened, and her fright becomes contagious. Mr. Archibald is so impressed with the desirability of fleeing the presence of their blue-stockinged mentor that he arises in the dead of night, and in company with his wife and ward, makes his escape. Freed from the importunate love-making of Miss Corona's hot-headed brother, Margery, having already sent the educated guide adrift, announces her engagement to the least obtrusive adorer, Mr. Harrison Clyde. In this condition the original Archibald party leave the wilderness, return to their billing and cooing daughter and son-in-law, and the curtain falls on the major act of the entertaining drama.

There is an epilogue. brief and interesting. Into Mr. Archibald's office not many days after, strolls the urbane "Bishop." From him we learn what took place at the camp subsequently to the stealthy departure of the Archibalds. Left alone with the irrepressible Corona, the clerical tramp stood little show. He retreated to Sadler's, but she followed on. "On Wednesday," said he, "I steeled my heart and told her I must positively depart the following morning. It was that evening, however, that we became engaged to be married."

"What?" cried Mr. Archibald, "Did you dare to propose yourself to that classic creature?"

"No," replied the other, "I cannot, with exactness, say that I did. It would be difficult, indeed, for me to describe the manner in which we arrived at this most satisfactory conclusion. Miss Raybold is a mistress of expression, and, without moving a hair's-breadth beyond the lines of maidenly reserve which always environ her, she made me aware, not only that I desired to propose marriage to her, but that it would be well for me to do so. There were objections, and I stated them, but they were overruled to my entire satisfaction, and she consented to become Mrs. Bishop." They concluded to continue the organization of Associated Hermits.

[The Associated Hermits. By Frank R. Stockton. Chas. Scribner's Sons. $1.50.]

Any communications for this department may be addressed to Ellis Worth, Waltham, Mass.

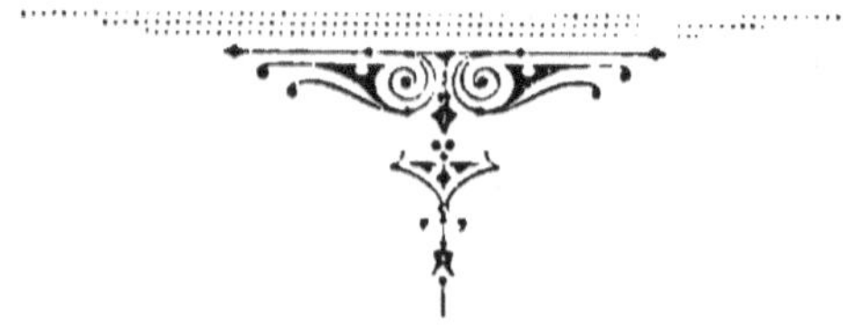

SELECTED MATTER.

S. W. FOSS.

The sun's heat will give out in ten
million years more,"
And he worried about it.
"It will sure give out then if it
doesn't before,"
And he worried about it.
It would surely give out, so the sci-
entists said,
In all scientifical books he had read,
And the whole mighty universe then
would be dead,
And he worried about it.

"And some day the earth will fall
into the sun,"
And he worried about it;
"Just as sure and as straight as if
shot from a gun,"
And he worried about it.
"When strong gravitation unbuckles
Her straps,
Just picture," he said, "what a fear-
ful collapse !
It will come in a few million ages,
perhaps,"
And he worried about it.

"The earth will become much too
small for the race,"
And he worried about it.
"When we'll pay thirty dollars an
inch for pure space,"
And he worried about it.
"The earth will be crowded so much
without doubt,
That there'll be no room for one's
tongue to stick out,
And no room for one's thoughts to
wander about,"
And he worried about it.

"The Gulf Stream will curve and
New England grow torrider,"
And he worried about it.
"Than was ever the climate of
southernmost Florida,"
And he worried about it.
"The ice crop will be knocked into
small smithereens,
And crocodiles block up our mow-
ing machines,
And we'll lose our fine crops of pota-
toes and beans,"
And he worried about it.

"And in less than ten thousand
years, there's no doubt,"
And he worried about it.
"Our supply of lumber and coal will
give out;"
And he worried about it.
"Just then the ice age will return
cold and raw,
Frozen men will stand stiff with arms
outstretched in awe,
As if vainly beseeching a general
thaw,"
And he worried about it.

His wife took in washing—a dollar a
day—
He didn't worry about it;
His daughter sewed shirts, the rude
grocer to pay,
He didn't worry ab   it;
While his wife beat her tireless rub-
a-dub-dub
On the washboard drum in her old
wooden tub,
He sat by the stove and he just let
her rub,
He didn't worry about it,

PROBABLY no people in the world eat so much meat as the Americans. The secretary of agriculture places the annual meat bill at not less than $900,000,000. Figures can be only approximate, yet a fair estimate would place the beef consumed at 5,000,000,000 pounds, pork at 4,000,000,000 and mutton at 800,000,000 pounds. With the poultry and game the total meat eaten annually cannot be less than 10,000,000,000 pounds, which is nearly two pounds a day for each family of five persons. At the same time the export of this product is enormous. Of beef 488,000,000 pounds went out last year, seven-eighths of which was consumed in Great Britain. Exports of pork products reached no less than 1,302,000,000 pounds. Germany took 15 per cent. and Great Britain 56 per cent. To the meat supply must be added the products of the rivers, lakes and oceans, aggregating probably some 800,000,000 pounds of various kinds of fish. The canned salmon alone is placed at 80,000,000 pounds.

———— ❖ ————

One of the most remarkable races that ever inhabited the earth is now extinct. They were known as the Gaunches and were the aborigines of the Canary islands. In the sixteenth century, pestilence, slavery and the cruelty of the Spaniards succeeded in totally exterminating them. They are described as having been of gigantic stature. Their food consisted of barley, wheat and goat's milk, and their agriculture of the rudest kind. They had a religion which taught them of a future state of rewards and punishments after death, and of good and evil spirits. They regarded the volcano of Teneriffe as punishment for the bad. The bodies of their dead were carefully embalmed and deposited in catacombs, which still continue to be an object of curiosity to those who visit the islands. Their marriages were very solemn and before engaging in them, the brides were fattened on milk.

———— ❖ ————

Frances Willard said in her will, "I have the purpose to help forward progressive movements even in my latest hours, and hence hereby decree that the earthly mantle, which I shall drop ere long, when my real self passes onward into the world unseen, shall be swiftly enfolded in flames and rendered powerless harmfully to affect the health of the living. Let no friend of mine say aught to prevent the cremation of my cast-off body. The fact that the popular mind has not come to this decision renders it all the more my duty, whe have seen the light, to stand for it in death, as I have sincerely meant in life to stand for the great cause of poor, oppressed humanity. There must be explorers along all the pathways; scouts in all armies."

———— ❖ ————

The States that rank first in the production of the following:

Sugar—Louisiana. Cotton—Mississippi. Rice—Louisiana. Corn, wheat; etc.—Illinois. Tobacco and hemp—Kentucky. Tar, pitch and turpentine—North Carolina. Nickel—Missouri. Coal and iron—Pennsylvania. Copper—Michigan. Gypsum—Arkansas. Gold and quicksilver—California. Silver—Colorado. Wool—Ohio. Cattle—Texas. Sponges—Florida. Lumber—Washington. Zinc ore—New Jersey. Salmon—Oregon. Marble—Vermont. Slate—Pennsylvania.

———— ❖ ————

Sugar alone will apparently sustain life for a considerable time.

———— ❖ ————

On an average every woman carries 40 to 60 miles of hair upon her head.

CHILDREN'S DEPARTMENT.

A Poem Postponed.

HELEN C. WALDEN.

I want to tell you about my kitten—
The prettiest kitten that ever purred;
But I've looked my speller through and through,
And I can't discover a single word
That rhymes with kitten,
    Excepting mitten,—
And that is old, and too absurd,
So the only thing for me to do
Is just to send you what I've written,
And wait till she grows to be a cat,—
There are ever so many to rhyme
    with that !
        —*St. Nicholas.*

HOW A BOY MEASURED A TREE.

He is not a boy in a book; he lives in our house. He seldom says anything remarkable. He eats oatmeal in large quantities, and tears his trousers, and goes through the toes of his boots, and loses his cap, and slams the doors, and chases the cat just like any other boy. But he is remarkable, for he asks few questions and does much thinking. If he does not understand, he whistles —an excellent habit on most occasions. There was much whistling in our yard one summer. It seemed to be an all-summer performance. Near the end of the season, however, our boy announced the height of our tall maple tree to be 33 feet.

"Why, how do you know?" was the general question.

"Measured it."

"How?.'

"Foot-rule and yard stick."

"You didn't climb that tall tree?" his mother asked anxiously.

"No'm, I just found the length of the shadow and measured that."

"But the length of the shadow changes."

"Yes'm; but twice a day the shadows are just as long as things themselves. I've been trying it all summer. I drove a stick into the ground, and when the shadow was just as long as the stick, I knew that the shadow of the tree would be just as long as the tree, and that's 33 feet."

"So that is what you have been whistling about all summer?"

"Did I whistle?" asked Tom.

FACTS ABOUT ALASKA.

Alaska is two and one-half times as large as Texas. It is eight times as large as all of New England. It is as large as the South, including Texas. It is as large as all the states east of the Mississippi and north of the Ohio, including Virginia and West Virginia. It makes San Francisco east of our centre. Its coast line is 26,000 miles. It has the highest mountain in North America. It has the only forest covered glacier in the world. The Treadwell is one of its greatest gold mines. It has the best yellow cedar in the world. It has the greatest sea fisheries. It has the greatest salmon fisheries. It has cod banks that beat Newfoundland.

Here is a bull from the nursery: "That's a terrible noise in the nursery, Molly," said the mistress. "What's the matter? Can't you keep the baby quiet?" "Shure, ma.am," replied Molly, "I can't keep him quiet unless I let him make a noise."

———

Wickwire—"You are about the most soiled specimen I have ever seen."

Dismal Dawson—"An' you bet every foot of it is good American soil."

———

Briggs—"I didn't know that you were near-sighted!"

Griggs—"Near-sighted! Why, I walked right up to one of my creditors yesterday."

———

Reverse Action.—The Elder Matron—"You shouldn't mind the baby crying a little. It strengthens his lungs."

The Younger Matron—Oh, no doubt; but if weakens his father's religion."

———

Irascible Lieutenant (down engine-room tube)—"Is there a blithering idiot at the end of this tube?" Voice from the engine-room—"Not at this end, sir."

———

"Do you know a good tonic for nervous persons, Simpkins?"

"No. What I want to find is a tonic for people who have to live with them."

———

"I thought you said you didn't care for him?"

"Well, I thought I didn't, but I didn't know then that the Smith girl in the next block is desperately in love with him."

———

Officer saluting—"I want to see General Grant."

Sentry, in a whisper—"He isn't here, but you can see General Fred Grant."

———

She—"The fact that I am a widow doesn't make any difference, does it?"

He—"Yes. I would't marry you if your husband was living."

———

Brownly—"How surprised we should be if we could see ourselves as others see us! Townly—"Yes; but think how surprised the others would be if they could see us as we see ourselves.

———

"A Half Memory.—Teacher—Who discovered America?" Street Gamin (after deep thought)—I disremember his name, but he was a Dago."

———

Said the anti-suffrage lecturer: "The roads up these mountains are too steep and rocky for even a donkey to climb; therefore I did not attempt the ascent."

———

Grandpa—"Why is little Tootles crying?" Guiltless Johnny—"Oh, she was yawning a minute ago, and she sprained her mouth."

When you want to ride first-class in a rail-
wa. train you get in the parlor car. When
you want to ride first-class on a bicycle you
select a Columbia Chainless, $75. If deter-
mined, however, to stick to the chain, see our
1899 Columbia Chain Models 57 and 58, $50;
or our Columbia Model 49 with 1899 improve-
ments, $40; Hartfords, $35, and Vedettes $25
and $26. Our 1899 Models are offered at
prices but little higher than the price of the
poorest.

Why Not Have the Best?
POPE MFG. CO.,   Hartford, Conn.

TALKS AND TALES,

A Magazine Published in the Interest of the Blind. . . . . 

The work of the magazine is largely done by the blind people and your interest and support is solicited, that its circulation may increase. Every subscription helps towards furnishing employment for the blind. Published by the Printing Department of the Institution, **334 and 336 Wethersfield Ave., Hartford, Conn.**

. . . Subscription Price $1.00 per year.

Talks and Tales.

VOL. II.   HARTFORD, CONN., MARCH, 1899.   NO. 6.

DEAR FRIENDS:—You will doubtless be somewhat surprised to find this number of our magazine devoted entirely to the presentation of one phase of our work for the Blind. I feel sure that when you understand how important it is that the results accomplished by the Industrial Home for the Blind at Hartford, Conn., during the past six years should be thoroughly known by the citizens of New England, you will forgive the departure from the usual style of our publication and for once, instead of fiction and the varied interesting and amusing matter which we have hitherto endeavored to furnish, you will be willing to read stories from real life.

We have arrived at the point when our plan to make our magazine accomplish the object for which it was brought into being, has received a serious and unlooked for check that will be exceedingly hard for our Institution to overcome unless our many friends come promptly to the aid of this most beneficent work for the Blind.

It will be remembered that the profit to be derived from publishing TALKS AND TALES is to be wholly devoted to uplifting and assisting such blind people as are unable to avail themselves of the privileges of our Institution and to furnish employment by the work rendered necessary in its publication, for friendless and hitherto dependent young blind women.

We have made the start and a goodly number of these young blind women are already enjoying the advantages which the carrying out of this plan has thus far made possible. We had counted however, upon being able after the first twelve or eighteen months of our existence to receive a considerable income from advertisers, and during the past six weeks we have been energetically pushing our canvass to obtain advertising patronage, but we meet on every hand the answer, "Your circulation is not large enough." We urge that we send out 5000 copies which go into towns in all parts of

New England, Northern New York and New Jersey, but they say, "You must have from fifteen to twenty thousand circulation before you can expect experienced advertisers to notice you." Now, dear friends, we greatly fear our whole project will be wrecked unless this circulation can be much more rapidly increased than it is possible for us to increase it by the methods we have thus far been able to employ. However, if every one of our present subscribers would send us just one new subscriber, we should then have ten thousand and if they could send two or three new subscribers our hopes would be immediately realized and our little ship would be sent bounding over troublesome waves with flying colors.

We therefore appeal to all subscribers of TALKS AND TALES to read this number through carefully and then ask themselves the question, "If I were blind how greatly would I appreciate a kindly act and service that would help along a work like this?" Then we would ask them to resolve to take this number of the magazine and show it to friends until they had succeeded in obtaining one, two or three new subscribers, as time and opportunity permits.

Few people understand what can be accomplished by and for the blind. This fact makes it all the more imperative that no stone be left unturned in order to place before the people of New England a faithful and true account of what has already been and is being accomplished.

For example, many persons are liable to regard the idea of a printing office for the blind as not practical nor feasible. To satisfy such persons we invited representatives from leading printing and publishing offices in Hartford to visit our printing department and judge for themselves. The Case, Lockwood & Brainard Co., Fowler, Miller & Co., and the printing establishment of C. M. Gaines complied with our request and as a result of their visit we were able to publish in the Hartford papers the following:

"This is to certify that the undersigned, by the request of the officials of the Industrial Home for the Blind at Nos. 334 and 336 Wethersfield Ave., Hartford, Conn., have this day visited and inspected the job printing department of said Institution, and we there saw a number of blind persons engaged in various kinds of work in job printing. Two were feeding power presses, two were printing on hand presses, another was binding pamphlets and showed his ability to take the work from the hands of the pressman and do all that was necessary to complete the work, making use of the wire staple binding machine in so doing, others were folding and making packages ready for the mail.

"The work was well done and in our opinion it is possible and practicable for one seeing person to keep from six to eight blind persons profitably employed in the job printing business. We also inspected the plant and outfit and upon being told that the cost did not exceed twenty-four hundred dollars, we are of the opinion that it was purchased exceedingly cheap and that the results attained fully justify the outlay."

MARCUS A. CASE,
Vice President C. L. & B. Co.
J. E. FLANIGAN,
Foreman, Fowler & Miller Co.
CHAS. M. GAINES,
Printer.

Hartford, May 28, 1897.

Just at this point we think will be a good place to reproduce the following:

"AS ITHERS SEE US."

A COMMUNICATION FROM THE PEN OF THE REV. F. F. THAYER, PASTOR OF THE BAPTIST CHURCH OF AYER, MASS., TAKEN FROM THE FITCHBURG "EVENING STAR," OF JAN. 24, 1899.

To the citizens of Ayer:—

"Believing that our townspeople who have of late shown their regard in a most substantial manner for one of our number, Edwin E. Warren, would like to know something of the Institution to which he has gone as the result of their kindly aid, I have taken the liberty to write the following as my impressions of that Institution: We arrived there at 1 o'clock, Saturday, January 14, and were invited into the music room by the superintendent. This we found a very delightful apartment, several pianos and other musical instruments being there, and used by the students, to many of whom we were introduced. Later in the dining room we found every thing in perfect order, and it is safe to say that after four hours riding, Mr. Warren and myself did justice to the very bountiful dinner provided. As one of the students said, who has been there several years, "the board and all in connection with the Institution is fit for a king." The kitchen was an equally attractive room and with the dining room constituted an excellent place to live and grow fat. At 2.30 we had the pleasure of once more meeting F. E. Cleaveland, President of the Institution, whom we met a few weeks before in Ayer at the concert so beautifully rendered by students of the Institution. They were at this time preparing for a similar trip to New Jersey. * * * I was greatly impressed by the great ability, kind-hearted and loving care shown by Mr. Cleaveland and his assistants. In one room young ladies were making baskets, in another running printing presses under the direction of Mrs. E. B. Kendrick, editor of their monthly magazine. Across the hallway was the store and a very bright, though blind young woman, dealing out goods to her customers in a manner so quick and ready as to put to shame some of our clerks who are blessed with sight. Next, in the rear, we found men making brooms and mattresses, and caning chairs. This was the department where Mr. Warren is to receive instruction from a blind man. In a few months Mr. Warren will be able to make from eighteen to twenty brooms a day, and so let the housekeepers of Ayer be ready to buy their brooms from our fellow citizen, when Edwin comes marching home again."

What follows above the signature of Mr. Thayer is a statement showing contributions received amounting to $186.85 to assist Mr. Warren who was a young blind man living in Ayer, Mass., and struggling to exist by occasionally getting a job of sawing wood.

The action of the reverend gentleman and other friends of the young man was the result of the visit to the town of Ayer, of the concert company from our Industrial Home for the Blind at Hartford, Conn., and the opportunity thus offered to explain the work of our Institution and the needs of the Blind. This is only a notable instance of what is happening right along, the only occasion for regret being our inability to keep pace with the demands upon our Institution.

Let us now introduce some statements from those who know and realize, better far than any seeing person can possibly do, the good the Industrial Home for the Blind at Hartford, Conn., is accomplishing along the line of the special work it has undertaken. We refer to those, the barren monotony of whose lives spent in an unending night, has been broken by the appearance of a ray of light which, through this Institution, has been shed upon their pathway.

For obvious reasons, in some instances, we refrain from giving more than the initials of the persons to whom these statements refer.

I am acquainted with John Sullivan of Willimantic, who became totally blind about nine years ago, while employed by the N. Y., N. H. & H. R. R. Co., through the carelessness of a fellow workman by the premature explosion of dynamite.

I applied for his admission to the Industrial Home for the Blind at Hartford, Connecticut, where he learned the trade of broom making. For the past four years, he has been carrying on business in Willimantic and has earned for himself a comfortable livelihood. This young man was without means and friendless, and but, for the opportunity thus afforded him by the Industrial Home for the Blind, would have been compelled to have spent the remainder of his days in the poor house, to which he had already made application.

A. C. ANDREWS,
Dealer in Music and Musical Instruments.

Willimantic, Conn., Feb. 15, 1899.

My daughter, S—— C——, who has been blind since her childhood, was educated at the Perkins Institution for the Blind at Boston. After losing my husband her support and care fell upon me.

My health for years has been very poor, but for a long time I labored faithfully to provide a home for us both, and whenever employed, I was compelled to leave her at home alone, as I had no other children to stay with her. No mother, until she has been in my place, can imagine the anxiety I felt for the safety of my child on these occasions. At the alarm of fire, it seemed as though my heart would cease to beat until I had counted the strokes of the fire alarm bell. The thought of dying and leaving my daughter alone in the world was simply unbearable, but now all is changed and this change has come to us on account of the opportunity which the Industrial Home for the Blind at Hartford has afforded my daughter to earn her own living. She is in every way a different person. Then she was the reverse of the animated, happy, and self reliant girl she now is. She now earns her own living aud for nearly ten months in the year, is paid a salary of six dollars a week, and many times when her mother has been ill and unable to work, she has furnished the money to meet home expenses, and how anyone can wish to deprive the blind, of the benefits which this Institution confers, by withholding from it, the support and patronage it deserves, I am unable to comprehend.

MRS. EMMA CLARK,

Hartford, February 16, 1899.

I am acquainted with C———— O————, formerly of Georgetown, Conn. He became totally blind some eight or nine years ago.

He learned the trade of broom and mattress making at the Industrial Home for the Blind at Hartford, Conn., and has been carrying on business for himself in Georgetown, and later in New Canaan, Conn., for the last four years, maintaining himself and family, consisting of himself, his wife and his mother.

I received a letter from his wife, who is my sister, less than four weeks ago, and she wrote that C———— was getting on finely with his business.

W. E. OFFICER,

Wethersfield, Conn., Feb. 16, 1899.

NOTE.—When this young man became blind he was the only son of a widow who depended upon him for support. He appealed to the Perkins Institute at Boston for admission only to be told that he was just too old to be admitted, owing to the rule which had fixed an 18 year limit.

In despair at what seemed to him to be the failure of his last chance to escape from being dependent upon his mother or spending his days in the poor house, he attempted to take his own life, but was discovered in time to prevent the consummation of his purpose. It was shortly after. that our Industrial Home was started and he became its first pupil.

I was formerly a pupil at the Industrial Home for the Blind in Hartford, Conn. I there learned the lesson that a blind person by the cultivation of self-reliance and business habits could readily become self-sustaining. Since I ceased to be a pupil at the Institution, though totally blind; I have during the past three years, in addition to supporting myself, saved from my salary an average of three dollars per week.

CHARLOTTE M. HINMAN,
W. C. A. Building, Church St.

Hartford, Conn., Feb. 15, 1899.

G—— P——, a former pupil of the Industrial Home for the Blind, after leaving the Institution commenced the manufacture of brooms, with the assistance of the Institution, in Danbury Conn., where he remained in business about six months, and then removed to Bridgeport.

When he entered the Institution his wife wrote him, that on account of his blindness she had been advised that it would not be judicious nor wise for her to live with him again. He was greatly depressed with this double affliction and for several months was unable to apply himself in a satisfactory manner to the acquirement of a trade.

Since leaving the Institution, his wife has consented to live with him again and they are now located in Bridgeport, Conn., where he expects, as soon as a suitable place can be procured to begin again the manufacture of brooms.

In a conversation with me to-day, he stated that when working at his trade, he could make eighteen first-class brooms in a day. These brooms when disposed of to consumers at the usual prices, would yield a profit of $1.50 per dozen.

JOHN A. NORTH.

Collinsville, Conn., Feb. 15, 1899.

I lost my sight when a mere child. Until I became a pupil at the Industrial Home for the Blind in Hartford, Conn., my home was first with one kind friend and then with another who provided for my needs. But while I was always kindly treated and well provided for, I longed to be able to take care of myself and to enjoy the satisfaction of knowing that I was neither dependent upon others nor expected at all times to conceal my preferences, fearing they might come in conflict with the plans which others had made for me. No one can imagine, what a source of happiness it has been to be able to feel that I could at last realize this dream and hope of my life.

I received voice culture, while at the Industrial Home for the Blind, which has enabled me during the past three years to support myself. I have been able not only to support myself, but have saved from my earnings a little over four hundred dollars.

EMMA L. PATTERSON.

Feb. 18, 1899, 3024 14th Street, N. W., Washington. D. C.

NOTE.—The advantages received by this young lady at the Industrial Home, were not limited to the development and cultivation of a naturally sweet and musical contralto voice; but, she acquired a good practical knowledge of printing which should her voice ever fail, would enable her to still maintain herself.

D. L. HONDLOW,
Foreman Printing Dept.

William D. Smith, was a pupil of the Industrial Home for the Blind at Hartford, Conn., and I was his instructor. He was a married man, having a wife and several children and was totally blind.

He was a very apt pupil and learned the trade of broom making thoroughly in less than four months.

We have kept up a correspondence since he returned to his home. He informs me that he has established for himself a good business and is taking care of himself and family.

I have also been in correspondence with Harry E. Whitten, a former pupil of the Institution, who was also a married man with a family. He also was totally blind.

When he left the Institution, he could make from eight to ten brooms a day and with the help of his children to sort his corn, would be able to make from twelve to fourteen brooms a day, which when sold to the consumer, would yield a profit of from a dollar and a half to a dollar and seventy-five cents per dozen.

From his letters I learn that he has not been quite as successful as Mr. Smith, for want of capital to procure stock, but under favorable circumstances would undoubtedly be self-sustaining,

ARTHUR SKINNER, 16 Preston St.

Hartford, Conn., Feb. 15, 1899.

NOTE.—The case of Mr. Whitten was one that would appeal to every person capable of any feeling for his fellow man, for in the statement which he made when he appealed for admission he says, "I lost my house by fire, my wife was removed to the hospital in a critical condition, and I became blind all within three months.

The following correspondence between Mr. Smith, Mr. Cleaveland, President of the Institution and Mr. Hondlow, foreman of the Printing Department, tell the whole story better than we can tell it in volumes.

It contains the whole argument for the existence and support of the Industrial Department of our Institution.

F. E. Cleaveland, President of the Pioneers Institution for the Blind, Hartford, Conn.

DEAR SIR—I am a young man, have been blind for the last ten years, not until two years ago did I learn of the Institution for the Blind at South Boston, Mass., at which time I made application, only to learn that I was too late. * * * I am strong and active, handy with tools, having done things that have puzzled seeing people. I am not afraid of work, having gone about sawing and splitting cord wood, but I am denied even that, the dealers doing it cheaper by means of their horses. I now submit the above for your careful consideration and humbly ask, if there is any possibility of my being instructed in some art in your institution that I may be enabled in the future to support myself. Can furnish references from either clergy or business men. Hoping that the only ray of hope that remains may not be crushed by your reply, I am your obedient servant,

W. D. SMITH, P. O. Box 120.

Sept. 6, 1897.

To the foregoing the writer sent the following reply:

MY DEAR MR. SMITH:

Replying to your favor of the sixth inst., just received, I would say that we will most gladly welcome you in our Institution just as soon as it will be possible for us to receive you without placing a greater strain upon its resources than they are able to bear.

If our young people meet with the usual success this fall in their concert work, or if the magazine, the publication of which we have just commenced, is favorably received by the public, we can undoubtedly make a place for you this winter.   Most cordially yours,

F. E. CLEAVELAND.

MY DEAR MR. HONDLOW:

Five months have passed since I left Wethersfield Avenue and not one week has passed that I did not at some time think of the promise so faithfully made that I should write and let you know how I was getting along, and cannot blame you if you have long since come to the conclusion, that the little Scotchman never intended to write at all. But after all I am convinced if you knew my circumstances you would be charitable enough to excuse the delay. I was without a dollar, requiring a workshop, machinery and broom supplies, and the worst of the jig was, the people did not think I had been long enough away to decently look over the Institution, instead of learning a business that was intended to support my family, but nevertheless I got what I required and started to make brooms last month. I have got small orders from most of the merchants and they have promised me all their trade when they sell the stock on hand. They all like my brooms and I have just received an order for twenty-five dozen from the paper company here, and if they suit I will get the trade. It is the second largest paper company in the country and use a pile of brooms and they pay a good price for them.

* * * * * * * *

Hoping this may reach you in good season, I am yours very truly,"

W. D. SMITH,
P. O. Box, 120.

Aug. 23, 1898.

"At the request of the President of the Institute for the Blind at Hartford, Conn., I visited the following named blind persons, who have received instruction at the Industrial Home. My first call was on James Girken at 1578 State St., New Haven, Conn. I found that he was out on business, but Mrs. Girken showed me his shop and in answer to my queries as to how he was getting on with his broom manufacturing business, replied: 'Very nicely indeed.' He is supporting his family, consisting of a wife and two children. He has a horse and wagon which he uses for delivering his goods and at the same time he takes orders for chairs to be caned by Burdett Knapman, who was also formerly a pupil of the Industrial Home at Hartford. Mrs. Girken was enthusiastic in her praise of the Institution and what it had done for her husband. Mr. Girken occupies as a work shop a store immediately under the tenement in which he lives. It is fitted up with all the appliances and machinery used for broom making, all of which I am told, was furnished him by money raised by the Industrial Home, to give him a business start after he had finished learning his trade at the Institution."

"I then called upon William Arion of 21 Avon St., New Haven, Conn. I had seen him at the Institution nearly two years ago and he recognized my voice at once. He also has a shop for broom making and chair caning nicely fitted up, and he has no trouble in getting all the work that he can do. He is self-sustaining and he spoke of the Institution and what it had done for him in the highest of terms, and when told that it was having a struggle to continue its work, he exclaimed, 'If I could do anything to help it along, I would go on my knees from New Haven to Hartford.' He regarded the Institution as one of the greatest possible blessings that had ever come to the assistance of the blind."

"My next call was on Thomas Donahue, corner of State and Newhall streets, New Haven. Mrs. Donahue met me and when I asked her how Thomas was getting along in his business, she said, 'Very well, indeed, he is out in the shop at work, now.' She added that he was very contented. I was then shown his shop which was built for his use in the rear of his dwelling. There was no light in the shop but he was busily working. He has a large family of children one of whom accompanied me with a lantern His shop was well fitted up with machinery and tools for broom making and in answer to my question asking how he was getting on, he said that he had all that he could do and was supporting his family by his own labor. He said, 'It was a God-send to me when I met Mr. Cleaveland at a fair the blind people gave in New Haven' adding 'If I had not met him I should have been crazy or dead before this time, for then I was sitting around brooding over my condition; without exercise my weight had increased until it was a burden, but since I have been at work at my trade learned at the Industrial Home in Hartford, I have got back to my old weight where I was when I worked at the Winchester Fire Arms shop before I became blind. The Winchesters buy all the brooms they use of me, and I supply the leading hotels of the city and the clock shops.' He also mentioned other customers. Mr. Donahue also spoke in the warmest terms of the Institution and said he would do anything in his power to help it on in the work it was doing for the Blind.''

Alexander Angus, 31 Warner St.,

Hartford, Conn., Feb. 17, 1899.

Note.—William Arion, referred to by Mr. Angus, was not a state pupil, as he was too old to be admitted, but while at the Institution he earned, besides his support, a sufficient amount to purchase his broom machinery and tools, with which he started in business. The Institution also furnished Thomas Donahue instruction, board, washing and mending for a year without receiving any compensation from the state therefor, he too, being considered at the time, too old to come within the provisions of the state law.

"In January of '98, the Connecticut Industrial Home for the Blind, opened its doors to Miss Grace Copeland, of Brooklyn, Conn.

Sickness had deprived her of hearing, and she was fast becoming blind. Owing to her last misfortune she had failed to gain entrance to the American Institute for the Deaf.

Under the instructions of the undersigned she was enabled to thoroughly learn the art of chair caning. On leaving us in June she had mastered the trade, and was equipped by the Institution with tools and cane for a proper start in business. Since that time she has written several letters to her teacher, speaking with much feeling of the great happiness which has come to her since she has been able to do something toward her own support.

In a recent letter she speaks of having finished seven chairs and was expecting more. All her letters breathe the gratitude she feels towards the Institution for placing within her grasp this means of self-support.''

C. M. Hinman.

"I became blind when a mere lad. I graduated at the Perkins Institution for the Blind, but was not fitted by my instruction there to enter upon any industry or employment by which I could earn my living, and I did nothing towards my support for seven years. I was living at the home of my father, when my brother-in-law, after visiting the Industrial Home for the Blind at Hartford, Conn., made arrangements for my admission. Four months after I was admitted, I began by my services to pay my own way, and have since earned on an average of $2.50 per week and my living expenses.

For the past nineteen months I have been using my spare time to study law. During this time I have transcribed into Braille, which is a point system used by the blind in reading, and I have mastered the contents of the following law books: Harriman on Contracts, Bigelow on Torts, May on Criminal Law, Benjamin on Sales, Mecham on Agency, Schonler on Domestic Relations, The Practice Art of Connecticut, Andrews and Fowler's Digest of Connecticut Reports of 1896.

I have also transcribed into Braille, about one hundred and fifty legal forms, with which I have become more or less familiar. I expect to apply for admission to the Bar, and I feel confident that I will succeed in my chosen profession.

I am sincerely grateful to the Institution and its management for the opportunity that has been afforded me to carry forward my life plans."

A. J. HOSKING.

"I was in the employ of the New York & New Haven Railroad Co., as Baggage Master at East Hampton, Conn., when I lost my sight. I was then about nineteen years of age. I applied to be admitted to the Perkins Institution for the Blind, but was refused admission on the ground that I was over eighteen years of age. I afterwards heard of and was admitted to the Industrial Home for the Blind at Hartford, Conn.

At this Institution I received instruction in music, and it is my expectation to earn my living by teaching music. While at the Industrial Home for the Blind I learned to print and bind pamphlets, that is, I could feed a power press, bind pamphlets on the power stitcher and do many other things about a printing office, so that if my preference ran that way I could undoubtedly earn my living at the printing business.

I am at present earning from four to five dollars a week, in addition to my living expenses."   HARRY L. BILL.

"Prior to my admission to the Industrial Home for the Blind at Hartford, I was living with my uncle in Wethersfield, Conn, this place being my old home. My uncle was giving me my living as I was able to do nothing for my support.

At the Industrial Home besides working in the mattress shop, I was instructed in vocal and instrumental music and since leaving the Institution, I have been self-sustaining. I am at present receiving a salary of five dollars per week and my expenses, with a chance of receiving more, contingent upon the profits of the business in which I am engaged.

The one thing which I consider was of the greatest value to me was the determination which I formed at the Institution to make a success of life and I am satisfied that every blind man, who has half a chance, with the right amount of push, can do this."

HARRY C. GREEN,

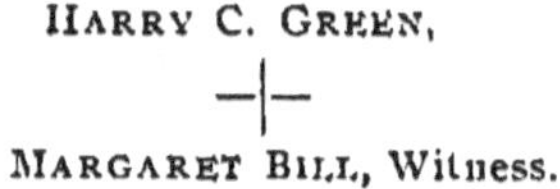

MARGARET BILL, Witness.

"My home is in New Haven, Conn., I became blind when about six years of age. Prior to my being admitted to that Industrial Home for the Blind at Hartford, Conn., I was supported by my parents. For nearly three years since I ceased being a State pupil at the Institution, I have earned my own living and an average of $4.50 per week. I am not very robust, and at present in quite poor health.

I am satisfied that nothing but ill health, will prevent my continuing to be self-sustaining, and I give the Industrial Home for the Blind full credit for giving me the chance to accomplish what I have."

THOMAS V. McCOY,

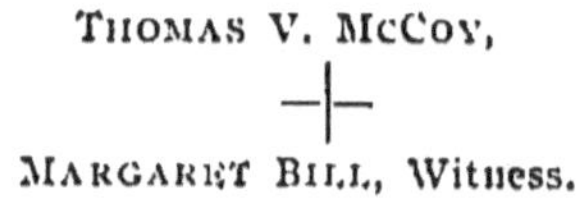

MARGARET BILL, Witness.

"I wish to state that I was a pupil at the Industrial Home for the Blind at Hartford, Conn. That while there I received instruction in music and that since ceasing to be a State pupil, I have had employment that has enabled me to support myself. With the exception of about two months in the summer, I am able to earn, and have earned from four to five dollars a week, over and above my expenses.

I know that the Industrial Home, at Hartford, has been a great help to other blind people. When I was in New Haven, about New Year's I saw Burdette Knapman, who is a friend of mine, who was also a pupil at the Industrial Home for the Blind. He told me he was doing a good business and I know he is earning his own living.

EDWARD NORTHROP.

MARGARET BILL, Witness.

"I learned the trade of broom making at the Industrial Home for the Blind at Hartford, Conn., and now consider myself competent to earn my own living, as soon as I can get a start in the way of broom machinery tools and broom material.

I am working for the Institution now and have been for the past few months, earning from two to three dollars a week. The Institution has been of great assistance to me and I am very grateful for the help I have received, as I have not been able myself to make any return to it for what it has done for me except by my labor. I am not totally blind, but so nearly so, that I am compelled to work as blind people do, and what sight I now have is gradually failing."

M. J. GILMORE.

MARGARET BILL, Witness.

NOTE:—The following letter was received from Miss Grace Copeland after the statement concerning her, by her teacher, Miss Hinman, was in print, but believing our readers would like to hear direct from our only pupil who was deaf, dumb and almost entirely blind, we have concluded to print the letter just received.

Mr. Cleaveland,

"Dear Sir:—The Institution has done a great deal for me. At the Kindergarten I learned to knit and crochet, and make hammocks. I also learned a little about sewing, and received the first lessons in chair caning there. Then I finished learning chair caning at the Institution, and when I came home last June, the Institution gave me a good start in business, by providing me with a complete outfit of tools and material, and I have earned quite a little since I came home, by caning chairs and crocheting slippers. And I cannot begin to tell you how happy it makes me to know that I am really earning something towards my own support. I am *very, very grateful* to those who have done so much for me. May God bless and prosper the Institution which is doing so much for the Blind."

Yours very gratefully,

GRACE M. COPELAND.

Brooklyn, Conn., Feb. 18, 1899.

"The Connecticut Industrial Home has recently taken up the new industry of basket making, which seems to be a departure of great promise for future helpfulness for the Blind girls.

An Indian woman was employed for two months, who taught them to make many different kinds of fancy baskets. Now they are going on with the work with very little help from one who can see, and after sufficient practice they will undoubtedly be able to do without help.

One great advantage of this work is that it can be carried on in their homes or boarding places. As one of the young ladies said recently, 'There is no place like this. The Perkins Institute educates them, but then they go home and sit down and do nothing, now we will have something to do to help at least toward our own support.'

Another advantage in their work is that it is light and pleasant and the girls enjoy it and consider it a recreation after the harder work of the printing office. Those who have the taste for it are studying music, both piano and violin, which will be of incalculable benefit in their after lives."

MISS M. E. GORHAM, Girls' Preceptress.

The volume of business done by the printing department, can be roughly estimated, from the fact, that in addition to over $800 charged on the books during the last year and four months, the cash receipts reported by Ella B. Kendrick, amounted to $6,439.17

NOTE.—Ella B. Kendrick, who makes the following statement and has charge of the work done by the Blind in the printing office and is also editor of the magazine, published by the Industrial Home for the Blind, had eight years experience in the printing business, before entering the employment of the Institution and no one can be better qualified to judge than she now is of the practicability of employing Blind people in the printing and publishing business.

"Before assuming the management of the Printing Department of the Industrial Home for the Blind, I had never been associated with blind people and had no knowledge of their capabilities. In fact, I rather shared the opinion prevalent among seeing people, that the Blind must of necessity be partially helpless. Consequently, when Mr. Cleaveland, in his enthusiasm, talked of his plans, I was sceptical, although willing to do all in my power to assist him to realize his hopes.

After nearly a year and a half in the work, coming into contact with many young blind people, who display all the different characteristics which belong to seeing people, I am satisfied in my own mind that under the right conditions a very large percentage of the Blind can be taught occupations to which they are adapted and that they can become self-supporting.

We have in our department young women who feed power presses, running at the same speed that our seeing people use; they do the same work that our seeing people do, which is the work of an average printing office. We publish a magazine, TALKS AND TALES, and the work rendered necessary by this keeps many of the blind pupils busy. One of the pupils gathers the forms, another we depend upon to stitch the books (she using a power wire stitcher) and we have also pupils who assist in covering the magazines.

All our pupils have learned to fold sheets and their work is well and rapidly done. Two of our young women operate a type-writer, using the same keyboard that seeing people use and doing good work.

The envelopes in which we send out our magazines, are all addressed by these pupils on a type-writer that is used by seeing persons and with no special arrangements for the use of the Blind.

It has been proven that our Blind girls can use type-writers exactly as seeing people do, learning the keyboard as we all learn the keyboard of the piano. They operate their machines with neatness and speed, taking care of them without assistance. After they become familiar with one machine they can readily use a different make. Feeding a cylinder press is also another work that our pupils have demonstrated can be done by the Blind

There are some parts of the work in a printing office that blind people cannot do, but I speak with conviction when I state that, given the same adaptability to the work that we require in a seeing person, blind people *can* earn a living in a printing office. The only difficulty in their way is the lack of faith on the part of seeing people.

Frequently, the question is asked me, 'Would anyone employ a blind person in a printing office?'

I have but one reply to that question: 'With my personal knowledge of the ability of the Blind, *I* would.'

I repeat, the only obstacle in the way of the blind person is the prejudice of the seeing person.''

ELLA B. KENDRICK,
Business Manager Printing Department,
Editor TALKS AND TALES.

Hartford, Feb. 23, 1899.

"I have had about seventeen years experience in the printing business, have been foreman in several printing offices and was foreman in the office of the "New England Home," when in existence, for four years.

Before I became foreman of the printing department of the Industrial Home for the Blind at Hartford, Conn., I should never have thought it possible for blind people to do anything in a printing office that would be of any practical value; but, with the opportunity I have had as foreman of this department for the last year and a half to judge, I now fully endorse all that has been said in the foregoing statement of Ella B. Kendrick, which I have carefully read, and should not hesitate if I were conducting a printing office to employ Blind people.

It may be thought by some that there is more danger of blind people being injured by machinery run by power in a printing office, than there

would be, to seeing people, but what danger there would otherwise be, has been eliminated. The belting that runs the power printing presses and stitcher all comes up through the floor, instead of the over-head system, and the gearings of all the machinery are covered so as to secure them from injury."
D. L. HONDLOW.

Hartford, Conn., Feb. 24, 1899.

"I am requested by Mr. Cleaveland, to give the opinion I have formed as the result of my observations of the practicability of employing the blind in the printing business. I have been the owner and publisher of several newspapers, and have had seven years experience in the business in every department from devil, to editor. For the last two years and a half I have been editor and part owner of the "Farmington Valley Herald, and Journal."

I have been in this printing office and seen the blind people at work scores of times; no one could have been more sceptical than I was of the possibility of a blind person working successfully in a printing office.

The foregoing statement by Ella B. Kendrick, has been read by me and I fully endorse all that she has said, concerning the work in this department by the blind."
JOHN A. NORTH.

Among the pupils who finished their course of instruction in the Industrial Department of the Institution last June, were two young men totally blind, one named Watson Higgins, the other Samuel Brooks, both from Greenwich, Conn.

Mr. Higgins was strong and became an expert broom maker, but Mr. Brooks was of a delicate constitution. Both, before they entered the Institution, were wholly dependent upon friends for support. With money raised by the Institution, a fine shop was fitted up with machinery and appliances for broom making and chair caning, for these two young men, and they started in with a flourishing business.

The writer has learned through Mr. Higgins and the friends of Mr. Brooks, that while Mr. Higgins is going on with business at the shop as usual, Mr. Brooks has removed his chair caning business to the house of his sister, where he makes his home. There is no question about Mr. Higgins being self-sustaining, and while Mr. Brooks lives with his sister, his time will be occupied and he will contribute very largely to his support, as I am informed he has plenty of work to do. But if this home should fail him and our Industrial Home was not in existence to receive him, this delicate young man, whose gentle, Christian spirit has won all hearts, would be doomed to end his days in the poor house, as he has not the physical ability to carry on any business by himself.

Thomas Connolley of Southington, Conn., another pupil of the Industrial Department, who finished his course of instruction last June, is in business for himself in Southington, and in course of conversation with the Town Clerk of Southington to-day, (Feb. 24,) the writer was assured that Connolley was self-supporting. Connolley for many years was an inmate of the poor house in Southington. He is a man of middle age, and his support might have cost the town of Southington during the remainder of his life, more than the instruction necessary to make ten blind men self-sustaining, would cost at the Industrial Home.

Two of the former pupils of the Industrial Department, namely, P. K. Root and Rose Nichols, gained their sight to such an extent that they have been able to secure employment as seeing people, the former as a traveling agent of the Singer Sewing Machine Co.; the latter as a domestic.

Two others, whom we will not mention by name, have not up to the present time, succeeded in becoming self-sustaining, the cause in neither case being lack of sight. One is afflicted by the same disease or condition of mind, which operates to make the career of seeing people unsuccessful, that is, using plain language, the only reason which the writer can assign, is a want of disposition to put forth an effort to succeed, and an indisposition to follow anything that requires any amount of labor or application. The other one has ambition enough for two people, but is lacking in good judg-ment, a character frequently met with in the seeing world, and possessed by persons usually spoken of as a "Jack of all trades and master of none."

THE DARK SIDE.

The reader of the foregoing statements, would undoubtedly, if he had an opportunity, ask these questions: Have all the Blind people who have become pupils of this Industrial Home, been successful? Are there no failures to record?

We should be compelled to answer, that there have been a few cases in which self-support thus far has not been attained, but the history of these cases furnishes the best argument for the continuance of the Industrial Home, as will be readily agreed to by the reader.

Two of the cases the writer has in mind, like Mr. Connolley, spent years in town poor houses. Both are able-bodied men, both after learning broom making have been started in business for themselves, one by the Institution, and the other by the selectmen of the town. Either of these men could have succeeded as easily as any of those above mentioned. Had the Industrial Home been open to them, when they first lost their sight, before they lost their ambition and self-respect, both of these men would have scorned to have received assistance from the town. Having once been supported by the town however, and knowing that they have only to ask for assistance to receive it, I am told that they are only partially self-supporting, as they frequently call upon the selectmen in the towns where they live, for assistance.

There are three other most unfortunate cases to mention. Two of these people, one a man of middle age, the other a young woman, had become so addicted to the use of opium, that the Institution could do nothing for them. The saddest case of all is that of a young woman who became blind at fifteen years of age, up to which time she had been proficient in her studies in the common school. It was the fate of this young girl to have this misfortune overtake her, at a time when it was no one's business in this State to look after the education of the Blind.

Being helpless and friendless she was sent to the poor house where she remained till she was twenty-four years of age, when she was brought to our Home by the overseer of the poor. Her condition was simply indescribable. To all appearances she was both a physical and mental wreck.

Our success with one other case of this kind, prompted us to see what could be accomplished in this case, but after three years of patience and perseverance on the part of caretakers and instructors, we are unable to report any more than partial success. The Industrial Institution, however, is the best place for her. She is no longer a charge upon the State, and whenever she seems to be sinking into the old condition of apathy, her instructors have only to mention that our Industrial Institution is not for idle people and that she will have to return to her old home, to obtain from her the very best service of which she is capable.

When the Industrial Home for the Blind was started in Connecticut by an association of Blind People organized under the name of The Pioneers, the legislature of the state was induced to create a State Board of Education of the Blind. This Board was to do for the Blind what the regular board was doing for the seeing children of the state. It was also to pass upon all applications of blind people for state aid to obtain an education. In six years our Industrial Home has been receiving about half of its income through this channel, but as was foreseen, the same selfish spirit which has always opposed every progressive movement, and which persistently opposed the establishment of free schools for the seeing, has manifested itself in Connecticut. There is now pending in the General Assembly of

Connecticut a measure to abolish the State Board of Education of the Blind, and withdraw all support from our Industrial Home. One of the principal reasons advanced by the opposition is, that no such provision is made by other New England States. We now present the defense of Mr. Cleaveland before the Connecticut Legislature in support of the progressive steps taken in behalf of the Blind in Connecticut.

To His Excellency, George E. Lounsbury, Governor, State of Connecticut.

SIR:—

"I have the honor to submit herewith the Fifth Annual Report of the State Board of Education of the Blind.

During the fiscal year ending September 30th, 1898, the number of State pupils coming under the care and supervision of the State Board of Education of the Blind was sixty-nine (69). Of this number, eighteen (18) attended the Perkins Institution for the Blind, at South Boston, Mass.

Twenty-five (25) were at the Kindergarten, one (1) being a day pupil, twenty-five (25) at the Industrial Home for the Blind and one whose attendance was divided, between the Perkins Institution and the Industrial Home. Of this number three were absent a portion of the time.

Assuring your Excellency, that the education of the young children in the Kindergarten, and the older children at the Perkins Institution, is progressing under the most favorable conditions attainable, we must refer those who would learn more concerning the methods employed for their instruction and the results obtained, to previous reports, the last of which will be found bound with the present report. These children have crossed the danger line and for the present are in a safe harbor protected by barriers raised by the humanity of a past generation, and the enlightened sympathy of the present. Our duty of the hour is to take our place by the side of those who were the children of yesterday, but who to-day are battling with the waves outside the breakwater. Waves made angry by the same spirit of selfishness that combated the establishment of free schools for the seeing, and has disputed every advancing step made by the vanguard of enlightenment, humanity and civilization. Waves that are made more angry in the impending struggle, by error born of prejudice and piqued by successive failures, into a persistent opposition. Six years ago the genius of Connecticut awakened to her duty, decided that she would no longer leave her blind children to a fate determined by chance, but that henceforth they should receive every advantage that had been gained and secured to her children whose days were brightened by the sunlight. Experience had taught her that it was not enough to establish free schools in which the children of the poor, might stand side by side with the children of the rich without being classified as paupers, but there must be a Board of Education established, charged with a duty of securing the attendance in such schools, of the children of slothful, careless or selfish parents.

What measure then in the light of experience would be more likely to secure the best results in the case of her less fortunate children, than to establish a Board of Education of the Blind? A Board, one member of which should be a woman, who with a mother's heart, stirred by tender and loving solicitude, would take in her arms each little neglected, sightless child, and with a knowledge prompted by love, fan the God-given spark of intelligence until it should illuminate the mind and thus strengthen and equip her little charge to begin its journey along the dark and sunless path, it must soon learn to walk alone. And when her charge, a young man grown, should reach the shore of the unknown and sunless sea, and be compelled to launch his frail barque upon its waves, he shall not, at this, the most critical time of his life, be deserted and abandoned to founder upon unknown shoals, for there shall be at hand a pilot, who, as master of his own ship, has sailed this sea for twenty years. A pilot, who, with chart in hand, shall point out the dangerous reefs, encourage and sustain her charge until, with confidence born of knowledge, he can be safely trusted with the helm. Nor should this work be undertaken until there shall be wise and just provisions made to safeguard the interest of the people.

Hence as members of this Board, the chosen chief magistrates of the State shall be entrusted to exercise a just and wise discretion and stand as guardians of the interest of the people, to prevent all unnecessary or unwarranted expenditures of public funds. Thus fortified, the genius of Connecticut stands forth the champion of this new and sacred trust.

Two years ago the Connecticut Legislature appointed a commission charged with the duty of examining into state expenses and making a report to the General Assembly of 1899, pointing out how these expenses could be reduced. This commission in order to save a little money for the State, proposes, among other saving measures, to withdraw the support which the state has hitherto granted to our Industrial Home.

Before considering what has been accomplished since the organization of the State Board of Education of the Blind, it will be well to understand how the blind people of Connecticut fared when everything was left to chance, and it was the business of no one to look after their interests, or to see that the money expended by the State accomplished the intended purpose.

A glance at the record shows that the number of State beneficiaries, up to the time the State Board of Education of the Blind was created, was fifty-seven, covering a period of twenty-eight years.

All of these were young children when they entered the Perkins Institution at Boston, and for every pupil the State paid three hundred dollars a year or any fractional part of a year. Of these, nine remained one year or less.

It is safe to say that over $11,000 expended by the State for the children who staid two years or less was practically thrown away.

The twelve who did not stay out their full time undoubtedly fell far short of the benefit they would have received had they completed their course. Of the whole number, not one-third as many became self-sustaining as the records of the Industrial Home will show as the results of its labors during the past five years.

This commission, however, proposes to dig a grave and bury therein the new born hopes and aspirations of the Blind. They have on their side this advantage, most people do not understand nor realize what it is possible for blind people to accomplish; therefore, when they say that what we claim can be done is not practical, and that we are attempting more than we can accomplish at the State's expense, they quite readily obtain converts to their ideas.

This commission in its report gives as one reason why the Industrial Home for the Blind should not be continued in Connecticut, that there is no such institution in Vermont, New Hampshire, Maine nor Rhode Island, and that Connecticut can send its pupils, as these other states do, to the Perkins Institute at Boston.

They fail to inform the General Assembly however, that no person over 18 years of age will be received as a pupil at that Institution and that our Industrial Home simply undertakes to cover the ground that the Institution at Philadelphia, which they commend, covers, and does not trench upon the ground covered by the Perkins Institution at Boston, but on the contrary, we send our own state pupils, after they finish their course in the Kindergarten and primary department, to the Perkins Institution.

Again, it is no argument to advance to the citizens of Connecticut, that they should wait for other New England states to perform their duty. Connecticut is proud of the part its citizens have taken in the progress of civilization and works of philanthropy. It was the citizens of Connecticut who formulated the first written constitution; it was in Connecticut that the first Institution in America, for the education of the deaf and dumb was established. It was a citizen of Connecticut, Mrs. Harriet Beecher Stowe, author of Uncle Tom's Cabin, who made converts by the thousands to the doctrine of anti-slavery and thus made the abolition of slavery possible; it was a citizen of Connecticut, John Brown of Torrington, who drew his sword and cut the Gordion knot that fastened the system of slavery to the backs of a people who had declared for freedom; it was also citizens of Connecticut who stoned the seminary where a brave Connecticut lady admitted a colored girl to equal privileges with white children, and it was a General Assembly of the State of Connecticut, that years after that act purged the State of this disgrace.

Now, when we are considering the advance work that is being done in this state for the Blind, is it any discredit to Connecticut that, at the recent bi-ennial meeting of the American Association of the Instructors of the Blind, where representatives from the old established Institutions for the Blind in Boston, New York and Philadelphia, as well as from all parts of the United States and Canada, were present, that a representative of this State was chosen chairman of a committee appointed to wait upon the Congress of the United States to secure legislation which by resolution of that assembly was deemed desirable.

One step further and we have reached the real reason that has plainly influenced the members of this commission to make the recommendations they have made and that is, they share with most seeing people the belief that blind persons are necessarily and irrevocably chained to a condition of hopeless dependence.

Upon this issue then, cleared of all obstructions, let the decision be reached by the present General Assembly. Before we proceed to discuss this question further, let us crave the sympathy of all fair-minded and considerate people. Not because we are blind, but because, despite the constitutional provision that no man's life should be twice placed in jeopardy for the the same offence, our cause is for the fourth time placed in jeopardy by the persistency of our opponents, after three times making good our defence before the chosen representatives of the people.

Does it count for nothing with this commission that the Board of Education of the Blind was created and its powers defined upon the advice and unanimous approval of the joint standing committee on Judiciary of the General Assembly of 1893, composed of such men as Senator Fox of New Haven, Messrs. Wood of Manchester, Hale of Glastonbury, Judd and Stoddard of Litchfield, Beardsley of Bridgeport, Corttis of Thompson, Palmer of Norwich, and Wilcox of Berlin.

Is the General Assembly aware that the whole subject of the advisability of the State lending its aid and encouragement to the work that is being done by this same Industrial Home for the Blind was thoroughly gone over and inquired into by the General Assembly of 1895, and that the Committee on Humane Institutions consisting of Senator Bernd, Messrs. Newton, of New Haven; Whiton, of Manchester; Fuller, of Suffield; Saunders, of Waterford; Lounsbury, of Darien; Barber, of Putnam; Battey, of Columbia; and Booth, of New Milford, after the most thorough canvass and consideration of the whole subject, made a unanimous report in favor of continuing the methods employed by the Board and favored an appropriation to the

Industrial Home for the Blind for the full amount it then asked for ?

Do the gentlemen of this commission know that their idea of abolishing the State Board of Education of the Blind and passing over its work to the Board of Education for the seeing did not originate with them, but that Judge Newton of New Haven, House Chairman of the Committee on Humane Institutions of the General Assembly of 1895, advanced this proposition, but, becoming thoroughly convinced that any such change would be unwise, he subsequently agreed with the committee, thus making their approval of the measure submitted to them unanimous.

Does it count for nothing with the members of this commission, that their opinions are opposed to those entertained by the late Governor Morris, Ex-Governor O. Vincent Coffin, Ex-Governor Lorrin A. Cooke and Chief Justice Charles B. Andrews without whose co-operation, sanction and approval the work they seek to undo could never have been carried forward ?

Does it count for nothing with them that their opinion and judgment is opposed to the opinion and judgment of such men as Mr. Rodney Dennis, President Connecticut Humane Society ; Rev. Joseph H. Twichell, Dr. Henry P. Stearns, Superintendent and Director of Hartford Retreat; Dr. G. Pierrepont Davis, General Arthur L. Goodrich, Ex-Lieutenant-Governor Ernest Cady, Colonel George Pope, Treasurer Pope Manufacturing Co.; Prof. A. R. Merriam, of the Hartford Theological Seminary and the Rev. Dr. George M. Stone, all of whom as members of the Advisory Board of the Institution, have become familiar with the affairs of the Industrial Home, and have had opportunities for judging the merits of its work during the past six years, a hundredfold greater than any information that the commission could have acquired through its sub-committee ?

In order that the State at large should be more fully represented on the advisory board of our Institution, the following named gentlemen with their consent and approval, have been added:

> Hon. George E. Lounsbury, Ridgefield,
> Major Richard O. Cheney, South Manchester,
> Hon. Allan W. Paige, Bridgeport,
> Hon. H. Lynde Harrison, Guilford,
> Lieut-Gov. Lyman A. Mills, Middlefield,
> Hon. Charles E. Searles, Thompson,
> Hon. Charles Phelps, Atty.-Gen., Rockville
> Gen. Louis N. Van Keuren, Bridgeport,
> Hon. Daniel N. Morgan, Bridgeport,
> Col. Norris G. Osborn, New Haven.
> Dr. S. B. St. John, Hartford,
> Richard G. Beebe, Stafford,
> Hon. J. Henry Roraback, Canaan,

> Erastus Gay, Farmington
> P. H. Woodward, Hartford,
> Dr. Jos. E. Root, Hartford,
> Herbert H. White, Hartford,
> Morris W. Seymour, Bridgeport,
> Charles M. Jarvis, Berlin,
> Ex-Gov. Thomas M. Waller, New London,
> Gen. Wm. B. Rudd, Lakeville.

Knowing this fact will the General Assembly not think that it will be as well to wait before undoing the work of the past six years until this board informs a future General Assembly that such action is desirable?

Is the commission not aware that all the reasons advanced in its report on which it bases its recommendations, were urged by the opponents of the work for the Blind before the General Assembly of 1897?

That, in addition to these reasons, all the evidence was in, including the advice of the State Board of Charities, which insists upon classifying the Blind with imbeciles, convicts, insane and paupers. That all this evidence was fully weighed and considered by Gov. Cooke before the writer, whose term of office expired in the following July, was reappointed to continue his labors in behalf of the Blind."

Resuming the argument, Mr. Cleaveland, to show what has been accomplished by the Blind in the past, and to point out that the lack of faith exhibited by seeing people in the ability of the Blind, is the greatest barrier to their success and chances in life, proceeds as follows:

"We therefore appear as an advocate before a Tribune of the people, who, we shall imagine, has all the prejudice and disbelief in the ability of the blind, shown by our critics.

"My first witness shall be your own REASON, from a different standpoint than the one you now occupy. When the hopes, aspirations and all that is worth living for in the lives of the blind are to be placed on one side of the scale, the Judge who is to hold the balance, should be an ideal judge. Let me therefore place over your eyes a bandage; for the wisdom of the age has created as its ideal a Goddess of Justice with bandaged eyes. Now that you cannot see, a Venus or Hebe might appear to testify and your judgment remain as undisturbed and dispassionate as though you were listening to a story of a poor but honest washer-woman.

"Again, while you are thus deprived of sight, let me for the sake of argument, ask you to imagine the limitation *permanent*. Have you any objection now to be classed with imbeciles, insane persons, paupers and convicts? If I should ask you if the loss of sight did not place you in as hopeless a situation as the imbecile or insane, would you not reply: 'No a thousand times, no! The eye is but the servant of the brain. I am far better off than the insane because my reason is not dethroned.'

"'Yes, you are right. Your REASON is like a king who in his palace sits enthroned. Your sense of sight is but one of five grand avenues of approach along which swift-footed messengers bring tidings of what transpires throughout your kingdom. You lose this sense of sight and you have but closed the palace gates of *one* of these grand avenues. But the messengers who are thus debarred, are only HINDERED, not dismayed. For quickly they approach the throne along the other four. Before you lost your sight you thought that little more could be accomplished for the blind than to provide them food, raiment and shelter, but now, with plenty of time to think it over and revise your former opinion, shall you feel compelled to resign the office you now hold and live in idle dependence on your fortune or friends, or perchance, if your fortune and friends should be swept away, will you be content to take a place in some neglected corner of a town poor-house? Or will you say in your mind, what blind men have accomplished may be again accomplished by the blind? Remembering Mr. Faucett, who was chosen by Gladstone as a Cabinet Minister, would you not say if it was possible for him to make an eminently successful Postmaster General of a great empire, will it not be possible for me to retain the office I now hold, and still find a way in which I can faithfully discharge my duty as a public servant?

"Would you think it possible for a blind man to use the eyes of others as men use spectacles, and become one of the most celebrated naturalists of his day? Turn to your encyclopedia and read the life of Huber, who is still the leading authority on the particular lines he followed out. Let us have his testimony in his own words on this point. We quote his language to a friend who could see.

"'I am much more certain of what I declare to the world than you are, for you publish what your own eyes only have seen, while I take the mean among many witnesses.'

"It is related of Michael Angelo that on an occasion when out walking with a friend, he pointed out a rough, unhewn rock, and inquired of his friend what he saw. The reply was, 'I see nothing but a huge, huge rock.' 'But I,' said Michael Angelo, 'see lying concealed in that rock the form of an angel.' And later, this celebrated sculptor released from its imprisonment the angel he had seen.

"But you reply, 'Michael Angelo was not blind. You do not mean to affirm that the blind can enter the domain of art successfully?' Yet note what is said of John Conelli, in a book entitled *Achievements of the Blind*, published at Rochester, N. Y., by Artman & Hall in 1872.

"'Perhaps the most complete triumph of tactual perfection over want of sight that history records, is to be found in the artistic skill of John Conelli, sometimes called Gambasio, from the place of his birth in Tuscany. This remarkable person lost his sight at the age of twenty, and after having been in this condition about ten years, he first manifested a taste for sculpture. His first work in this art was to imitate a marble figure representing Cosmo de Medici, which he formed of clay, and rendered a strikingly perfect likeness of the original. His talent for statuary soon developed itself to such a degree that the Grand Duke Ferdinand, of Tuscany, sent him to Rome to model a statue of Pope Urban VIII, which he completed to the entire satisfaction of his patron. It is supposed that this is the same famous blind sculptor whom Roger de Piles met with in the Justinian Palace where he found him modeling in clay a figure of Minerva.

"'It is related that the Duke of Bracciano, who had seen him at work, doubted much that he was completely blind, and in order to set the matter at rest he caused the artist to model his head in a dark cellar. It proved a striking likeness. Some, however objecting that the Duke's beard which was of patriarchal amplitude, had made the operation of producing a seeming likeness too easy, the artist offered to model one of the Duke's daughters which he accordingly did, and this also proved an admirable likeness. Among his numerous other works is a marble statue of Charles I of England, said to be finely finished.'

"Let us now ask you to turn once more to your Britanica, and read that James Holman, an officer in the English army, after losing his sight, became one of the most famous travelers of his time; that in 1835 he published a four volume edition of his travels entitled *A Voyage Around the World*, of which the author of the article in the Britanica writes:

"'The works of Holman, besides the interest attaching to them from his incidental references to the peculiarities of his circumstances arising from his physical defect, and his methods of triumphing over his difficulties, occupy a unique place in literature as products of very extraordinary energy and perseverance, while on account of the variety of their information and their frequently graphic descriptions, they are of considerable value as books of travel.'

"Entering the domain of poetry and history, it is hardly necessary to ask you to recall that Homer completed the Illiad and composed the Odyssey after he became blind. That it was not until after Milton was turned from his political career by his becoming blind that he wrote *Paradise Lost*, and that our own Prescott, author of *Ferdinand and Isabella, Conquest of Mexico*, and *Conquest of Peru*, gathered his material and produced these valuable contributions to history after losing his sight.

"We are living in an age of wonderful achievements of the mind, and the triumph of inventions. If any noted scientist should announce that he had opened up communication with the inhabitants of another planet, *who* among us would stake our lives or fortunes that he could not demonstrate the truth of his declaration? And yet, let me summon the most noted scientists and inventors of this generation before you and ask them if they have not seen more that was of service to them in their labors when their heads were lying on their pillows and their eyes were closed, than at any other time.

"Did you ever consider that the messenger whom we are now able to send around the world in thirty minutes was never seen by Mr. Morse or any of his successors in electrical experiments, and that it was to his sense of hearing and not to his sense of sight that the world is indebted for the invention of the telegraph?

"Blind men as clergymen have attained to the greatest eminence. Thomas Blacklock, D. D., who was born in Scotland, lost his sight while an infant, but became an eminent divine and author. (*Achievements of the Blind*, page 70.)

"The Rev. Richard Lucas, D. D., was a noted divine and author. (*Achievements of the Blind*, page 52.)

"There is to-day a physician in active practice in the city of Hartford, holding an important office under the law, who is so nearly blind that there could be found many pupils in any institution for the blind whose percentage of sight is very much greater.

"William E. Cramer, of Milwaukee, as a journalist and at one time editor of the *Albany Argus* and later editor and proprietor of the *Evening Wisconsin*, at Milwaukee, ranks among the distinguished men of that vocation in this country.

"Mr. Herreshoff, of Bristol, R. I., has held the palm against all seeing competitors. The yachts made after his designs and under his supervision have proudly borne the stars and stripes, leading in every contest with the swiftest sailing yachts constructed by the most skillful of our British cousins.

"The *Mentor*, a work published in Boston, and devoted to the interests of the blind, records the following instances:

"'Printing and book-binding successfully attempted. (Vol. I, page 121.) 'Successful Telegraph Operators.' (Vol. I, page 356, also Vol. III, page 313.) 'Farming and Mining.' (Vol. I, page 251.) 'Typewriting' (Vol. I, page 17.) 'Piano Tuning.' (Vol. II, page 263.) 'Stenography and Editorial Work.' (Vol. II, page 56.) 'Crystal Cutter.' (Vol. III, page 221.) 'David Wood, of Philadelphia, an organist at the head of his profession.' (Vol. III, page 41.) 'John Metcalf, Yorkshire, England, remarkably successful as a contractor and builder.' (Vol. III, page 25.)

"'Watch and Clockmaking, by William Huntly and William Kennedy.' (*Achievements of the Blind*, page 250.)

"To these the more ordinary pursuits of brushmaking, basket making, chair caning, mattress making and broom making may be added.

"In England there has existed for a number of years an association of philanthropists, known as the the British and Foreign Association, who have charged themselves with the work of creating opportunities and facilities for furnishing employment for the adult blind.

"In Connecticut, we have had many associations for the prevention of cruelty to animals, and a State Board of Charities, but until the friends of the present work which has resulted in the establishment of a State Board of Education of the Blind, began their labor, no one, not even the State Board of Charities, had made it his business to look after the elevation and advancement of this class of our citizens.

"An interesting account of the founding of an institution in Brazil will be found in Vol. I, page 130, of *The Mentor*, from which we select the following:

"'In 1872 was laid the foundation of a building sufficiently large, when completed, to receive six hundred pupils,—four hundred boys and two hundred girls. The annual receipts of five lotteries were appropriated to this institution, this sum, with the accumulating interest and various donations which would be given, to constitute a fund for the maintainance of the establishment.

"'The accommodations thus provided for six hundred pupils are far from meeting the needs of the country. Recent statistics show the number of blind children, between the ages of six and fourteen years, in the Empire of Brazil to be about 12,000. Accordingly, six other schools for the blind are to be established in the chief towns of the provinces of Para, Pernambuco, Bahia, Minas-Geraes, Sao Paulo, and Rio Grande de Sul. In connection with each of these schools a workshop will be provided to give employment to those who cannot earn a livelihood by music or the liberal professions. The Institution at Rio will then become a training school to furnish teachers for the provincial establishment.

"'The pupils of this institution are supported and educated at the expense of the government. The first teachers were seeing persons, and their appointments were for life. In 1886 three vacancies occurred, and these were filled by former pupils of the school who had been assistants. The religious teaching is given by an ecclesiastic, and in three other branches—namely, natural sciences, playing of wind instruments, and the needlework for girls—the training is given by teachers who have sight ; but in all other departments of the school—in the elementary classes in Portugese, arithmetic, algebra, geometry, geography, history, French, the piano, harmony, piano tuning, printing and book-binding,—the instruction is given by blind teachers.

"'Among the successful graduates of this school are cited two wealthy farmers; one man who has earned a competency by raising stock; another, a poet, novelist and musician, who is organist in the richest church in Rio; a fifth who is a teacher of the French language; and a sixth who, as a piano tuner, music-teacher, and conductor of an orchestra, has reared a family in comfortable circumstances and will probably become rich. Among the girls who have graduated, are mentioned one who became a distinguished pianist and another who is a charming vocalist.

"Now, then, if it please the Court, let us stop a moment, and see where we are.

"Are we assuming too much if we claim that we have succeeded in maintaining the following propositions: First, that *blindness itself* is not an impassable barrier preventing a person with this limitation from becoming a self-reliant, self-sustaining and useful member of society? Second, that the only reason why all blind people who are otherwise mentally and physically sound, do not become self-sustaining, is not because they are *blind*, but because the general belief entertained by all their seeing friends, (including their parents,) has in the case of children, robbed them of that training and discipline essential to a successful career even on the part of those who can see, and in the case of the adult blind operating to confirm *them* in the belief that they are rendered helpless by the loss of sight. Third, that Connecticut, in its labors for the blind, (to say nothing of what our sister states have done,) is twenty years behind even our neighbors in South America.

"It is possible that we may not have sufficiently emphasized the importance of educating the seeing public on these points. So important, however, is this phase of the work, that all else sinks to insignificance compared with it. You may teach the blind as much as you please, they may become even more skillful and proficient in what they undertake than any of their seeing competitors, as Mr. Herreshoff undoubtedly is. But, when you send them forth into the world and they run up against the solid wall of public disbelief in their ability to accomplish anything without sight, they in ninety-nine cases out of a hundred will give up the struggle and settle back into a condition of idle dependence. Now this same public will receive them without question, where, in their apparent helplessness, they but serve to confirm the public in its erroneous belief.

"Some years before the locomotive had found its way into Utah, a small army of Mormon proselytes started to march from Denver to Salt Lake City, drawing their luggage and supplies with them in handcarts. This march, known in history as the Handcart Expedition, was begun later in the fall than was expected and before they had covered half the distance winter had set in. The extreme cold, driven by the bleak winds, chilled the very marrow in their bones and their trail was easy to follow for years after by the skeletons of those who perished. Only a mere handful out of that large company ever reached their goal.

"The blind persons who have attained success, in spite of the disbelief of the world in their ability to do so, may be compared with the survivors of this ill-fated expedition.

"Just what a train of cars drawn by a locomotive over the iron rails that now bind Denver to Salt Lake City would have done for these poor, perishing Mormons, the education of the seeing public on the point in issue will do for the blind ; and if I could summon before the Tribune the two thousand successful blind people out of the sixty-two thousand in the United States in 1890, every one would tell you the same story that the brave girl writes me in a letter which I here introduce :

" 'I graduated in the Ohio School for the Blind in the class of 1889 and entered the Cleveland College of the Western Reserve University, in the folfowing September.

" 'It was my ambition on leaving college to obtain a position in some seeing school, to teach those branches which I had found by careful investigation, that a properly trained blind teacher could teach seeing pupils quite as well as a seeing teacher. I felt sure that if I could succeed in this, I might open a field for those of the blind who could fit themselves for such work, and break down a little of the aversion to our doing anything practicable. It is hardly necessary however, for me to say that, though I did my utmost, and though I had the best of commendations, I failed to find anyone who would give me a trial. There were plenty of seeing teachers seeking employment, and those who had positions to give either did not believe that I could do their work, or they were unwilling to try the experiment. Perhaps if I had had influential friends in some of the schools, it might have been otherwise.

" 'In the meantime, I maintained myself by private teaching, tutoring and writing, until my failing health made it necessary for me to have country air and out-door exercise. I believe that the blind, properly trained, and conveniently located, can do nicely in each of the above named fields, and it is easier to overcome prejudice where only the individual is concerned.

" 'At present I am not doing much of anything but trying to regain my strength. Yet I hope to be able to go to work soon. Like yourself, I am deeply interested in our class, and I hope we may become better acquainted. It is hardly necessary for me to add that if I can be of any assistance to you in your work I am entirely at your service."

Yours truly,

ROBERTO ANNA GRIFFITH.

"We have several times cited a book entitled *Achievements of the Blind.* I now ask you to receive in evidence the testimony of its authors on the point we are now considering. We take the following from the introduction:

"'We will not weary the reader's patience with an elaborate preliminary, nor with apologies for offering the present work to the public. We have been induced to enter the arena of book-makers by a desire to disseminate a more correct and extended knowledge of blindness and its effects upon mental and physical development than the reading public has hitherto possessed. In this way we hope to remove some of the most formidable obstacles that hedge up the way to usefulness and independence for all who are placed in this condition; a condition to which, by the vicissitudes of life, every person is exposed, and in whose dark and inauspicious night more than five hundred thousand of our race are at present enshrouded, in almost every state of our Union, as well as in those of Europe. Charity, with her angelic hand, has raised within the present century institutions dedicated to the sacred purpose of giving the light of science and a knowledge of some of the useful arts to those who behold not the beautiful earth and serene sky. But sad experience has taught us that until society in general better understands and appreciates the abilities of the blind, all the knowledge and skill we can acquire at these establishments are not available as means of self-support, but tend only to awaken a keener sense of our privation and dependence. To illustrate: A young man graduates at one of our institutions for the blind, after receiving a thorough course of instruction in the theoretical and practical sciences. Elated with the hope of henceforth being able to earn for himself a respectable livelihood as a teacher of music, or of some other science, he hears of a vacant situation and makes the necessary application, but is informed that as he cannot see, he cannot, of course, discharge the requisite duties. The next time an opportunity offers he determines to go in person, say a hundred miles, and in winter too, to show that he is qualified. If a knowledge of music is required, he performs with proficiency; if of literature, philosophy or mathematics, he is ready and clear and proves himself competent to the discharge of all the duties of the employment that he seeks. But the idea that one who can see is more serviceable than one who cannot, still erects an impenetrable wall between him and success. And thus the prejudice which his condition creates opposes him on every side.

"'Without hesitation we say, that all the most painful disadvantages with which we have been obliged to contend under the absence of sight, have arisen entirely from ignorance on the part of communities of our capability and resources.

"'Sympathy, like the atmosphere, surrounds us on every side, but like the atmosphere, is too light to sustain life. To acknowledge that our present work may have faults and imperfections, is only to admit that it has been produced by human agency. But we certainly cannot ask to have them excused or loved in consequence of our peculiar condition. No; attribute them to our ignorance, carelessness, or stupidity, but we pray thee, reader or critic, attribute them not to blindness, for this we must deem rather an advantage than an inconvenience in the art of composition.'

"After a quarter of a century's experience, during which time we have taken an active part in the affairs of life, and attained a certain measure of success, we here solemnly affirm that nine-tenths of the difficulties experienced have been due to the unwillingness of the public to believe in our ability to accomplish what we undertook. And now, Your Excellency, turning from our imaginary Tribune, we propose to take the public somewhat into our confidence. We confess that we foresaw that as soon as the work for the blind in Connecticut assumed the proportions that it was bound to assume if we discharged our duty faithfully, we should meet with serious opposition from those who did not understand the importance of the work, and from those who have always stood in the way of human progress, just as the public school system (which is the proudest monument Connecticut has ever erected to bear testimony to the enlightenment and civilization of her people,) was persistently opposed.

"'It was in order that we should be prepared to meet the storm when it came, that we have labored in season and out of season, and that our young blind people have given exhibitions in nearly every town in the State, so as to raise up friends for the work, who would understand and appreciate its importance and who would stand by us when the battle was won.

"'We felt that we had accomplished what we had undertaken, when we were able to support our recommendations by a memorial to the General Assembly containing such names as, Ex-Gov. Charles R. Ingersoll, Pres. Dwight, of Yale College, Theodore S. Woolsey, Rev. Newman Smythe, Rev. T. T. Munger, Ex-Gov. H. B. Harrison, Judge Simeon E. Baldwin, of New Haven, and Bishop Williams and Ex-Gov. O. Vincent Coffin, of Middletown, Henry C. Robinson, James G. Batterson, Rev. Francis Goodwin, Dr. Chester D. Hartranft, John R. Buck, and Chas. E. Gross, of Hartford, with twelve hundred and fifty prominent and representative names from all the principal cities and towns in the state, standing not only for a large majority of its voting population, but representing three-fourths of the grand list of the State. These memorials referred to the committee on Appropriations, formed but a part of the hearing, a report of which appeared in the *Hartford Courant* on the morning following the day assigned, and which report we here quote:

"After referring to the presentation of the needs of the Institution for the Blind, by the secretary of the State Board of Education of the Blind, the report proceeds as follows:

` " 'Rodney Dennis spoke in favor of the appropriation and viewed it from he standpoint of duty the State owed to the Blind.

" 'The Rev. J. H. Twichell said: 'By making this appropriation, the State will only be following where others have led. Many individuals have put aside comfort in order to help the blind. Of course it is a matter of pity that we are obliged to come before the Committee in the present state of affairs and ask for money. A good father once admonished his son not to be a spendthrift but to keep within his salary if he had to borrow money to do so. If necessary, we should do that way, rather than neglect the crying wants of humanity.'

" 'Ex-Lieut-Gov. Cady said that one thing that should lead the State to aid the blind was that they were doing all they could to help themselves. Other unfortunates had been provided for, but none could be more worthy than these poor people. They had got into debt and asked for aid. It seemed to him there was an obligation the State ought to assume.' In closing, he said: I hope the appropriation may be met as far as you gentlemen see fit.

" 'The Rev. Dr. G. M. Stone called attention to the fact that the blind movement started in the slums. This fact should be especially considered in its favor. The object was such a worthy one that he felt it would be rightly met.

" 'Prof. A. R. Merriam, of the Theological Seminary, had for a long time been interested in watching the blind work go on. The reports of their work were most favorable and the State should help them obtain the pecuniary aid they needed.

" 'Prof. J. J. McCook favored the bill and urged that the requirements be met. 'The most we can do,' he said, 'for these poor people is to bring the light of enlightenment to them.'

" 'T. M. Crowley, speaking for organized labor, said he was heartily in favor of the appropriation and was willing to do all he could as an individual to aid its being brought about.

" 'A blind man spoke of how he had been benefited by learning the trade of broom-making at an Industrial School for the Blind.

" 'Mrs. Foster, Ass't. Secretary of the Board of Education of the Blind, related instances where the blind had been helped and stated that in certain cases blind eyes might be opened by giving them proper care. Others who spoke in favor of the appropriation were Mr. Job Williams (head of the School for Deaf-mutes,) Mrs. Whitmore, and Mrs. Olmsted.

' 'Mr. Cleaveland exhibited articles showing the work the Blind are capable of doing; he also showed a printed abstract of the names of prominent people of forty-five cities and towns who supported the bill. The list represented two-thirds of the grand list of the State and half the voters, he said.'

"From this it will be seen that to all appearances we were prepared to show good reasons why the State should go steadily forward with the work for the blind and make amends as soon as possible for past neglect."

———

To the objection that other states in New England have not as yet taken up the work for the adult blind, Mr. Cleaveland says:

Again, it is no argument to advance to the citizens of Connecticut, that they should wait for other New England states to perform their duty. Connecticut is proud of the part its citizens have taken in the progress of civilization and works of philanthropy. It was the citizens of Connecticut who formulated the first written constitution; it was in Connecticut that the first Institution in America, for the education of the deaf and dumb was established. It was a citizen of Connecticut, Mrs. Harriet Beecher Stowe, author of Uncle Tom's Cabin, who made converts by the thousands to the doctrine of anti-slavery and thus made the abolition of slavery possible; it was a citizen of Connecticut, John Brown of Torrington, who drew his sword and cut the Gordion knot that fastened the system of slavery to the backs of a people who had declared for freedom; it was also citizens of Connecticut who stoned the seminary where a brave Connecticut lady admitted a colored girl to equal privileges with white children, and it was a General Assembly of the State of Connecticut, that years after that act purged the State of this disgrace.

Now, when we are considering the advancé work that is being done in this state for the Blind, is it any discredit to Connecticut that, at the recent bi-ennial meeting of the American Association of the Instructors of the Blind, where representatives from the old established Institutions for the Blind in Boston, New York and Philadelphia, as well as from all parts of the United States and Canada, were present, that a representative of this State was chosen chairman of a committee appointed to wait upon the Congress of the United States to secure legislation which by resolution of that assembly was deemed desirable.

STATEMENT OF DISBURSEMENTS

—FOR THE——

FISCAL YEAR ENDING SEPTEMBER 30TH, 1898.

The total amount disbursed under the direction of the State Board of Education of the Blind was $22,569.96 as follows:

1.	Amount paid Perkins Institution for the Blind	$5,325.23
2.	Kindergarten for the Blind	7,406.64
3.	Industrial Home	6,489.00
4.	Salary of Secretary	1,200.00
5.	Salary of Assistant Secretary	600.00
6.	Traveling and Office expenses of Secretary	70.69
7.	Expenses reported by Assistant Secretary	137.97
8.	Traveling Expenses, Chief Justice Andrews	5.50
9.	Cash paid for clothing and transportation of Pupils at Industrial Home (Pioneers)	255.99
10.	Stationery	10.30
11.	Cash expended for transportation and clothing of other State Pupils	750.34
12.	Printing Report and Expense	318.30
	TOTAL	$22,569.96

DR. STEARN'S LETTER.

The following letters have been received by the Hon. Joseph L. Barbour, who is counsel for the managers of the Industrial Home:—

Hon. Joseph L. Barbour.

My Dear Sir—Having been a member of the advisory board of the Industrial Home for the Blind in this city, and also one of the auditors during the last four years, it has been my intention to be present at the hearing before the committee on appropriations, which will relate to the interests of this Institution. As, however, I am to be absent from the state and cannot be present, I desire to say a word in behalf of its management.

I have been probably in a better situation than anyone else except my associate, Governor Cady, to understand and appreciate how much has been accomplished by the management, and with what limited means, and I unhesitatingly affirm that instead of careless financial management, deserving adverse criticism, those in charge of it are deserving of credit and commendation. It is my opinion that they have made the most of the means at their command, and that the results of their work, both in the Kindergarten and industrial departments, compare very favorably with those of any other similar institution in the country.

I further beg to say that in my opinion the state cannot afford to withdraw its support from the industrial department of this Institution, which has already passed the period of its existence which always tests the character of its usefulness more fully than any other is likely to do. Moreover, I have no question as to the practicability of the industrial education of the blind, especially where it is commenced during the period of adolescence or early adult life.

The brains of some blind persons may not be capable of receiving an education which would render them self-supporting, but the same is true of some adults who are not blind; besides many hundreds of the blind have been educated so as to become self-supporting, and they nearly always take much pride and satisfaction in being able to support themselves.

A retrograde movement in the education of the blind would in my opinion be a serious mistake. It certainly would result in no saving to the state and would be a loss, as it would necessitate doing the work over again at some future time under a reorganization, thus losing the advantage of experience already had and of disbursements already made.

I have the honor to be, very truly yours,

Hartford, Conn., March 6, 1899.   H. P. STEARNS.

The following is from ex-Lieutenant-Governor Cady, who has been associated with Dr. Stearns as auditor of the institution accounts:—

I fully endorse the above and foregoing letter.

Yours truly,

ERNEST CADY.

March 8, 1899.

The following is from the acting treasurer of the institution:—
HON. JOSEPH L. BARBOUR.

Dear Sir—I have read the accompanying letter from Dr. Stearns concerning the work and interests of the Industrial Home for the Blind.

Although not having been connected with it as long as he, as far as my experience and knowledge go I fully endorse his words.

Yours very truly,

HERBERT H. WHITE

Hartford, March 1899.

NOTE—Dr. Stearns is well known throughout New England as the director of the Hartford Retreat for the Insane and his experience as director of this old established institution for more than a quarter of a century, eminently qualifies him to pass judgment upon the financial management of the Industrial Home.

Hon. Ernest Cady is the former Lieutenant-Governor of Connecticut and Mr. H. H. White is secretary of the Connecticut Mutual Life Insurance Co. of Hartford.

ABSTRACT.

Showing signatures of prominent citizens of many of the principal cities and towns in the State, in aid of Senate Bill No. 88; pending before the General Assembly, entitled An Act Concerning the Instruction and Employment of the Blind.

To the members of the joint standing committee on appropriations, and through them to the members of the General Assembly.

GENTLEMEN:—This abstract has been prepared to afford a ready reference to a list of names which we believe will impress you as being worthy of your consideration as evidence that the people of this State are in hearty accord with what has been done and what it is proposed to do for the elevation, enlightenment and general welfare of the Blind.

HARTFORD.

Joseph H Twichell
Rodney Dennis
Ernest Cady
G Pierrepont Davis
Francis Goodwin
Henry C Robinson
Arthur L Goodrich
Frank L Burr
George M Stone
Jonathan B Bunce
H P Stearns
Charles M Lamson
George Pope
Jacob L Greene
Meigs H Whaples
Ralph W Cutler
George F Hills
Atwood Collins
James Nichols
Thomas W Russell
Chester D Hartranft
W B Clark
J G Batterson
Charles E Gross
John R Buck
Henry L Bunce
Samuel G Dunham
John Addison Porter
Charles E Chase

Herbert H White
Miles B Preston
Waldo S Pratt
Edwin Knox Mitchell
S. B. St John
Job Williams
Henry Ferguson

NEW HAVEN.

Pierce N Welch
Oliver S White
Charles R Ingersoll
Charles E Grases
Newman Smythe
T T Munger
Wilbur F Gay
A W DeForest
Morris F Tyler
Henry F English
Henry G Newton
E Hayes Trowbridge
Ezekiel G Stoddard
Francis Wayland
George P Fisher
S E Merwin
E B Bowditch
Henry T Blake
H B Harrison
John K Beach
A D Osborne
Eli Whitney

Gardner Morse
Leonard M Daggett
George D Watrous
L. W. Cleaveland
Henry C White
Timothy Dwight
Theodore S Woolsey
Simeon E Baldwin
Henry W Farnham

BRIDGEPORT.

Frank E Clark
A Stewart
Fred Seeley
William A Barnes
James Staples
Benjamin Fisk
J B Prindle
John T Sterling
Russell I Whiting
H M Knapp
John Neal
Richard B Coggswell
F W Marsh
Henry H Pyle
George Comstock
J H McMahon
C V Beach
W B. Beach
P W Wren
W W Starr

R C Giddings
Bernard Keating
F C Mullens
A W Wallace
W S Wilson
F Garrett
Joseph Smith
H G Scofield
L N Middlebrook
T B Ford
C F Washburn
Lyman W Wilson
Frederick E Stevens
James Richardson
Frank D Bell
Edward T Bartram
J E Foster
C K Macomber
C R Brothwell
Walter B Bostwick
R S Neithercut
M Moody Downer
Phillip L Holzer
Frank W Beers
D M Rowland
Orland Smith
Wm H May
F W Storrs
Walter Nichols
Louis Van Deusen

WATERBURY.

F J Kingsbury
F W Kellogg
H L Wade
Leroy Upson
E L Frisbie Jr
A M Dickinson
J Richard Smith
Earl Smith
E C Lewis
G W Beach
John D Elton
Gilmore C Hill
B G Bryan
A I Chatfield
Thomas D Barlow
Nathaniel Brouson
J M Burral
R N Blakesley

MIDDLETOWN.

O Vincent Coffin
Richard L de Zeng
Simon Spear
James Donovan
Isaac Spear
Geo A Coles
Henry Woodward
Conrad G Bacon
W U Pearne
Eldow B Birdseye
Geo T Meech
E E Ellsworth
C H Lewis
Lucien R Hazen
Chas Reynolds
C Barrows
G Burr
W D Thayer
Jas J McNulty
J A Broach
A Jameson
R C Kelsey
Wm E Hale
Henry Burnhart
A W Bidwell
J W Stenck
J S Fairchild
Wilbur A Snow
Ernest King & Son
Richard Murphy
Christian Bischel
Richard Cody
James Young
John Conway
Henry S Beers
J Williams
Samuel Russeil
Joseph J Noxon
Wm S Whitney
M B Copeland
Seth H Butler
Arthur B Califf
Daniel J Donahoe
John T Walsh
Orrin D Stoddard
John D Ryan
Geo A Craig
Edward G Camp

Earl C Butler
F G Chaffee
Samuel T Camp
Geo Bull
O H Cone
T F Nolan
P M Camp
John J Murphy
Michael Wall
James Lawton
M Lawton
J H Seiferman
W B Griswold

WESTFIELD,

Rev D B Hubbard
Albert Bacon
Marcus Wilcox
James H Ross
Julius C Atkins
Wm H Wilcox
T M Carckin
Edgar H Burns
Geo Goodrich
A L Congdon
Henry Wilcox

NORWICH.

Anros T Otis
C H Preston Rich
A L Story
Charles F Thayer
Gilbert S Raymond
J H Welles
F T Sayles
Nathan Small
Ira L Peck
C L Hopkins
D L Underwood
Stephen H Hall
Charles B Chapman
Henry D Johnson
Hans Rasmusson
William S Hemstead
Adam Reid
Hull Brothers
D T Ruby
W H Cardwell
Porteous & Mitchell

Joseph S Cunningham
A W Pearson,
Editor Bulletin
Lewellyn Pratt
Jonathan Trumbull
H H Gallup
A H Brewer
Archibald S Spalding
Luther S Eaton
D H Hough
C J King
Charles C Caulkins
O H Reynolds
E R Thompson
Charles Bard
Henry W Bard
Lewis A Hyde
Henry L Bennett
W F Crandall
Nathaniel A Gibbs
Warren K Dowe
George W Swan
S B Meech
C C Johnson
Charles D Foster
Frank Hempstead
George D Coit
Edward Harland
John M Brewer
George E Bachelder
Charles W Comstock
Henry H Burnham
Paul B Greene
Stephen D Moore
A A Browing
Franklin H Brown
Andrew Miller
James Duggan
H I Palmer
C W Hill
James A Brown
Samuel H Freeman
George E Parsons
F L Osgood
Irving N Gifford
Justin Holden
Sidney L Geer
L W Carroll
F L Klein

Nathan D Bates
N Douglas Sevin
Patrick Cassidy
George W Kies
H O Rallion
Edson S Bishop
Charles W Gale
W A Briscoe
John T Wait
F T Brown

MERIDEN.

W N Catlin
R S Norton
A Chamberlin
C S Perkins
J J Anderson
C L Upham
Phillip C Rand
George A Fay
S J Hall
John L Billard
John Ives
F J Wheeler
Walter Hubbard
George M Curtis
Frank A Camp
George Rockwell
E B Everett
C E Stockder Jr
S T Thomas
A J Fletcher
Asher Anderson
Samuel Dodd
Levi E Coe
Wilbur F Davis
Edwin W Husted
G W Miller
Wm W Wheeler
Herman Hess
E B Moss
Charles H S Davis
F H Cushing
W R Mackay
John McWherry
C W Cahill

NEW LONDON.

James P. Johnson,
Mayor of City

P Hall Shurts
F H Parmlee
H A Hull
T W Potter
C A Benjamin
Isaac Knowles
W H Rowe
F E Barker
Arnold Rudd
George M Coles
Alfred Poole Grint
Benjamin Stark
F D Crandall
John E Darrow
William F M Rogers
A T Hale
W G Wilbur
Geo T Strong
C A Williams
Edmund S Neilan
A T Hatch
E D Stone
Walter Davis
Daniel Latham
Charles H Goss
W H Bentley
C J Vick
D T Morsh
E N Caulkins
R S Smith
Clark E Smith
Charles W Strickland
Henry H Stoddard
Herbert L Crandall
Lee S Denison
Franklin G McKeever
John C Nichols
H H Daboll
H J Civiker
H E Harris
C S Broddock
B F Mahon
D J Lucy
W H Chapman
E D Barker
William T May
Charles B Ware
Henry D Stanton
S Leroy Blake

KILLINGLY.
Anthony Ames
W H Chollar
C C Young
A D Putnam
Joseph W Stone
George C Foote
Edward Dexter
Samuel D Danielson
J Q A Stone
F W Chapman
James E Keech
R R James
H H Green
C P Backus
E L Palmer
J A Gilbert
E J Mathewson
R F Lyon
C H Burroughs
C E Carpenter
Frank T Preston
E O Wood
W F Bidwell
W E LaBelle
E M Randall
W C Darrow
A B Potter
M P Dowe
H M Clemons
Clarence E Young
H F Clark
O W Bowen
C H Bacon
G P Hall
Rev H S Brown
S S Waldo
E S Carpenter
James H Potter
John W Law
H C Atwood
L S James
S R Gilbert
W F Day
W P Kelley
Frank W Bennett
Rev. John Deans
H L Hammond M D
William Y Harrington
H J Miller

BRISTOL.
J F Chidsey
W W Russell
John S Lyon
W Hart
Williard E Goodwin
George W Mitchell
W T Shepard
Samuel M Steele
Charles H Buck
Thomas M Miles
H B Cook
L M Bennett
A B Judd
C B Abell
S K Montgomery
George W Baker
Miller Card
Arthur G Muzzy
William B Adams
W T Smith
C S Cook
M E Wilden
William Madden
James D Rowe
F W Whitman
Perry M Holley
Lee Roberts
W B Hinkley
W S Jones
H O Palmer
William H Adams
H S Bartholomew
Stephen N Wells Jr
George P Allen
R B Codling
L G Mesick
M D Edgerton
Francis O Lewis
Edson M Peck
T H Patterson
Epapheoditus Peck

WINSTED.
Rufus E Holmes
Henry Gay
Lucius V Pinney
Ralph W Holmes
Darwin S Moore
M H Marines

Wm P Gladwin
J J Whiting
A W Healy
H Skinner
C Halstead
C A Bristol
Rev G W Remington
H C Price
Edward Ferris
George S Rowe
D C Roraback
Geo H Spencer
Edward Jones
Fred H York
John W Moore
G L Fancher
Charles J Ryan
C S Foster
K L Preston
H S Rising
E W King
J R Griswold
Sam S Newton
James C Kelley
S N Lincoln
J O Houlihan
W H Gillette
Charles Pulver
David E Jordan
John F Coffee
W M Johnson
H O Atkins
Wallace Persons
S H Alford
E Larkin
W J Sparks
F G Gates
W C Plant
John P Cook
L C Colt
J T Morgan
H B Stevens
W H Miles
A W Clark
J C Burwell
S C Wheeler
J H Alvord

MANCHESTER.
Thos J Gardiner
Wm S Hutchinson

A L Geer
W B Porter
W H Coates
J G Trotter
John P Cheney
Charles Cheney
Edward Cadman
S T Bidwell
Rich O Cheney
K D Cheney
James W Cheney
Saml Richmond
William C Cheney
Geo Davidson
Alex Miller
B J Bartlett
Loren Davis
James Britton
H. G. Brown
John Wright Jr
Wm Dongan
Charles McKee
Edward McKee
Frank Hobley
James Fallow
Geo W Ferris
J B Grimes
L B Bade
John Hickey
Harry Nelson
Arthur Sault
Geo H Acheson
Wm H Wright
Henry W Leidholdt
John M Shewey
B A Cadman
John Wright
W W Cheney
H F Brown
Wm Ferguson
Frederick Waldo
Theo H Bidwell
D C Y Moore M D
Thos S Cadman
Jos Watkin
John Cadman
L N Hebner
Wm N Keating
M L Chapman
B F T Jenny

Chas F House
Fred W Mills
C L Leacey
James Hutchinson
James H Miniken
Arthur W Cone
C Tiffany
A H Skinner
D Wadsworth
J H Bilser
Isaac M Quinn
F H Ladd
O B Taylor
Wm Arnoth
Alexander Arnoth
Thomas P Aitkin
Thomas Simms
W H Grant
C G Watkins
Julian S Wadsworth
Wm E Keith
A E Peterson
F A Verplanck

SOUTHINGTON.

Stephen Walkley
E E Stowe
John Heminway
Enoch Nichols
Edwin G Lewis
Hial S Grannis
Rev T C Hanna
L E Southwith
W S Gould
Geo S Allen
Geo W Blakeslee
Theo Buckley
Wm H Cowles
R W Cowles
A W Lewis
T B Atwater
Chas W Bushnell
W H Cummings
W A Finch
H D Smith
Wm Cook
W G Steadman
E W Twitchell
E P Hotchkiss
L C Clark

Jno C Breaker
Ralph T Ives
J H Martin
A N Cheney
J H Pratt
O D Woodruff
L K Curtis
N A Barnes
Chas D Barnes
William Hutton
T H McKenzie
O N Lamson
T E Barnes
J Bond
J H Baldwin
Wallace A Johnson
C F Hamlin

PLYMOUTH.

George Langdon
W M Bull
Arthur Beardsley
A S Beardsley
Frank Blakesley
Rev C H Smith
M W Beach

BERLIN.

A A Barnes
Benj K Field
Charles W Janes
E W Stearns
Geo H Sage
J B Barnes
Arthur W Upson

SOUTHBURY

Wm H Barrows
Sherman Tuttle
A W Guthrie
D M Wheeler
H H Brown
J P Welch
H R Stone
Herman Perry
B M Tuttle
Theodore Mallory
George A Smith
William E Beecher
J S Bennett
H A Mathews

S L Tuttle
Henry B Russell
Timothy Reynolds
Charles E Smith
James E Baldwin
Benjamin S Hicock
C S Brown
H W Beecher
H V Peck
Samuel O Barton
Stephen Collins
Joel U Strong
Oscar W Ambler
C W Wheeler
Charles K Osborne
Walter Hicock
William Morris
C O Hine
E P Hine
A L Hine

STRATFORD.

Joel S Ives
William B Cogswell
W H Smith
M Fryer
F W Judson
Paul A Carey
John R Lattin
William Chichester
Lewis Curtis
Charles Sanford
James A Sanford
Perry Beardsley
William H Feyer
George T Jewell
E M Wells

NOANK.

Robert Palmer
John E McDonald
R P Wilbur
Amos R Chapman
J E Stark
C I Fitch
William E Spencer
Gurdon L Daboll
W A Fraser

UNION.

Benjamin B Hopkinson

J W Winch
W G Howard
E W Upson
R B Horton
E M Horton
George Wallace
Rev O Sherwood Terry
George W Crawford
A T Allen
Fayette Crawford
G W Thayer
Chelsea Young
Williard Richards
F B Johnson
F S Upham
N B Booth
C R Webster
L M Reed
H F Corbin
D C Mathews

NEW HARTFORD.

Edwin R Carter
Edgar H Lane
J P Hawley
W C Woodruff
C E Moorehouse
Frederick R Jewell
Frank P Marble
Calvin Aldrich
R G Foster
Frederick M Tarrill
George W Barrempt
Walter M Smith
Orrin Fitch
Fred O Clark
P N Chamberlin

POMFRET

Francis H Bird
Ezra B Pike
Edward L Williams
Joseph E Stoddard

CROMWELL.

A N Pierson
R Ludwig
P Anderson
W B Hallock & Son
E S Coe
R S Griswold

C R Frisbie
William E Hurlburt
George S Wilcox
Russell Frisbie
W R McDonald
M W Austin
George P Savage
C E Bush
H G Marshall
George W Stevens
William G Keighley
W A Bugbee
C E Penniman
Arthur Boardman
Thomas Beaumont
Maguire Pierson

ELMWOOD.

George T Goodwin
P A Sears
R N Francis
N E Sears
Charles E Lord
H B Goodwin
Cyrus Brown
Fred A Handall
Charles W Perry
J H Raymond
J W Hayer
H L Lamb
J M Shaw
H Hurlburt

NEWINGTON.

Joshua Belden
F H Belden
Mary E Belden
Julia M Belden
Agnes W Belden
John S Kirkham
Mary K A Kirkham
Minnie L Petsuer
Edwin Stanley Wells
Daniel W Fish
J N Merrill
G N Downs
C M Kilbourne
Gaylord Morgan
Erastus Kilbourne
R S Kilbourne
Horace Kilbourne

S H Kilbourne
C L Bayington
Fred H Bayington

SIMSBURY.

C D Shaw
George O Butler
A S Chapman
F N Hoskins
Edwin Chase
George H Noble
Burton J Noble
William C Mather
A Eberg M D
Nelson St Thomas
E D Jones
W S Holcomb
S H Alger
J T Monks
Geo W Carr

TARIFFVILLE.

J E Heald
C A Ensign
Morton Ensign
Wm H Pease
H Higinbotham
Harvey Tucker
J L Dewey
S M Griffin
A Buncus
Frank Wilkinson Mfg Co
Fred Jones
C M Wooster

NEW FAIRFIELD.

I S Knapp
J K Hatch
J J Ticadwell
R J Scudder
Henry Barker
H O Leach
David S Barnum
John A Waldron
H H Wildman
S E Knapp
E Jennings
A M Couch
H W Jennings
W B Yale
S B Gilbert
A B Brush

G W Trusdale
J F Myer
Emory Kirk
D J Gross
A A Brush

ASHFORD.

Henry C Barlow
Anson G Barlow
Cicero D Chapman
Geo H Whitaker

SAYBROOK.

Amos S Chesebrough
John T Bushnell
J H Mannip
W C Booth
D A Kellogg
O H Kirtland
Edward E Bacon
Robert T Chuther
J H Chase
Thos C Aston Jr
John Sangle
G A Bushnell
W R Bushnell
J D S Pardee
D W Clark
Isaac N Devoe
F F Bradley
F A Curtis
D C Spencer
N D Spencer
John Allen
Sam H Pratt
G Walker
N L Kelsey
Robert Chapman
Joseph M Pratt
Joseph L Hayden Rept.

E. WINDSOR HILL.

George O Clapp
Wm B Parmelee
Frank Bancroft
J D Weyart
J W Clark
C Z Parmelee
W R Wood
J R Noble
D Busbee
R M Burnham

Henry Chapman
Geo S Bissell

ESSEX.

James Phelps
Thomas D Coulter
Chas D Hubbard
Percy I Fenn
J T Mather & Co
Chas Harrison
Mack & Burrows
G W Hayden
W H Parmlee
S M Morley
N H Williams
P Murdock
M W Johnson
J E Knowles
Charles Neitzel
L L Wooster
E E Dickinson & Co
Louis P Parker
Julius L Wilder
L H Parker
H T Phelps
Geo A Dowd
F Halliday
Wm Halliday
S W Ingersoll
Wm Bowen
Edwin T Pratt
James L Pratt
Selden Spencer
Edwin Pratt
N F Stevens
B E Case
Chas E Pratt
Henry R Stevens
Alfred A Pratt
Henry L C Stephenson
Wm P Chapman
Wm E Williams
E C Williams
A C Fenn
J T Lancaster
J Minke
W E Peabody
N E Gladding
M J Beebe
Geo D Dickinson

E C Strong
W E Stephens
Chas Munger
A Shaffer

NORTH HAVEN.

M D Marks
Wm S Stiles
Jas H Halligan
W P Leetes
Wm Lush
H P Smith
C G Malmgieth
Amos A Tuttle
Ezra L Stiles
E D L Goodyear
E A Heminway
H F Potter
L P Tuttle
G W Doolittle
F Hayden Toddy
P A Alson
A F Austin
Theopilus Eaton
D L Clinton
G F Cooper
C O Saxton
Henry C Terrill
D W Tucker
E L Ball
R Harrison

ROCKY HILL.

H R Merriam
F C Warneu
E F Belden
R W Griswold
John North
Geo H Bugbey
A P Shipman
Timothy Gilbert
W A Hammond
Elizabeth Gilbert
Jane Blinn
Geo E Belden
Henry D Trinkous
Fred E Fowler
Chas A Fowler
Elmer E Brown
Wm G Robbins
Geo Risley

Geo B Stillman
Frank G Sherwood
Fred Morton
M J Merriam

NORTH BRANFORD.

F Countryman
Geo C Linsley
Andrew J Russell

EAST HARTFORD.

Edw F King
A G Olmsted
Joel H Brown
E O Goodwin
C P Risley
J E Cawall
Chas Merriway
F W Richardson
G W Darlin
John L Jinks
Wm Duff
Wm G Stoughton
Henry L Goodwin
D C Burnham
W F Bartlett
J W Elmer
M J Hickey
L P Gale
E C Walker
F E Hyde
F H Hammer
P S Bryant
Edward P Carroll
Jos O Goodwin
James S Forbes
C R Forbes
Wm N Lowey
E W Pratt
H W Vinton
Sam O Goodwin
S A Barrett
John Houghton
William A Foley
Charles W Roberts
William S Jasman
L H Forbes
W E Truesdell
W H Chapman
Julius Levy
William J Foley

J W Forbes
Charles Olmstead
John McVay
E Ackerly
F C Gould
Abner Track
L V Lister
D E Lane
William B Noble
William P Stanley
Norman S Brewer
Alme Von W Wickham

NEWTOWN.

Rev Otis W Barker
Allison P Smith
 Editor Newtown Bee
George T Linsley
 Rector Trinity Church
Chas Northrop Treas
 Newtown Saving Bank
M J Houlihan
M J Bradley
 Judge of Probate
H S Clark
N S Clark
W A Leonard
A G Baker
R H Beers (merchant)
Edgar F Hawley
Charles H Peck
Aaron Sanford M of H
M F Houlihan M of H

SALEM

A Morgan
Rev Jarius Ordway
N E Miner
Donald Macrus
Rev E W Merritt
J A Rix
F S Dewolf
G F Allyn

CHESTER.

E W Smith
Ira C Tucker
C H Watrous
E K Cone
J H Wilcox
C A Wright
I L Abbey

E W Clark
J Egerter
F Y Sallum
J A Parker
S E Ackley
E G Smith
W L Bates
C N Smith
R B Jones
Henry C Scoville
E W Tyler
H C Lewis
G W Warner
A Cooper
E C Hungerford
Julius Smith
George W Smith
A L Osborne
Fred Summer Smith
Fredrick W Silliman
John B Hardy
Rudolf Davis
J K Dennison
H D Selden
W A Warner
C E Smith
H H Clark
A J Smith
H K White
H C Parker
E F Alexander
C Holmes
S G Arnold
W A Foster
D F Hood
H B Crok
James S Deuse

PUTNAM.

Chauncey Morse
F D Sargent
George E Shaw
F W Perry
W C Sharpe
J R Champlin
C A Smith
F W Sewall
E G Wright
E F Whitmore
E C Bohamm

A W Bowen
Edgar M Warner

TERRYVILLE.

William Alfred Gay
Henry E Hinman
M P Robinson
Frederick T Cook
George A Scott
O D Hunter
A D Gaylord
Jason C Fenn
T F Higgins
H A Barton
F E Williams
H Plumb
J A Russell
C H Baldwin
M A Shurts
Otis B Hough
Frank L Mather
E E Baldwin
P Salmon
C K Palmer
A B Beach
Geo M Bayington
W D Duffy
J N Keefe
W Atwater
C W Plumb
H D Allen
W A Tilden
J M Gilbert
E I Barnes
Wm C Bates
Albert Griffen
John E Knox
W T Goodwin
Wm L Norton
Charles W Judson
George F Carr
C E Chapman
William W Carr
H O Sullivan
W S Webb
A P Clark
A C Holcomb
Arthur P Clow
F H Pond
E Clayton Goodwin

E Goddard
F R Alford
J M Clemens
A A Place
William Robinson

GRISWOLD.

Clayton T Williard
W Moulding Baker
C F Griswold
J D Welles
George Harris
C H Dilling
S N Woodside
Stephen Churchill
Levi B Churchill
Fredrick G Churchill
H D Shepard
W E Griswold
R S Griswold

WOODSTOCK.

C H Hiscox
H R Lowe M D
G N Lyon
Prescott P Hammond
R F Williams
Rev George L Putnam
F L Corbin
J T Hall
Frank R Jackson
G Clinton Williams
C E Tomburd
N D Skinner

FARMINGTON.

S Porter
M M Porter
E G Porter
Mr & Mrs F L Scott
E F McKien
Mr & Mrs D R Hawley
F H Root
J S Porter
Richard H Gay
M A Howe
M H Smith
M C Gay
Edward H Deming
Alfred Hardy
J Backus

PUBLISHER'S NOTES.

This number of TALKS AND TALES has been delayed that we might place before our friends an outline of the situation that confronts the workers who are seeking to better the condition of those who are in perpetual darkness, thus giving our subscribers an insight into the difficulties with which these workers are contending.

We consider that we can accomplish this in no better way than to give excerpts from the report recently issued by the Secretary of the Connecticut State Board of Education of the Blind.

We are confident that the many kind friends who have sent to TALKS AND TALES during the past months letters of cheer and encouragement will expect no apology, but only this explanation. The work for the Blind is progressing in spite of some opposition,—or perhaps because of some opposition—as many new supporters have come to the assistance of the workers, within the past year. As is the history of new movements, opposition is necessary to our best growth.

Will our subscribers please bear in mind that our magazine wrappers are addressed a month in advance so a change of address must be delayed for a month at least.

It is necessary for a subscriber wishing a change made to send former address as well as new address, some of our friends forget that little necessity.

We have on our desk at present a slip which a subscriber sent with neither present nor former address; and also a letter in which one dollar was inclosed. with no name.

We intend soon to begin a series of articles on "An Ideal Government" and How to Attain it. Writers of prominence will contribute their views on the subject.

We wish to call attention to our new department "At the Heart of Things," in which all the better books of the day are summarized by a literary critic of recognized ability. This is a valuable addition to TALKS AND TALES and will be appreciated by our subscribers.

As the months go by and our subscription list increases bringing better facilities for our work, we hope and intend to meet the expectations of our friends by giving them better service and by giving them more about the work which is being done in the United States for the Blind.

In our next issue we shall publish an article by Mr. Samuel Brazier, Secretary of the New England Anti-vivisection Society. We trust our readers will read carefully the evidence against vivisection, which humanitarians name the next great moral question.

Elizabeth Stuart Phelps says: "I believe that the urgent protest against vivisection which marks our immediate day, and the whole plea for lessening the miseries of animals as endured at the hands of men, constitute the 'next' great moral question which is to be put to the intelligent conscience, and that only the educated conscience can properly reply to it."

Rev. Geo. Leon Walker, D. D., also says: "I am glad you have called attention to the vivisection horror in your annual report to the Humane Society. I am almost afraid, however, to say I hope it will be widely read. I hope it will be by people whose nerves can stand it; but the facts you present have haunted me like a nightmare ever since I read it. We read in Parkman's volumes with a shudder his description of the tortures of the Jesuit missionaries by the Indians, but no Algonquin or Iroquois savage ever surpassed in cruelty many of the scientific experimenters in physical suffering of whom you speak.

"As brutal as Sioux or Comanche are the Doctors Chauveau, Castex, and Watson, whose terrible studies in the art of torture are self-recorded, to their own shame. Science has taught them better than the wild Indians how to wring the last throb of agony out of their victims, but the experiments of both classes seem about on par as to utility, and not to differ as to the hardness of heart implied in each.

"We have been congratulating ourselves on the mellowing influences of later civilization; but the distinct revival in two or three years past of popular interest in brutal pugilistic exhibitions, and the extensive and horrible practice of vivisection are fitted to chasten our self-esteem. The savages are not all dead, or all in savage lands."

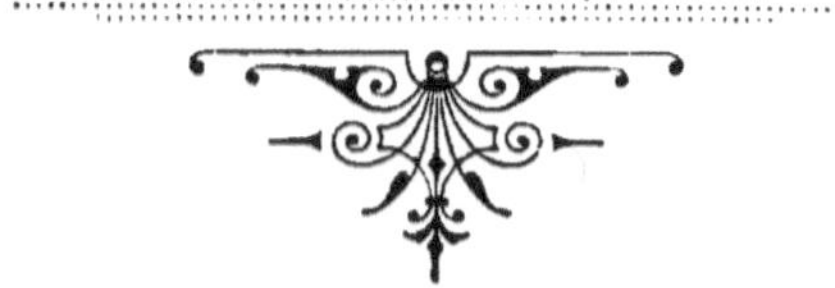

TALKS AND TALES,

A Magazine Published in the
Interest of the Blind. . . . . . 

The work of the magazine is largely done
by the blind people and your interest and support is solicited, that its circulation may increase. Every subscription helps towards furnishing employment for the blind. Published
by the Printing Department of the Institution,
334 and 336 Wethersfield Ave., Hartford, Conn.

. . **Subscription Price $1.00 per year.**

TALKS AND TALES.

A MAGAZINE

——PUBLISHED BY——

The Conn. Institute and Industrial Home for the Blind,

Nos. 334 and 336 Wethersfield Ave.,

HARTFORD, CONN.

F. E. CLEAVELAND, President.

Edited by Mrs. ELLA B. KENDRICK.

One Dollar a Year,   -   Ten Cents a Copy

PRESS OF
THE CONN. INSTITUTE AND INDUSTRIAL HOME
FOR THE BLIND.

Table of Contents.

The Connecticut Mutual
Life Insurance Company
1846--1899.

To those who desire to do fully, at its least cost and to the utmost of their financial ability, their duty to their families, and to use life insurance for their protection and not for a speculation for themselves, THE CONNECTICUT MUTUAL offers the utmost that life insurance can accomplish, in its simplest, clearest forms, of perfect equity and perfect mutuality, on the soundest basis of any, and at a lower cost than has been achieved by any other company. Greater service can no life insurance company render.

JACOB L. GREENE, President.   HERBERT H. WHITE, Sec'y.
JOHN M. TAYLOR, Vice Pres't.   DANIEL H. WELLS, Actuary

A. T. RICHARDS, General Agent, Room 16, Company's Building, Hartford, Conn.

THE OLD MILL.

TALKS AND TALES.

VOL. II. HARTFORD, CONN., APRIL 1899. No. 7.

CHAS. H. S. DAVIS, M. D., PH. D.

TWO of the most remarkable achievements of human ingenuity during the present century has been the decipherment of the Egyptian hieroglyphics by Champollion and of cuneiform script of Babylonia by Grotefend, Rawlinson and other scholars. A literature has been recovered which already far exceeds in compass the whole of the Old Testament Scriptures, and a new and unsuspected world of culture and civilization has been opened to us, and the history of the world has been carried back to at least seven thousand years before the Christian era. Notwithstanding discovery after discovery has been rapidly crowded upon us, yet the surface of the ground has only been scratched over, and very much more yet lies under the ground awaiting the explorer, than has been brought to light. The Hilprecht expedition to Babylonia has recovered 32,000 cuneiform tablets, representing syllabaries, letters, chronological lists, historical fragments, astronomical and religious texts, votive tablets, inventories, contracts, etc., and we learn all about the social life of the ancient peoples who lived four or five thousand years ago; and we are enabled to write some of the earliest and most important chapters in the history of our race.

We learn from the inscriptions in Egypt, that 5000 years ago, when all of Europe was sunk in barbarism, that the Egyptians were a reading and a writing people, with considerable literary culture, and a wonderful knowledge of architecture and sculpture. The first knowledge we have of the Egyptians of 5000 years ago shows that their culture and wisdom was of the highest character. All of the arts were known and practiced, and life was comfortable and even luxurious. In fact, the farther back we go the more perfect we find it. No more striking evidence of the high civilization of ancient Egypt can be produced then that which is seen in the condition of the women, and the respect with which they were treated. Her activities were many, her liberty great, her position often exalted. In some of the most solemn religious ceremonies of the nation, women took an official and public part.

The position of women in ancient Babylonia was very independent, and they were allowed to transact business and bequeath their property. Among the deeds discovered on the clay tablets are many, such as that of a mother transferring her property to her daughter, the deeds of gift by a father to his daughter, and a brother and sister to a brother-in-law.

The Egypt Exploration Fund has recently published a volume of papyri obtained from Behneseh in Egypt, which gives us an excellent idea of the inner life of a town in Egypt some two thousand years ago. Some 1200 texts were recovered from the ruins, among which were several verses of the first chapter of Matthew, some were fragments of Sappho, and a great number of contracts, deeds, letters, etc. There were a number of invitations to dinner such as follows: "Herais requests your company at dinner in celebration of the marriage of her children at her house to-morrow, the 5th, at 9 o'clock."

"Greeting, my dear Serenia, from Petosiris. Be sure, dear, to come up on the 20th for the birthday festival of the god, and let me know whether you are coming by boat or by donkey, in order that we may send for you accordingly. Take care not to forget. I pray for your continued health."

A father breaks off a betrothal as follows: "Forasmuch it has come to my ears that you are giving yourself over to lawless deeds, which are pleasing neither to God nor man, and are not fit to be put in writing, I think it well that the engagement between you and her, my daughter Euphemia, should be disolved, seeing that, as is aforesaid, I have heard that you are giving yourself over to lawless deeds and that I wish my daughter to live a peaceful and quiet life. I therefore send you the present deed of dissolution of the engagement between you and her, my daughter Euphemia, by the hand of the most illustrious advocate aforesaid with my signature, and I have taken a copy of this document, written by the most illustrious advocate aforeraid (Anastasius). Wherefore for the security of the said Euphemia my daughter, I send you this deed of separation and dissolution, written on the 11th day of the month Epeiph in the 11th indication.

"I, John, aforesaid father of Euphemia, my daughter, send the present deed of separation or dissolution to you Phœbaummon, my most honorable son-in-law, as is above written."

Among the papyri are those for repairs of public buildings, appointments of guardian, orders for arrest, receipts for wages, sales and leases of land, contracts of working men, etc. "A Promise to be Honest" is a contract

between Aurelius Menas, head watchman, and Flavius Apion the younger,
by which Menas undertakes to pay twenty-four solidi should he be proved
to be a party to any theft of the agricultural plant under his charge.

Palestine is covered with mounds awaiting the spade of the explorer, in
fact, Ancient Jerusalem is one vast mound, upon which modern Jerusalem is
built. Students of the Bible are watching with great interest the uncovering
of the mounds and the explorations in Egypt and Babylonia, Palestine and
Arabia, Assyria and Asia Minor, for these lands were closely connected with
the history of Israel. The records already discovered confirm, explain and
illustrate the Scripture records, and the historical portions of the Bible are
now read with an entirely new interest. All light is surely welcome that can
make clearer the conditions of social life and progress, and illustrate the
phraseology of the people of Bible times. What is said in Genesis and
Exodus of the character of the country, its government and its court, and
the customs of the people, Egyptological research shows are pictures
faithfully drawn from life. In regard to Palestine, the Palestine Exploration
Fund has done and is doing a remarkable work. Magnificent maps have
been made, and many biblical sites identified,—cities, villages, mountains,
valleys, brooks, fountains, and caves have been located. Future revelations
from the soil of Palestine will no doubt throw great light upon the early
history of the inhabitants of that country.

This Fund was organized in 1865, and is under the patronage of Queen
Victoria. Explorers are kept constantly in the field, and the publications of
the Society now number twenty eight volumes, and ten maps.

A great work is being done by the French, German, and English Exploration Funds towards systematically exploring and excavating the hundreds
of ruins in Egypt. The English Fund, founded in 1883, has during fifteen
years sent out every season two and sometimes three explorers, and each
year has been fruitful in discoveries. Much has been done towards the res-
toration of the ancient topography of Lower Egypt. The sites of famous
cities have been identified and discovered, and thousands of papyri, and
inscriptions have been discovered and deciphered.

Fourteen magnificent quarto volumes have been published. Each donor
of five dollars to the Fund receives not only one of these volumes, but the
illustrated "Archæological Report," and also the annual report. Since its
organization, America has contributed over seventy thousand dollars to the
Fund.

Connected with the Exploration Fund is an Archæological Fund and a
Græco-Roman Branch, both of which issue annual publications.

NOTE. Dr. Davis, who is local Honorary Secretary of the Egypt Exploration Fund, will send to any person interested a prospectus of these
various societies which are doing such excellent work in Palestine and
Egypt. His address is Meriden, Conn.

HOW WE GOT A PIANO.

CARL LOUIS KINGSBURY.

"**I** wish that we had an organ," said Lottie at the breakfast table.

"What for?" demanded Uncle Silas, pausing in the act of spearing a potato, and looking at her inquiringly.

"To play on, of course. You know what Aunt Maria said when she was here last month."

"That she'd pay for your lessons if you had an instrument to twiddle on? Yes, I recollect, Maria always did have more'n her share of foolish notions; I'll say that for her if she is my sister. What good would the thing do you? I call playing on them a sinful waste of time."

Lottie sighed, and said no more. When Uncle Silas spoke of anything as a sinful waste of time, there never was anything more to be said. Even Aunt Lois, who usually had a will of her own, and a placid way of achieving her own ends, always subsided into silence or changed the subject when he took that tone.

Uncle and aunt were very good to us. The doors of their wide, roomy, old farm-house were thrown open to us poor little homeless tots on the day that our widowed young mother, uncle's youngest sister, died, and they could not have shown greater love or care for children of their own, if they had had them, than they gave to us. But as we grew older we developed tastes that uncle, who believed in useful things, pronounced trivial. Chief among these contraband tastes was one for music.

On these secret and furtive occasions when we found opportunity to try it on some favored schoolmate's instrument, we each displayed a natural aptitude for playing, and our longing to become the possessors of some kind of a musical instrument grew apace. We were quite sure that Aunt Lois sympathized with our longing, although she was far too wise a woman to say so in opposition to her husband's expressed disapproval.

Uncle was a very upright man; to say simply that he was honest does not begin to describe his uncompromising fidelity to his word, to any promise, however slight. The thing that he had said he would do, that and no other, without equivocation, amendment, or retrocession, was the thing to be done.

I know now that Aunt Lois was a wonderful woman. Her husband's stubborn adherence to the slightest promise he had either made or imagined he had made must often have caused her serious annoyance; but she was always cheerful, and never seemed to oppose her domineering lord by word or look or action. Yet, remembering how invariably it was her side of any case that won, I recognize and offer tribute to her generalship.

Lottie and I did not know until long after the organ episode was disposed of that uncle had been bred a Quaker, and that that sect is, as a rule, peculiarly averse to musical expression of any kind. Once, when Lottie, who found it hard to relinquish her wishes, remarked somewhat pertly that even the angels sang, uncle retorted:

"Yes, but the Scripture don't speak of their having pianos and organs. Such things are most gen'lly s'posed to be inventions of Satan."

Then we girls, without a word, ran along to school. The schoolhouse stood on one corner of uncle's farm; he had, in fact, given two acres there for its use, and a foot-path led from the house through the fields to the schoolhouse door.

When going home on the evening of the day on which Lottie and uncle had had their unprofitable discourse in regard to organs, we came upon a little stray pig, squealing forlornly in the edge of the oat-field. Since he was on our land, the natural inference was that he must be one of ours gone astray. He was a tiny pink morsel, apparently given over to grief and home-sickness, for he shook and trembled with one or both, or with cold, as I picked him up and started homeward.

"Isn't it a cute little thing?" queried Lottie, touching the moist little snout with an inquisitive forefinger. "Its nose is as cold as a dog's. Are pigs' noses always cold?"

"I suppose so. See how he snuggles up to me, poor little thing! I'm going to ask uncle to let us keep it for a pet."

Lottie caught at this suggestion gleefully. Uncle had just come in from the field as we reached home; he was washing his hands at the kitchen sink, and we carried our new-found treasure straight to him.

"See what we found down by the oat-field, uncle," I said, holding the little creature up against my face, where he nestled contentedly.

"Oh, one of those Chester white pigs! Must have got out of the hog pasture somehow. Put it into that covered box on the back stoop, and I'll send it back when Jake goes to feed the pigs."

"Oh, uncle, mayn't we keep it for a pet? It's so cunning!"

"For a pet! Well, now! I guess you'll get tired of it soon enough. I shouldn't think you'd want a pig for a pet."

"But this one is so little and so clean, and we'll keep him washed up just as nice!" I said, coaxingly.

Aunt Lois had not spoken; she surveyed the scene and the pig silently; her face wore a thoughtful expression.

"Why, a pet pig's the worst bother—" uncle was beginning, when she interposed. "Let them keep it if they want to, Silas. It isn't as if it was a musical instrument."

"No, it isn't;" uncle admitted, rather gruffly. "It's of some use. Well, do keep it; I don't care."

"Oh, thank you!" we both cried in a breath. "May we have it for our very own?"

"Of course, it's yours; nobody else's got a right to say a word about it," he explained, with a knowing smile.

We named our treasure Jehoshaphat; why, I do not know, unless it was that the name had an unctuous sound and seemed to fit our little friend, who, however, was fast ceasing to be little. He grew with amazing rapidity. We fixed a box for him to sleep in, and he had the run of the front yard. We cared for him solicitously at first, feeding him at all hours, and on everything we could get hold of; but in a few days he began to forage for himself so successfully that our care became, not to furnish things for his refection, but to save them from that insatiable appetite.

Nothing came amiss to him,—not even Aunt Lois's prized light brahma chicks and young turkeys; he ate them with no sense of shame whatever, and would come running to meet us, on our return from school, with the dress feathers of his latest victim clinging to his chops.

Aunt Lois was fond of her brahmas, and took pride in her big bronze turkeys, but she submitted to the destruction of their young without a murmur; and when uncle, moved to wrath by Jehoshaphat's depredations, would have consigned him to the company of his fellows in the far pasture, she reminded him:

"You promised the girls that they should do just as they pleased with their pig, you know, Silas, and they seem to like to have him around."

"Like to have him around! Why, he's a perfect famine! He's a devouring lion! There isn't a thing on the place that's safe from his snout. If I set a pail of milk down while I am putting up the bars, when I turn around there's that pig with his head stuck into the milk up to the eyes, gulping it down, and his tail wiggling with joy.

"I wish I'd cut his tail off when he was little," uncle went on. "It makes me mad to see it. If I leave the barn-door open a minute, he's in the wheat-bin; when he isn't rooting up the garden, he's sucking eggs, when he isn't sucking eggs, he's eating chicks or turkeys; when he isn't eating something that's worth more'n a dozen pigs, he's lying in wait to trip me up. I can't step out of doors after dark but here he comes, woof-woofing, so all-fired glad to see me that he knocks me down. I wish to goodness he'd eat something that would kill him."

"He is some trouble," aunt admitted. She was at the moment engaged in putting new sleeves in one of uncle's shirts. Jehoshaphat, who liked starch, had chewed off the original ones as they hung on the clothes line. "But then," she went on, "you know you promised the girls not to interfere with him."

Uncle groaned. "I s'pose I've got to keep my promise, but if things keep on this way much longer, we'll have to give up the management of the place to that pig. There won't be room on it for him and me, too."

"He *is* some trouble," aunt reiterated, biting off her thread, and gazing reflectively out of the window, which revealed a darkening view of Jehoshaphat surrounded by some of his recent works. "But then, you know you *promised*."

She never allowed uncle to forget that.

Jehoshaphat, in return for our kindness, was devotedly, even distressingly, attached to us. He would leave the most delightful wallow in the horses' watering-trough,—they sniffed at the water after one of his baths and refused to drink it, thus obliging uncle to pump a fresh supply,—or a cool siesta in the tulip bed, to follow us to school, or to church, or to make neighborly calls, or wherever we chanced to be going. The climax of insult was reached when an audacious schoolmate included him in the politely written invitation to her birthday party.

For his dear sake we refused that party, and in anger, for, of course, the annoyance and trouble that he caused us had the usual result. The more he tried our patience, thus keeping the remembrance of him continually in our minds, the fonder we were of him. We quite exhausted our ingenuity in framing excuses for his misconduct.

In the privacy of our own room Lottie and I did comment with some wonder on Aunt Lois's complacent endurance of the devastation wrought by our uncouth pet, but we were too selfishly glad of it to offer to relieve the household of its growing burden.

When it became so cold in the fall that the house doors were closed, and Jehoshaphat could not stretch himself upon the porch and watch our movements through the screen doors, his affection became more intrusive than ever. He would, in spite of his bulk,—and he had now grown to be very large,—slip noiselessly into the house whenever a door was left open. It was impossible for him to hide his satisfaction when his strategy succeeded, and his triumphant "woofing" would presently proclaim his whereabouts.

We had all gone to bed one November night, when a neighbor rapped at the door to ask if uncle and aunt would go and sit up the rest of the night with another neighbor who was ill. Of course they agreed to do so.

Aunt called up-stairs to us, after she was dressed, telling us where she was going. "We'll be back by daylight—before you are up," she said.

She had set a pan of bread dough to rise behind the dining-room stove, which held a fire all night. We heard her move the pan, and knew she was taking a speculative look at it before she started. Her bread, set overnight, was usually ready to "knead down" by daylight.

Aunt and uncle put out the light and climbed into the neighbor's wagon, but in a moment the door was unlocked again, and we knew by the blast of cold air that came up the stairway that it had been left open. We heard some one groping around in the darkness.

"Is that you, uncle?" I called.

"Yes; your aunt wants her big shawl. It's colder'n we thought for. Here 'tis. Don't lie awake now. Good-by!"

We heard him close and lock the door, heard the wagon rattle away over the frozen road, and then fell asleep again. We did not sleep long. I awoke with a start as Lottie clutched my arm.

"What is that?" she whispered, breathlessly.

I listened. Some one was walking about down-stairs. There could be no mistake about that.

"Uncle locked the door; I heard him!" breathed Lottie.

"So did I. H—ush!"

We fancied that the intruder must be cold; he was probably crouching over the stove when he knocked the tin pan off from over the bread bowl. It fell with a terrific clatter. Lottie and I crouched under the bedclothes, and lay there, trembling, for a long time; but we were eventually forced to come to the surface for air.

A considerable time passed, during which we heard no sound. Then the moving about began again; the steps went into the parlor, which opened off the dining-room. There was a good deal of the restless walking about and then there came a groan, low, distinct, unearthly!

"May—maybe—some one is dying down there!" chattered Lottie.

"Sounds like it," I admitted, recklessly. "Any way, they shan't come up here to die!"

With the words I crept out of bed, quaking in every limb, and softly crossing the room, locked and bolted the door. Lottie did not fail to remind me, as I crept into the bed again, that the person whoever he might be, had gained access to the house in spite of the locked doors.

We could not hear the dreadful sounds with our door closed. We lay awake a long time, listening, but being young and unused to lying awake, we fell asleep at last, in spite of our terror, and slept until awakened by Aunt Lois's voice proclaiming in hollow tones, "Well, if this isn't the cap-sheaf!"

We sprang out of bed, dressed with nervous haste, and ran down-stairs. Aunt Lois was right, as a glance at the room convinced us. Jehoshaphat had reached the cap-sheaf of his many misdeeds; he had been making a night of it in the house! Lottie and I surveyed his work in awed silence, too much overcome to venture upon any excuses.

He must have slipped into the room when uncle opened the door to look for aunt's shawl, and in the darkness remained unnoticed. Safe inside, with the family away or asleep, he proceeded to look about for something to eat. He found the bread bowl, and evidently appreciated the dough—at first. But Aunt Lois's yeast was sure to rise, put it where you might. Jehoshaphat presently made that discovery, and it was one that made him very sick, too.

Seeking for a comfortable place in which to lie down, he finally took refuge in the parlor, where we found him still lying in one corner, and still very sick; and very, very large, for the bread had not done rising. He looked at us, and "woofed" a piteous greeting as we gathered around him in consternation too deep for words.

The havoc he had wrought in the tidy rooms was fearful. Uncle, his face white with wrath, seized our suffering pet by the ears, and dragged him squealing from the room.

"He'll be all right in an hour or two, I am sorry to say," he observed, coming back and surveying the rooms, over whose pretty carpets trails of bread dough meandered like a series of gigantic spider-webs.

"Girls," he continued, "will you sell that pig to me? Of course, you don't expect to keep him always. I'll buy him; just name your price; I don't care what it is."

That was a reckless speech. Poor Uncle Silas!

"I guess they'll sell," aunt spoke up. She looked meaningly at us.

"How much do you want? Name your price!"

Abashed by the mischief our pet had wrought, neither of us was ready with a reply, and aunt said, cheerfully, "Maybe you'd be willing for me to set a price for your pig, girls, if you really think you'd better sell him."

"I suppose we'd better sell," I faltered. "You—you may set the price, aunt."

Then Aunt Lois rose to her feet, and to the occasion. She looked at her husband, and her eyes glowed.

"You are a well-off man, Silas Worden, and these two are all the children you've got. Girls can't be young but once. They've had their hearts set on getting an organ for nigh a year, as you know full well. But you said an organ was an invention of Satan, and so you gave them a pig instead. If you've realized any more satisfaction out of that pig than you'd been like to have done out of an organ, I tell you fair, I haven't. He's been a sore trial to me, that pig has, but I've borne it as patiently as I could, for I thought— yes, I did, Silas—that this day would come, and that being a neat, tidy man, who liked to see things decent about you, which is a thing you haven't done since the fourteenth of last June, which was the day that the pig came among us, you'd be willing to give any price, *any price*, Silas, to be rid of the creature.

"The girls want me to set a price on their pig. The price that I set," she took up a catalogue of musical instruments, which had suddenly and mysteriously appeared, and glanced at it, "is four hundred and fifty dollars."

Uncle Silas sank into a chair. "Four hundred and fifty dollars!" he gasped, weakly.

"Just that," returned Aunt Lois, inflexibly. "You are a well-off man, and four hundred and fifty dollars is the exact price of this cabinet grand piano—they paying freight charges."

Lottie and I stared at our relatives open-mouthed. Never before had mild Aunt Lois so asserted herself. Great beads of perspiration broke out on uncle's forehead; he looked sick, ghastly.

I rose from my chair, and approaching him, began to falter, "We—we might take less for Je—"

"Sit down and keep still!" commanded Aunt Lois, pointing to my chair with a rigid forefinger; and I subsided. There was a moment's silence.

"Well, Lois," uncle groaned at last, "a promise is a promise; you've took advantage of that. How do you want the money, in bills or a draft?"

The battle was won; the strained look on aunt's face vanished. "I guess you'd better tend to the money part of the business, Silas," she said, with a sigh of relief. "I don't understand such things very well."

"You understand some others well enough to make up," uncle assured her, with a grim smile.

"Maybe I do, but I keep my knowledge pretty close to myself, as a general thing. Now I'll sit right down and write to Maria that she can make ready to pay for those terms of lessons."

"No, you don't, Lois!" said uncle. "A man that can afford to pay four hundred and fifty dollars for a pig can afford to pay for his girls' lessons, I guess; anyway, we'll try it."

An hour afterward Jake, the hired man, and uncle were loading Jehoshaphat into the wagon preparatory to taking him away somewhere. His remonstrant squeals, as they dumped him unceremoniously into the box, so wrung our hearts that we ran out to say good-by to him, and to promise that we would often visit him in his new quarters, which was simply a pig-pen beneath the farthest of Uncle Silas's barns. But the piano came in a few days, and in our preoccupation with it, we neglected to make the promised visit until nearly two weeks had slipped by. And when we did go to call on Jehoshaphat, his fickle affection had already been transferred to his fellows; he would not even look at us.--[Youth's Companion.

A TRANSFORMATION.

ADELAIDE KEEN.

SHE was heartsick and discouraged, weary in mind and body. She—who? A little woman with crimpy brown hair and clinging ways, but very dowdy and unkempt in appearance.

Her name is Miss Legion, and so we shall call her. No doubt you know her, and guess her heart's history. Just the same as ever so many others; a summer flirtation, short and sweet—a dream which faded into the cold reality of winter. The man who admired her, danced with her, walked with her under the sun by day and the moon by night, was as far off as if she had never known him. And through it all she had behaved like a modest girl, which she was; and he, manlike, forgot her in a host of stylish and irresistibly pretty girls.

Thanksgiving Day came, with its turkey and family reunion. She had no cause for thanksgiving, poor little Miss Legion, except a few sweet memories, of which no one could rob her. Christmas came with all its greetings and presents; no gift worth having for her. For what matters the whole world without love, especially when one has tasted the sweets of life? And Love, the crafty fellow, had flown away from her like a summer butterfly; and shaken his wings and waved his arrows as he fled away, laughing. These are the tricks he likes to play, and he finds plenty of tall "six-footers," bearded and strong as lions, to do his bidding.

New Year's Day came, with plenty of calls, but none from him, who was miles away amusing himself, as the woman—the world over—sits and thinks, and wonders and weeps.

"To-day," said Miss Legion, examining the calendar, Jan. 2, "to-day I turn over a new leaf. I am twenty-four; love is a serious thing, but I am going to forget it for work; crush it out, stamp it out; obliterate and crowd it out. I am going to be a new woman. That!" she snapped her fingers, "that for him! I will conquer myself, and rule the world. I cannot bring him back by will power (haven't I tried it?) but I can compel my brain and hands to change circumstances—and he can go to anyone who wants him!"

Miss Legion looked at her face in the glass, a strong light reflecting two gray eyes flashing blue fire, and a faint color shining in her pale cheeks. Anger, genuine emotion of any kind was becoming, when controlled.

"Let me examine my stock in trade: Complexion, muddy and unpromising, but my skin elsewhere is white and fine; neck long, shoulders fair, but bony; figure slight; walk ungraceful, and hair good in color, but arranged in an old-fashioned and unbecoming way—easy to do up. Hands well-formed, but nails stubby and pale; lips full, but not red enough; teeth fair, and her eyes large, but dull in expression; eyebrows irregular, and lashes long, but not thick enough. Here we are, and no flattery; a very sad and haggered look over all; clothes good enough in material, but lacking individuality and style."

Miss Legion left no stone unturned to accomplish her end. Two faithful aids were at her right hand. Patience and Perseverence, these are the guides, the props of the long path which winds tortuously around the mount upon which Beauty sits enthroned, and, Venuswise, looks proudly down on the valley, where amorous swains and envious nymphs regard her with never-failing interest.

"I will be mistress of myself," said Miss Legion, with her chin perked up defiantly, and her mouth resolute, "and mistress of my own little world. Let me be advanced and obtain my rights. We are no longer in the dark ages. Science, art, nature—kindly as of old, but more clearly understood— are ready to assist those who wish to renew themselves and their lease of life and love—for love is life, and until a woman loves she does not begin to live."

Miss Legion's home is in the city; she does not even have the advantage of the country air, but her two little feet learned to take her daily into the city for a long bracing walk. She used to lie in bed in the mornings, but she stopped that the first thing; she got up at seven and took a cold sponge, lasting ten minutes, including the vigorous dry rub. Then she exercised for fifteen minutes with light dumb-bells, performing every movement imaginable which would develop latent curves. She first went through the neck movement, then the arms, throwing, fencing, sparring; then the hips and waist; then the knees and ankles. She read up about gymnastics in every available book in the library, and wrote out a course of training selected for especial use. Then she read several volumes on lotions and their chemical properties, and their effect in health and disease. She obtained these at the free library, availing herself of an opportunity hitherto neglected. In fact, she was astonished to find how much she had missed, how many sources of pleasure and help she had ignored.

She found out just how much food she needed, of what kind and proportion. She soon knew that anything else was unnecessary and harmful, as it gave the digestive organs, already taxed too far, more work, and did not furnish the elements of bone and muscle.

For without a sound constitution as foundation, which ought to be laid in childhood, or rather before birth, in ancestors strong and cleanly, it is impossible to have good health. A weakly constitution is something to be remedied, not resigned to as a visitation, or ignored as a disgrace, but bravely faced and conquered. All moral, mental, and spiritual health has its root in this animal health, and the sooner this fact is recognized, the sooner will the material obstacles to success be pushed away.

Miss Legion began to find this truth very fascinating, for truth she sought for daily and hourly, however discouraged by seemingly fruitless efforts. She investigated the subject of baths, and at first went to extremes with the water cure, so enthusiastic was she, and so anxious to secure a rose-leaf skin at once. The whole family ridiculed this perpetual running of water, and laughed at her attempts to reform; but Miss Legion kept quiet about her hopes and failures, and soon adjusted things moderately and regularly. She took a bath and rubbing each day; sometimes with hot water and scrubbing-brush at night, and always with cold water in the morning. She tried salt water and alcohol; also cologne-scented dips. Turkish baths she took about once a month, as often as she could afford.

How did she manage it? She put all the money she had previously spent in tram-fares, candy, flowers, and matinee tickets into this scheme for health, and found it well invested. She did not buy even a bunch of violets; she put that money into perfume for her bath, and said to herself, consolingly: "Never mind, I shall make some one buy me flowers next winter. When I am as sweet and fresh as a rose myself, I shall make some one give me roses."

She was sure of her success, every day of her training; she never wavered, though she made many mistakes, and progress was slow. She bought a pound of orris root, and a quart of bran, and a large box of almond meal. With two yards of cheese-cloth she made a dozen luxurious bags, each of which made a delightful bath.

To be clean, healthy, strong, and well-groomed is the secret of success and just how much time, money, and patience it takes, you must discover for yourself.

One of the means used to purify and enrich the blood was long and deep breathing when out of doors. Drugs she left entirely alone; she pinned her faith to nature. Her sleeping-room and bed-covers were well sunned, and underwear as fresh and as frequently renewed as her means allowed.

She aimed for perfect digestion and circulation, and gained wisdom by experience. She was very careful about her diet, in spite of a teasing brother, incredulous sister, and parents anxious lest she should starve. She avoided the rich food of the family table, and confined herself to fruits, green vegetables, fish, eggs, and meat once a day. She ate bran bread, onions, spinach, and tomatoes in abundance—tomatoes are said to contain atropine, which brightens the eyes. She gave up hot biscuit, pies, cake, candy, pickles, salt fish, and all spiced sauces. Ice-cream she sometimes ate during summer, but sparingly. She gave her face a good scrubbing in hot water and soap every night at bedtime; this was washed off with cold water, and the skin rubbed gently with a pure cold cream which she made herself. She discovered that all cold creams (except a few expensive French ones) are made of lard or tallow, a cheap substitute for vegetable oils, and injurious to the skin, as they turn rancid.

At first, under the new régime, Miss Legion's complexion became less beautiful, it must be admitted, owing to the sudden stirring up of the blood caused by vigorous exercise and cold baths. Like the ladies of the court of the Georges, who feared to wash their faces because their bodies were neglected, Miss Legion's complexion became more muddy and broken out. Gradually, however, it began to clear, for she had always enjoyed good health, and had nothing to keep her from being beautiful, except lazy and luxurious ancestors.

Within six months she found a decided improvement. Her skin was clearer and her eyes brighter, and her whole body felt so invigorated that she actually looked about eighteen. She had always been young in heart and wise in head, and she had now the essentials of an attractive woman. She took up the study of dress, compared colors and forms, and educated her eye; lastly, she went regularly to a good hair-dresser, who massaged her scalp and taught her how to arrange her hair becomingly.

The family, like the poet of old, gave her "no honor in her own country," but they at last began to hear a great deal of curious and admiring conversation about the change in the patient and hard-working little sister. It was a long, rough road to travel, every step up hill, but at the end of a year she stood on the heights and blissfully enjoyed her happiness, for, whatever the world may say, an attractive or unattractive appearance makes a wonderful difference to a sensitive person.

By that time she had gladly forgotten the faithless one, whose behavior had stimulated her to improve herself, and another, better in every way, had met her and appreciated her. And strange to tell, the first one met her one day when she was attended by her new lover, and, struck by surprise, and, perhaps, remorse, sought to renew old relations. Miss Legion, with wide-open eyes, passed him by, looking up to the one she knew she could trust.

Her skin is now clear and fresh; her hair arranged to suit her face; her figure improved in grace and outlines, and her dress is in perfect taste. If you should meet her, she would tell you that success is worth every effort, however hard. —[Dawn.

MRS. DALE'S INOPPORTUNITY.

ELIZABETH PRESTON ALLAN.

IT was a blue Monday at the Glade-Spring Manse; one of the bluest. The preacher felt stiff and sore in mind and body and in spirit. Regularly once a week he felt that his work was all in vain, and that it would be better to be hoeing corn; and then the tired body and mind and spirit rallied, and on Tuesday he thanked God and took courage, or perhaps he took courage to thank God.

But in addition to Mr. Dale's sore muscles, his wife had a nervous headache, and could not lift herself up to brighten the Monday sky, as she was apt to do, by producing a new book, borrowed for the occasion, or by suggesting some sort of picnic suited to the parson's taste. For Mrs. Dale insisted that the Fourth Commandment required a seventh rest day, and since her good man worked on Sunday, he must as a good Christian rest on Monday.

Moreover, it was raining hard to-day, with the dreariness of November, and the hopeless chill of approaching winter; everybody felt depressed; the cook in the kitchen, over her bread that was refractory; the children, missing the mothering that usually sweetened life; and most of all, the preacher himself.

And then the door-bell rang. Mrs. Dale lifted her aching head to listen, but eight-year-old Roger did not leave her long in doubt: "A book-agent, mamma?" he said, coming back from the study, with an amusing imitation of the despair a book-agent generally awakens.

"Did he come in, Roger?"

"Oh, of course he came in. Papa took him right to the fire and dried him off; he was wet as everything."

Half an hour went by, and not a sound from the study. Mrs. Dale turned restlessly on her pillow and sighed. Some one had lent her "Seats of the Mighty," and she had hoped to have her morning enlivened by the tonic of this fine historical romance: how could a book-agent think—Ah, there was the study door! But only the preacher crossed the hall, and softly opened his wife's door. He came in with a flush of pleasure on his handsome face; and a great light in the deep-set grey eyes.

"Wife," he said, with a boyish ring in his voice, "I have come to ask a favor of you. I know things are upsidedown with us just now, but I want you to let me keep this lad with us a few days."

"The book-agent, John?"

"Yes; poor fellow, he isn't any book-agent to hurt; he is just a thoroughly homesick, heartsick, discouraged boy, who set out with high hopes of earning some money for a college course, and who has lost money instead, and is miserable. I am sure I know a thing or two that will help him, if I can keep him by me a while; in fact, Isabel, I want very much to keep him; I look upon him as an opportunity."

It was as well, perhaps, that our country parson did not recognize the adoring admiration that shone upon him from the white face on the pillow; what he did *not* miss, was the sweet mirth of his wife's answer.

"Of course you shall have your book agent, John—as if you needed to ask leave! But you will have to let me say that *I* look upon him to-day as an *in*opportunity."

The preacher went back to his study laughing, and Mrs. Dale felt that the book-agent had after all proved a better tonic than the story of Quebec. All day long she heard the cheerful sounds of entertainment going on, interspersed with visits to the cellar for apples, and to the woodshed for nuts. After the early dinner—fortunately there was a good supply of Sunday's extras left over—Mr. Dale took his young guest out visiting in his tight little buggy, regardless of the rain.

The wife was on the sitting-room couch when they got back, and her gentle, bright welcome went straight to the desolate boy's heart. He felt a most boyish desire to have a good cry when she took his hand and said how nice it was to have him at the Manse.

Well, it rained and rained, and all those wet days Mr. Dale held on to his guest, though he was too busy now for much entertainment.

On Thursday morning the sun shone brightly on a drenched world, and our young book-agent left the manse, refreshed in mind and body, with a new hope and courage, and an undying belief in the loving kindness of Christian people. A letter or two passed between him and his entertainers, at intervals, and then they lost sight of him for long years.

But one day at a meeting of Synod, Mr. Dale—no longer the handsome young man you saw that rainy Monday—brought up a stranger to speak to his wife: he had preached the night before, but she had failed to catch his name; and what a strange introduction it was: "Isabella," said her husband, "did you ever see this gentleman before? This was your *Inopportunity*, my dear!"

Then Mr. Dale went away and left the stranger sitting by his wife, and it was to her, of course, being a sympathetic woman, that he opened his heart, and the story he told made the tears run down her sweet face. For she had not dreamed what a turning-point that stay at the manse had been to a discouraged young life; nor how it had made the lad desire to be what seemed to him the noblest thing he had ever known, a Christian pastor.

He had now reached the goal he had then set himself; he was a country pastor; life was even fuller of precious opportunity than he had then dreamed, and he owed it all to that rainy Monday, when with a sick heart and crushed hopes he rang the bell at the door of the Glade-Spring Manse.

I do not know what points of order, or tenets of belief that meeting of Synod settled, but one attendant went home with new views concerning her *inopportunities!*—[American Messenger.

A Good Motto.

PRISCILLA LEONARD.

Is life a fret and tangle,
  And everything gone wrong?
Are friends a bit disloyal,
  And enemies too strong?
Is there no bright side showing?
  Then—as the sage has said—
"Polish up the dark side,
  And look at that instead!"

The darkest plank of oak will show
  Sometimes the finest grain,
The roughest rock will sometimes yield
  A gleaming golden vein;
Don't rail at Fate, declaring
  That no brightness shows ahead,
But "polish up the dark side,
  And look at that instead!"

AUNT BINA'S QUILT.

MRS. O. W. SCOTT.

AUNT BINA EMERSON had pieced the quilt from bits of calico given her by the women and girls in Eden that she liked. It was the lone woman's "love-quilt," with her shades of affection deliberately outlined in tiny triangles.

"I wont have any pieces in it that call up anybody that's stingy, or stuck-up, or meddlesome, or cruel," she said. "I'll have it just as near like fresh air and sunshine as it can be so, when I'm sick, it'll seem like a nice, bright story."

But, you needn't have counted every stitch," protested her sister, Mrs. Billings, in whose home she had her cozy room.

"Anybody would think you were an astronomer counting stars, to see how particular you've been," added pretty Hetty Barton, for whose benefit the quilt was now exhibited; and she looked at the paper, covered with cabalistic figuring, which was Aunt Bina's actual record of stitches set.

"Well, stars or stitches, we like to see how many we've got, and counting is only a pastime. The minister says we can't think of two things at the same time, but, somehow, I can count my stitches and have most profitable thoughts right along. I like the way I've disposed of my lights and darks, don't you?" Aunt Bina shook out the great square complacently.

"It is beautiful!" Hetty exclaimed. "Why, you've got a piece of my light blue in the middle; and here is my pink, and there is my dark blue!"

"Yes; that's because I—" Aunt Bina had almost said "love you," but she was not in the habit of expressing herself in that way.

The young girl looked at her, questioningly, then suddenly stooped and dropped a kiss upon her forehead.

"Don't be foolish, child," said Aunt Bina.

When the last minute triangle was finally set in its corner, Mrs. Billings made a "quilting," to which every woman came who was invited, for it was well understood, by this time, that goodness as well as gowns—according to Aunt Bina's measurement—was represented.

"She ought to know who amongst us is angelic, after being in our sick-rooms and kitchens so many years," they said.

In those days quiltings were supposed to be enlivened by much gossip, but the women who gathered that afternoon, in the spring of 1862, wore anxious faces and had but one theme of conversation, the sacrifices that the overburdened nation seemed to be preparing to ask from them.

"They have opened a recruiting office," said one to another.

"Captain Pillsbury's in charge. His furlough is almost up, but he means to get a company enlisted before he goes back," was the next bit of news.

"I should think we were far enough out of the world to be let alone," said Mrs. Hastings, as she snapped the cord, wet in starch water across the triangles.

"That's crooked!" interrupted her neighbor, referring to the work: then she added, coming back to the topic, "but I don't wonder you feel so, with three grown sons to worry about."

"We've no boys to spare, here in Eden," added Mrs. Thurston; but Massachusetts hasn't failed to do her part so far, and I've expected our time would come."

"Her John'll be one of the first to enlist, now you see!" whispered two busy workers on the opposite side of the quilt.

And so it proved; for when, at twilight, the husbands and brothers came in to partake of Mrs. Billings' bountiful supper, bringing the Boston papers and the news of the day, they gave the names of those who had enlisted that afternoon, and the first one was John Thurston's.

"And probably Harry Thurston will join that company before it's filled; but his mother needn't know about John now," they said. So it was whispered in the room where she sat; but she understood the message that passed from eye to eye. Hetty Barton understood, too, although she did not raise her eyes from the line where she was setting small, even stitches. The air-waves were full of echoes in '62, and Hetty did not need even John's words, which came later in the evening, to confirm their dire prophecies.

Then how the war fever spread through Eden! Around the recruiting office where a large flag proudly floated, on the store steps, at the post office, out on the country roads, and beside the fences while horses stood still in the furrows, men gathered to talk about the boys who were going to the war. The village paper printed a long list one week, and, as it was read with tear-dimmed eyes, the people said, "It seems as though all Eden is going."

Then, one bright June morning, the sun shone upon a company of eager, young soldiers, in new blue suits with shining brass buttons. It fell upon the fathers, and mothers, and friends, who stood grouped near the long wagons which were ready to take "Company I" to the nearest railroad station. The white-haired old pastor offered the last prayer, and with fluttering flags, beating drums, huzzas, and waving caps, the brave soldier boys were borne away.

A strange hush fell upon the small town. It had always been a staid and sober place, but now it almost seemed as though life had gone out of it. Hard work became a blessed necessity to old and young.

The girls learned to drive horses that were not "steady," to ride mowing-machines, to help plan the farm work, to do "everything but sing bass," which they could not learn to do. But the real life of the place depended upon news from the boys, after all; and the coming of the old yellow stage, twice each day, quickened heart-throbs as did nothing else.

Two years passed, and the suspense was not yet over. Some of the Eden boys had gone beyond the sound of bugle-call, a few were in hospitals, but most of them were in action that dreadful spring of '64, when news of battleafter battle flashed over the land.

Eden was at its height of anxiety as the people gathered for worship in the white church, one Sunday morning, the last of May. Hymns, Scripture reading, and prayer were over, and the old pastor arose, but instead of beginning his sermon, he said:

"Late last night word came that there is great need of everything for use on battle fields and in hospitals. The sanitary commission begs us to send cotton and flannel garments, socks, sheets, quilts, old cotton and linen —everything we can gather, at once. It would be cruel to keep you women, who can use needles, here with hands folded over your Bibles, when the need is so great. You are invited to gather, immediately, at the home of Mrs. Grow for work, and may God's blessing go with you."

There were children in that congregation who still remember how, with one impulse, all the women arose and reverently left the church.

The law of Sabbath observance in Eden was Puritanic, but those who would not sew on button under ordinary circumstances were soon seated, needle in hand, wearing the exalted look which meets a greatemergency.

Mrs. Grow was president of the Soldier's Aid, and her husband kept the village store. This was opened, and necessary materials were taken from it. The only two sewing-machines in the village were already there, and were soon clicking an accompaniment to the subdued voices of the busy workers.

A delegation, one of whom was Aunt Bina, was sent out to gather whatever could be found, ready for use.

"I'm glad to get out in the open air," said she. "It stifles me to sit there like a funeral in Mrs. Grow's parlor. Seems as if it would kill me to see the look in Mis' Hastings' eyes since Harry was shot."

"They knew you could tell just where to go for supplies," replied Mrs. Kent. "We must get sheets and quilts and old linen. Have you any quilts to spare at your house, Aunt Bina?"

"I'm sure sister has some, and—yes, I've got an extra blanket or two. Come in."

While Mrs. Billings was collecting her contributions, Aunt Bina was in her room upon her knees. When she entered the parlor again a few minutes later, she bore in her arms a pair of soft, white blankets—and her love-quilt.

"Bina Emerson!" exclaimed her sister. "You don't mean that you're going to send that quilt?"

"Yes, I am!" cried Aunt Bina, her face quivering. "Nothing's too good for our boys. I won't send 'em old things I don't want; they shall have this."

It was useless to argue, nor in that hour of supreme devotion did any one care to do so; but when it was known that Aunt Bina had sacrificed her treasure, it aroused a splendid rivalry which brought together just such stores as were needed.

All day the good work went on, and at night the men, weary of their enforced idleness, packed barrels and boxes ready to ship in the early morning.

Aunt Bina reached her room again at twilight, taking with her Hetty Barton. "You know I've sent my quilt to the soldiers?" she asked hesitatingly.

"Yes, they told me so. I think it was so generous of you," Hetty replied, in an absent-minded way, as she twisted the plain gold ring on her finger.

"I had planned to give it to you, Hetty. There's nobody I like so well as you and John; but now—"

Hetty's eyes were full of dumb agony. Suddenly slipping from the chair to her knees, she buried her face in Aunt Bina's lap. "Oh! oh!" she sobbed, "you needn't think about that. It has been two long weeks since I heard from him. John wouldn't neglect me so, Aunt Bina, unless—" and then the girl could say no more.

Aunt Bina's tears fell upon the brown braids. "There, there! don't give way. I guess John is all right."

"Oh, but he always wrote! He wasn't careless, like some of the boys. Do you know his father and mother are almost sick. They think he—is—"

"There, there!" comforted Aunt Bina. "I believe John will live to come home; that's my faith. Why, we've got to believe it, Hetty! If we didn't how could we live through it!"

.   .   .   .

Even while they wept and talked, John was lying in one of the Washington hospitals. He had been terribly wounded, and after many delays was brought there with one leg amputated and his right arm disabled. His nurse, a bright little woman from Maine, tried in every way to arouse him.

"I believe he wants to die," she said to the surgeon. "I can hardly persuade him to eat."

"Probably he does," replied the weary-eyed man. "He had a magnificent physique, and such a fellow feels that he cannot face life maimed in this fashion. I've often had such cases. If you can only get him past this first shock—"

The busy man hurried away without finishing his sentence, but the nurse understood.

A few nights later a lot of boxes arrived in response to the urgent call for hospital supplies, and John's nurse eagerly claimed some of their precious contents. "I need blankets in my ward," she said, "and oh, here is a beautiful quilt! This will cheer my poor boys like a boquet of flowers."

The nurse from Maine was one of the best in the hospital, and no one objected when she carried away the quilt and placed it gently over her favorite patient.

"Perhaps it will keep his eyes off the blank wall," she said to herself, with a sigh.

When the first morning light shone in through the long, narrow windows, the young soldier opened his eyes, almost resenting the knowledge that he had slept better than usual. As he looked languidly to see if his nurse had given him an extra blanket, he saw the new quilt, and at the same moment was conscious of a faint perfume of rose-leaves, perceptible even in that sickening atmosphere.

He closed his eyes and saw the bushes under the parlor window at home, laden with great red roses, as they had been the morning he left Edēn. He had started out that morning with a bud in his button-hole, and another between his lips—"decked for the sacrifice," he thought, with a spasm of bitterness.

With his left hand he pulled the quilt nearer. It was made of many, many small triangles! "Mother's dress!" he murmured, placing his finger upon a brown bit, with a tiny white spray in it. "*Hetty!*" and a wave of color rose to his pale face, as he caressed a triangle of pink.

For the first time since he was placed upon that cot, great tears rolled down his cheeks. The spell of despair was broken. Life was sweet after all.

"Mother and Hetty won't mind if I am a poor one-legged fellow," he sobbed.

All the bitterness and rebellion melted out of his heart as he lay there quietly crying; and when his nurse came in he greeted her with a smile that transfigured his face.

"This is Aunt Bina's quilt!" said he. "I don't know how it got here, but it is. Now, nurse, bring on your broth, for I'm going to get well."

It's better than medicine," the delighted woman declared to the doctor. "He's given me his address, and I have already written to his mother."

"And I've shown that quilt to all my boys, and told them about the dear

old maid who counted all the stitches and thought so much of her 'love-
quilt,' and how hard it must have been to give it up. They're all brighter
and better for it. 'Why,' they say. 'do the folks at home think so much of
us as that?"

Years have passed since that day, and John and Hetty are elderly people
now, with boys and girls growing up around them. John found that his
brains could do better service for him than even physical energy, and has
become a successful and conscientious lawyer. In their busy, happy lives
they have never forgotten the woman whose sacrifice meant so much to
them, and when Memorial Day comes round, and the veterans gather to dec-
orate their comrades' graves, John and Hetty reserve the choicest flowers of
their garden for Aunt Bina's humble resting place.

And the quilt? Through the thoughtfulness of the nurse from Maine, it
was returned to the generous donor, who bestowed it, as she had intended,
upon her young friends. If you had the privilege of examining the contents
of a certain chest in the Thurston homestead, you would find a soldier's cap
and suit of faded blue, and very near it, carefully wrapped in tissue-paper,
Aunt Bina's quilt.—[Youth's Companion.

THE DEACON'S TEMPTATION.

WILLIAM LYNCH.

(A blind boy, 17 years old.)

Lawyer Greene had finished his hard day's work, had eaten his supper, and was now seated with his family before a cheerful fire, in a small but cosy parlor.

"How shall I amuse you this evening, my children?" asked the father, as he placed his six-year-old son on his knee.

"Tell us a story about your boyhood," replied his eldest daughter, a bright-eyed girl of twelve. "You cannot imagine how much we should enjoy it." As the other children agreed to their sister's proposal, Lawyer Greene settled back in his great easy chair and began:—

"What I am going to tell you happened when I was about fifteen. At that age most boys are inclined to be mischievous, (or at least I know I was), and for that reason I was not much of a favorite with many of the girls. The older people considered me rough, and some even rude. A few of the more pious even went so far as to say that I was on the broad road to destruction; and among these was Deacon Brown, the one with whom our story is concerned.

"He was known by the boys as 'the scare-crow;' but whether he merited the name or not you shall judge for yourselves.

"His age was about fifty. He was tall and rather slim, had a slightly stooping figure, and a quick, springy gait. The wrinkles in his face much resembled those in the skin of a shriveled up apple except that the ones in the former were by far the more numerous. His beard and mustache were red, though here and there they were slightly tinged with grey. The eyes were jet-black, and it always seemed to me that they read my inmost thoughts. He had a large, well-shaped head, covered with a scanty growth of spiky, red hair, which, in spite of all that comb and brush could do, would stand erect, giving its owner somewhat the appearance of an enraged porcupine. The mouth was very large, and it was said that a horse and carriage might drive through with ease, but as the experiment was never tried, I cannot say as to the truth of the statement.

"The deacon's friends pointed him out as an exemplary Christian; but his enemies (among which were most of the boys), considered him a proud, boastful, miserly, old crank.

"His property consisted of a dilapidated old house and an apple-orchard, which, to speak the truth, had not its equal in the surrounding country. The owner knew this, and so did certain other persons, with whom he waged constant war.

"Now I had a grudge against the deacon because he had accused me of stealing his apples, and had told father so. Of course he did not believe the story; but nevertheless I was angry with my accuser, and determined to get even with him in some way or other.

"I did have long to wait for the opportunity.

"It happened one evening that I attended a prayer-meeting, why I cannot tell, (for at that period of my life I was not much given to church-going); and by good fortune Deacon Brown had charge of the service. His subject was 'Temptation,' but I must confess that I heard very little of what was said, until suddenly a sentence caught and held my attention. It was this: 'For my part I am certain that whatever temptation may overtake me I shall win the victory.' I heard no more of what was said, for I was too busily engaged in concocting a scheme whereby the deacon should not only have an opportunity to try his boasted strength, but I be revenged on him for the wrong that he had done me.

"It seemed as if the meeting would never come to an end, but at last it did; and without waiting to speak to anybody, I rushed from the church, ran at full speed to the house, and darted into my room just as my brother was getting into bed.

"'What's the news?' asked my brother in surprise, 'You are all winded,' What mischief have you been up to?'

"'None,' I replied as soon as I could get breath enough to speak, 'but I have a plan.'

"'Is it about the deacon?' inquired my brother, (for he knew that the scare-crow and I were not on the best of terms), 'if it is, let's hear it, and I'll help you.'

"Rejoicing that I had so soon found a helper, in as few words as possible I told him my design.

"I knew that the deacon always conducted the Tuesday evening service, and I determined, if it could be done, to execute my plan on that night. So the next day (which was Saturday), I sought out four of my most intimate friends and requested their aid, which, after a little hesitation, they promised.

"All were ready at the appointed time, and just as the clock struck nine, we started for the deacon's orchard.

"There were two ways in which this might be gained; one, by crossing several fields which separated our land from that belonging to the object of our plot; the other, by following the main road for about six hundred feet below my home, and then taking a by-path from which the orchard was only separated by a high wall.

"We chose the latter, and in a few minutes after starting were safely over the wall. Here we stationed a sentinel to warn us of our enemy's approach, while the rest of us, stretching ourselves at the foot of a great tree, ate and chatted to our hearts' content.

"We had not been in this position more than ten minutes, when a low whistle, (which was the appointed signal), caused us to spring to our feet, seize a soft apple in each hand, and hurry to our companion's side. Yes, sure enough, there he was coming slowly down the road. How we longed to get a whack at him! At length he came within reach; and yelling like a company of fiends, we hurled our missiles, and waited to see what effect they would have.

"We were not kept long in suspense, for with a 'Confound those rascals!' he began to climb the wall, and how we did pepper him. We had no mercy, but hit him whenever we could get a chance.

"At length the deacon reached the ground in safety, and judging that discretion was the better part of valor, we scampered across the orchard, hotly pursued by our foe.

"One, two, three fields were crossed in quick succession, the deacon still pursuing, and slowly but surely gaining. There was but one hope. Almost in the center of the next field was a deep ditch! Oh, if the deacon would but fall into it. But alas! there was as much chance of one falling in as the other. We could but trust to fortune. And she did not forsake us, for hardly had the last boy crossed, when the deacon, catching his foot in the long grass that grew at the edge of the trench, went in all over. Giving vent to a perfect volley of oaths, he picked himself up and once more gave chase. But further pursuit was useless, for already we had put a barb-wire fence between ourselves and our enemy.

"Thus I had had my revenge, and the pious deacon had been tried and found wanting."

MR. WILSON'S SUPPLY.

MAY BELLEVILLE BROWN.

"IF I could only go out and do something to help earn money!" said Mrs. Wilson wistfully.

Mr. Wilson laughed fondly, as one shows amusement at the vagaries of a child, and patted his wife's cheek playfully.

"The idea of a little woman who has been sheltered all her life, as you have, going into the world as a money-getter! You make a first-class wife and mother, but that doesn't demand a knowledge of the principles of business. No, we will get along with what the man of the house is able to earn, even if we cannot buy the corner lot; so do not let your mind stray from the province in which you dwell so successfully to work that you would not be able to perform. My wife does not need a business head."

As her husband left the house, Mrs. Wilson walked to the window and looked after him, with her mouth drawn into a firm scarlet line.

"So I do not need a knowledge of business principles, Asbury Wilson!" said she, apostrophizing his retreating form. "You must have forgotten that I have had to make use of them for a number of years; that twice a year I look up the tax receipts and pay the taxes, often out of my own spending money; that I look after all our insurance; that I always kept up the interest on the mortgage until we paid it; that I keep all the accounts of the family, and that every claim is submitted to me for payment, to say nothing of the business knowledge necessary to make one dollar do the work of two—a problem that a man seldom tries to solve. It's all right, of course, and I must put up with being considered a business cipher; but if there is anything in the doctrine of re-incarnation, I hope you will be re-born as a woman, to see if brains are not as necessary for a wife and mother as for a husband and father!"

After this spirited speech Mrs. Wilson went about her work, which, that morning, was the construction of a stylish spring jacket for twelve-year-old Edna out of Mr. Wilson's light overcoat of two seasons back, meaning a saving of from eight to twelve dollars toward the June tax assessment.

Mr. Wilson occupied the position of traveling salesman for a grocery house, and had been able to provide his family with a comfortable home and a good living. It was no business crisis that brought forth Mrs. Wilson's wish to earn money, but the chance to purchase a certain piece of property at a most advantageous price. She could see the advisability of such a transaction, and of her desire to see the investment made was born her wish. Mr. Wilson was proud to term himself a "self-made man," and the idea that his wife's work might have a commercial value, or that he might be compelled to receive such aid from her, would have been distasteful to him. He was a most generous man, giving freely and unasked, yet always conveying the feeling that he considered the money used by the family as his alone.

Through all the afternoon, Mrs. Wilson could not help a little feeling of resentment against her husband for so coolly setting aside the idea of her capability; but the feeling vanished suddenly, when, at supper time a closed hack drove to the gate and two men took from it a stretcher. She flew to meet them, and the man they were carrying opened his eyes to say to her,

"It's only a broken leg, Chick, don't be frightened."

It proved to be "only a broken leg," but how serious the effects would really be to him she only knew late that night, after the broken bones were set, and the doctors gone.

"The worst of it is, Chick," he said, dolefully, between groans, "I was to start to-morrow on that two weeks' trip up north, and it's the most important one of the season. It takes in Great Bow, Hinesville, Robinson and several other smaller towns, all comparatively new to our house, and I had timed my dates just ahead of the man from the Occidental Grocery Co. He'll get every one of them, for the house wouldn't have time to send a supply in my place, and it may be the means of putting me on a poorer route, since I lost last month for them, because of that *la grippe*."

In spite of his wife's efforts to quiet or cheer him, the man worried himself through a restless and feverish night. The next morning when he opened his eyes. Mrs. Wilson stood beside him, in her out-of-door costume

"I've found your supply, Asbury," said she. "I sent over for mother last night, you know, and she will stay here while I go up north in your place."

"*You* go in my place? Great Heavens! Mary Wilson, you do not mean such a thing!"

"Indeed I do, Asbury," said she, undaunted by the horror in his face and voice. "I can go over the ground, and if I don't do as well as you would, I will save the route for the house, and for you, anyway. It is two hours yet until train time, and I can sit here for an hour and a half, with your lists and books, and find out where to go, and how to handle each man, and about the prices—though I have helped you so often with your writing that I could find out about the prices myself, I think."

"But, Chick," interposed Mr. Wilson, "you don't know what you are offering. You'll have to travel on crowded trains, and put up at strange hotels, and talk to the grocers themselves. You've led such a sheltered life that you don't realize anything that would be expected of you."

"I've traveled on crowded railway trains more than once, Asbury, when I had three babies to take care of, and had to drag them around while I bought tickets and re-checked baggage, and I've put up at strange hotels with them, too; and as for talking to grocers—if I haven't learned how to do that, after fourteen years of marketing, I need this experience to teach me. Oh, it's no use, Asbury, I am going, and you needn't waste any more of our hour and a half in arguing the question. Mother is a better nurse than I am, and the children love her so that they will be as good as gold, so none of my duties will be neglected. Here are your books and papers; hurry and tell me what I must do about things."

Mr. Wilson spent a lonely and worried two weeks, though in the bottom of his heart, he did not doubt that his wife would be successful—he had seen her meet too many perplexities to lack confidence in her ability. In his heart, also, he knew that all his assumption of her dependence upon his superior judgment was but a pretty play of his own, whereby his value to her seemed enhanced.

Promptly to the day Mrs. Wilson returned, bright and fresh from what had been to her a vacation from the indoor life she had been leading, joyous at seeing the family, and elated at her success. For it had been a success, as the well-filled pages of the order-book testified.

"Only two of your customers refused to buy of me, Asbury," she announced, as she quite breathlessly relieved herself of the details of her venture, "and they were old Mr. Green, of Hinesville, who 'reckoned he'd wait for the Occidental Co.'s man,' and a man up at Great Bow, who talked through his nose, and who said he 'didn't consider no woman fit to sell groceries.' The rest were all so polite—at first, I think, because I was a woman, but afterwards they really seemed to like to order from me, as I have had practical experience with so much of the goods that you carry, I could add my knowledge to what you had told me, and so my orders grew amazingly."

Mr. Wilson was enthusiastic over his wife's suceess, and as he praised her unstintedly, the thought went through his mind that when a rosy little woman, with bright eyes and a dimple-cleft chin, held the order-book, a merchant would need some of the adamant in his nature to keep his orders from growing.

During the weeks that he was confined to the house, Mrs. Wilson came and went over his route, with the result that when he could take his place again, the firm for which he worked sent an offer of steady employment to M. A. Wilson, the non-committal name that Mr. Wilson's supply had signed to her orders, with the astounishing information that she was "just the kind of a man they had been wanting."

Did she go? No; because, you see, this happened in real life, where duty and poetic justice do not go hand in hand. She went back to her home and babies, to the remodelling of old clothes, and the cooking of groceries instead of the selling of them.

"I might be able to hire a housekeeper," said she, "but never a mother, nor an economizer. It takes business judgment to be a housekeeper, wife, mother, nurse, dressmaker and general economizer, all in one, just as it does to run a government, or to sell groceries."

"You're right, Chick," said Mr. Wilson, approvingly, "and a great deal more, I think, for here is a housekeeper who can sell groceries, and here is a salesman who couldn't be a housekeeper. And you deserve a salary for your work, just as I do for mine, so hereafter, half the income of this family is your own, and I'm ashamed that I had to be brought to a proper sense of the value of your work by such an experience as this, though I must say that I deserved it all."

Which was a great deal for Mr. Wilson to say, and, although, quite the most satisfactory thing, also, from Mrs. Wilson's point of view.—[Woman's Journal.

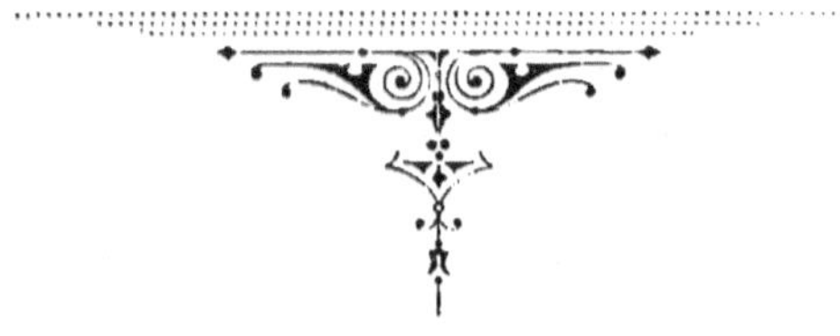

THE MODERN COLLEGE WOMAN.

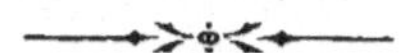

FOR the sake of the young women who are looking with eager eyes toward a college course, but shrink half dismayed at the thought that they have no money, this article is penned.

To-day, in the west, two requisites will put the average young woman through one of our universities. These are health and determination. A brief study of this question in a college town will soon satisfy one that the opportunities are more numerous for women than for men. This is because the life of the average woman has a wider range of duties than that of the average man.

Before setting out to work her way through college the young woman should make up her mind that if she can pay her way through in five or six years she is doing well.

She may be able to take an inexpensive room, perhaps the roomy attic chamber with good light and good air.

One of the easiest and pleasantest ways of earning her board will be to aasist in the care of young children.

One girl whom I know used to do a large baking every Saturday and served Sunday dinners for a small family who did light housekeeping and who had no room for a servant. For this she received $2.00 a week. Another planned her studies so as to recite afternoons and then worked up a good line of customers and spent five forenoons a week sweeping and dusting parlors. These were in the homes of people who preferred to pay fifteen cents an hour for skilled fingers to move and dust costly bric-a-brac.

Waiting on table at a private boarding-house twice a day paid one girl's board and the care of two little girls each evening while their mother went to post up her husband's books, paid for her room and the use of a piano.

Another university girl who was taking an expensive course, paid her living expenses for two years by boarding her brother and cousin. She is now practicing medicine in Chicago.

Two clever girls once took a room near the ladies' dormitory and upon the college bulletin-board announced their desire to clean and repair gloves and clothing. They did not make up their minds to attempt a college course until late in the fall and so found the girls with much work of that sort to be done. They spent a week in presenting letters of introduction and settling themselves in two third-floor rooms. An oil-stove, a set of flat-irons, and a gallon of gasoline together with well-equipped work-baskets comprised their stock. Soon they were doing a thriving business and before the middle of the semester had accumulated sufficient money for matriculating fees.

One girl made enough money to buy her books and pay her tuition by laundring fine handkerchiefs, ties, and collarettes. She gradually worked into a lucrative trade by pressing dresses. A little borax water and a hot flat-iron by her deft fingers gave gowns the appearance of new ones. She charged twenty-five cents a piece and could sometimes do ten on Saturday.

So I could go on enumerating the varieties of work, some more pleasant than others, and some more lucrative than others by means of which the girl of to-day, with the freedom given her, may reach the much coveted prize, the university sheepskin.—[Wisconsin Citizen.

If any little word of ours
Can make a life the brighter;
If any little song of ours
Can make one heart the lighter;
God help us speak that little word
And take our bit of singing,
And drop it in some lonely vale
    To set the echoes ringing.

If any little love of ours
May make a life the sweeter;
If any little care of ours
May make another's fleeter;
If any little help may ease
The burden of another;
God give us love, and care and strength
    To help along each other.
        —[*Selected.*

ANTI-VIVISECTION.

SAM'L BRAZIER.

(Secretary New England Anti-vivisection Society.)

THIS term signifies literally the cutting up alive of animals, but has a much wider application in common use. It refers to a hundred different modes of torture practised on living animals in medical laboratories daily in this country and throughout the world. It is called by its advocates "scientific research", "physiological investigation", and other euphemistic terms; but it everywhere involves inconceivable agony to living things. The "imaginary horrors" which anti-vivisectors are falsely accused of inventing are all taken from the printed reports of vivisectors themselves. The volume and page of the "Lancet," "Journal of Physiology," "Vivisectors' Directory," or other authority, could be given for each in the following short list, among hundreds of other experiments on dogs, cats, rabbits, horses and other animals—their hearts exposed; their kidneys dissected out; baked alive; eyes inoculated with poisonous matter; brains exposed, galvanized and burned; starved to death slowly; nerves of ears tortured with acids; hooks fixed in their hearts; dipped in boiling petroleum; lungs cut out; crucified with hundreds of nails; and so on without number and without end. It is impossible to exaggerate the horrors of vivisection. The details are scarcely fit for publication. Yet the public should know that paralysis, suffocation, spasms, fainting, piteous moaning, and piercing shrieks of agony are amongst the commonest results of vivisection in America to-day.

In palliation of this cruel practice its advocates say that only a few animals are used; only a few tramp dogs, for instance. How false is this assertion their own records abundantly show. The most awful experiments were performed on 585 animals by Paul Bert. Majendie tortured 4,000 dogs to prove a theory, and then 4,000 more to disprove it. In Florence, in about two years, Schiff vivisected 70,000 animals. Orfila poisoned 6,000 dogs. Between 1850 and 1882 there were 26,000 dogs, 25,000 cats and rabbits, and 5,000 horses, asses and cattle vivisected in Vienna alone. The extent to which vivisection has been practised is intimated by Dr. Harndall, who says: "There is no proof that the millions of animals that have been cruelly tortured and sacrificed to the whims of scientists, have produced the slightest benefit to science." In America some of the medical schools possess instruments and facilities for vivisection as costly, and on as large a scale, as those in Europe. They are, of course, intended to be used. There can be little doubt that in this country vivisection is carried to a much greater extent than the public is aware. It is a cruel and needless crime, and is carried on behind doors locked and barred against the humane public. The perpetrators of these horrid cruelties dare not let the light of public inspection into their torture chambers. If the public knew what vivisection involves it would be abolished at once.

But comparatively few people imagine what inconceivable agonies are inflicted on helpless animals in medical laboratories. And efforts are constantly made by vivisectors and their advocates to deceive the public. Quite recently a symposium has been going the round of the papers in which Dr. Shrady and others, either ignorantly or intentionally, endeavor to deceive the public as to the very little pain involved in vivisection, and as to the benefits it is supposed to have conferred on science and mankind. Let us consider these two points separately.

The value of testimony depends to a large extent on the character of the witness. If a witness in a court of justice should boldly declare that he did not think there was any harm in lying or perjury, he would be regarded as a discredited witness. Just as worthless, I submit, is the testimony of a vivisector as to the painlessness of vivisection. Professor Yeo is being widely quoted in the symposium I have referred to on this point. The Professor has a very high opinion of vivisectors, whom he praises as "humane men" for whom he feels great regard. Some of these "humane men" appeared before the Royal Commission in London, which was appointed to investigate the matter of vivisection. Their opinions are printed in the Report which the Commission issued. From these "humane men" we learn that "frogs do not suffer when boiled alive." "Baking animals to death does not give them much pain." "Baking cats would not cause them any very extraordinary suffering." "Nor freezing them to death; indeed, this would be the reverse of painful." "A frog had his back slit open, and a hole drilled through his skull, a needle was run into the brain and another into the spinal marrow. It was pinned to a board, the breast cut open, and the heart exposed. The amount of pain the frog suffered would be extremely small." "The screams and struggles of animals under experiment are no indication of pain." "Animals or men, when prevented from moving, suffer no pain under experiments or operations." "Dogs do not suffer if they are tied down and prevented from moving, not even when cut into." "A dog was starved for eighteen hours. It was paralyzed with curare. Its throat was cut open, and the tube of a bellows inserted in the windpipe to maintain artificial respiration. Its stomach was next cut open, and a tube' inserted into bile duct. This operation lasted half an hour. In this condition the animal was kept for eight hours, its

stomach being repeatedly opened and substances injected into the bowels."
The doctor who described this experiment declared "that he did not think
the dog suffered anything more than trivial pain." Dogs, cats and other
large animals had the tops of their skulls sawn off, and their brains stimulated by electricity for periods of several hours. They uttered "long continued cries and screams," gnawed their own legs, and exhibited indications
of intense agony. Yet these experiments were described as "not at all
painful." If it were at all possible to doubt, it would seem incredible that
human beings could become so utterly indifferent to the pain they inflict.
But one of these medical witnesses, Dr. Clein, boldly declared before this
same Royal Commission, and repeated his assertion that, "he had no regards
at all" for the sufferings of the animals under his knife. This frank declaration, and many other expressions of medical opinion and feeling, or entire
want of feeling, amply justify the physician, who declares his belief that
vivisectors have no more regard for the victim on which they operate than
if it were a piece of inanimate matter.

But this indifference to the sufferings of animals is inseparable from a
like indifference to the sufferings of human beings. Medical brutes who do
not care for a dog will not care for a man. Before the Royal Commission
medical witnesses declared that "human beings, when starved to death, do
not feel anything more than discomfort; and that "shipwrecked sailors
exposed to cold and starvation do not suffer anything more than discomfort
and inconvenience."

When men, moving in respectable society, habitually practise such
horrible cruelties that they become perfectly oblivious to the sufferings of
their victims, and even believe, or profess to believe, that dogs or men tied
down and prevented from moving do not feel any pain, even when cut into,
it becomes a serious question whether it is safe to admit such men, or
medical men who defend them, into our homes. Are patients safe in the
hands of such monsters? Are the poor safe in our hospitals? We know
they are not. Dr. Wentworth of Harvard University informs his scientific
associates that he has experimented on forty young infants, puncturing
their spines when no such operation was necessary except to gratify medical
curiosity. One of the children thus experimented on "clutched at her
hair, tossed herself about the bed and uttered sharp cries. He was unprepared for such a result and did not know but that it would terminate
fatally." I do not know whether any of these children died or not; but if
they did, should not this miscreant have been tried for murder? Operations
of a painful and dangerous character have been and are carried on in this
country on patients, without their knowledge and consent, and for no other
purpose than experimentation. To what extent this crime is perpetrated it
is impossible to say.

Here is the calm, cold blooded statement of Dr. Janson, of Stockholm, who inoculated human beings with the poison of black small pox. He says "When I began my experiments with black small pox poison I should, perhaps, have chosen animals for the purpose. But the most fit subjects, calves, were obtainable only at considerable cost. There was, besides, the cost of their keep, so I concluded to make my experiments upon the children of the foundlings' home, and obtained kind permission to do so from the head physician, Professor Medin." Do not facts of this kind warrant the opinion that the medical profession, under the influence of the craze for experimentation, is fast becoming a menace to the health and lives of the public? Poor women, without their knowledge, have had their breasts inoculated with cancer that the doctors may study the progress of the disease. And patients in asylums, sometimes without their knowledge, and sometimes fiercely resisting the doctors, or piteously pleading in vain against it, have been inoculated with all kinds of filthy and dangerous diseases. Sometimes the sufferings of a patient were prolonged for the purpose of studying results. And a patient who was certain to die has been made to undergo painful operations which were altogether unnecessary. I am quite justified in asserting that health and life are not safe in the hands of medical men who are infected with the cruel craze for "scientific research."

Instead of vivisection being almost painless, as Professor Yeo, and Dr. Shrader and others assert, it is attended by the most diabolical cruelty that any human being can inflict. I confess I am dumb with horror when I learn the details from the printed reports of vivisectors themselves. And it may be asked if vivisection is as painless as its advocates pretend, why do eminent physicians in this country and in Europe denounce it as horribly cruel and useless? Why, for instance, should Dr. John Anthony, formerly a pupil of Sir Charles Bell, speaking of practices which are common in medical laboratories, exclaim : "No sum would tempt me to go and see these things performed."

It is too plain to be denied, except by men who are trying to deceive others, that vivisection is the cruelest crime that men can commit, and is constantly attended by inconceivable agony to helpless animals.

And what has the world gained by all this agony inflicted on millions of creatures? It has gained nothing. Dr. John Bowie denounces vivisection as "a vile fraud under the name of science." Dr. Claud Bernard, the prince of vivisectors, himself declared as to results : "Our hands are empty." "The most eminent medical authorities in the world denounce it." "Vivisection has been tried and found wanting."—Dr. James Macaulay. "I am not aware of any of these experiments on the lower animals having led to the mitigation of pain or to improvement as regards surgical details."—Sir

William Fergusson. "As a surgeon I have performed a very large number of operations, but I do not owe one particle of my knowledge or skill to vivisection. I challenge any member of my profession to prove that vivisection has in any way advanced the science of medicine or tended to improve the treatment of disease."—Dr. Charles Clay. "I have never derived one item of assistance from the doings of vivisectors. On the contrary, I am convinced that whatever is bad, erroneous, narrow-minded or hard-hearted in my profession has some root drawing nourishment from the vivisecting school."—Dr. Garth Wilkinson. "Vivisection has done nothing but wrong."—Professor Lawson Tait. "Young men had to unlearn at the bedside what they had learnt in the laboratory."—Sir Thomas Watson.

These testimonies, which might be multiplied to any extent, entirely dispose of those wonderful claims of benefits resulting from vivisection, which exist only in the imaginations of those who repeat the falsehoods. There are no such benefits, but on the contrary, thousands of human lives have been lost (so the best authorities assure us) from the false light that vivisection has shed on medicine and surgery.

It is to be feared that this craze for opening living animals is extending in this country. Efforts are made to introduce it even into the public schools. The degrading and brutalizing influence cannot fail to affect injuriously the whole of human society. It is time the public conscience informed and aroused ; and this cruelest and most cowardly of all crimes should be visited with the condemnation and punishment it deserves. But the best and most permanent antidote to this great cruelty is that nobler spirit of humanity which teaches us

> "Never to blend our pleasure or our pride
> With sorrow of the meanest thing that feels."

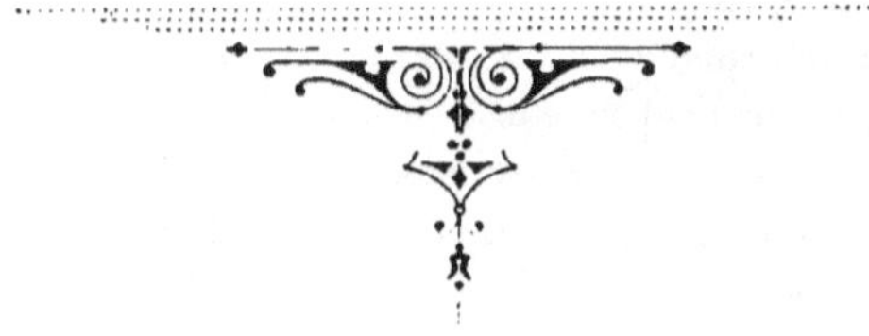

FREE LIBRARY FOR THE BLIND.

PHILADELPHIA many years ago saw the necessity for extension to the Blind of the privileges accorded the public at numerous free libraries of the city, but from lack of room, was compelled to hold the matter in abeyance.

Recently the Trustees of the Free Library of Philadelphia have made provision for a complete stock of literature for the blind and a new building adjoining their property on Chestnut street has been fitted up to meet the needs of this new department.

A similar work has been carried on for many years by the Bible House, and a society entitled the Philadelphia Home Teaching Society.

The librarian, Mr. John Thompson, says in his recently published report:

"By mutual arrangements between the Free Library and the Home Teaching Society an agreement has been effected under which the work will henceforth be maintained as a department of the Free Library. The Home Teaching Society will provide teachers who will visit the homes of the blind and instruct them how to read, and they will also take the books to and from the homes of the borrowers in cases where they are unable, owing to expense or otherwise, to fetch their own volumes. A room with suitable shelves for the bulky books which form reading for the blind will be set apart for the purpose in view, and as soon as the volumes are catalogued and prepared for the readers the work of circulation will be commenced. There will be over two thousand volumes in the Library when the department is opened to the public. Of these, between one thousand and one thousand five hundred are the property of the Home Teaching Society and have been handed over to the Free Library to be used by them according to their rules so long as the joint work of the two institutions shall be continued. The Free Library has purchased between three and four hundred new volumes which have just been received from England. The Library will be entirely free to the blind and conducted for their benefit without distinction of age, sex, race, or color. The books are of a varied character, and, in addition to copies of the Scriptures and religious books, comprise biographies of Captain Cook, Columbus, Franklin, Nelson, Livingstone and Washington. A variety of books of history and elementary science and selections from the poems of Scott, Burns and others are also included.

It is intended as early in the year as possible to organize a series of readings for the blind, which will be given at the Free Library upon stated afternoons. This plan has been very successful in several large libraries, notably in the Congressional Library at Washington."

JUST BETWEEN OURSELVES,

The "purpose novel" is quite the fashion of late years. "Sugar-coated sermons," some one has called them. A good deal has been said pro and con upon the subject, but I suspect that you and I judge of this particular class of novels just as we do of novels in the mass,—we like some of them and we don't like others. One story appeals to us, another does not. While we are reading the former, we are realists and theorists; while reading the latter we are idealists and romanticists.

* * * *

Mrs. Deland is the striking example of the purpose-novelist. And some of us like Mrs. Deland's work; perhaps some of us do not. I am one of her admirers. It is more than ten years ago that "John Ward, Preacher" brought her money and fame. It is probable that it would have achieved greater glory had not "Robert Elsmere" come across the sea just then, bearing a letter of introduction from Mr. Gladstone. *That* was the purpose-novel *par excellence.* Every page was a sermon, and the sugar-coating was pretty thin. It is wonderful how many people swallowed the nauseating dose—or pretended to. People who never read anything more weighty than the daily papers felt that their duty to society demanded the perusal of this theological work of fiction, wherein a poor, uninteresting love story meandered through a swamp of uninteresting discussion concerning things in heaven and things on earth, and was, for the most part, utterly lost.

This takes us a long way from what I started out to say, but before retracing our steps let me say a word about reading things because we are expected to do so by society. Now and then a book becomes a fad. It is "Robert Elsmere" or "Ships that Pass in the Night" or "Trilby," and we read them because we are goaded to it. Think of the countless multitude, as ignorant of French as a babe unborn, that wandered through "Trilby." About all in the book that was worth reading was in French, but I imagine it was just as well that not many people understood it. "Trilby" was a masterpiece, but there were some things in it that were better written in Sanscrit. For my own part, I have come to the place where I resolutely decline to read a book because "everybody" is reading it. It may betray ignorance to confess to numerous friends that we have not done so, but that is a more honest course than to join in the chorus of praise of something we really detest; and it is more conducive to self-respect.

* * * *

This brings me around quite naturally to what I started out to say. Which is, that a book with a moral hidden away like a dagger beneath a cloak, may at the same time be quite worthy to live just as a story. "John Ward, Preacher" I believe to have been one of this class. I took it down from the shelf not long ago, blew off the accumulated dust of ten years, and read it again. And I do not hesitate to say that it was more interesting than when I read it with the ink scarce dry. It is a hard test for any book, this re-reading. Few books can stand it. But Mrs. Deland's masterpiece is quite equal to the test. Even that caricature of Calvinism, John Ward himself, has an interest all his own that is entirely apart from the dreadful theology he tried to live. There is something of the romance here; the romanticists will tell us that it is because of this that it has lived ten years.

*   *   *   *

And now I want to say a word about Mrs. Deland's later work, partly because it is a pleasure to speak of something that has given me pleasure, and partly because I believe that every man and woman will be the better for reading such stories of common life. We are rushing and hurrying a great deal in these days; we are almost too busy to give expression to those deeper and sweeter currents that flow somewhere beneath the most humdrum and ordinary life. "Old Chester Tales" are certain, whether so designed or not, to educate and bring out that sweeter, smoother aspect of our existence.

*   *   *   *

We do not undertake to speak in detail of these tales of men and women,—for they are men and women, not lay figures, nor straw stuffed scare-crows. The latter charge was brought against John Ward. We were told that no man could be the embodiment of such theological notions, that even Jonathan Edwards was a weak and puny exponent of Calvanism compared with this young man of intense convictions. There was something of truth in the criticism. But it does not apply to Dr. Lavender, or Willie King or Mr. Horace Shields. They live and breathe, and the village street in Old Chester is no creation of wooden men and women, such as we used to create in our childhood's day; they live and move and have a being. Their joys are ours, and their griefs find ready sympathy. Even the hardened cynic must admit that here is genuineness and sincerity, love and charity, virtue and righteousness, worthy of the name.

*   *   *   *

Where do we get nearer to "The Heart of Things" than in the March number of this magazine? As we noted two months ago, there is a literature of fact and a literature of power: last month's "TALKS AND TALES" was both. It spoke of facts, wonderful facts, too, every one of them. Of the utilitarian side of the matter Mr. Cleaveland seems to have left no loop-hole for question. It is a practical benefit to the State to take its blind paupers and make self-supporting citizens of them. But what is self-support compared to self-respect? *That's* the great thing. It's a pathetic beginning, those stories of destitution and distress; of the alms-house refuge; of the ray of hope dying out and blank despair creeping in. But what a glorious ending, wherein an avenue of escape is opened through the Industrial Institution. That story, told in simple words, by a dozen letters, ought to move a heart of stone. It ought to get to the people of the State of Connecticut, and it ought to reach her Legislature. "No other state does this work in New England!" What of it? By what law is Connecticut bound to ride at the tail-end of the procession of progress? Better keep up in front near the band-wagon. Let us trust that Mr. Cleaveland's argument struck home.

ELLIS WORTH.

THE HEART OF THINGS.

CORONA AND CORONET.—Did you ever read Lady Annie Brassey's "Voyage in the Yacht Sunbeam?" If so, you enjoyed it. Possibly we ought to say that with a reservation. Dean Stanley went to Switzerland, saw the Alps, and wrote home that they were "huge, unmeaning masses." So it is possible that you might not feel the charm of that estimable lady's simple and unpretentious style. But if you were of those who did read the book and admired it, you will likewise be of those who have a treat in another woman's simple story of a voyage across the sea.

That other woman is Mrs. Mabel Loomis Todd the wife of Prof. David P. Todd, who fills the chair of Astronomy at Amherst College. "The daughter of one astronomer and the wife of another," she humorously describes herself, so that she has scientific blood in her veins as well as being married to it. Now the great event to astronomers as to common folk, is the eclipse of the sun. And because of this importance it is the desire of every astronomer to see every eclipse, not merely because it is a sublime spectacle, but because an eclipse affords the only opportunity for studying the Corona. Now it is probable that you do not know any more about the Corona than I do, and that is very little; but it is the name given to the mysterious flashing, or tongued radiance about the sun. This can be studied only during the brief period of total obscuration. So far as our

interest in Mrs. Todd's book goes, this is enough for us to know, because it is a book of travel and not an astronomical treatise.

The sun is not at all accommodating in the matter of the time or place of his temporary extinguishment. Now it is somewhere in the United States, now it is in Africa, now in South América, or, as it was in 1896, in Japan. On the latter occasion the Amherst expedition were favored by having the beautiful schooner yacht "Coronet" at their disposal. She sailed around "the Horn" but the party went overland and took possession at San Francisco. And of that delightful sail across the Pacific, Mrs. Todd has written. They put in at Honolulu and spent several days of unalloyed pleasure in those semitropical isles, since become a part of our own land. Sailing westward to Japan they found the Pacific a sea of glass. They reached Tokyo, however, only after meeting some rough weather. In the typhoon some of the expedition remembered a little story at which they had laughed earlier in the voyage.

"Friends," said the captain of a steamer laboring in a fatal storm, "We must prepare for death. We shall go down in an hour."

"Heavens," groaned a passenger, "must we live an hour yet!"

The eclipse was due to pass over the extreme north of the islands. The particular spot chosen as a station by the Amherst party was the little town of Esashi, on the north coast of the island of Yezo. Here they assembled and awaited the coming of the eventful day. Alas for the hopes of the scientific members of the party, whose chief thought was the photographing of the corona. The 9th of August came, and with it haze and partial cloudiness. The eclipse as a spectacle was sublime but the photographs were a failure.

And so I suppose some dry-as-dust, scientific individuals may have thought the whole journey a waste of time and money. But to some foolish people whose minds are not seasoned to the scientific way of looking at things, it will seem that the voyage was fruitful indeed. It furnished the materials for a delightful book of travel, and as we read we think we learn something of the greatest science of all. For we learn of men; we visit another land; and we come back from the trip refreshed and invigorated. And not least thankful are we for the charming society of her by whom we were personally conducted.

[Corona and Coronet. By Mabel Loomis Todd. Houghton, Mifflin, & Co. $2.50.]

*   *   *   *

Any communications for this department may be addressed to Ellis Worth, Waltham, Mass.

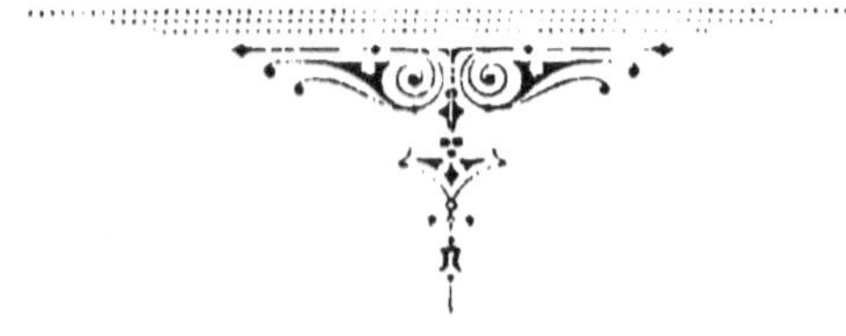

SELECTED MATTER.

The Point of View.

MARTHA SHEPPARD LIPPINCOTT.

This world is as we make it,
I often hear them say,
If we are sad and tearful,
The world will seem that way;
And if we seek the dark side,
Where everything goes wrong,
And see mole-hills as mountains,
Our lives will seem too long.

But if we seek life's sunshine,
Sweet joy to others give,
And gaily climb life's mountains,
As though we're glad to live:
To overcome disaster,
And sunshine 'round us shower—
To make our dear friends happy—
Then joy will be our dower.

The world is but a mirror,
Reflecting each one's mind.
If we look at it crossly
To us t'will not look kind;
But if we smile upon it,
It will be joyous, too;
No matter how we see it,
'Twill give us our own view.

So, when the world seems dreary,
And life seems bitter, too,
Just ask your disposition
If it can better do;
And, if it turns to sunshine,
The world will look so bright
That you will be forgetting
How dark has been the night.

THERE is no kind of false wit, says Addison, which has been so recommended by the practice of all ages as that which consists in a jangle of words, and is comprehended under the general name of punning. It is, indeed, impossible to kill a weed which the soil has a natural disposition to produce. The seeds of punning are in the minds of all men, and though they may be subdued by reason, reflection, and good sense, they be very apt to shoot up in the greatest genius that is not broken and cultivated by the rules of art.

* * * *

Punsters, in the opinion of Steele, very much contribute towards the sardonic laugh, and the extremes of either wit or folly seldom fail of raising this noisy kind of applause. "As the ancient physician held the sardonic laugh very beneficial to the lungs, I should, methinks, advise all my countrymen of consumptive and hectical constitution to associate with the most facetious punsters of the age."

* * * *

Erskine was reproached with his propensity to punning, and was told that puns were the lowest kind of wit. "True," said he, "and therefore they are the foundation of wit."

* * * *

At a time when public affairs were in a very unsettled state in France, M. de G——, who squinted terribly, asked Talleyrand how things were going on. "Mais, comme vous voyez, monsieur." (Why, as you see, sir.)

In preaching a charity sermon, the Rev. Sydney Smith frequently repeated the assertion that, of all nations, Englishmen were most distinguished for generosity and the love of their species. The collection happened to be inferior to his expectations, and he said that he had evidently made a great mistake, for his expression should have been that they were distinguished for the love of their specie.

*   *   *   *

George Colman was an admirable punster. Sheridan once said, when George made a successful hit, "I hate a pun; but Colman almost reconciles me to the infliction." He was once asked if he knew Theodore Hook? "Oh, yes," was his reply, "Hook and I (eye) are old associates."

———— ✦ ————

That silk may be produced from certain mussels or shells is a fact long known, but only recently renewed attention was called to the matter by the receipt at the Berlin Royal museum of a pair of golden brown silk gloves made of byssus silk. This silk is obtained from the small silky tufts protruding from the byssus shell, which they use for holding fast to the ground or rock under water. The fibre is silky and changes in color from greenish yellow to dark brown. The single threads are from two to three inches long, and after being cleaned and dried they are spun into yarn. Byssus silk woven into material is still a great curiosity, for the supply of material is so scarce that industrial development of the manufacture is out of the question. Only in certain settlements on the coast of Sicily there is some effort to work with this material, the shell used being the so-called Pinna. Fishermen tear the shells with nets from the rocks,

and, after cutting the tufts, return them into basins of shallow water; the tuft will grow again within a year. It takes between 3000 and 4000 shells to obtain a pound of fibre.

———— ✦ ————

Rudyard Kipling has announced his conversion to the prohibition cause. In "The Young Man" he gives an account of having seen, while in this country, two young men make two young women drunk, leading them afterward down a dark street. "Then," he writes, recanting previous opinions, "I became a prohibitionist. Better is it a man should go without his beer in public places, and content himself with swearing at the narrow-mindedness of the majority; better is it to poison the inside with very vile temperance drinks and to buy lager furtively at back doors, than to bring temptation to the lips of young fools, such as the four I have seen. I understand now why the preachers rage against drink. I have said 'there is no harm in it taken moderately,' and yet my own demand for beer helped directly to send these two girls reeling down the dark street to—God alone knows what end. If liquor is worth drinking, it is worth taking a little trouble to come at—such trouble as man will undergo to compass his own desires. It is not good that we should let it lie before the eyes of children, and I have been a fool in writing to the contrary."

———— ✦ ————

An interesting experiment in egg storage was recently tried at Leith. In June a batch of 50,000 Scottish, Irish, and Danish eggs were sealed up in a storage apparatus, and were opened and examined four months afterward, and only a small proportion of the eggs were found unfit for use. In this method the eggs are kept cool and the air is allowed to have free access around each egg, which is kept in an upright position. The eggs are turned periodically, so that the yolk of the egg is constantly embedded in albumen. This is accomplished by placing the eggs in frames which, by the action of a lever, can be inclined in different directions as needed. In this way 23,000 eggs can be turned over in a minute without any chance of breakage.

* * *

There were but three or four women lawyers in New York when the Women's Legal Educational Society was incorporated in New York, in 1890. Its first work was to induce the University of New York to allow a course of law lectures to be given to women under its sanction. Ten women each gave $100 to pay the salary of Dr. Emily Kempner, a young graduate from the University of Zurich, who delivered the lectures for the first year. The following year the University opened its law classes to men and women alike. There are now several hundred women lawyers in New York City, and recently Miss Anita H. Haggerty won a case before the Supreme Court which involved $10,000.

* * *

Mrs. Kidder, of New York, has been lecturing on "Mistakes of Women," instead of the "Mistakes of Moses." "One of the gravest, most far-reaching mistakes good women make," she says, "is encouraging bad men. Be charitable, but what you mete out to women mete that out also to men. Another of the mistakes of women is in not knowing how to rest, and still another in not knowing how to eat. What women don't know about both has built ten thousand hospitals. Consider the ways of men and be wise. Women worry too much; they hurry too much; they are misers of jollity; and they nearly always die leaving a large account in the Bank of Merriment."

* * *

Dr. Leipziger of New York tells this story in connection with recent efforts to obtain a clue to the kind of books children really want to read: In the Colorado investigations into children's habits of reading, sheets of questions were distributed on which each child wrote the answers. Most of the pupils were serious in their answers; but one facetious girl rather threw the educators off the track by answering the question, "What books have you found most helpful?" by saying: "The dictionary, the cookbook and pocketbook."

* * *

The wearing of spectacles is not confined to the human race. Nearly 40,000 pairs of smoke colored glasses are said to be worn by the cattle on the Russian steppes, where the poor beasts manage to subsist on the meagre tufts of grass that appear through the snow. The dazzling brilliancy of the snow would cause blindness were goggles not worn. The average Russian rustic may be a rude fellow, but he appears to have some mercy on his beasts.

* * *

One of the most notable congresses to be held in 1900 at Paris is the proposed gathering of newspaper men and women. This is the first meeting of the world's journalists ever called. Invitations have already been sent to all of the principal newspapers asking for delegates to be present.

* * *

Oliver Wendell Holmes used to be an amateur photographer. When he presented a picture to a friend, he wrote on the back, "Taken by O. W. Holmes & Sun."

CHILDREN'S DEPARTMENT.

The Funny Little Brays.

ELLA RODMAN CHURCH.

Four of them,—
beginning
with Sue,
And next came
Teddy and
Joe;
While last of all
was toddling Lou,
Who lisped and blundered so.
They meant to be good, those little
Brays,
But they sometimes made a mis-
take;
And this happened on so many days,
That their mamma would often
quake,
When visitors came, lest Joe or Sue,
Or Teddy or Lou, might chance
to say
The thing they should not—and say
it, too,
In the most unexpected way.
The innocent dears intended no
harm,
And it seemed to them very queer
That grown-up people could see no
charm,
In making things plain and clear.
A silver tea-set was bought one day,
And spread out for the children to
see
Before the guests came, who were to
stay
For a sociable cup of tea.
"Now remember," said mamma to
her flock,
"How often you've tried me be-
fore;

And at the table don't give me a
shock
By all saying at once, in a roar:
'Ma's got a new tea-set!'—it's ill-
bred,
And would sound like a rough lit-
tle set."
"Yes, dear mamma," the little Brays
said,
And were sure that they would not
forget.
The visitors were the two Misses
Green,
Such very fastidious people!
They were high of birth and yet so
lean—
As high and thin as a steeple.
The new silver tea-set was very fine;
And when all were fairly seated,
Sue began at the head of the line
And thus distinctly repeated:
Ma's got a new tea-set!"—Teddy the
same—
And Joe piped clearer than ever:
"Ma's got a new tea-set!"—until it
came
To Lou, who thought that she'd
never
Get a chance to speak, and hurried
to say:
"Math dot a new tea-set!" Poor
Sue
Had invented this very nice way,
Of telling their guests what they
knew;
For hadn't mamma especially said:
Don't speak all at once!—But why
Did papa look queer, and mamma
turn red,
And the Misses Green make no
reply?   *—Good Cheer.*

THINGS TO REMEMBER.

1. Never to stick pins into butterflies and other insects, unless you would like to have somebody stick pins into you.

2. Never to carry poultry with their heads hanging down, unless you would like to be carried in the same way.

3. Never throw stones at those harmless creatures, the frogs, unless you would like to have stones thrown at you in the same manner.

4. That nearly all snakes are harmless.

5. That earth worms are harmless and useful, and that when you use them in fishing they ought to be killed instantly, before you start, by plunging them in a dish of boiling water.

6. That it is very cruel to keep fish in glass globes slowly dying.

7. That it is kind to feed the birds in winter.

8. That bits should never be put in horses' mouths in cold weather without being first warmed.

9. That it is cruel to keep twitching the reins while driving.

10. That when your horse is put in a strange stable you should always be sure that he is properly fed and watered, and in cold weather that his blanket is properly put on.

11. That you should never ride after a poor-looking horse when you can help it. Always look at the horse and refuse to ride after a poor-looking one, or a horse whose head is tied up by a high check-rein.

12. That you should always talk kindly to every dumb creature.

13. That you should always treat every dumb creature as you would like to be treated yourself if you were in the creature's place.—*From Angell's Lessons on Kindness to Animals.*

HOW SANDY SAVED HIS MASTER.

A gentleman who lived in an apartment house in New York City had a Scotch terrier by the name of Sandy. One night he went to bed and tried to sleep. Sandy happened to smell smoke in the house and he gave a series of short, quick barks, so as to alarm his master. He was annoyed and told him to stop barking. But Sandy did not understand and again barked. In the darkness his master reached under the bed and got one of his boots and threw it at Sandy. Sandy was surprised but he again barked. His master reached under the bed and snatched another boot, throwing it at Sandy. He still wondered why his master threw it at him. But he kept on barking so that the third time his master got his boot-jack and threw it at him. Again Sandy did not understand, but in spite of his master's indignation he continued to bark. His master being tired of his dog's continued barking, arose to see what the matter was. Suddenly he smelt the smoke and immediately gave the alarm to the occupants of the house. He looked for the fire and soon put it out. Had Sandy not persisted in barking the house would have been destroyed and several lives might have been lost.—[Selected.

WISE AND OTHERWISE.

"Why, of course, they have chills and fever in Cuby," said old Mr. Squeehawkett. "They wouldn't have named that place Santy Ague if they hadn't."

———

Cannibalism—"Where are the children, Susan?" asked a visitor of the nurse. "The ladies up at the parsonage has got them all for dinner to-day, ma'am," was the reply.

———

Judge—"Well, doctor, what is the condition of the burglar's victim?" Doctor—"One of his wounds is absolutely fatal, but the other two are not dangerous, and can be healed."

———

"Do you think I'm a simpleton, sir?" thundered a fiery Scotch laird to his new footman. "Ye, see, sir," replied the canny Scot, "I'm no' lang here, 'an I dinna ken yet."

———

"Are you engaged?" inquired the lady of Bridget at the intelligence office.

"No, mum, but—but I have regular company four nights o' the week."

———

"That is a pretty big buckwheat cake for a boy of your size," said papa at breakfast to Jimmie-boy. "It looks big," said Jimmie-boy, "but really it isn't. It's got lots of porouses in it."

———

"I suppose by this time, Bobby, you know both French and German?" said the visitor.

"Well," said Bobby, "I can't say I know 'em, sir, but—I'm aware of 'em."

"What a lucky man Jones is !" exclaimed Beadle. "He is an A. B., A. M.. and LL. D:, and I see by this card that he is now an R. S. V. P. He's a lucky dog !"

———

"What is the money to be used for that the church is raising?" Harlem Man—"It's to send the minister away, and give the congregation a much-needed vacation."

———

A gifted young lady asks, "Why is Uncle Sam's latest achievement like a woman's throwing a stone? Because he aimed at Cuba in the West, and hit Philipines in the East."

———

"I never argy agin a success," said Artemus Ward. "When I see a rattle-snaix's hed sticking out of a hole, I bear off to the left, and says I to myself, that hole belongs to that snaix."

———

Burgin—"I see the scientists claim that strawberries are ninety-one per cent. water."

Ralston—The scientists are away off. Strawberries are ninety-one per cent. box bottom.

———

Tommy —"I dunno whether that new boy nex' door is a coward or jist smart."

Mr. Figg—"What have you been up to now?"

"Tommy—"W'y I called him a Spaniard, an' he said I ought to go in the house an' get him something to eat."

TALKS AND TALES.

A MAGAZINE

—PUBLISHED BY—

The Conn. Institute and Industrial Home for the Blind,

Nos. 334 and 336 Wethersfield Ave.,

HARTFORD, CONN.

F. E. CLEAVELAND, President.

Edited by Mrs. ELLA B. KENDRICK.

One Dollar a Year, - - Ten Cents a Copy

PRESS OF
THE CONN. INSTITUTE AND INDUSTRIAL HOME
FOR THE BLIND.

Table of Contents.

The Connecticut Mutual

Life Insurance Company
1846--1899.

To those who desire to do fully, at its least cost and to the utmost of their financial ability, their duty to their families, and to use life insurance for their protection and not for a speculation for themselves, THE CONNECTICUT MUTUAL offers the utmost that life insurance can accomplish, in its simplest, clearest forms, of perfect equity and perfect mutuality, on the soundest basis of any, and at a lower cost than has been achieved by any other company. Greater service can no life insurance company render.

JACOB L. GREENE, President.   HERBERT H. WHITE, Sec'y.
JOHN M. TAYLOR, Vice Pres't.   DANIEL H. WELLS, Actuary.

A. T. RICHARDS, General Agent, Room 16, Company's Building, Hartford, Conn.

"O'ER HILL AND DALE TO QUIET"

TALKS AND TALES.

VOL. II.   HARTFORD, CONN., MAY, 1899.   NO. 8

ALEXANDER CAMERON.

(A Blind Student at Yale.)

MINNESOTA is one of the larger states in the Union. It has an area of eighty-four thousand square miles, with an average length of three hundred and fifty miles and a width of two hundred and fifty. Its greatest length is three hundred and eighty-five, and greatest width three hundred. There is a point of land projecting into Lake of the Woods which goes beyond the forty-ninth meridian and so makes Minnesota the most northern state of the Union. It is in the centre of the continent from east to west. It has a population of thirteen hundred thousand. The largest city is Minneapolis which has over two hundred thousand population and the capitol is St. Paul, which has a population of a hundred and seventy thousand. These two largest cities are so near one another that their boundaries touch and they are called the twin cities. Jealousy keeps them from uniting.

My knowledge of Minnesota consists of my stay in four places in the state: Duluth, in the northeastern part on the shores of Lake Superior, Faribault, a little south of the centre, Northfield, thirteen miles north of Faribault, and Kasson in the southeastern part. I shall describe these four points.

*_**   *_**   *_**

DULUTH Is situated at the head of the Great Lakes, and therefore has a very fine commercial location. Five years ago every one in Duluth believed the city was going to rival Chicago at the beginning of the twentieth century, but I rather think they have relinquished that hope now, seeing Chicago has a population of nearly a million and a half while Duluth has only seventy thousand. It is the first duty of everyone making a speech in Duluth to comment on the wonderful possibilities before the city and the duty of its inhabitants to make sure the foundations of a city that is going to be the metropolis of the Northwest.

The city is located on a hill, which, in the western part, rises very precipitously from the St. Louis bay. At the steepest point the hill makes a rise of five hundred feet in about half a mile. At this point there is an elevated street car line to convey people to the top of the hill. This line is literally pulled up and let down the hill. At the top of the hill there is a power house by means of which the cars are drawn up the hill. There is a strong cable which draws the cars up. One car is always going up while the other is coming down. In summer evenings I have often been on one of these cars when there were two hundred passengers on it.

If the cable should slip when one of these cars was at the top of the hill very few of that number could escape with their lives. The cable did slip once or twice when the car was near the bottom and a few were injured. At the upper extremity of this street car line there is a summer pavillion. This is a most delightful place in the summer. It takes the place of the opera house and all other places of amusement summer evenings. Vast throngs meet there every night to enjoy the band music and various other means of amusement furnished. On a clear day one can see twelve miles down the lake from this point. In the evening the lights from Duluth and West Superior make the scene beautiful. West Superior is in Wisconsin just across the St. Louis bay from Duluth. There are a good many dwellings being erected now on top of this hill back of the pavilion.

The western part of the city which is the business portion, borders on the bay, while the eastern portion, which is the resident part, borders on the lake. The bay is formed by the St. Louis river, which enters the lake at this point. Between the bay and the lake is a long narrow strip of land, the full length of which is ten miles and the greater part of it only a quarter of a mile in breadth. About four miles of this strip belongs to Duluth. The rest of it is included in West Superior.

This strip of land makes the St. Louis bay one of the finest harbors in the world. The portion of this natural breakwater which belongs to Duluth is called Park Point, and has been made into an island by a canal which was dug at the point where the land begins to get narrow. Through this canal the great whalebacks are continually passing to and fro, going or returning to or from Buffalo and the other lake ports. At West Superior these whalebacks are made. The inventor of these boats, Alexander McDugal, resides in Duluth, and would gladly have established the ship yards in his own city if room could have been found along the bay shore for the works. There were already so many docks, for shipping wheat, coal and iron ore along the bay shore that no room could be found for the extensive ship yards. It is probably known to all my readers that a few years ago extensive iron mines were opened fifty miles north of Duluth, and these mines furnish new material to be shipped down the lakes. At the time when the mines were opened the excitement in Duluth was frantic. Everyone who had five dollars invested it in stocks in the mines. The stocks were continually rising in value, and as fast as the people sold their old stocks they bought new ones. While this excitement lasted, about a month, the stocks reached a point at which they could go no higher.

People who bought stocks at the high water price were obliged to keep them. They began to look about to see where there mines were located and of course they found their stocks were worthless. People who had been buying recklessly simply to get a chance to sell again at a higher price now found they were deceived. A few men who started the work had all the money and began work on the mines. The money was furnished by the persons in Duluth who had a little and lost that little. Three or four mining villages grew up rapidly. These villages are typical mining towns. The people rough, without education or religion. For two or three years no schools or churches existed in these towns, but they have been introduced lately and the people are assuming a more civilized aspect. When the financial crash came in 1893, the Merit brothers who own the mines, found it impossible to continue the work in the mines and dismissed their crew of Italians, Polanders, Finlanders and all other fierce tribes without their pay. This crowd came swarming into Duluth threatening to rob all the banks in the city if they did not get their pay. After two or three weeks these men were paid and scattered. During this time most of them camped near the depot watching every train for the arrival of their money.

Another panic, but of a different character, took place in Duluth in the fall of '94. All have probably read about the terrible forest fires which took place in northern Minnesota, Wisconsin and Michigan in that year. At the town of Hinkley about fifty miles south of Duluth, toward St. Paul, occurred one of the worst forest fires perhaps ever known. The woods around had been burning for a month, but the people had managed to keep the fire away from the village and thought there was little danger but what they could continue so to do. Saturday afternoon, September first, a heavy wind began to blow and soon turned into a regular whirlwind. It picked up the burning trees from the forest, and poured flames all over the village. In ten minutes a village of two thousand people was literally blotted out of existence. Of course, hundreds of the inhabitants were burned. A train from Duluth came to the village at this critical moment, and the engineer at great risk, crossed a burning bridge and rescued about all the people who were saved. The first intimation the people in Duluth had of the fire, was the dense smoke which the wind blew into the city. At three o'clock in the afternoon the city was shrouded in almost complete darkness. All the street lamps had to be lit. Following the smoke came cinders which fell in the streets like snow. In some places they were an inch deep.

The thick smoke and the falling cinders combined with the doleful fog horn, which blew all day on account of the smoke, made a most terrifying situation. Some of the more timid thought the world was approaching its judgment. I was at a hotel where one of the servant girls was in tears all the afternoon fearing that every moment would be her last. The news of the terrible catastrophe at Hinkley arrived at six o'clock in the evening, and soon after rescue trains were sent out. During that night and the next week Duluth was turned into a hospital. The survivors of the Hinkley fire came to the city without homes, money, and many of them without clothing. They were burned and some were crazy with fear and anxiety. In the fire they had got separated from their friends, and fathers and mothers had lost their children. The smoke had blinded them so that they could not see where they were going. Many parents never found their lost children, and many children never found their parents. All the restaurants in the city fed the rescued party, and every home was open to receive them. Many died in the city hospital and many more remained there for months, finally recovering. Hinkley was not the only village which perished at this time. Two or three smaller villages were burned at the same time in Wisconsin. The third of September I went through the region which was burned in Wisconsin. The fire was still raging along the railroad track so that we could feel the heat through the windows. Many times the train was obliged to stop for fear they could not get through the fire. The telegraph lines were all down. We passed through one village which was all destroyed and the ground was burning. There was a woman on the train who said she had lost her husband in that village, and when the train reached it she was determined to get out although the fire was still raging. The conductor was obliged to keep her in the train by main force. She told of how she had been saved from the village only two days before.

I have got away from the description of Duluth in my account of this fire, but will return. The narrow strip of land between the lake and the bay which I have said was made an island by the canal, is a famous camping ground in the summer. There is always a gentle breeze blowing across it from the lake or bay which makes the hottest days pleasant. There is a horse-car line runs the full length of Park Point, and this furnishes the only street. Along either side of this bordering on the lake or bay, are the tents or cottages where the people spend their summers. I have known over twelve hundred people to be camping there at one time. In many places the land is not more than three hundred feet wide.

East of the city, which I have said is the residence portion, the hill disappears, and many large and handsome dwellings are being erected there now. Many gardens are being developed there also, which furnish the city with fresh vegetables.

Sixteen miles from the mouth of the St. Louis river are the beautiful cascades of that river, and this too, is becoming famous as a summer resort. An island in the river two or three miles below the cascade, is occupied by these summer visitors who wish to get further removed from the city than Park Point will allow.

As I have given more space to my description of Duluth than I originally intended it will be necessary for me to abbreviate my description of the other three places in the state which I have visited.

_   *_*   *_*

FARIBAULT Is situated in the southeastern part of the state about fifty miles south of St. Paul. At Faribault are located three state institutions. The schools for the blind, deaf and feeble minded. Besides these there are three Episcopalian schools. The Shattuck, a school for boys, is a particularly good military school. More emphasis is laid on military drill than on study. The students at this school are of a careless irregular character. Many of them are obliged to attend this school by their parents who want them under strict discipline. They are being constantly punished for various breaches of conduct. The St. Mary is a school for young ladies. The young ladies here correspond to the young men at Shattuck. They are kept under strict rules but still are often in trouble for breach of conduct. The third Episcopal school is a Divinity school, called Trinity. There are only twenty or thirty students attending this institution, and they are not much seen in the town. They seem to spend most of their time smoking. I believe the school does not rank very high. Faribault is a town of seven thousand inhabitants and is surrounded by hills, a tiny stream called the Straight River flows through it. The name of the river reminds one of what was said about the Holy Roman Empire, that it was neither Holy, Roman, nor an Empire; so we may say that the Straight River is neither a river nor straight. The amount of water in it is so small in the summer that it can be crossed on the stones at dry seasons, and it is so far from being straight that it makes a tolerably good S. On the east side of the river rises a high bluff on which are located the schools for the blind and the feeble minded and the Trinity Divinity school. The town is on the west side of the river. At the school for the blind, there are or were in '96, sixty-five students. Perhaps my readers would be interested to have rather a detailed description of this institution. My description will be rather old as I have not visited the school since the spring of '96, and then only for an hour or two. I graduated from the school in '92. The Superintendent is Prof. James J. Dow, who with his wife, composed all the members of the first class of Carleton college. So the school is strongly Carleton in its tendencies. There is a ten year course allowed for the students at the school, and during that time they are taught broom-making, mattress-making, piano tuning, bead work, besides a very full course in ordinary grammar school and high school work. The institution fits one for college except in the classical languages.

Instruction is also given on various musical instruments to those who have any musical ability whatever. The high school work of the institution is very ably carried on by Mr. Shattuck, who is an untiring worker and takes a personal interest in all the students. The Kindergarten work is managed by Miss Hoffner who is also very faithful in her interest and labors. There is usually an orchestra in the school which furnishes very good music. For fuller accounts of the school I will refer my readers to the bi-annual reports of the institution. I wish my knowledge of the school were more up to date so that I might give a more interesting account of the institution. There is nothing more to be said about Faribault, it is an ordinary country village with some manufacturing work in furniture, shoes and flour.

*_**   *_**   *_**

NORTHFIELD Is a city of 3,456 inhabitants, thirteen miles north of Faribault. There are two colleges at Northfield, Carleton college, which is under the Congregational church, and the academy, college, and music department altogether have about three hundred students. The college is a Norwegian college called St. Olaf. There are less than a hundred students at this college.

Probably all know that one-third the population of Minnesota is Scandinavian, that is either born in Scandinavia, or born of parents who had their early education in Scandinavia. There are as many Swedes at Carleton as there are Norwegians at St. Olaf. The Scandinavians are among the best emigrants who come to this country. They are industrious and desirous of an education. At Carleton we find the Swedes are among the most interesting people at the school as well as among the best in the classes. They are a strong healthy race, and make "Good foot ball timber" as the students say.

Carleton college is co-educational, and many a love romance has occurred there, sometimes with rather disastrous results. I spent three years at the college, graduating in '96. Northfield has nothing especially interesting about it. The Cannon River flows through it which is more of a river than the Faribault stream, but still is nothing to brag of. There is a hill of considerable height rising on the west side of the river where St. Olaf is situated. The people in both Faribault and Northfield are of New England descent largely. These are among the oldest towns in the state and have not as much of the foreign element as are to be found in the northern parts.

_   *_*   *_*

KASSON Is fifty miles southeast of Faribault. It is a town of twelve hundred population. I spent the summer of '96 preaching there. There is nothing special to be said about the town, but while staying there I learned something about farming, as my congregation was largely farmers. The land in southeastern Minnesota is very fertile and the farmers in the past have accumulated considerable wealth in this part of the state. Prices are so low at present however that there is not much chance to save money. Wheat has been raised on the land so long without fertilization, that it will not produce as abundant crops of that nature as formerly. The summer that I spent at Kasson the farmers had large quantities of flax planted, and I found it to be the same throughout the southeastern part of the state. Some farmers had flax and wheat planted in the same land, and each helped the other. The best of the land still produces twenty-eight bushels of wheat to the acre. The army worm made destructive inroads into the flax crop in the summer of '96. This worm is a long worm of about an inch in length. It is oily in its substance owing to its food which is the oil from the flax.

The worm crawls up the stalk of flax and bites off the head of it and gets its food out of the head. Sometimes in a day they will thus clip the heads off of a whole field of flax. They go in swarms and so are called the army worm. When going to a new field they cover the road so thickly that one thinks he is walking through mud to pass through the swarm. They said at Kasson that they come once in four or five years and usually remained all summer. There is always some sort of an insect to bother the farmers. Either the grasshoppers, the potato-bug, the chintz-bug, the army worm or some other. They never go together but one follows the other.

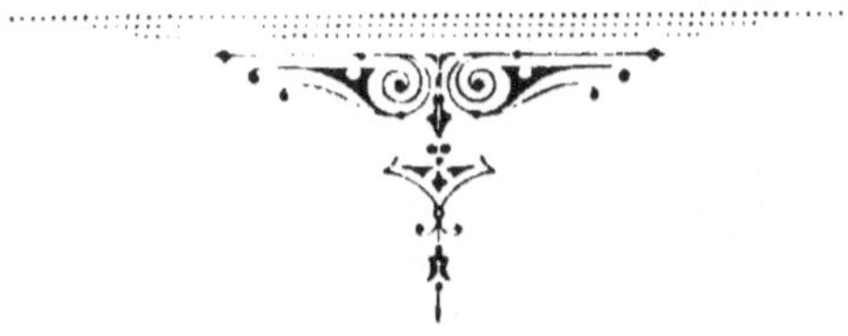

NED AND NELLIE.

ESTELLE BAKER.

THEY were twins—both rosy and plump, but she rather the more robust of the two. They were popping corn on the kitchen stove. Every now and then a kernel popped out of the popper on to the stove, where it perished, to the regret of the children. Suddenly a score did what they had many precedents for doing—leaped from bondage to death. The children could not permit all that destruction without some effort to prevent it, so both reached out a hand to save a few kernels, and each hand obtained—a burn. Both children started, crying, to the sitting-room, to tell their father, who sat reading; but Nellie's dress catching on the oven door, Ned reached him first with its tale of woe.

"Well, my son," said his father, as he looked up from his magazine, "you have learned that a hot stove burns."

As Ned crept into a corner, blowing his smart, Nellie arrived on the scene, and, climbing into her father's lap, rained tears on his open book as she said: "It hurts awfully, papa." And her father said, "It was a naughty stove to burn my little girl;" and he kissed the little fingers.

Ned hated his father, and hated Nellie—for an hour.

Nellie had a reason for avoiding contact with a hot stove, but Ned had two.

Ned and Nellie had each a "Flyer" which would fly down a snow-covered hill, but not up. On one of their flying trips they espied at the foot of the hill a man coming towards them, and Ned steering his flyer to the right and Nellie guiding hers to the left, they essayed to encircle him; instead of which they each appropriated one of his legs, which caused him entirely to envelope them both. When the man regained his feet, he had both acquired and lost—acquired a very red face and lost his cane. He quickly found the latter, without relinquishing the former, and gave the flattened Ned three energetic strokes, before he could make himself cylindrical enough to roll out of the way. Then he turned to the frightened Nellie, saying, "Poor little girl, I hope I did not seriously hurt you. Take this nickel, and run across the street and get you some candy."

Ned ever after looked carefully about before he took a fly down a hill, but Nellie—well, it would be absurd to say that candy isn't a bit like a pickle.

One day Ned lay back in his yellow cart, driving his beloved Punch along Oak Avenue. He didn't hate his father, or Nellie, or anybody. The clouds seemed so friendly up in the blue sky, and the castles up there were so beautiful and real, too—he knew he could make them real. He would be great, but he would be kind and helpful to all who were not great; he would forgive injury, and nothing but peace should dwell——

His head was nearly snapped off backwards. Punch was rearing, and another horse was trying to break its halter. The wheels of his cart were locked into those of the carriage attached to the other horse. A policeman, No. 46, ran up and jerked Punch back by the bit, hurting his mouth awfully, Ned knew, and then No. 46 struck Punch on the nose, so that it brought tears to Ned's eyes, and ended by saying, "You little idiot, don't you know anything? Go home and tell your mother to put long dresses on you!"

But that wasn't all. Ned remembered that last week he and Nellie were out in the same cart, and Nellie was driving just as he was to-day, that is, not driving at all, when they were suddenly jerked back by this same No. 46, just as a street-car swept by, and No. 46 had said to Nellie, "Excuse me, little lady, if I gave you a start, but there was no time to speak." And when Nellie thanked him, he had answered, "Nothing but my duty, Miss."

And Nellie believed him.

Ned, remembering this, resolved that he *would* adopt dresses for his future clothing, short ones now, and long ones later on.

Nellie, with the bright face of seventeen and its soft brown eyes, round red cheeks, full, smiling mouth, curling locks on brow and temples, and all framed with a large dark blue velvet hat, stepped into the First National Bank to get a check cashed. The cashier handed her a fifty-dollar bill. She started to put it into her purse, then hesitated, saying, "*Would* it be too much trouble to give me five tens instead of this?"

"No trouble at all; delighted to do it," answered the cashier, as he handed her five ten-dollar gold pieces.

Nellie gazed upon them a moment, then opening her red lips, and thereby uncovering four pearls—they are teeth in an older woman—said, "I *ought* to have said that I wished paper money. Oh, I am so unbusinesslike! You must be disgusted."

"Deliver my sex from businesslike women," said the cashier with a cordial smile, "and you can just as well have what you want as not, for we have all sorts and conditions of money here;" saying which, he handed her five ten-dollar bills.

Every one in the bank remarked simultaneously, as she closed the door, "A bewitching girl!"

Two conversations were going on at the same time—and possibly another one somewhere in the world. One was in a down-town office. "He knows what he is about," said the old book-keeper. "Though he is not twenty-one, I see in him a stockholder here at no distant day."

"Almost everybody *does* know what he is about, after a year down-stairs under Pettison, and Ned has had that discipline," said the operator; "but I agree with you that he is a bang-up smart boy."

"Well, holding a man or woman wholly responsible for every act is the only way to have them come out with a spinal column," said the old book-keeper. "If we could exemplify the divisibility of matter by eternally dividing Pettison and distributing him in every home, perhaps the market would not be so flooded with mollusks as it is at present, especially that half called the softer sex. How *can* a mollusk be hard?"

The other conversation was on a street-car.

"Oh," exclaimed a sweet voice, which came from between two red lips, located below two soft brown eyes. Then she crossed the car. "Oh, Mr. Clarkson, *won't* you have the conductor stop the car? I ought to have got off at Ninth Street."

Mr. Clarkson looked up with a delighted glance, and sprang to the rear of the car, which had just started on, after a stop at Ninth Street. It stopped again, and Mr. Clarkson got off to walk back with the lady to Ninth Street.

"How troublesome women are!" she said; "but I am so accustomed to Ned's care that I am not a bit self-reliant."

"It is the 'troublesome' women that are agreeable," he returned, with a happy smile. "May I ever be preserved from the 'self-reliant' woman!"

Mr. Clarkson had become "James." It was moonlight, and she was "driving." A bicycle shot past them; the horse jumped; the lines fell out of the carriage, and, before "James" could spring to the horse's head, the vehicle had two wheels resting upon air; but he got them on terra firma before the complete overthrow of the carriage. When he was seated once more beside her, she said: "I am just an irresponsible, and useless for an emergency!"

He looked down on her with shining eyes, and said: "Oh, sweet 'irresponsible!' Don't you know that is why we men were made—for emergencies?"

And she believed him.

They had been married six months, and were keeping house. He had been out of town for a week. He went down cellar for a hod of coal. He returned with the hod. "Why, Nellie, there isn't a pint of coal down there," he said, with a blank face.

"Oh, yes!" exclaimed Nellie. "Kate told me day before yesterday that we needed coal, but I forgot all about it," and two lips as red as ever uncovered four pearls as pearly as ever, below two soft brown eyes, as soft brown as ever, as she leaned complacently back in her chair, with her arms over her head, to drink in the words: "Well, sweetheart, we'll just have to draw so much heavier on our hearts' warmth, till I can order some."

She watched his mouth. His lips parted. He said: "The fire won't last till midnight, and it will be beastly having to dress in the cold."

The fire went out then, for Nellie.

They had been married three years, and the house had for one year contained two jewels, brighter than diamonds, and more dear; duplicates of herself and Ned,—twins. Her cheeks were neither round nor red now, for those two fat, heavy, red-cheeked babies had every disease that children thrive on, and not one night's unbroken rest had she had since their arrival. She did not dress so well, either; for they were saving to buy a home of their own; a house with a yard, where the "jewels" could roll on the grass and "play house" under a tree.

She went down town to get a check cashed, for Christmas was near. The same kind cashier of a time some years before was bringing her the money, when she said, with the old-time sweetness: "I forgot to ask you to bring it all in paper except one five-dollar gold piece."

With a weary air, he turned back to comply with her request. He turned towards her again. "I beg your pardon, but I wanted *two* five-dollar gold pieces. I am *so* sorry to make you so much trouble, but I want them for Christmas gifts."

He stood still, and looked coldly at her; then he folded his arms across his chest, and said: "Are you quite sure that this is your final decision?"

And all her answer was in the color which rose, and in her eyes, which drooped.

The president of the bank had stood near, and, when Nellie left, he volunteered: "That fine young man who just deposited the $10,000 for Cross & Co. is her brother. They are twins, and when they were children I used to visit their father in his home. Then, she was fully her brother's equal, if not more; but there seems to come a time—and an early one—when a boy shoots ahead, while the girl stands still, if she does not deteriorate. The law of sex will show itself."

"James" was coming home to his midday meal. About two blocks from home he came upon No. 46 and a crowd surrounding a smashed carriage and a broken-legged horse, which he recognized as his own. No. 46 was saying: "The woman went into the house, and left him unhitched. I could see that he was a horse that wouldn't stand without tying, and before I could reach him he turned around, got frightened at his own footsteps, and began to run. For total absence of judgment in all matters of common-sense, just give me a woman. Ain't that so?" he concluded, turning to James.

"I wish I could dispute it," James replied, bitterly. Then, with a start, he saw, a few steps away, a woman lying on some coats. It was Nellie with her leg broken, too, and she had heard every word.

Next day, as she lay where she would lie for many a long week, James said: "How *could* you have left Jim, when you know he won't stand a moment?"

"I just came in to bring Mary the sugar, and was going back downtown for some other necessaries. When I saw him turn, I ran out to stop him, but No. 46 caused him to shy towards me, and he knocked me down, and then the carriage wheels ran over my right leg. Besides," she continued, "I didn't feel that much damage could be done if he should start to run, with policemen everywhere."

"Policemen 'everywhere !'" repeated James, scornfully. "Most people hold quite opposite views on that subject. Well," concluded James, in the tone of the schoolmaster who says, "Now stand up and take your punishment," "well, this postpones the house for another year."

Her bed had been put in the back parlor, and that evening she interrupted James, as he sat reading the newspaper, by saying: "James, what would you think, if a man should plant onions, and water them, and weed them, and say, over and over and over, that he liked them above all vegetables, and then, when they were grown, be angry because they were not cabbages?"

He looked at her a little anxiously, and then said: "I wouldn't talk if I were you." Then, to himself, "She's getting flighty."

"Oh, I know what you think," she smiled, "but I am perfectly clearheaded, as I shall prove by giving you a conundrum. You know you like riddles."

"I confess I have a weakness for them," he said, his face brightening.

"And you are so good at solving them," she went on.

"The 'boys' seem to think so," he returned, in a pleased tone.

"Well, listen," said Nellie. "Why is irresponsibility called cunning in childhood; in girlhood, bewitching; in maidenhood, charming; and in wifehood, imbecility?"

He gazed at her as though the condition suggested by the last word had taken hold upon his brain; then he looked far into the coal stove

"Well," said Nellie, at last, "this is my solution—it is imbecility all the way up."

James went down cellar for a hod of coal.—[*Scott County Argus.*

IN THE HOME.

HARRIET FRANCENE CROCKER.

THANKFUL DELIGHT PENROSE looked about her sunshiny room with a satisfied smile on her sweet old face. It was a pretty, dainty room, with plenty of photographs on the walls, and two or three quaint and precise landscapes done in oil by Thankful Delight's own hands more than forty years ago. The white-covered bed, with its pretty ruffled shams, and the gay crazy quilt of silk, satin, and velvet, which lay across the foot in all its visiting-day splendor, spoke of Thankful's order-loving soul and artistic tendencies. Bunches of paper morning-glories hung from the electric burner beside the bureau, and pretty bits of fancy work here and there spoke of busy fingers.

Thankful Delight's happy face beamed approvingly upon the room and its furnishings.

"It's all complete," said she, "except a vase of heliotrope on the table. I'll just go down to the garden and get some."

Slowly and carefully she went down the long flight of winding stairs with the handsome stained-glass windows at the half-way landing, which was one of the charming features of the Old Ladies' Home—slowly, because she was in no hurry this lovely morning, and carefully, because her rheumatism had been troubling her of late.

On the stairs she met her friend of No. 40, two doors from her own room, and stopped to chat a moment. "A lovely morning, my dear," she said. "I'm so glad it's Tuesday, aren't you?"

Isabel Bemis hesitated. "Well, I suppose I ought to be glad, but I can't say I enjoy Tuesday very much. Nobody ever comes to see me. There's Mrs. Abby Star, her little grandchildren come up every Tuesday, and always bring her something nice, and there's Mrs. Delforth, she has more visitors than she's got chairs to put 'em in. I think it's too bad, Thankful, that you and I can never have company like the rest. I declare, Tuesday makes me real lonesome and homesick."

Thankful Delight smiled at her friend's doleful face. Come, come, my dear," she said, "cheer up! Let's take comfort in seeing the others have company. I'm going down now to pick some heliotrope. I want to make my room sweet."

Isabel proceeded slowly up the stairs. "Well, my neuralgia bothers me some, this morning," she said. "I hate to leave my door open every day, because I'd a sight rather slip on my old wrapper an' lie down; but that's the rule, and as long's I'm not sick I'll have to do it."

"I'll bring you some heliotrope when I come," said Thankful, as she daintily lifted her best black alpaca skirt and descended the wide stairs, making a sweet picture in her soft old laces and waved silvery hair.

Several old ladies were sitting in the wide, breezy hall, all dressed in their Sunday best. "Good morning, Miss Penrose," said one, looking admiringly through her glasses. "Going after some flowers?"

Thankful nodded cheerily to them all, with a pleasant word to each, and passed out through the great arched doorway into the garden.

The soft air tempted her to sit a while on one of the rustic seats before she picked her heliotrope, and as she sat silent in the morning sunshine she thought of Isabel's words. "She spoke truly, indeed," said Thankful, to herself, musingly, "there is not one soul to come to see us two. Let me see, I'm sixty-one and she's sixty. Poor girl! She's never got over that early loss of hers, and I don't wonder she's lonely at times. If all had gone well, and Robert had come home from the war, Isabel would have been a happy grandmother now, instead of the lonely old maid she calls herself. And—" Here Miss Penrose paused, while a faint color showed itself in her soft, wrinkled cheeks,—"if he had known that the foolish girl who let him go without a word after that first quarrel—if he had guessed that her heart went with him, and has been with him all these years—if David had known how sorry I was, and how proud I was—too proud to call him back—why, I should be a grandmother myself, and not the solitary old maid I am. But Isabel, poor girl! has grieved these many years for the boy in blue who never came back, and I have tried to bury my little romance under a gay outside. Nobody dreams, not even Isabel, that I keep that little old daguerrotype of him safe and snug in my writing-desk. Wouldn't they smile at the silly old thing's romance if they knew?"

Thankful Delight smiled herself at the thought, and arose to gather her heliotrope. "I declare, I love it better than any flower in this whole garden. I wonder if it's because he used to like it? How ridiculous I am! But how well I remember that moonlight night! It was out in the front yard, and there was mother's great heliotrope bush. My, how sweet the air was! I recollect I had on that straw-colored lawn dress of mine,—he always admired it,—and he put a sprig of that deep purple heliotrope in my ribbon belt. And not ten minutes after that we quarreled, and that was the end of everything. Forty-three years ago! Dear! Dear!"

Thankful aroused herself with a little shake. "But what in the name of sense do I mean by thinking and dreaming about the past the way I do this morning? If Isabel hadn't turned my thoughts in that direction, I should be up-stairs now, fixing my heliotrope, instead of idling away my time down here."

Ten minutes later, the fragrance of freshly-gathered heliotrope scented Thankful's pretty room. It was the finishing touch to No. 38, and Thankful was satisfied. After she had peeped into her mirror, and put on her dainty white apron—her "Tuesday apron," she called it—she took up her "crazy-work"—all the old ladies at the Home were very fond of crazy-work as a pastime—and settled herself in her rocker by the window.

She knew how it would be—how it had been for the last year in which she had been an inmate of the Home. The visitors who came on Tuesday would pause at her open door, look in with pleased smiles, perhaps step inside and look around, politely curious, and after a few common-place words depart to the next room. That was pleasant, in a degree, but what would it not have been to have some one come especially to see her, some one who really cared!

"I declare, I don't wonder at Isabel's feeling so!" she thought, as she heard across the hall the hearty kiss and "Well, mother!" with which her married daughter greeted old Mrs. White. "Well, lonely old maids must not expect much," said Thankful to herself, with a smile and a sigh.

In the long corridor the matron was saying, "Now Major, I'm going to take you to see our sunshine, for that is just what she is. This Home's been a different place this last year since she's been here. Never a gloomy, fault-finding word out of her! Always cheerful and pleasant, and ready to help somebody in some way. She's a perfect treasure."

The matron laughed softly as she paused at No. 38, and tapped on the open door. "Good morning, Miss Penrose; heliotrope as usual, I see. Here is a caller for you—Miss Penrose, Major Lewis."

The matron sat down on the edge of the snowy bed. Thankful came forward as was her wont, and gave her hand cordially to the major. She looked into his face as she bade him welcome, and he looked interestedly into hers. Then he settled himself comfortably in the chair she offered him.

"In my early days," began the major, "the name of Penrose was quite familiar to me. I had a friend by that name, a dear friend of whom I long ago lost sight. I often wonder if it is among the possibilities that we may ever meet again. I hope so—I hope so. I may say I was deeply attached to her.' Perhaps you may be some connection of hers. Her name," he went on, turning politely to the matron, "her Christian name was a singular one. At her birth her parents were so delighted and thankful that they called her Thankful Delight."

The matron gave a little gasp, and excused herself abruptly. Outside in the hall she leaned against the wall quite weakly. "Well, I never!" she whispered to herself. A romance right here under our very noses, and we never suspected it!"

In No. 38 the roses of long ago were aflush in Thankful Delight's soft cheeks, and she was smiling tremulously. The tears were not far behind the pleasant brown eyes.

The major looked at her through his gold-rimmed glasses. "The perfume of this heliotrope reminds me," he began, but Thankful could wait no longer.

"David," she said, quietly, "don't you remember Thankful Delight?"

The matron peeped in just then. She couldn't help it. But neither the major nor Miss Penrose knew. They were leaning forward from their chairs with clasped hands, looking into each other's faces as though to read the story of all the years that had been lost to them.

A little later Thankful Delight with a little laugh, opened the old-fashioned writing-desk and took from it an old daguerrotype in its shabby leather case. She opened it and set it on the little table beside the heliotrope. The major smiled, and began to search in an inner pocket. "Not much left of it now," he said, "but here it is," and he carefully drew from a long, old-fashioned pocketbook a folded paper. A few faded fragments clung to the paper as he opened it, but Thankful knew what it was—a sprig of heliotrope picked in the front yard of the old Massachusetts home forty-three years ago.

"So you see, Thankful Delight," said the major, "we both remembered. What was that little quarrel of ours about? I declare I can't tell to save my life!"

"Neither can I!" said Thankful; and then they both laughed.

Later, when the matron had told all she knew to the occupant of No. 40, Isabel sighed despondently. "That's the way it always is, every one has Tuesday visitors but me, even Thankful Penrose! Of course I'm glad for her, glad as I can be, but—" and Isabel sighed again.

The matron rose to go. "Well, I rejoice for her, I'm sure," she said heartily, "she's like sunshine in the Home, but I suppose the major will carry her off now. They say he has bought a lovely house here in this very city, and has decided to spend his last years in California, so it will be just the thing for you. For, don't you see, Miss Bemis, you'll have Tuesday visitors yourself after this, because the major and his wife won't forget you."

Nor did they. Every Tuesday after the quiet, pretty wedding which occurred in the parlors of the Home, the major and his sweet-faced wife came up the familiar staircase and along the corridor to No. 38. And Isabel knew that whatever was new and dainty in the line of fruit or interesting in the way of reading matter was sure to come with the major and his wife

And always she noticed a spray of heliotrope in the laces of Thankful Delight's soft silk gown.

And the matron, as she says good-bye with a warm hand-clasp at the wide arched doorway when they depart, thanks her stars that in this busy, practical age of ours there lingers still a touch of romance.—[*Portland Transcript.*

OUR BROTHER.

JOAQUIN MILLER.

Is it worth while that we jostle a brother
  Bearing his load on the rough road of life?
Is it worth while that we jeer at each other
  In blackness of heart !—that we war to the knife !
  God pity us all in our pitiful strife.

God pity us all as we jostle each other;
  God pardon us all for the triumph we feel
When a fellow goes down 'neath his load on the heather
  Pierced to the heart; words are keener than steel,
  And mightier far for woe or for weal.

Were it not well, in this brief little journey
  On over the isthmus, down into the tide,
We give him a fish instead of a serpent,
  Ere folding the hands to be and abide
  For ever and aye in the dust at his side?

Look at the roses saluting each other;
  Look at the herds all at peace on the plain—
Man and man only makes war on his brother,
  And laughs in his heart at his perils and pain;
  Shamed by the beasts that go down on the plain.

Is it worth while that we battle to humble
  Some poor fellow-soldier down into the dust?
God pity us all! Time oft soon will tumble
  All of us together like leaves in a gust,
  Humble indeed down into the dust.

Miss Elizabeth's Calendar.

HATTIE LUMMIS.

THE smile which had brightened Barbara's face in the sick-room gave way to a frown as soon as the door closed behind her, though the frown indicated perplexity rather than vexation. She went down stairs with a deliberation far from habitual, and, having reached the landing, turned into the sitting-room, as though she had come to a sudden resolution.

Miss Sophia was crocheting lace, and Barbara scrutinized the somewhat intricate pattern with an air of polite interest.

"It must be a great deal of work," she observed. This was politic of Barbara, for she did not like crocheted lace, nor, to tell the truth, did she like Miss Sophia.

"It is very agreeable employment," returned Miss Sophia, not unbending in the least; and Barbara, having come to the end of her limited diplomatic resources, plunged into the subject uppermost in her mind.

"It seems to me that Miss Elizabeth is feeling rather depressed. Don't you think so?"

"I am not aware," said Miss Sophia, with an alarming increase of dignity, "of any reason why that should be the case."

"I'll tell you what I'd like," continued Barbara, irrelevantly. "I'd like to give a reception for her, invite her old pupils from far and near, and have them come by the hundreds. She's got to thinking"—here Barbara's voice suddenly grew husky—"that they've forgotten her, that all her lovely, self-denying, helpful life has counted for nothing. I'm sure it isn't strange that she feels so, either, shut up in that cramped little room, where the love and gratitude of her friends can hardly reach her."

Miss Sophia felt that it was her turn now.

"You must be crazy, Barbara," she expostulated. "A reception to an invalid! Hundreds of people here in this little house!" Her voice grew shrill in its protest. "Surely you are not serious."

Barbara jumped to her feet, realizing that her appeal had been useless, if nothing more.

"Oh, that was only a flight of fancy," she explained. "Miss Elizabeth's pupils are scattered all over the globe, and we could hardly expect them to flock here, even to attend a reception. No, we shall have to try the next best thing."

There was a flash of mischief in her eyes as she took her leave of Miss Sophia, for she guessed rightly that that excellent woman would spend many anxious moments questioning what Barbara's "next best thing" might be.

"If she finds out, I hope she'll tell me," Barbara said to herself. "For I'm sure I haven't the faintest idea."

As it proved, however, it was Barbara herself, not Miss Sophia, who solved the important problem. The inspiration came to her when she waked one morning, as if some obliging dream-fairy had brought it.

"Just the thing!" she cried, springing out of bed, and beginning to dress hastily, as though no time was to be lost. "If I can only carry it out, it will be perfect."

As the weeks went by, Miss Sophia ceased to worry over the unpleasant possibilities in Barbara's "next best thing," and concluded that the girl had either forgotten her careless words, or else had meant nothing by them. And up-stairs, in her narrow room, Miss Elizabeth lay, thinking that the outside world had forgotten her. Twenty-five years she had taught in the little weather-beaten academy on the river-bank, never forgetting that she owed a higher duty to the boys and girls under her charge than just to instruct them in the rudiments of geometry and Latin grammar. How she had planned and prayed for those wayward boys! How her heart had yearned over those flippant, heedless girls! "I've tried hard," said Miss Elizabeth, wearily, to herself, "but I don't seem to have accomplished anything. My life has been a failure, I'm afraid."

The last day of the year Barbara Willis dropped in, carrying a good-sized package, the exterior of which gave no hint as to its contents.

"It's a New Year remembrance," she explained, eagerly, "not to be opened till to-morrow. Inside you'll find a letter, telling all about it. You must promise, Miss Elizabeth, that you'll follow directions faithfully."

Barbara knew, instinctively, that this mild mystery would contain a certain charm for the invalid, but she little guessed how many times that restless night Miss Elizabeth's thoughts turned towards the brown paper package. By three in the morning she concluded that this was "to-morrow" for all practical purposes, and she turned up her night-lamp in order to read Barbara's letter.

DEAREST MISS ELIZABETH:

A few months ago I was wishing that I could invite all your old pupils to come together, and tell you how much you had done for them. As that seemed impossible, I have tried the next best thing. Your boys and girls, north, south, east, and west, have sent you their tributes, expressed in other people's words sometimes,—and I have put them together in the shape of a calendar. Just think, there are three hundred and sixty-five of them!

Of course, you will be tempted to look them all over the first thing, but I shall be very firm on that point. There is one for each day, and one a day is all you can have. Every morning there will be something new. Dear Miss Elizabeth, I hope this will help to make your New Year happy. Your loving pupil, BARBARA.

Miss Elizabeth's hands trembled as she removed the wrappings from Barbara's gift. There seemed to be twelve squares of white cardboard, and as she held the uppermost to the light she saw "January" printed at the top in gilt letters. Underneath thirty-one squares of paper of uniform size had been arranged in a compact block, tied through with a white ribbon.

"One for each day," repeated Miss Elizabeth. "Now I wonder what there is for to-day."

Something dimmed her eyes so she could not see for a moment. Then she laughed softly, congratulating herself that she was alone, and turned the lamp a little higher, to read her New Year greeting:

> Thine was the seed-time. God alone
> Beholds the end of what is sown.
> Beyond our vision, weak and dim,
> The harvest time is hid with Him.
>
> Yet unforgotten where it lies,
> That seed of generous sacrifice
> Though seeming in the desert cast,
> Shall rise with bloom and fruit at last.
>
> JAMES FELTON FOX.

"Jimmy Fox," said Elizabeth, in a whisper. "The naughtiest of my boys and the dearest! How he used to vex me, and how I loved him in spite of it all!"

She shut her eyes and let the starting tears have their way for a little. The face of the old-time "Jimmy" rose up before her, the frank, freckled face which nobody could help liking. She had been disheartened about the boy countless times, and his early manhood had been such as to confirm her worst fears. Later she had heard that in the Western city which he had chosen as a home he had made a gallant fight for purity in municipal affairs, and had won the esteem of his fellow citizens. Could it be, Miss Elizabeth wondered, that her patient teaching, dropped like seed into the heart of that heedless boy, could be in any degree responsible for this fruitage of manly courage in defending the right.

In spite of a bad night, Miss Elizabeth was unusually cheerful that New Year's day. Once or twice she amazed her sister by laughing softly. She was recalling one by one the pranks of the irrepressible Jimmy. And more than once through the day she smiled with unmixed amusement over the childish eagerness with which she was looking forward to the coming of the morrow, and the reading of the second leaf on the Calendar.

The sentiment for January second was signed Henrietta Stowe:

"I should know who it was by the way she crosses her t's," said Miss Elizabeth, with that curious mixture of emotions for which the veriest trifles are frequently responsible. Henrietta had always been a good girl. Nobody was surprised when she went as a missionary to China, Miss Elizabeth least of all. She lay for some minutes with closed eyes thinking over old times before she roused herself to read Henrietta's tribute:

> Men hearkened to her words
> And wondered at their wisdom and obeyed,
> And saw how beautiful the law of love
> Can make the cares and toils of daily life.

"I don't know why I'm crying," said Miss Elizabeth, feebly, but in her heart she knew. It was over the sweet suggestion that this brave and successful life owed something to a humble teacher's having tried to make her daily toil beautiful through the law of love.

It really seemed that the good angels must have had something to do with the arrangements of Barbara's Calendar. How else did it happen that when Miss Elizabeth had been tried almost beyond endurance by her sister's peculiar ability to be irritating, that on this particular morning she should read—

> From the field of her soul a fragrance celestial ascended,
> Charity, meekness, love and hope and forgiveness and patience.

Elmer Taylor had written that. He had tried her patience often enough to have sound faith in its endurance. And his confidence helped Miss Elizabeth, as confidence always does.

It may have been coincidence, but you could not have made Miss Elizabeth believe it, that when one day she fell to brooding over the thought that her life might have been fuller and more successful if her mother's health had not kept her from leaving the country village where she was born, that the Calendar silenced her discontent with this message:

> Faithfulness in the humblest past
> Is better at last than a proud success.

That year of suffering was nevertheless a happy year to Miss Elizabeth. Many of her old-time pupils, who through Barbara had learned of her illness, sent her long letters full of the appreciation for which her heart had hungered. Her room was adorned with photographs of her "boys and girls," and of their boys and girls as well. The marks which pain and weakness had furrowed on Miss Elizabeth's face seemed to pass away, and in their place came the peace which is the token of victory.

On the morning of the last day of the year, Miss Sophia, who was about to enter her sister's room, checked herself on the threshold. "She's sleeping late," she said.

But there was no need for Miss Sophia to close the door so gently. Miss Elizabeth had passed where the jars of earth would no longer fret her tired nerves. Her Calendar was in her hands, and she had fallen asleep to the music of these words:

> And in the morning when she shall wake
>   To the spring-time freshness of youth again,
> All trouble will seem but a flying flake,
>   And life's worst sorrow, a breath on the pane.

—[Chicago Advance.

WORTH WHILE.

ELLA WHEELER WILCOX.

'Tis easy enough to be pleasant,
  When life flows along like a song;
But the man worth while is the one who will smile
  When everything goes dead wrong;
For the test of the heart is trouble,
  And it always comes with the years,
And the smile that is worth the praise of earth
  Is the smile that comes through tears.

It is easy enough to be prudent
  When nothing tempts you to stray;
When without or within no voice of sin
  Is luring your soul away;
But it's only a negative virtue
  Until it is tried by fire,
And the life that is worth the honor of earth
  Is the one that resists desire.

By the cynic, the sad, the fallen,
  Who had no strength for the strife,
The world's highway is cumbered to-day;
  They make up the item of life.
But the virtue that conquers passion,
  And the sorrow that hides in a smile—
It is these that are worth the homage of earth,
  For we find them but once in a while.

STEW FOR THE MILLION.

N. A. M. ROE.

HE didn't believe in woman suffrage, and almost the first sermon he preached after reaching the place was on that subject.

Now the women of Quincetown did believe in suffrage, and when a pastor's first sermon does not meet with the approval of the ladies of his congregation, it is a sure sign that he will only stay one year.

But the minister's wife was "lovely," and it would of course, hurt her feelings if they said a word against her husband, so what could they do?

The Reverend Arthur Kenney let it be known on all occasions and in all places that he considered a woman's place to be at home, looking after the children, mending the clothes of the family, getting the dinners, and otherwise making herself useful. The lovely wife of the Reverend Arthur Kenney let it be known in a very quiet way that her opinions and his were very different, and then the ladies were more at a loss what to do than before. The men knew that something was disturbing the even tenor of Quincetown life, but as their wives were not much given to worrying their men folks with troubles they could not appreciate, they never knew what a ferment was going on in the breast of every woman in the town.

Finally a meeting of the Ladies' Social Circle was held, and at this meeting the whole affair was thoroughly canvassed. The sermon of the pastor had been announced two Sundays before, and the day it was given there was not a vacant seat in the church. The galleries were filled, and a row of chairs were brought in and set behind the last row of pews on the floor of the audience-room. No minister had ever filled a church in that town before, and the trustees and other prominent members congratulated themselves on having secured such a man.

After that Sunday a gloom seemed to settle over the female portion of the town. The men remarked one to another that the minister was pretty hard on the women, and one said he "guessed his wife wouldn't like that sermon."

Dr. Beals and his wife were looking forward to attending the Philharmonic Concert on Monday evening. The tickets were expensive, and they couldn't go to many such things, so they picked out the best and enjoyed it heartily, contented to give up minor entertainments in order to save money for this treat.

Monday night his wife hardly spoke a word at the tea table, and when the doctor inquired anxiously if she felt well, she threw herself on the lounge and cried--cried hard. The doctor was almost frantic. He could be very calm when it was sickness in another man's family, but when his own wife was suffering—and he was sure she never would cry so about nothing— why, that was a very different matter. He soothed and questioned, and finally found out that she had been struggling with herself all day, debating in her mind whether she ought to go to the concert or not.

"I want to go awfully— it's almost the only thing all winter we do go to —but Mr. Kenney said it wasn't a woman's place out in public with the men, and she ought to stay at home and mend and bake; and he's been to college, and of course he's studied up all these things, and he's here to teach us about temporal things as well as spiritual, and—I just wi-wish he'd waited till after the concert;" and then she cried harder, till a nervous chill was the result, and Dr. Beals spent the evening putting her to bed and looking after her.

Next morning she stayed in bed till nearly noon, and when Dr. Beals passed the minister, he did not ask him to "jump in and ride a piece," but used the whip on his horse till he was out of sight, while Mr. Kenney wondered who was dangerously ill that the doctor was in such a hurry.

Mr. Hammond and his wife were never known to absent themselves from the Wednesday evening prayer-meeting, and of course Mr. Hammond was much astonished that his wife continued her sewing so late. He fidgeted awhile, and then said:

"It's most time to go, Martha."

"I thought I wouldn't go to-night. I have a big pile of mending to do, and I shall have it nearly done when you come back."

"Well, I'll read the new *Scribner's*."

"Oh, you must go; we can't both be absent. I want you to tell me about it.

He went, and his wife was waiting to hear about it, but he sat down without saying a word.

"Did you have a full meeting?"

"Full of men," was the laconic answer. "I asked Carroll where his wife was, and he said he left her mending stockings, but she insisted on his coming; and then I asked Jennings, and his wife said the minister said the women ought to stay at home and do the mending, and she was going to stand by the minister if it took a leg, so I didn't say any more; but there wasn't a woman there, and I'm free to say the meeting wasn't what it ought to be."

Nellie Cordis was ill, and Mr. Kenney called on some of the leading ladies of the church to ask them to visit the sick girl, but each one had some home duty to attend to, so she could not possibly go. He felt sure of Hannah

Keen, but though she said there was nothing she could not readily put off, she fully agreed with him that a "woman's place was at home," and she ought not to interfere in any way with man's work. Nellie had the doctor and the pastor, and she understood they had notified her young man, and she didn't see that they would need any of the women.

Mr. Kenney made no more calls that day.

Then it was told in the village that the great concert had not been a financial success and the singers would hereafter give Quincetown a wide birth.

Sundry errands that Mrs. Kenney had been accustomed to do herself were transferred to her husband's shoulders. He now was required to do the marketing, because the last number of the *Woman's Home* said it was man's work, and he should attend to it.

Sunday came, but the women of the town didn't come—to church, at least. The children were all in Sunday school, but one little girl said they'd had "company dinner every day that week;" and another volunteered the remark that "Papa said he couldn't pay the bills if they lived so high all the time, and mamma said she was just going to spend all her time, now she hadn't to do any more church work, in getting things to eat; and papa said 'Hang it !' "

Nobody could be found to get up the supper at the church; the secretary resigned, the treasurer resigned, and the president drew up a set of resolutions to the effect that as so many of the ladies had increased home duties, it would be well to disband the church circle. The resolutions were adopted, but at Mrs. Kenney's request they were laid on the table in order that the members might think the matter over. The secretary and treasurer agreed to hold the office till their successors were appointed.

John Carey expected to marry Alice Green. Everybody in town knew it and, moreover, everybody said it was a splendid match—both members of the church, both prudent, helping the good cause in every way possible; both anxious to do right and help others on the same road. John went to make his usual call on Alice, and was told that she had gone to bed with a raging headache, and had left a letter for him. IIs wondered, but opened the letter, finding therein his ring and a formal dismissal, giving as a reason that she must remain at home and take care of her parents, and that her mother agreed with her.

"John, I didn't see you at church last Sunday. I missed you."

"I shall never go to hear you preach again. I don't believe in a man who thinks a woman can't go for pleasure or business where her husband or lover can; and when it comes to breaking engagements and spoiling homes with your nonsensical ideas"—he turned away, afraid he should say something the minister would not like to hear.

"Why—why, John—but John was gone.

He heard from his wife that Alice had broken her engagement, and he heard from another source the reason of his depleted audiences, and there were enough to tell him why Dr. Beals had seemed less friendly—there are always people to tell of things.

One day Mr. Kenney brought a roll of manuscript to his wife saying, "I want you to take care of this and put it where I shall never see it again. I preached on that subject in all sincerity, and I know you, at least, believe me when I say it; but I also want to say that the views I put into that sermon do not fit this day and generation, and I do not hold them myself now, as suited to *this* church. I ought never to have given that sermon.

He went to his study, and the roll went into the kitchen range.

After dinner Mrs. Kenney made a few calls.

.　　.　　.　　.　　.　　.　　.　　.　　.　　.

Some weeks after, Mr. Kenney gave a notice from the pulpit to the effect that a vote was to be taken at the Wednesday night prayer-meeting to decide whether women should be admitted to the Conference on the same footing with men, and he hoped everybody would go and vote for the ladies. He believed them to be efficient workers in the church; they had filled well all the places they had tried to fill, and he knew of no reason why they should not do as well in other places.

The official board will ask for the return of Mr. Kenney another year.— [*Zion's Herald.*

THE BUBBLE BOY.

CHARLES BATTELL LOOMIS.

GEORGE TRUESDELL had been a naughty boy. His mother had said that as soon as his father came home he was to be punished. George sat in his little attic room and looked anxiously out of the window for his father's coming.

Mr. Truesdell had gone to town with a load of cabbages—he was a farmer—and George knew that when he came home and heard that he had been naughty he would tell him sorrowfully but firmly to go out in the wood-shed and—he hated to think of what would follow. "I wish I had a twin brother who didn't mind a licking, and then when I cut up papa'd attend to him and think it was me."

What is that speck, rising out of the birches, southeast of the road? Is it a cow? No, it looks like a bubble as large as a pumpkin and of all the colors of the rainbow. Then a gust of wind blows it into his room. It hits the shade cord as it passes it and bursts, and presto, there stands a little fellow the exact counterpart of George.

"Hello!" said George. "Who are you?"

"I'm a boy that loves to be punished. I love hard work. I love to study. I love to be sent to bad a half hour ahead of time"—

"Why, then, you're the fellow I'm looking for," said George impulsively, "because I hate all those things. What'll you take to live up here and get punished for me and do all my hard work?"

"I'll do it for my board and keep."

"bully for you! "What's your name?" said George.

"Better call me George, as long as that's your name. I'm only two minutes old and I hadn't thought of a name. But you understand that your folks are not to know that I'm here. Whenever I'm needed you'll hide and I'll take your place. The rest of the time I'll stay up here and hide under the bed if anybody comes into the room."

"But won't you be hungry and want exercise?"

"Oh, I'll exercise at night and you can smuggle food up to me. I won't need much."

Just then George looked out of the window and saw his father driving home in the ox cart. His "Gee, haw" floated through the calm of the October afternoon in a drowsy tone. But George knew that the tone would be anything but drowsy when he learned that the boy had been naughty, and he groaned aloud.

"What's the matter?" asked his double, the Bubble Boy.

"Oh, I've been bad and papa's going to flog me."

"Oh, let me be flogged instead. You don't know how I long to feel a little pain. I think I'll like it as much as you like pie."

George looked at him in astonishment. "You're a queer fellow. It doesn't seem exactly right, but papa wouldn't know the difference, and I'm sorry I was naughty; so you may go down and get punished, and I'll stay up here."

A few minutes later Farmer Truesdell drove his team into the barnyard, unyoked the oxen, leaving them to wander off down the lane. Then he came into the kitchen where his wife was preparing dinner. ";Hello, Molly! Sold 'em all early. People seemed hungry for cabbages to-day. Those medicine Indians was on the flat and I bought a bow an' arrow for George. He's been pesterin' me for one, an' seein' to-morrow's his birthday I bought 'em. Where is he?"

Mrs. Truesdell shook her head. "He's up in his room, where I sent him. He's been very trying to-day. He teased Cynthia and when I scolded him he was impertinent to me. And then to cap all he broke the pantry window throwing stones at the chickens, although I told him not to."

Mr. Truesdell put the bow and arrow into the north pantry. "I don't know what gets into that boy sometimes," said he. "I suppose I'll have to flog him."

Seth Truesdell went to the foot of the attic stairs and called "George!"

"Yes, sir."

"Come down."

"You go," said George, and his double went gleefully down the stairs. George took up his station at his window, where he could command a view of the woodshed. But first he locked the door for fear his mother might come up and find him.

The double walked into the kitchen.

"My boy," said Mr. Truesdell, "I'm sorry to have to punish you when I come home, but your mother tells me that you have been impertinent and disobedient, so come out into the woodshed."

George's double, with never a word, walked out to the woodshed. Mr. Truesdell took a birch rod down from its resting place on two nails and told the boy to hold out his hand. Up in the window George was staring wildly and feverishly breathing.

Swish! came the rod. Phew, what a resounding whack! George heard it distinctly. He would have cried out, but his double never winced. Four cuts of the rod and then the double flung his arms around Mr. Truesdell's neck and hugged him. "Thank you, thank you," said he. It has been a pleasure to him. "As good as pie," as he had told George.

Mr. Truesdell was overjoyed to think that the boy could take his punishment in so good a spirit, so he returned the caress.

Then the Bubble Boy went into the kitchen and kissed Mrs. Truesdell and said, "I'm sorry I was naughty."

She had half repented having told her husband about George's misdemeanor and she patted the boy's shoulder and kissed him and said, "Well, I'm sure it won't occur again."

According to schedule he should now have gone upstairs to relieve George who was wondering what was keeping him, but this Bubble Boy was having too good a time to go up into the hot little room. He saw cake and pies and he smelt a good chicken dinner cooking and, as he had never eaten in his short life, he determined to stay and have something.

"Dinner most ready?" asked he. "I'm awful hungry."

"It'll be ready in ten minutes," said his mother. Mr. Truesdell had gone out to feed the hens and the double sat down by the kitchen window and sniffed longingly at some apples.

"'N I'll have 'napple?" said he. He seemed to have mastered small boy dialect in a surprisingly short space of time. His mother—she thought she was his mother, although as we know he had no mother—gave him an apple, and when dinner was served, soon after, he ate three times as much as George did and was so jolly withal that Mr. and Mrs. Truesdell didn't know what had come over their boy.

"George, after dinner I wish you'd harness up Jack," said the farmer. "I've got to drive over to the Gages to get a book on hens that he promised me. I'm going to give you some hens and let you see what you can make out of them with the aid of the book. I don't take much stock in hen books myself. I've always made 'em lay without any book, and I don't believe but what hens laid before the first book was printed, but I'll give you something to be interested in, and you won't be so apt to break windows if your time is more occupied."

"The Bubble Boy smiled but said nothing. He was too busy with his third slice of pumpkin pie to talk. After he had finished it he said: "Can I ride over with you?"

"I dunno. Kinder late for you. Well, seein' to-morrow's your birthday I'll let you."

So it happened that a few minutes later, George, who had been weeping in his room, not daring to go down and expose the trick he had played upon his father, and yet feeling very hungry and contrite, heard a sound of wheels in the yard and looked out of the window. There in the dusky light he saw the Bubble Boy backing Jack into the Concord wagon. He worked like an old hand, and in a few minutes his father came out of the house and got into the wagon, and then they rode off, his double driving.

This was too much for the poor boy. If there was one thing he liked before another it was a ride with his father, and at night of all things. He cast himself upon the bed and sobbed as if his heart would break. What a wicked boy his double was. Here he'd offered to board and keep him, to take all his troubles off his shoulders and he was taking his pleasure as well. Oh, how hungry he was. Cold chicken would taste good.

He rose from the bed and walked as noiselessly as he could down the attic stairs, but his mother, who was putting Cynthia to bed, heard him, and called out in an alarmed tone: "Who's there?"

It's me," said George, in a weak voice.

"You back so soon? Why; what's the matter? (Seeing he's been crying.) Has anything happened to your father? Tell me, child!"

"I didn't go with papa," sobbed George. "That's why I've been crying."

"Why, George, I saw you go," said his mother.

"It wasn't me; it was a bubble boy that floated in this afternoon."

His mother looked bewildered. "What's the matter with you? Are you crazy? said she.

At this moment the sound of wheels was heard in the yard and George said "There they are. They'll be in in a minute."

In less than a minute his father came in.

"Oh, here you are," he said to George. "You ought not to jump out of the back of the wagon in that way in the dark. I stopped and called to you and you didn't answer and I thought you were hurt. And then I saw you running toward the house."

"That wasn't me. That was the Bubble Boy."

His father didn't notice what he said. "Where's that hen book? I want to show your mother that picture of the Wyandotte."

"What hen book?" asked George, mystified.

For the next few minutes his answers were so bewildering to both parents that they finally told him sharply to go to bed.

"It doesn't do to keep a growing boy up late," said his father.

As for the double, they wouldn't hear another word about him.

George went upstairs by way of the pantry, and appeased his appetite somewhat. When he entered his room he half expected to see his double. But, as we all know, Bubble Boys have short lives. He looked out of the window. A silvery moon was riding through steamy clouds and he thought he saw an iridescent bubble floating by its side.

"I guess I'll take my own punishments and pleasures after this," said he, as he took a bite of drumstick. "I know I don't want any more mean old doubles like that one."—[*New York Sun.*

A Tribute to Bishop Williams.

JULIA H. BANCROFT KEENEY.

BISHOP WILLIAMS who has just "passed beyond," was one of those men whom one could not meet without being impressed by his goodness and sincerity.

It was my privilege to hear his address to the students of Trinity College, at the last Baccalaureate, delivered on June 23, 1878, in the old college buildings on Trinity street, before they were removed to make place for our State Capitol. His theme was, "Life a Stewardship, Faithfulness a standard by which it is measured." He said, "Faithfulness will involve many self denials, much self-sacrifice, many subjections of tastes, inclinations, wishes and purposes, to the severe demands of duty. But let it be remembered that every subjection, be it however small, tells powerfully on human character, makes the man who does it manlier than he was before, lifts him up to the very loftiest freedom, and be it said with reverance, moulds him more and more entirely on the pattern of Him whose self-abnegation none can conceive.

Take these truths with you as the parting charge of your academic mother, take them with our blessing and our prayers, and be assured that whatever the future may have in store for you, whether your life's pathway is to lead you over the dusty and heated highways of the world, with their noise and tumult, their wearying burdens, and disturbing labors, or to conduct you through the green pastures and beside the quiet waters which God allots to some, more favored than they know, still, if you take these truths into yourselves and work them out in your lives, those lives will be such as will be worth the living, the world will be better for them, and instead of being dragged down to the level of an age that is marked by sordid selfishness and petty aims, you will rise above it and do something, —how much the end will show—towards lifting it up with you. More than this, what good things you give out from yourselves will come back to you with manifold increase, they will strengthen your manhood, deepen your characters and crown your lives with golden and glorious harvests. May it be yours, dear brethren, to say,

'Now let the poor short-sighted mob of men
Laugh on and have an echo for their cheer,
But we will live our lives for future days;
Content to know that, though despised and mocked,

> We in communion with the noble dead,
> And with applause from unseen ministers
> Aye, with the strengthening smile of God Himself,
> Do hold in His high service our still sway,
> Having within us all our journey through
> And in his home at last, our high reward.'

These farewell words to you mingle with our farewells to this sacred place and our collegiate home. I had thought in preaching the last sermon that will be preached in this place * * * that I would make those memories my theme. It is forty-five years since I first entered these walls as an under-graduate, but the service comes back to my recollection fresh and clear to-night, and as it comes I not only recall the place as it then was, but I re-people it with those among whom I stood as a stranger, little dreaming of all the ties which in future years were to bind me to our college.

When I tell you that of the officers of instruction who occupied the desk where that altar stands, two only are among the living, and when I further tell you that of less than threescore students who were here that day, nearly half are starred on the college roll, you will not wonder I am sure, that I shrank from the purposed theme. I do not mean that only sad memories and associations would have come to mind, far from it. And yet what a mysterious ordering it is of human life and of this world's story, that they never present a line of joy, but a line of sadness runs beside it, that never a rainbow glitters but a dark background of cloud looms up behind it.

Then beside, time would fail me and your patience with it, had I tried to speak of even a part of what comes thronging to my memory, so abandoning that purpose, my thoughts turned next to the place which this chapel has occupied in our collegiate life, and the unchanging lessons it has been teaching for more than half a century. That place will not be annihilated, nor will the lessons cease, because these honored walls are so soon to be removed, because the places that have known them shall know them no more forever. The old creed that we have uttered here, the familiar prayers and psalms, and chants that have lived before us through ages of glorious life, and will live on forever, the old lessons of truth and duty, shall all be transfigured to a statlier home where I hope and trust they may be even more to coming generations than they have been to us. * * * We are all going from the cherished home of our early manhood, some of us from the more cherished home of our later years, as we go, and whenever we go, let it be with the prayer of the great King of Israel.

'The Lord our God be with us as He was with our fathers; let Him not leave us nor forsake us; that He may incline our hearts to Him, to walk in all His ways and to keep His commandments, and His statutes and His judgments.'"

A LETTER.

The following letter came to us through the courtesy of Mr. W. Wade, Oakmont, Pa., to whom it was written. Miss Haguewood is a deaf and blind girl of Iowa.

I thank you for sending me the box of books. There were ten books in Braille. Miss Chappell sent me two books and two magazines. I shall write to her to-day and thank her. I wanted to ask Miss Mattice at Vinton for an English History, but Miss Donald says I may ask Miss Chappell for it. I should like to visit Cambridge Square in London, England, but I cannot go now. If I have English stories, I can find out about it. I am so glad that you like to send me books. There are twenty-five stories in one of the readers. I read one every afternoon. One is about sugar. I like it. The story told me about the sugar-canes, where they grow, and how sugar is manufactured. Louisiana is noted for sugar plantations. It grows there because it is adapted to a hot climate. The French make sugar of sugar beets. Another story is about a boat. I have read it and it made me think of little waves in the lagoon at the Exposition in Omaha. The little waves will be happy when the weather is pleasant. They are frozen now. I am very sorry for them, but the warm sun will shine again soon and make them melt. Then they can creep around the boats and whisper to the happy people in the boats. I am always happy when I am in a boat on the water. Another story is about catching monkeys. I do not like monkeys because they are not nice and I am afraid of them, but I want to know who catches them. So I shall read the monkey story to find out. The monkey men will take off the monkey's fur skin and clean it after it is killed. I do not know what "magpies" means, but the story will tell me. Do you want me to be educated about all these things? George Washington's birthday came last Wednesday. Mr. Simpson gave us a masquerade party. I wore some masquerade clothes. I was dressed like an English May Queen. I was very happy. I danced with Miss Donald. I let my hair float around my shoulders like Star's hair. Star is Captain's little girl, and her hair is like a cloud of yellow gold. Captain January makes funny mistakes. I am studying about the North central states in Geography. I can name the states and their capitals. I am studying about Captain John Smith in History. He liked anything wonderful. I like Geography better than History. History is not interesting because it is about such old people. I am going back to Vinton next year. Miss Mattice has a library full of books. I could go and read in there. It will be all right. I wish you would be there to explain the new words. I am always your loving friend,

LINNIE HAGUEWOOD.

Sioux Falls, S. D., March 1, 1899.

STATE NAMES.

ALABAMA is named from an Indian tribe. It is said that an exile chief, with his people, reached the shore of the Alabama River, struck his spear in the ground and said, "Alabama"—here we rest. This is not authentic. Arizona comes from Arizonac, the native name for a locality near the head of the Rio Altis. Arkansas is the name of an Indian tribe, but its meaning has been lost. California is a word invented by a Spanish novelist, who, in 1510, wrote a story about an imaginary island of California, "where an abundance of gold and precious stones is found." Colorado is the past participle of the Spanish verb, colorar, to color, and was given to the Colorado River because of its high color. Connecticut is an Algonquin compound word, meaning "the land on the long tidal river," Delaware is a corruption of the title of Lord De la Ware, the first Governor of Virginia. An explorer sent out by De la Ware named Delaware Bay in honor of his chief. Florida means land of flowers. It was named by Ponce de Leon, who discovered it on Easter Day, which the Spaniards call Pasena Florida, the flowery festival. Georgia is named in honor of King George II. Idaho is said to be an Indian word meaning "the light on the mountains," referring to the splendor of the peaks at sunrise. Illinois is a French corruption of the Indian Illinwik meaning "we are men." Indiana is simply the Indian country, just as Georgia is King George's country. Iowa is an Indian word of disputed meaning, but supposed to signify "Here is the place to dwell in peace." Kansas is an Indian tribal name meaning probably the people of the wind. Kentucky is another disputed word, some say it is a Shawnee word meaning "at the head of a river;" others, that it means "the dark and bloody ground." Louisiana was named in honor of Louis XIV, of France. Maine was called "The Maine" originally by English sailors to distinguish it from the Northern islands. Maryland was named by King Charles I. in honor of his wife, Henrietta Maria. Massachusetts is an Indian compound word, meaning the place at the great hills. Michigan is derived from two Chippewa words one meaning "great," the other "lake." Minnesota comes from two Dakota words, signifying "water blurred," and is supposed to refer to the peculiar aspect of Minnesota skies when they seemed filled with water. Mississippi is Algonquin for "Great River." Missouri is from two Indian words meaning "big muddy." Montana, the mountain land, is a word of Latin origin. Nebraska is the Indian name of the Platte, and means "shallow water." Nevada takes its name from its mountains, which were named for the Sierra Nevada in Southern Spain. New Hampshire, of course, like New York, is named for the old country in England. New Jersey is named for Jersey in the Channel Islands. New Mexico for old Mexico. North and South Carolina derived their names from a French settlement, made near Beaufort, and named for Charles IX. of France. North and South Dakota preserve an Indian word meaning "allied." The Dakotas were a confederacy of Indian tribes. Ohio is a corruption of an Indian term, meaning "how beautiful," which was applied by the Senecas to the Ohio River. Oklahoma is Indian for "beautiful country." Oregon is in much dispute, both as to meaning and origin. Oregon is Spanish for "big ear" and said to have been given to an Indian tribe. Pennsylvania means the woods of Penn; Rhode Island takes its name from the Island of Aquidneck which was renamed in 1644 by Colonial act the Isle of Rhodes. This is supposed to have been done in honor of the heroic defense of Rhodes against the Turks. Tennessee is a Cherokee word, meaning "a bend in the river." It was originally the name of the village of the Cherokee tribe. Texas represents the name of the ancient Tajas or Atayos Indians, whose name meant "friendly." Utah is Indian for "a home on the mountain top." Vermont comes from the French Verts Monts, "green mountains." Virginia was named in honor of Queen Elizabeth the virgin Queen. Washington needs no explanation. Wisconsin takes its name from the chief river, but the meaning of the name has been lost. Wyoming is of Indian derivation and means "broad plains."—[*The Dawn.*

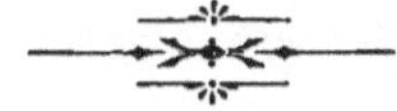

THE SUNNY SPOT,

The clouds may rest on the present,
  And sorrows on days that are gone,
But no night is so utterly cheerless
  That we may not look for the dawn.
And there is no human being,
  With so wholly dark a lot,
But the heart by turning the picture,
  May find some sunny spot.
                    —*Selected.*

JUST BETWEEN OURSELVES.

Sickness is a species of affliction and affliction makes the whole world kin. When the patient is a great public character it brings most unexpected sympathy. Some of us remember the days when Gen. Grant was making his brave fight for life. Those who shed the most tears and uttered the loudest lamentations were those who not many months before had been busy describing him as a menace to the liberties of the people. It is a special and beautiful dispensation of Providence that we forget and forgive in the presence of affliction.

*　　*　　*　　*

I do not know that Mr. Rudyard Kipling ever had a large host of ill-wishers at any period of his career. But some critics, a few actuated by conscientious reasons, a few by envy, have always protested that the young Englishman was not an artist, that he did not exhibit real genius, that his work was lacking in the elements of permanence. But when he lay close to death a few weeks ago the grand chorus of sympathy had no discordant note and now no one dares dispute his place as a leader in the world of letters.

*　　*　　*　　*

Some things are not to be overlooked in Mr. Kipling's case. One is his great versatility. There seems to be no branch of literature to which he can not turn a successful hand. His range is from Browning-esque poetry to children's stories, and in all he achieves success. Another thing which is likely to be overlooked in the hey-day of his prosperity, is that he has attained his rank by hard labor. He did not awake to find himself famous. By grinding, tedious labor he has won his place. Let us be fair and applaud liberally.

*　　*　　*　　*

The evidence of hard work is to be seen in his own productions. He has developed from the first. "Plain Tales from the Hills" was not lacking in power. The genius was there, most assuredly. But the polish was lacking. So with his poetry. People shrugged their shoulders when "Barrack-room Ballads" appeared. "Good fun, doubtless, but not poetry." Surely it was a boyish performance, but it was rugged and strong. I have never been able to get some of the lines of that book out of my head, so they are running there yet, and I am not sorry. They are lines which show a deep insight into human nature. They are something more than "good fun."

*　　*　　*　　*

Another man is at the point of death, so the papers say, for whom I keep a warm place in my heart. That is Mr. Chas. Dudley Warner. One of the first books of essays in lighter vein that I ever read was his "Back-Log Studies." I suppose they are *passe* now; a younger generation does not trouble to read the book, but I doubt if they find a more interesting or more wholesome substitute. Nor do I think anyone will find truth and humor more cleverly blended than in the story of the new gothic church. One good man told me that he seriously objected to "My Summer in a Garden," because it derided a most useful branch of industry, but that man was deficient in the sense of humor. I have tried amateur gardening myself and fully appreciate that passage in the trial balance, wherein he gives as an asset some hundreds of potatoes at two cents each. "Some people," said Mr. Warner, "will think the estimate high; but I ought to know what they are worth, I raised them."

*   *   *   *

There is one prospect, not devoid of pleasurable anticipation, in advancing years,—a man who moves in the center of stirring events as a youth and man, may in his old age write his reminiscences. He will have a chance to tell some things of the country's secret history that everybody wants to know. Senator Hoar in the February Scribner's, gives the history of four national conventions of the Republican party, and the article makes wonderfully interesting reading. In the March number of the same magazine he tells of the birth of the same party; an account replete with new views of the Free Soil movement. Few men write a simpler style than Mr. Hoar, and, consequently, few of our American statesmen address so large an audience when they have something to say.

*   *   *   *

Just now the printing presses are groaning with the labor of printing the libraries that are being written on the Spanish-American war. It looks as though every man who saw the shores of Cuba last summer felt that he was inspired to write a book. Certainly many of them are doing it, inspired or not. Some of them are worth reading, others are of interest only to the authors and their friends. Among the former are two noted at length below. Of the latter class, the less we write the more paper saved.

*   *   *   *

The New York papers report a meeting of the retail book sellers of that city, who find that their trade is gradually diminishing under the pressure of competition from the department stores. No doubt the outlook is a serious one, but no more so for the book seller than a hundred other small tradesmen. So he must take his chances with the rest. It does not fall to me to suggest the way out of the economic problem created by this centralization of trade. The simple fact is that the department store sells a $1.50 book for $1.20 or even less, and does it at a profit. They buy in large quantities for cash and are able to undersell the small dealer. While we are sorry for the latter individual we must not forget that the department stores are making it easier for people of moderate means to buy books. Let that be remembered to their credit.

ELLIS WORTH.

THE HEART OF THINGS.

WITH KITCHENER TO KHARTUM.—
Since Mr. Kipling set forth "The
White Man's Burden" in eloquent
phrase we of America have begun to
understand that there was something
more than poetry in the subject.
One of my friends is the father of a
promising son of some four years
growth. The child came home
recently with tearful eyes, and seeking out his father told his tale of
woe. He had engaged in a fight
with another youngster and his first
essay in pugilism was not encouraging. He received scant sympathy
from his father, who told him to
"stand up and face the music." The
boy did not disguise his contempt
for the advice; he looked up through
his tears and blubbered out, "There
wan't no music there !"

We have discovered that fighting
semi-savages is not always a matter
of dress display with an orchestral
accompaniment. Our Anglo-Saxon
cousins across the sea could have
told us that years ago. England has
found that not all savages haste to
embrace advancing civilization. Particularly in Egypt has she found to
her cost that "The White Man's
Burden" is anything but light. Over
here, where no one had an interest at
stake in the contest, the past sixteen years have fled rapidly, and I
doubt not many of us forget that the
fall of Khartum and the death of
Gordon was but the beginning of a
fourteen years campaign against the
Mahdi,—that all-powerful despot of
Upper Egypt Yet that is just the
length of time England has taken to
mass her forces, train them, open
the way for the advance, until that
bloody day on the field of Omdurman
in September last, when El Mahdi's
power was shattered and Gordon
avenged. The cost in, money and
blood is fearful to contemplate. Mr.
G. W. Steevens, correspondent of the
London Daily Mail has told the
story in vivid language; told it with
a brutal frankness that conceals
nothing. There is a kind of awful
fascination about the tale, and its
gory realism is somewhat relieved
by the author's innate humor. The
mind would reel with sickening description of the battle field did we
not once and again get a breathing-
spell from a passage like this:

"Our side, too, was thick with mimosa and dom-palm, and tufted with
grass—great coarse bunches, mostly
as thick as straw and as yellow; but
a few blades maintained a bloodless
green, and horses and camels went
without their sleep to tear at them.
The camels eat the mimosa too—
elsewhere a bush that grows thorns
and little yellow honey-breathing
fluff-balls, but on the fruitful atbara
a cedar spreading tree, with young
leaves like an acacia's. The camels
rear up their affected heads, and ec-
statically scrunch thorns that would
run any other beast's tongue through;
their lips drop blood but they never
notice it. And the blacks eat the dom-
nuts—things like petrified prize apri-
cots, whose kernel makes vegetable
ivory, and whose husks, they say,

taste like ginger-bread; though, having no ore crusher in my kit, I cannot speak for that. But lanky Sambo was never tired of shying at them as they clustered just above the dead leaves and just below the green, and Private Atkins lent a hand with enthusiasm. Then Sambo would grin all round his head and crack the flinty things between his shining teeth, and Thomas would stand staring at him, uncertain whether he was a long-lost brother-in-arms or something out of a circus."

Mr. Steevens' report of the battle of Omdurman has been published all over the world. It is worth reading, as is every chapter of his book. But it makes us tremble lest we have begun a like prolonged and bloody contest in the far East. Let us hope not, but in any case we are likely to find that there is no retreat, having once begun. "Let not him who putteth his hand to the plow look backward," must be our motto in the Phillipines as it has been England's in Egypt. Having begun we must fight it out. We only trust our army may find as worthy a chronicler as has the Anglo-Egyptian.

[With Kitchener to Khartum. G. W. Steevens. Dodd, Mead and Co. $1.50.]

THE WAR IN CUBA.—Of course I mean *our* war in Cuba; the field of battle lying about Santiago. In another place I have spoken of the literature on the subject, perhaps too disparagingly, but I am afraid there are many others who have heard all that they care to hear about that interesting episode of American history.

I trust I may be correctly understood. We are patriotic enough; we glory in the triumph of American arms; we are glad that this nation did what she did. The fight between Spain and her rebellious subjects in Cuba had gone on until the time came when humanity was forcing us to say "Stop!" We are proud, or we were proud, of the part these United States took in the stopping operation. We might be quite as proud to-day except that a fierce and bitter partizan squabble (no other word describes the situation) has been going on between "the staff and line," until we are pretty well disgusted with both parties to the controversy. The glory of the achievement is lost in the disgraceful *denouement;* the smoke of battle, rising thick from those antiquated Springfield rifles was less offensive than the dust rising from the scuffle still in full tilt.

In this heated controversy as to the merits of the commanding general, the secretary of war, the quality of food served the soldiers, the cause of lack of medical supplies, there are two sides. Every controversy, in the nature of the case, has at least two sides. Naturally these fluent authors have chosen each of them a side. Some of them declare that everything was planned and executed in the most efficient and satisfactory manner: others flatly deny this. Mr. George Kennan, known to the world through his exposé of the Siberian prisons, says that nothing was planned right. Mr. Stephen Bonsal says that while there were mistakes, they were the mistakes any finite being is likely to make on the battle field. So there you are, as we say; but it were more correct to inquire, "Where are we?" It certainly is puzzling, but these two books are about the best of the lot. It is a good plan for one to read both of them before deciding. They are both about equally interesting, probably they are as valuable as any books on the same subject will be or can be under the limit of a quarter of a century hence.

[Campaigning in Cuba. By George Kennan. The Century Co. $1.50. The Fight for Santiago. By Stephen Bonsal. Doubleday and M'Clure Co. $2.50.

WHERE BREEZES BLOW.—Stories of the sea are always rated among the best of stories of adventure. Beginning with Tobias Smollet, the sea story has always offered the novelist an excellent opportunity for displaying powers of description and portraying thrilling situations. Our own country gave to English literature one of the best of sea-novelists in Fennimore Cooper. He stands to-day without a rival, except the idol of English lovers of maritime adventure, Captain Marryat. Mr. W. Clark Russell has in these later days, in some of his best work, rivaled both his predecessors in the same field. Now comes a new claimant for public attention in the person of Mr. T. Jenkins Hains, who puts out a volume of sketches with the title "The Wind-Jammers." The title is enigmatical enough to the land-lubber, but we do not read far without discovering that a "wind-jammer" is a deep-sea sailor. Mr. Hains writes unequally. Some of the stories in this collection are a great deal better than others. I do not think that one reading the first story in the book would feel impelled to go on. But there are some good things beyond, none the less. Such a story as "The Treasure of Tinian Reef," for example, is a fine blending of fun and adventure. A whaler comes to Tinian Reef, a coral island in the Pacific, peopled by savages under the rule of Sangaan, who lives in the royal village of Sunharon, in the pride of his manhood and a grass-thatched palace. The ship sends a boat ashore

under the charge of the mate Garnett. Pulling the stroke oar is Gantline who figures in several stories as an independent, quarrelsome, able seaman, productive of much trouble to his officers and much amusement for the reader. The mate espies a piece of whale blubber floating near the shore and orders the mass inspected. It is pulled in and discovered to be a hundred pound lump of ambergris, worth fifty dollars a pound anywhere on the West Coast. Gantline claims a share in the find, and as he and Garnett dispute, the boat is caught in the surf and they all go ashore in light swimming order.

The errand on which they come to the island is the landing of supplies for the Rev. Mr. Easyman, who is laboring to save the souls of the natives and incidentally to make something material out of the job. And as they made their undignified landing, they perceived the majestic form of Sangaan approaching them accompanied by the Reverend Father Easyman himself.

The sailors had a pretty clear conception of Easyman's real character, and were not altogether sure about the safety of that piece of ambergris. And their anxiety was not without cause. Easyman sighted the lump and proceeded to investigate, and to the disgust of Garnett and Gantline turned it over to Sangaan for safe keeping; and closely packed in an empty keg, it was carried off to the mission.

And that night, which by reason of the stove boat they were forced to spend on shore! Sangaan got at the missionary's store of rum and he and his followers held high carnival until daylight. Garnett feared for the lives of himself and his companions, but the day came and brought safety to the sailors and enlarged heads to the natives. When finally the boat was repaired and the visitors were about to leave, the keg and its precious contents were put on board. Garnett and Gantline hardly expected such good luck. They even regretted having entertained suspicions of the good missionary. With a hearty will they pulled away and were soon on board ship.

They explained the cause of their delay to Capt. Foregaff, and appealed to him as to the proper division of the spoil. Gantline wanted half; Garnett declined to share the booty with any one.

"Well, where, in the name of Davy Jones, do I come in on this deal?" bawled Foregaff. "Ain't we running this business on shares, I want'er know?"

The mate growled, but the captain seized an iron belaying-pin and made a hasty examination of the contents of the keg—"It's ill smelling stuff and its value is according to its smell." Garnett took a good whiff of the contents, sprang to his feet, roaring, "Gord A'mighty! Pig grease! s'help me, the scoundrel's robbed us!"

"'Tis as good lard as ever fried doughnuts," said the skipper, as he stuck his finger into the mass and then drew it through his lips.

Revenge and retaliation was the thought of skipper and men. They cleared away the gun forward and stood in toward the white line of surf. In his anger Garnett aimed the gun at the "sky-pilot's" house but the antiquated piece was not equal to the task imposed on it. The shot struck the crest of a comber, and ricochetted on to the sand, where a native picked it up and danced a peculiarly aggressive dance while he held it aloft in his hands.

The flag on the mission dipped gracefully three times while Garnett loaded for a second shot.

"If I only had a shell I'd make those niggers see something," he muttered, as he rammed home the charge.

"Fire!" and the gun banged again.

The flag dipped again in the breeze, and several natives, joining hands, danced wildly to and fro.

"Keep her off!" bawled the skipper, with a broad smile on his face. "Done by a nigger chief," he muttered to himself. "I want'er know, I want'er know."

That's but a poor report of a good story. Get the book and read it as it is.

[The Wind-Jammers. By T. Jenkins Hains. J. B. Lippincott Co. $1.25.

———

Any communications for this department may be addressed to Ellis Worth, Waltham, Mass.

SELECTED MATTER.

The Kicker.

Kicking in the morning
  Kicking all the day,
Kicking if he's busy,
  Kicking at delay.
Thus the chronic kicker
  Fills his life with woes,
Frowning, grumbling, wrangling,
  Everywhere he goes.

Nothing ever suits him,
  Always finding fault:
Every kind of pleasure
  He is sure to halt.
Scowling at the children,
  Growling at his wife:
Turning peace and comfort
  Into constant strife.

Kicking if the weather
  Happens to be dry;
Kicking when the rain is
  Tumbling from the sky.
Kicking in the summer,
  Heat has then no charm;
Kicking in the winter,
  Then he'd have it warm.

Kicking every mealtime,
  Glaring at the meat;
Often he is saying:
  "Nothing fit to eat."
Kicking when he's reading
  Grumbling at the light;
Now and then denouncing
  Everything in sight.

Kicking in the morning,
  Kicking all the day;
Kicking in the evening,
  Kicking should he pray.
Kicking while he's thinking,
  Kicking when in bed;
Wonder if he'll keep on
  Kicking when he's dead.

WHEN Massachusetts was a colony long ago, there were a great many lazy Indians who annoyed the settlers by begging. One of the Indians was arrested and taken before the judge. "Why are you lazy?" asked the judge. "Me lazy?" said the Indian. "You lazy, too, you sit on chair all day. No work." But the judge told him that he worked with his brain, to think about the law and how to punish the people. "Mine is brain work," added the judge. The Indians said "Oh!" Then the judge wrote a note and told the Indians to take the letter to the jail keeper. In the letter was written: "Give the bearer ten lashes." The Indian took the letter out of the court-room but did not go to the jail. He went to the judge's home and gave the letter to the judge's hired man. He told the hired man that the judge wanted him to take it to the jail-keeper. The hired man suspected nothing and took the note to the jail. The jail-keeper read it. It said, "Give the bearer ten lashes." The jail-keeper whipped the hired man very hard. In the evening the hired man told the judge about it and asked why he was sent to be whipped. The judge was very angry at the Indian. The next day the judge had the Indian arrested. He asked the Indian what he meant by deceiving the hired man. The Indian replied, "Brain work, Judge; me do brain work." But the judge sent him to jail.

THE learned are aware that there are many languages in the world, but the actual number is probably beyond the dreams of ordinary people. The geographer Baldi enumerated 860 which are entitled to be considered as distinct languages and 5,000 which may be regraded as dialects. Adulgums, another modern writer on this subject, reckons up 3,064 languages and dialects existing and which have existed. Even after we have allowed either of these as the number of languages, we must acknowledge the existence of almost infinite minor diversities; for almost every province has a tongue more or less peculiar, and this we may well believe to be the case throughout the world at large. It is said that there are littleislands lying close together in the South seas, the inhabitants of which do not understand each other. Of the 860 distinct languages enumerated by Baldi, 89 belong to Europe, 114 to Africa, 123 to Asia, 417 to America, 117 to Oceanica—by which term he distinguishes the vast number of islands stretching between Hindoostan and South America.

IT is quite important, when speaking of the longest day in the year, to say what part of the world we are talking about, as will be seen by reading the following list, which tells the length of the longest day in several places. At Stockholm, Sweden, it is eighteen and a half hours in length. In Spitzbergen, the longest day is three and one-half months. At London, England, and Bremem, Prussia, the longest day has sixteen and one-half hours. At Hamburg, in Germany, and Dantzig, in Prussia, the longest day has seventeen hours. At Wardbury, Norway, the longest day lasts from May 21 to July 22, without interruption. At St. Petersburg, Russia and Tokolsk, Siberia, the longest day is nineteen hours, and the shortest, five hours. At Tornea, Finland, June 21 brings a day nearly twenty-two hours long, and Christmas one less than three hours in length. At New York, the longest day is about fifteen hours, and at Montreal, Canada, it is sixteen hours.

A WELL known chief engineer of the navy, who weighs about 300 pounds, was recently ordered to one of the smaller gunboats on the Pacific station. He did not particularly like the assignment, but he made no protest—at least in words. He simply sat down and made a sketch of the exceedingly narrow doors that lead into the engine rooms of the gunboat to which he was ordered, marking the dimensions of the doors in figures on the sketch. Below his drawing of one of the engine room doors this jolly chief engineer made a neat sketch of himself, full figure, not exaggerating his Falstaffian paunch a trifle. He attached his own dimensions in feet and inches circumferentially to this sketch of himself. Then he put the sketch in an envelope and "respectfully submitted" them to the bureau of navigation. It was a sort of document that occasionally makes a hit.

THE Sunday *World*—not especially noted for its piety—preaches quite an orthodox sermon on the inconsistency of certain high-class New York churches that rent property for saloon purposes. It says that the rents from Manhattan's 6,216 saloons pay for the pews in which the ornaments of the Four Hundred sit in church; for the dole of charity which gloved hands drop into grimy ones; and for the subscription written with a gold pencil at a temperance rally. In a list compiled from the records of the state license department, are given the names of property owners who rent to the highest paying ten-ant without regard to the consequences upon the community. This list includes church deacons and men whose names are prominent on the subscription records of the Church Temperance Society.

M. Tissot, the French painter of the remarkable pictures of the life of Christ, now on exhibition in this country, was fifty years old when he undertook his real life work. Leaving Paris where he was famous as a painter of fashionable life, he spent ten years in Palestine, where he studied every aspect of ruin, nature and humanity, that he might catch the spirit and the environment of Him he wished to trace. His success emphasizes Capt. Mahan's ironical remark that a man's opportunities are hardly over at fifty. Lord Dufferin, at the age of seventy, has recently set about the acquisition of the Persian language, thereby rivaling his queen, who at the same age began to study Hindoostanese.

Josiah Strong says that there are no arts, no gymnastics, no cosmetics which can contribute a tithe so much to the dignity, the strength, the ennobling of a man's looks as a great purpose, a high determination, a noble principle, an unquenchable enthusiasm. The soul that is full of pure and generous affections fashions the features into its own angelic likeness, as the rose by inherent impulse grows in grace, and blossoms into loveliness.

The publishers of a German novel once did a neat thing in the way of advertising. They caused to be inserted in most of the newspapers a notice to the effect that a certain nobleman of wealth and high position, desirous of finding a wife, wanted one who resembled the heroine in the novel named. Thereupon every marriageable woman who saw the notice bought the book in order to see what the heroine was like, and the work had an immense sale.

A very widespread error is that Edwin Arnold, author of the "Light of Asia," is the brother of Matthew Arnold. The latter, who has no fancy for the former as a man or a poet, was deeply chagrined while in this country to hear so often of his brother Edwin, and felt called upon to deny indignantly that they were in any way related. Nor does Edwin admire Matthew. In plain language, the two men detest one another Matthew calls Edwin a poetizer and a Philistine. Edwin styles Matthew an egotist and pedagogue.

London binders often get orders to fill library shelves by the running yard. To do this cheaply they bind up patent-office reports in handsome covers and back them with such titles as "Macaulay's Essays," "Walpole's Letters," which are subsequently put in bookcases, the keys of which are conveniently lost.

The Nevada Legislature has distinguished itself during the session just closed. It defeated a woman suffrage amendment, repealed the "purity of elections" law, checkmated an attempt to repeal the bill legalizing prize-fights, and provided for a State lottery.

"Daniel Webster is not loquacious," Carlyle wrote to Emerson in 1839, "but he is pertinent, conclusive; a dignified, perfectly-bred man. As a logic-fencer, advocate, or parliamentary Hercules one would incline to back him at first sight against all the extant world.

A COMICAL incident is related of an eminent English nobleman who was presiding at a press dinner. He concluded his few feeble remarks by proposing the "health of Gutenberg." Some one pulled his coat-tails and whispered that he was dead. "I regret," continued the nobleman, "to announce that intelligence has just been received that Gutenberg is dead."

RUSKIN uses confusing titles to some of his books. "Notes on the Construction of Sheepfolds," was largely ordered by the well-to-do farmers of England, who were not a little disgusted to find that it related to church matters.

BAYARD TAYLOR, at nineteen, borrowed $140 and started on his famous travels, which extended from 1846 to 1874. His books of travel, condensed from the record of nearly thirty years, were published in eleven volumes

THURLOW WEED never made a dollar until after he was fifty. Horace Greeley was poor as a church-mouse until about the same age—or until after the *Tribune* became a success.

OLIVER WENDELL HOLMES is as ready to pop up at a dinner and read his poem on the occasion as he was thirty years ago. And the poems have grown rather longer as the years roll on.

WILKIE COLLINS was not a very rapid worker, and seldom wrote more than ten pages of manuscript a day.

IN the United States there are the following number of women bread-winners:

Practicing medicine	2,500
Preaching	275
Postmasters	6,000
Earning livings	3,000,000
Have secured patents	2,500

As NEARLY as can be approximated the population of the globe is 1,500,-000,000. According to religions this population may be divided as follows: Protestants, 150,000,000; Greeks, 110,-000,000; Jews, 7,000,000; Mohammedans, 206,000,000; heathen, 796,000,-000.

IN New York city alone 27,000 women support husbands. These independent women, carrying life's responsibilities, citizens of the United States and the state wherein they reside, are governed without their consent.

WHEN Queen Victoria ascended the throne, more than fifty per cent. of the British people, it is said, could not write their names. Now only seven per cent. are illiterate to that extent.

CONGRESS passed the bill providing that all matter with the raised point letters for the blind should go through the mails as third class mat: ter, which gives a rate of one cent per pound.

AT the recent exhibition in Berlin of the Vegetarian Society, sixty children were shown who had never tasted meat.

Grandma and I.

My grandma talks of the "good old days"
To me and my little brother Ben;
But if you won't tell, I'll whisper to you
That I'm awfully glad I didn't live then.

My grandma's doll couldn't shut her eyes,
For you see they were only daubs of paint,
And her hair was made of raveled yarn,
I tell you, I'm glad that *my* dolly's ain't !

Such funny books as they used to have,
And the pictures weren't pretty a single bit;
The old New England Primer was one,—
I guess you'd laugh if you looked at it.

There weren't any furnaces in church,
And sometimes grandma would almost freeze;
And she says, when she was a child like me,
She never had seen any Christmas trees.

My grandma is dear, and wise, and good,
And I love her a lot, but anyhow,
I think that the good *new* times are the best.
And I'm glad that, Benny and I live *now*.

—*Selected*

DEWEY, THE SCHOOLBOY.

JUST across the street from where I write stands the old Johnson academy, where Dewey was a schoolboy in his teens, in the early fifties A gray-haired man, who was one of Dewey's chums, tells us this anecdote of him:

"Three or four of us, including George, used to go to school in company and we would meet daily a crowd of smaller boys on their way to the district school. They got into the habit of making it interesting for us whenever we met, by pelting us with snowballs and insulting remarks. Some of us were disposed to retaliate, but George would say, 'Oh, come along, boys. Never mind those little shavers.'

"But the 'little shavers,' unable to appreciate such forbearance, seemed to imbibe the idea that we did not dare to attack them, on account of their superior numbers, so grew daily more annoying. One day an immense snowball hit George square on the side of his head, filling his ear with snow.

"Handing me his books, in a twinkling he had caught the ringleader of our tormentors, and administered such a spanking as the chap would not forget in a hurry. If he is alive to-day he is probably proud of having been spanked by Dewey, though at the time he howled like mad. The crowd were so dazed at this sudden attack that they stood as if paralyzed, and George pushed several over in the snow, and scrubbed some faces cleaner than they were wont to be, I dare say, before the rest of the enemy gathered their wits enough to take to their heels.

"'Father once told me,' said George, as he brushed of the snow and took his books again, 'never to fight unless I was obliged to. But if you have to fight, fight in earnest!' he said.

"We had no further trouble with the district school boys that winter. The lesson Dewey gave them was as effectual, in its way, as the lessons he has given some boys of larger growth, at Manila."—*Selected.*

SLY-BOOTS.

Tommy was very happy when he came home from school with a tame crow perched on his shoulder; but to tell the truth he was not so proud of his pet after a closer acquaintance. Sly-boots—that was Master Crow's name—soon learned a great many tricks beside those that Tommy taught him.

Biddy Topknot was bringing up a large family of fluffy white chickens, and Sly-boots did covet them so! He knew that Biddy was stronger than he, but he set his wits to work, till his sly little brain contrived a plan for getting a chicken dinner.

So he flew down to the grass where Biddy's children were playing "Hunt the cricket," and opened his mouth as if he meant to devour them all.

Of course Biddy drove him away, but he soon came back, taking care to keep out of reach of her bill and claws. Over and over again he tried this manœuvre, till poor Biddy's patience was quite exhausted.

At last she bristled up her feathers, and chased him clear across the garden into the meadow. When she had left her brood far behind, Sly-boots suddenly took to his wings, and, reaching the poultry-yard first, carried off the fattest little chicken.

Biddy saw her mistake too late, but the very next day she lost her temper again, and so lost another of her children.

"Oh, dear!" sighed Tommy; "If she could only remember not to get mad! But I can't always remember that myself, when the boys tease me; and I s'pose I mustn't expect a hen to know more than I!"

Poor Biddy could never learn to keep her temper, and so Sly-boots had to be banished to his native woods.—[*Golden Days.*

SAM JONES says this is the greatest country on earth for a young man, A. T. Stewart taught school at twenty-one. Cornelius Vanderbilt didn't have two shirts when he started his ferry; Jay Gould peddled rat traps in New York; Elihu Burritt's wife taught him his letters after he was married. Leland Stanford's father was sent adrift without a cent; Carnegie worked for a dollar a day forty years ago; Abraham Lincoln mauled rails on an Illinois farm. This country is all right if you want to be a man. If you don't you can find lots of company.—[*Ex.*

ONCE a little girl saw in the home of a neighbor a beautiful picture of a mother just in the act of putting her babe in the cradle. Calling at the same house a few weeks later, she looked in surprise at the picture and said, "Mamma, that woman hasn't got her baby to sleep yet!"

WISE AND OTHERWISE.

An Irish shoemaker advised a customer, when he complained of his new boots being tight, not to put them on until he had worn them for a day or two.

———— ✦ ————

Bennie had spoken aloud in church, and to mamma's caution against doing it again he exclaimed, "But, mamma, when my mouth's so full of talk I can't help its leaking some."

———— ✦ ————

"Aren't you afraid that your daughter will come home from college knowing more than you do?"

"Why, we shall consider our money thrown away if she doesn't!"

———— ✦ ————

"Oh, my dear daughter" (to a little girl of six), "you should not be frightened and run from the goat. Don't you know you are a little Christian Scientist?" "But, mamma" (excitedly), "the billy-goat doesn't know it?"

———— ✦ ————

Superintendent (to citizen sweeping the streets in the hot sun)—"You'd better put on your hat, Mike. This blazing sunshine will affect your brains."

Mike—"Sure, do you think I'd be sweeping the street, if I had any brains, sir?"

———— ✦ ————

An old Scotswoman, when advised by her minister to take snuff to keep herself awake during the sermon, replied: "Why dinna ye put the snuff in the sermon, mon?"

A lady of charitable disposition asked a poor man if she could not help him by mending his clothes. "Yes, madam," he replied, "I have a button, and you would oblige me greatly by sewing a coat to it."

———— ✦ ————

"Didn't you tell me you could hold the plough?" said a farmer to an Irishman he had taken on trial. "Be aisy, now," says Pat. "How could I hould it an' two horses pullin' it away? Just stop the craytures, and I'll hould it for ye.

———— ✦ ————

A little Parisian, Gontran by name, was taken out to see a regiment marching past, with a band of music at its head. "Oh, it's fine!" he said, clapping his hands; "but what's the good of all those fellows who aren't playing any instrument?"

———— ✦ ————

Lady (in a crowded street car)—"Thank you, sir; but I don't like to deprive you of your comfortable seat."

Gallant Irishman (who had risen to offer a seat)—"Be th' powers, ma'am, it was comfortable no longer when Oi saw you standin'."

———— ✦ ————

A little girl had a kitten. She was very fond of it, and it was a great delight to her to hear it purr. One night she was restless; and her mother said, "Cynthia, why don't you lie still and go to sleep?" "I can't," answered the little one, "papa purrs so loud."

TALKS AND TALES.

A MAGAZINE

——PUBLISHED BY——

The Conn. Institute and Industrial Home for the Blind,

Nos. 334 and 336 Wethersfield Ave.,

HARTFORD, CONN.

F. E. CLEAVELAND, President.

Edited by Mrs. ELLA B. KENDRICK.

One Dollar a Year,   -   -   Ten Cents a Copy

PRESS OF
THE CONN. INSTITUTE AND INDUSTRIAL HOME
FOR THE BLIND.

Table of Contents.

The Connecticut Mutual
Life Insurance Company
1846--1899.

To those who desire to do fully, at its least cost and to the utmost of their financial ability, their duty to their families, and to use life insurance for their protection and not for a speculation for themselves, THE CONNECTICUT MUTUAL offers the utmost that life insurance can accomplish, in its simplest, clearest forms, of perfect equity and perfect mutuality, on the soundest basis of any, and at a lower cost than has been achieved by any other company. Greater service can no life insurance company render.

JACOB L. GREENE, President. HERBERT H. WHITE, Sec'y.
JOHN M. TAYLOR, Vice Pres't. DANIEL H. WELLS, Actuary.

A. T. RICHARDS, General Agent. Room 16, Company's Building. Hartford, Conn.

REPUBLISHED BY REQUEST.　　　THE ORIGINAL CONCERT COMPANY, FROM THE HARTFORD INSTITUTION.

Talks and Tales.

Vol. II.   Hartford, Conn., June, 1899.   No. 9

FANNY BULLOCK WORKMAN.

A TRIP by bicycle, to interest the general public, must be something out of the ordinary in these days of bicycle traveling. Fanny Bullock Workman has presented to the readers of *The Woman's Journal* such a pleasant description of some parts of India reviewed from a bicycle that we reprint portions of her article. Referring to Mrs. Illrath who has also traveled extensively through India, this writer says:

"We heard of the McIllraths in Agra, Delhi, and other places along the Grand Trunk road, which is usually traversed from Calcutta, northwest, by smot "around-the-world" tourists. This is one of the best roads in the world, provided with provisioned bungalows every twelve or twenty miles.

"We did not hear of them in our zigzag wheel trips across South India, where a run of eighty miles must often be made in order to find a place to sleep, nor did we hear of them as we cycled over the Nilgiri Hills, 8,000 feet above the sea, meeting in twenty or thirty miles only now and then a wild Toda man or woman, a stray member of the aboriginal tribe of these mountains. Nor did we hear of them as we pursued our solitary journey through the fever jungles, that flank the northern side of the Nilgiris, nor on the deep, sandy roads of the vast plain of Mysore. As a matter of fact, these jungles, with the exception of a hut or two every fifteen or twenty miles, are inhabited mostly by elephants, foxes, jackals, and other wild beasts. In one deep jungle, where we were busily engaged in forcing our bicycles over the narrow, sandy road, we spied our own servant, who had been sent three days ahead of us with luggage, in a bullock cart. To the surprised inquiry as to why he was not two days further on, he replied that he and the driver had been so frightened by three antic wild elephants that they had remained fifteen hours in the same place, afraid to proceed.

"As I said above, we did not hear of the McIllraths here, nor from the officials in charge in towns or villages which were passed through on our way to remote and beautiful temples. As in isolated parts of Spain, all sorts of simple questions relative to the machines were asked by the Indian officials, who said they had never seen any one before on such a vehicle.

"I do not vie with Mrs. McIllrath or any other 'around-the-world' tourist, nor have I done so in the seven years during which I visited many countries; but I believe I am a pioneer woman cyclist in India, as I was in Italy, Sicily, Algeria, and Spain. By that I mean pioneer in visiting thoroughly all the most interesting parts of these lands, whether for studying architecture, people or nature. Study of these three subjects is usually the goal of my distant wheel journeys, and the satisfying of this desire in India is giving me no easy or short trip.

"Since I last wrote the *Woman's Journal*, after a deeply interesting three months in South India, we cycled north to Rawal Pindi, at the foot of the Punjab Himalayas. From this northern English station we crossed the outpost Himalayan chain, 7,700 feet high, and cycled up and down passes for 200 miles to Srinagar, capital of Kashmir.

"From here we made a six days' wheel-journey into Moore's "Vale of Kashmir" to the quasi-Greek quasi-Hindu temples of Martened, Payech, and Avantipur. Here, in this rose-laden valley of Kashmir, it was interesting, while leaning on my faithful bicycle, to trace in the graceful plinth supporting one of the temples, distinct lines of the Chalukyan architecture, 2,000 miles away to the south, to and from which my wheel had borne me in a few months. At Srinagar we had finished 4,000 miles of our Indian trip, called by the Indian papers and many English residents already a large and unique record.

"This is, however, only part of our intended journey in India. When we have finished the long tent trip through Kashmir, Ladakh, Nubra, to the border of Turkestan, we hope to need our cycles again, and pass another winter in studying North India from East to West. Even now, I believe, I have made a pioneer journey of my kind in India, and later on, if climate, health, and other obstacles (which are many) allow me to do what I wish, I shall still more claim this pioneership.

"For the benefit of the few who may not know, I will describe briefly the large upland province of Ladakh, in different parts of which I am passing a few months.

"Ladakh lies northeast of Kashmir, to which it virtually belongs. In its boundaries it includes Rupshu, Zanskar, and Unbra, from which latter province I am writing, also the great plains north to the Karakoram. It is the highest inhabited country in the world, no part of it lying lower than 9,000 feet. I have, however, since entering Ladakh, not been so low as that, but have been camping and marching at heights varying from 11,000 to 18,000 feet above sea level.

"A march of fifteen days from Srinagar, in Kashmir, brings one to Leh, the capital of Ladakh. Although nominally under the Maharaja of Kashmir, the province is still greatly influenced by Tibet, to which it formerly belonged. Half way from Kashmir, after crossing a high pass, you come into this curious and most interesting Tibetan country.

"In a distance of five miles the nature and the people both change. You leave behind the green meadows and long mountain slopes of Chenar, and its deodar trees, and enter a land of sandy valleys, treeless spurs, and lofty mountains piercing the sky at over 20,000 feet. You also leave behind the turbaned, servile, crooked-nosed Kashmiri, and have in future as pony driver the short, thick-set, Mongolian-featured Ladakht, clad in dusty, loose homespun and thick felt shoes. He bears two sure signs of his nationality—a thin pigtail supplemented at the end by cotton of the same color, and a small cap lined with sheep skin, the fur ear-flaps of which he usually turns up in summer, thus rendering his appearance most comical. Like the Kashmiri, he is of light color; but there the resemblance ends, for he is as jolly and loud-voiced a savage as the other is taciturn and cringing.

"I have said Ladakh is greatly influenced by Tibet: and this comes through its lamaseries filled with Lamas, who are divided into two classes— those who look after the spiritual and those who largely control the temporal affairs of the villagers. There are no large towns, Leh itself not being one, and each village, nay, one might say each height, has its good-sized lamasery perched upon a wild rock.

"These Lamas irrigate and cultivate tracts of land, which they are supposed to account for to the government of Kashmir, and are large owners of sheep, yaks, and the celebrated pachmino goats, which supply Kashmir with its shawl-wool. Also they own isolated spots which they irrigate and turn to good account, but never report to the government. · The Lamas acknowledge the supremacy only of the Delai-Lama, and, like the clergy of Spain, but in a greater degree, by keeping the people in ignorance, they preserve an almost unlimited power over them. Lamas here are almost as numerous as brahmans in India, and every family, even of the poorer classes, tries to get one son into a lamasery, where he leads an easy, lazy existence for life.

"It seemed to me, in Ceylon, that the outward manifestations of Buddhism were very different from what they are supposed to have been in the days of Prince Siddhartha. But after visiting the lamaseries of Ladakh, and particularly the religious festival at Hemis, near Leh, Ceylon appears in comparison with this land to be still a fairly pure fountainhead for the teachings of Buddha. Of course this is judging from the outside. Of the inner meaning, the deep, mysterious bearing of the mummery ceremonies that go on before the public at Hemis and elsewhere, I have no knowledge. I can only testify that the Lamas dance in elaborate and picturesque China-silk robes, and cover their faces with most ingenious and expressive masks. What they really wish to tell us during their various monotonous, minuet-like dances, it is said they themselves do not know. Yes, in this land of chortens, manis, and praying-wheels, Buddhism has reached a degenerate stage.

Hemis and a few other lamaseries possess real skooshoks, or incarnations, who, educated in all the erudition of Buddhism until fifteen or sixteen, at Lassa, come to be spiritual heads of the larger monastaries of Ladakh. But they do not apparently raise the tone of religion here. One pony driver, in passing the long lines of manis, or praying walls, on the march, is no longer so particular about having them on the right side, lest his soul be detained by demons from entering Nirvana; nor does one hear him murmur even faintly to himself that wide-spread prayer, "Om mani patmi om," as he is supposed to do on passing a mani. Prayer-wheels are at a discount: except on festival occasions, and the average Ladakhi, or Nubran, is more often found twirling his spinning-wheel than reeling off prayers on the road.

"A Ladahki's explanation of why he no longer carried a praying-wheel, is perhaps as near true as any: 'The lamas take care of all that. If we go to the festivals and use our wheels there, that is all that is required—the lamas do the rest.' But dare we scoff at the Ladakhi for neglecting to use his wheel? Is not some of the lip service in the Christian churches quite as wanting in vital feeling as the prayer whirled off on the Buddhist prayer-wheel?

"It is a curious fact, that in a country where the clergy exercise so much power, women should be free and independent. I do not mean that they are particularly intelligent. As for education, they possess none; but as compared with their Mohammedan and Hindu sisters in India, their privileges are great. In the first place, polyandry is as firmly established throughout this province as polygamy is in Baltistan; according to the missionaries, to the detriment of the general morality; according to others, who have studied the conditions of life in Ladakh, to the material advantage of the inhabitants.

"Owing to the great elevation of the whole country, the Ladakhis cannot stand the climate of lower regions, and thus do not emigrate as do the Baltis, nor, on account of their peculiar habits and religion, so different from those of any other province, could they do so and be popular. Then again, the cultivated ground is *nil* compared with that of Kashmir for instance, and is confined to small areas of irrigation about the villages. These facts seem to furnish a ground for establishing a custom that limits the population and diminishes poverty.

"The eldest son shares his wife with his two younger brothers, who are minor husbands, and often stand little better than servants in the family circle. Should the chief husband die, the wife can rid herself of these husbands. If there is no son, the eldest daughter inherits the family estate, and, being an heiress, is not obliged to marry an eldest son and his brothers, but can choose her husband, and if she pleases have but one. This husband, or magpa, as he is called, is the property of his wife, and should she tire of him, he must go, content with a few sheep or a small sum of money. These marriage customs are all fully sanctioned by the lamas.

"Women go about unveiled, working in the fields and looking after the herds of sheep and yaks. In their long loose gowns belted at the waist, and chogas, or capes of sheep skin hanging from their shoulders, they are not without a barbaric picturesqueness. Their head-dress, or peyrak, brought directly from Tibet, is very peculiar. It consists of a long piece of leather covered with rows of turquoises from Chinese Tibet, more green than blue in color. A woman's wealth can generally be estimated by the elaborateness of her peyrak, which, in the case of an heiress, is often supplemented by long strings of coral on the left side. The pure Ledakhi woman is very difficult to civilize or educate, even in an elementary way, let alone Christianize. There is a small colony of hard-working Moravian missionaries at Leh. They tell me the zenana work is peculiarly discouraging, and has to be carried on chiefly among Mohammedans or half castes. They have as yet been able to establish but a few schools, and these only for boys and among half caste Mohammedans.

"Work among women must be done in their own homes, and consists chiefly in telling them stories and showing biblical pictures. The field here is not ripe for first educating, then Christianizing, as in places in Southern India, and it is to be feared will not be in a long time.

"The Moravian missionaries of Leh appear to me to have more to contend with in regard to opposition and ignorance than any I have seen in India, and certainly deserve all praise and help for braving the climate of Ladakh, which knows but three short months of summer, and in zealously working for a cause, which up to date is so hopeless that mild forms of philanthropy alone are efficacious."

The Minister's Bedquilt.

SOPHIE SWETT.

"THEY voted to ask for his resignation," said Milt; and although he was seventeen, he swallowed a lump in his throat, and did not care even if Martha Ellen knew that there were red rims around his eyes. As for Martha Ellen, the pink actually wavered in her firm cheeks as she stood under the hop-vine in the porch, and her face seemed to lengthen dolefully, from the widow's peak—just like grandma's—to the little peaked chin.

Martha Ellen was not pretty; some people did not think she was "smart," but Milt did. He was in the habit of looking at Martha Ellen to see what she was going to do about things, but in this case it was clear to Milt's mind that she could do nothing. It had been voted in the church-meeting to ask the Rev. Gilbert Longley for his resignation as minister of the Gilead church. A great deal the deacons cared what he and Martha Ellen thought about it!

When Martha Ellen's peaked chin quivered piteously, Milt pulled himself together and essayed to comfort her, as became a man.

"We have never cared a particle about the ministers before, whether they came or went," he said, philosophically.

"There was old Doctor Turkey—he was nice," said Martha Ellen, meditatively. "He always forgot who I was, but he would give me a peppermint out of his vest pocket to make up for it; and Mr. Spence—"

"Oh, they were well enough!" said Milt, with a savor of condescension. "But when they ask Mr. Longley to resign, it's something to us."

"Yes," said Martha Ellen, dolefully; "that's the difference."

She sat down upon the step and tucked her chin into her hand reflectively. Those reflective moods of Martha Ellen's were, in Milt's experience, so likely to bring something to pass that, for a moment, he actually looked hopefully at her.

"I'm going to make him a bedquilt," said Martha Ellen firmly, at length.

A bedquilt! Milt flung away in disdain. If that wasn't exactly like a girl!

"Not a crazy-quilt, you know," explained Martha Ellen; "everybody is tired of those; nor with texts, because two or three people are likely to choose the same.　Over at Corinth, when I was at Aunt Lupiry's, three people wrote on their squares, 'The Lord taketh not pleasure in the legs of a man;' and it wasn't nice, anyway, for the minister was very tall.　Besides, it isn't easy to write on silk, and I mean to make it of silk."

"There isn't much silk in Gilead, and besides, what does a man want of a bedquilt?" said Milt, who could be a wet blanket upon occasion; he called it being reasonable.

"Every one has a little bit of silk; even the boys have old neckties.　I sha'n't care if it isn't handsome, nor he won't; that isn't the idea.　You don't exactly understand," said Martha Ellen, slowly, which was pretty well for a fifteen-year-old girl.

"They'll all want to give," she continued, "all the people he has been so good to—even the Purgatory people and the Ferry people."

Milt shook his head sagely.　"That's the trouble; he's been too much out to Purgatory and down to the Ferry.　Purgatory is a rough place to go to, and he was out there one Sunday night so late that they had to delay the prayer-meeting.　And he didn't give any particular account of himself.　And he plays checkers in that old shanty af Gilkup's down at the Ferry every Saturday forenoon!　You can't blame the deacons for saying that doesn't look well for a minister."

"Are you turning against him?" demanded Martha Ellen, in startled reproach.

"I guess I'm not!" said Milt.　"I—I never was much of a fellow for sermons, but when Mr. Longley preaches, a fellow feels as if he meant *him*. It gets right hold of him, somehow."　Milt spoke huskily, and the red rims appeared around his eyes again.　"And when you know that there isn't such a pitcher anywhere around!　He never did it but once—the day Ken Robertson sprained his wrist.　Some people said it wasn't dignified for a minister, but it saved the day for the Gileads!"　With that Milt went away; he didn't seem to think the bedquilt was worth talking about.

Martha Ellen shortly afterward presented herself before grandma and grandpa with the color high in her freckled cheeks and her eyes shining.

Grandma was willing to give a whole breadth of her snuff-colored brocade for the minister's quilt, and as every one knows, snuff-color is beautiful for a quilt; and grandpa wished to give a piece out of his wedding waistcoat that was brocaded with blue satin roses.　Martha Elen said, rather grandly, that she was afraid she must limit them each to a little piece, because every one would wish to be represented in the minister's quilt.

Grandma looked at grandpa as Martha Ellen went out of the room, and said, "Poor child! she's young; she has got to get used to disappointment."

But Martha Ellen was not daunted, even by that.　She set out that very afternoon, with grandma's large, old-fashioned reticule on her arm, to collect pieces for the quilt; and the very first person whom she called on was Mrs. Deacon Crisp, whose husband was the leader of the opposition to the minister.

Mrs. Crisp wished to be a leader, too; the deacon had grown rich, and she thought she ought to lead. Martha Ellen went to the front door, and so impressed Mrs. Crisp by her dignity that she was invited into the parlor; and while Martha Ellen modestly but firmly explained her errand, Mrs. Crisp rocked emphatically in the only plush platform rocker in Gilead, and uttered exclamations of astonishment.

"Why, we ain't on that side! Being a little girl, I suppose you haven't heard. We don't approve of the minister!" she said, as soon as Martha Ellen gave her an opportunity. "Look here Lyman, little Marthy Ellen Snow thinks we're goin' to help make the minister a silk bedquilt!"

The deacon was a little man; at this moment in his shirt-sleeves, and a twinkle in his eye. He brought in a kitchen chair,—he said he hadn't confidence in jouncing springs,—and set it near to the platform rocker, as if for moral support.

"If he hain't enough bedclothes, we won't send him out into the cold without 'em," he said, facetiously.

Martha Ellen took heart of grace, although the color burned in her cheeks. "I thought perhaps every one would like to give him a pleasant remembrance of Gilead," she said. Then falteringly she added, "I thought maybe one of Olly's neckties—"

Olly was the deacon's only son. It had been his mother's great ambition to send him to college; he had been dull in mathematics, and it was only by the minister's patient, persistent help that he had passed the examination. Olly had died in his sophomore year, and the minister had watched with him the night before he died. The deacon shuffled uneasily in his chair, and his wife's face flushed.

"I thought a border of neckties would be kind of pretty, all 'round, and the boys all think so much of him!" faltered Martha Ellen.

Mrs. Crisp turned suddenly to her husband, and her chin quivered. "It wouldn't be saying we thought he was what he ought to be, and--and—maybe Olly would have liked to have it so. And perhaps I'd better give her a little piece of grandma's plum-colored pelisse, too; grandma thought so much of him. You see that was when he first came, seven years ago, and he was so young we couldn't tell how he would turn out."

The deacon shook his head doubtfully. He said he didn't want to encourage checker-playing, ball-pitching ministers; but still, seeing he was going away anyhow—

Martha Ellen's heart thrilled as she went away, tightly clutching her reticule, for it contained four precious bits of silk from the leaders of the opposition—four, for Mrs. Crisp had said she thought it wouldn't look well for the deacon, the foremost man in the church, not to be represented, and his purple Sunday neckties, the only finery he ever permitted himself, looked so much like him that one of them seemed just the thing to put into the quilt! And it might be a duty to give a piece of her new brown satin, since there were so few people in Gilead who had silk or satin dresses.

Little Miss Scammon wished to give all the silk accumulations of twenty years of dressmaking, and begged to be allowed to furnish a silk lining out of her slender purse, because the minister had been so kind to her mother while she was slowly dying of cancer.

Miss Lucia Prime, next on the list, thought the minister too strict in doctrine, but gave a piece out of her changeable parasol to show that she was not bigoted. And after that there was Mrs. Abijah Lamb, who found the minister wofully lax in doctrine, but gave a piece of yellow silk out of the middle of her parlor tidy, because she was not going to be outdone by anybody in Gilead.

Some people kissed Martha Ellen and cried about the minister; others said things so harsh that they made her cheeks burn; but all finally decided to give a bit of silk to the quilt—the minister would be obliged to resign anyway, they said, and they were only following Deacon Crisp's lead. Yet, as she went homeward, with the great reticule plump and heavy upon her arm, Martha Ellen's heart was not light. Not one of the opposing party had shown the least sign of softening towards the minister.

Milt would say that he did not know why she should have expected it. but Martha Ellen had felt in her heart that she might be able to recall the minister's kind acts to the minds of some people who had forgotten them.

Of what comfort to Mr. Longley would be "a testimonial of their regard" when they were going to send him away? Perhaps Milt was right to scorn bedquilts. She sat down on the gnarly roots of the great butternut-tree at the end of their own lane, resolutely brushed away the rising tears, and put on her thinking-cap.

Half an hour afterwards she was spreading the pieces of silk upon the table for grandma and grandpa to see, and relating her adventures. Grandma could guess to whom almost every one of the bits of silk had belonged, and grandpa recognized the neckties, and they had such a good time over them that they seemed quite to forget the minister.

But Martha Ellen did not forget. She presently unfolded a plan, her homely little face so full of eagerness that it looked as if a candle were alight behind it. They could sew the pieces together on the machine in such a little while, she said, breathlessly; it would not be like old-fashioned quilt-making, and the minister was not to be asked to resign until the end of a week. Couldn't they have a quilting-party in the great unfinished barn chamber, that was sweet with drying herbs, and already decorated with festoons of drying apples and pumpkin, and ears of red and black and yellow corn? Only the women and the girls to quilt industriously in the afternoon, but in the evening the men and the boys, the children even, everybody in the parish—and the minister!

A party! Grandpa and grandma looked at each other in consternation. Why, they hadn't given a party since their own son and daughter, long since dead, were young—not for twenty years! And, under the circumstances, wouldn't it be unseemly, or at least embarrassing, to bring the opposing factions, and also the minister, together? Martha Ellen saw the dreaded "no" in their faces, and ran out of the room because she could not bear to hear it spoken.

It was Milt who came to the rescue. "If Martha Ellen has an idea, you'd better let her carry it out," said he, wagging his head sagely. He shut the door softly, and stood with his back against it. "It wouldn't do to let her know it," he whispered, impressively, "but I tell you for a girl she is *some!*"

There was a quilting party. "To quilt the minister's counterpane," the invitation read, and the people looked at each other, and said they didn't know what to make of it. Some went to find out; some went because there used to be such good times at Deacon Snow's; some, because they felt, with Mrs. Deacon Crisp, that merely to attend the quilting would not be saying that they thought the minister was what he ought to be.

Those were the opposition; the other side went joyfully, for love of the minister. So it happened that the great barn chamber, where the quilting-frame was set up, was filled with busy workers—women who made guesses about the pieces, and admired the pattern, and remembered old times, and tacitly avoided discussion of the minister; and when the shades of evening began to fall, those who were not to quilt, but to have a good time, came in such numbers that the great barn chamber, where they all flocked first to see the quilt, was fairly overflowing.

When the last stitches were taken, and all were preparing to go down to supper, the door opened suddenly to admit some unexpected guests—a delegation of Purgatory boys and men, with Derrick Rudd, the ringleader in reckless deeds, at their head. Behind them there slipped into the room a little old woman, Terry Neil's mother—Terry was another leader of thegang.

Martha Ellen's heart stood still; she had wished to ask these boys to contribute to the minister's quilt, but Milt had seriously opposed it. "Where would they get silk?" he asked. They would probably jeer at her; it wasn't safe to approach such rough fellows, anyway, he said.

Derrick Rudd unfolded a great roll of silk that he carried, beautiful crimson silk that must have cost a great deal, thought Martha Ellen.

"We want this put into the quilt !" said Derrick Rudd, in a harsh, strained voice. "You didn't ask us, but we have a right, for he's our friend. None of you Gilead folks ever troubled yourselves about us, except to threaten us with the law, but he came right among us, and took us by the hand to show us better ways. And if he is a minister, he's every inch a man ! And Terry Neil—you'd better believe we won't forget what he's done for Terry !"

"The great rough fellow swallowed a lump in his throat, and the little old woman took advantage of the pause to bob a courtesy to the hushed assemblage, and pipe shrilly, "I'm Terry's mother that's blessing the minister this day !"

"He'd play checkers with Terry," began the leader again, "to keep him from going across the river to the drinking shops, every Saturday when Terry brought in a load of wood. Terry has a head for such things, and for figures; the minister has got him a place to help the accountant in a great manufactory. He's gone there with him now, and not a drop has Terry drunk for six months, and has given the minister his word—we'll none of us break our word to him !"

The old woman was crying softly. "I've brought the old man's handkerchief; 'twas all the silk we had." She held up a great square of dingy yellow silk, with faded red spots. "If you could have put it in somewhere, Terry would have liked it well."

"We're coming to church to hear him preach," Derrick Rudd's voice rang out firmly. "We never thought much of churches or ministers, but we're coming. We would have come before, only you'd all stare as if we were wild beasts !"

"I'll come with 'em myself," declared Terry Neil's mother, "to show 'em the ways of churches, for once I knew 'em well."

No one had presence of mind to say much as the rough fellows left the room. Martha Ellen did call after them that their silk should be made into a lovely ruffle all around the quilt, and grandma sent Deborah, the hired girl, to ask them to stay to supper—an invitation which they declined.

The minister looked weary and depressed when he rose in the pulpit next Sunday morning, and at the close of the service, in a voice that faltered, he read his resignation. He had received a call from a Western church, he said, and it seemed expedient for him to go. He was influenced to this decision by the knowledge that he had given dissatisfaction to many by a zeal which, perhaps, had not been always according to knowledge—in work which might be thought to lie outside his parish, but which was very near his heart.

There was a hush all over the church, and then a murmur, tears, even suppressed sobs. Deacon Crisp arose suddenly to his feet. He began to speak formally, but his voice broke: "We aren't going to hear anything of it! We won't let you go anyhow! And there isn't anybody that'll try to hinder you in—in the work that's near your heart."

A swelling murmur arose all over the house, a chorus of "Amens!" and a very strange noise from the long back seat away back behind the stove. They ought to know, even those rough fellows from Purgatory, that applause is not seemly in church. The little old woman at the head of the seat—she who had once known church ways—arose and shook her finger at them, and said, "Sh! Sh!" frantically. If they had had their own way, every one knew what a hurrah would have gone up from that back seat!

Orrin Scammon, the leader of the choir,—he was the dressmaker's brother,—relieved the tense situation by starting the anthem.

"Blessed are the peacemakers," they sang. They had not rehearsed it, and Martha Pine broke down in her solo, "For they shall be called," and no one felt quite sure whether peace had really been made by Martha Ellen Snow or by that rough crowd on the back seat; yet to many besides Martha Ellen the music seemed to soar straight to high heaven, and carry them with it.—[*Youth's Companion.*

FOR A DAY.

WILLIAM WATSON.

Just for a day you crossed my life's dull track,
   Put my ignoble dreams to sudden shame,
Went your bright way, and left me to fall back
   On my own world of poorer deed and aim;

To fall back on my meaner world, and feel
   Like one who dwelling 'mid some smoke-dimmed town,—
In a brief pause of labor's sullen wheel,
   'Scaped from the street's dead dust and factory's frown,

In stainless daylight saw the pure seas roll,
   Saw the mountains mirrowing the perfect sky,
Then journeyed home, to carry in his soul
   The torment of the difference till he die.

Mrs. Winthrop's Deception.

R. S. HITCHINS.

MRS. WINTHROP was short, fat, and a widow. Her friends sometimes
called her, sub rosa, the "Cottage Loaf;" her head being the small
loaf at the top, and her body the big loaf at the bottom. She had little
green eyes, and a very wide mouth that turned up slightly at the corners,
and she waddled as she walked. She was about thirty-six years old, and she
had a great deal of money. In addition to this she was the possessor of a
pretty, bird-like voice, with a note of surprise in it, as if it could not help
being perpetually astonished at belonging to plump Mrs. Winthrop.

People said Mrs. Winthrop meant to marry again. She was decidedly
greedy of admiration, despite her lack of good looks, of which she appeared
to be totally unaware, and she decidedly amused men. She had an odd
little laugh that seemed to come from high up in her head, and her funny
face and curious small eyes, that always looked at some spot just above the
person whom she was addressing, had a certain attraction for many people.
In fact, Mrs. Winthrop was quaint, very quaint indeed, and she was not
without admirers.

There was one man, however, among the widow's acquaintances who
could not endure her. He was a barrister, rather briefless than otherwise,
and not too well dowered with this world's goods. He was a good looking
man, and a man of considerable talent. Yet he did not get on. Perhaps his
gravity stood in his way. He took life rather seriously, and seldom smiled
without definite reason. And he did not find reasons for smiling on every
trifling occasion. Reginald Ormethwaite could not endure Mrs. Winthrop.
He considered her the silliest woman he had ever met. He disliked her
waddle, which was certainly undignified.

He thought her high-pitched laugh—which he dubbed giggle—intolerable. In fact, her entire personality irritated him. And the widow, with
the perversity of her sex returned his dislike with adoration, worshiped the
ground he walked on, and longed to do him a service. She was always
asking him to dine with her in Cadogan Place, but he was always engaged,
and at last she began to despair of ever advancing a step in his good graces.

It was tea-time one day in the season. Mrs. Winthrop had just come
waddling upstairs from a drive in the park, and was now closeted with her
particular friend and parasite, Mrs. Jameson, in whom she placed much

confidence, and to whom she was a decided benefactress, for Mrs. Jameson had a husband and no carriage, so that an acquaintance who had a carriage and no husband was a distinct boon to her. For, had there been a Mr. Winthrop in existence she could hardly have lived in Cadogan Place so much as she did.

Mrs. Winthrop had waddled into the dining-room and plumped down into a large frilled armchair by the tea-table. It was a hot day and she felt the heat much, although her round form was clothed in white muslin and her head was covered with a large, shady hat profusely adorned with showers of blush roses.

"Catherine," she said, continuing a conversation, "he is really poor, I believe. It seems odd that such a clever man should have no practice. Does he get no briefs at all?"

"Really, darling, I don't think he does," said Mrs. Jameson. "Cream, please. You always have such delicious cream—country cream."

"Never mind the cream I have," interrupted the widow, abruptly, "I want to talk about the briefs that poor man doesn't have. I'm not a fool, and I know a clever man when I see one. Mr. Ormethwaite is clever. If he got his chance he would take it. And then he is wonderfully handsome."

"Wonderfully, darling," assented the other.

Mrs. Winthrop sat quite silent for a moment, sipping her tea and rolling her small eyes about in an abstracted manner. Then, on a sudden, she gave vent to a shrill ripple of laughter, and her wide mouth curled upward,

"I should like to give him a chance," she cried. "I should love to be defended by him. Catherine, I have a plan," and again she laughed till the teaspoon rattled in her saucer.

"Catherine looked mystified but receptive.

"What is it, darling?" she murmured.

"Listen," said Mrs. Winthrop, "Would you do much for me, Catherine? '

"Almost anything, darling. You know that."

"Then listen, and I will tell you what you can do. You know that lovely, old enameled watch of mine?"

"Yes, dear."

"Well, you must steal it.'

Mrs. Jameson jumped and protested.

"But I couldn't," she said, in amazement. "Besides—why? If you wish me to have it, it would be much better to give it to me."

"That wouldn't answer my purpose. I will lose it, if you prefer, and accuse you of stealing it. You shall bring an action against me for slander and then, just at the end of a fashionable trial, in which Mr. Ormethwaite has made his name as my counsel, I shall find the watch hidden somewhere and make you an ample apology. Now that is settled. Leave the details to me. Dear Catherine, you shall not regret your part in the affair, I promise you. I shall pay all your expenses and give you the watch into the bargain."

But the parasite was not to be won over quite so easily, and it was only after a long discussion and many promises of ultimate reward and'emolument that she consented to become a party to this plot for the making of a briefless barrister's legal reputation.

Reginald Ormethwaite sat in his rather old-fashioned rooms in the temple, smoking a pipe and meditating sadly upon destiny and the irony of fate. It was rather a wet day, and the room looked dark and dreary despite its sofa and warm chairs, and Reginald Ormethwaite felt dreary, too. It is dull work for an energetic man to wait, and especially when he is waiting for something that may never come.

"Oh, for a chance of distinguishing myself and making a name!" he murmured. "This inaction will waste away all the powers of my mind. Oh, for a chance!"

There was a ring at the bell, and a footstep, an odd footstep, and a rustling outside. Another moment and Mrs. Winthrop was ushered in, waddling as usual, and apparently in some agitation.

Reginald was very much confused and very much disgusted at this advent. Mrs- Winthrop bored and distracted him at the best of times, and to-day he felt especially unprepared for small talk and aimless frivolity. However, he was gravely polite as usual, brought forth his cosiest armchair and promptly extinguished his pipe with an apology and an inward bad word.

Mrs. Winthrop sat down, gazed just above his head, and exclaimed in a piping voice:

"Oh! Mr. Ormethwaite, you must save me!"

The handsome barrister looked frankly astonished

"Save you, Mrs. Winthrop! Why, how can you be in danger?"

"I am indeed," she said, in a tone expressive of despair, and then she unfolded her plot, and told him about the theft of her watch, her accusation against Mrs. Jameson. Mrs. Jameson's indignant denial, and the action for libel and slander that was now pending against her.

"And, oh! Mr. Ormethwaite," she cried, in conclusion, "I want you to come with me at once to my solicitor, and he will—what do they call it?—instruct you. If any one can save me I know you can. Oh! don't say you are too busy to take up my case."

Too busy! Ormethwaite could hardly refrain from laughing outright.

"You know," the widow continued, "it will create a terrible scandal. Everbody is talking about it already. They say it will throw even the Brinkton case into the shade."

The barrister's eyes began to sparkle. Was fate going to be kind to him at last? He could scarely believe it. Still it was possible. For the first time in his life Mrs. Winthrop interested instead of bored him. He drew his chair close to hers and quite forgot the rain pattering so dismally outside. He fixed his dark eyes on her face, and wished she would not look just over his head, as he said, in his most sympathetic voice:

"Will you state to me all the facts of the case as clearly as possible? And then I will give you an answer."

A thrill ran through the widow's heart as she proceeded to tell her story afresh, with all the ingenious details which her busy little brain had invented to make the supposed theft seem probable. Mr. Ormethwaite listened with rapt attention till she had finished. Then he said slowly:

"You have a very strong case."

"And you will act for me?"

He answered by another question:

"May I see your solicitor?"

Mrs. Winthrop got up.

"I am going to him now. Will you come with me?"

Two minutes later they were driving to Oxford Place, where the great man lived, and as they talked, it already seemed to Mrs. Winthrop that the barrier which had always divided her from the handsome barrister was being swiftly broken down.

As the day for the trial drew near, the heart of the poor parasite, Mrs. Jameson, sank lower and lower. A thousand times she wished that she had never been born, or had never been led into deception, and consequent ignominy, by her keen desire for that lovely watch. She knew, of course, that her reputation would be eventually cleared, but meanwhile she had much to endure—the reproaches and suspicions of her at all times cross-grained husband, the eager curiosity of her quondam friends, and the impertinence of strangers.

For the Jameson vs. Winthrop case was already attracting a great deal of attention. Many and many a time Mrs. Jameson was on the point of going to Mr. Ormethwaite and telling him the whole truth, but she was held back by her sense of duty to the friend whom she was prosecuting, and also by a still greater dread of what the consequences might be to herself. She was an unlearned and weak-natured creature, knowing but little of the law, and having vague and terrible notions of the punishments meted out for "collusion," she held her tongue and endured. But the worst of it all was that she could not turn for sympathy to Mrs. Winthrop. They were, of course, not on speaking terms. No more did Mrs. Jameson drive in the Winthrop carriage. The humble 'bus received her miserable form. She was indeed, undergoing heavy affliction.

Mrs. Winthrop, meanwhile, was happy. She was growing fonder and fonder of Reginald Ormethwaite, and he had no longer to deplore his endless engagements. No invitation of hers was ever refused by him now. He dined in Cadogan Place frequently; and, although, of course, their intimacy was to some extent a business intimacy, there was little doubt but that the barrister was getting over his dislike of the widow. He knew her now beyond her mannerisms, as it were. He had left them behind, and so, insensibly, they had almost ceased to trouble him. He certainly wished at times that her mouth was a little less wide, her eyes just a little less green, and her laugh a little less high pitched. Still he was growing to like her. In fact, a decided change had come over the spirit of the barrister's dream, and Mrs. Winthrop noted it with a throb of delight that caused her fat little form to tremble. All was going well.

One evening, nearly a fortnight before the day fixed for the trial, Reginald Ormethwaite was dining alone with the widow in Cadogan Place, and in the drawing room afterward, when they were drinking their coffee, he said:

"There's one thing that nerves me for the encounter more than anything else."

"Yes," said the widow, "what's that?"

"The knowledge that we are in the right; that we have truth on our side. The weight of evidence against Mrs. Jameson is overwhelming. She must have stolen your watch. There cannot be a shadow of doubt about it. There are a good many barristers, Mrs. Winthrop, who pride themselves more upon the winning of fishy cases than of sound ones. They love to drag a verdict out of the fire by sheer force of cleverness and ingenuity. They would sooner win a wrong one than a right one, because it seems to set a larger seal upon their ability. I cannot feel that. I am afraid that if I were on the wrong side, I should not be able to put any heart into my work. It is a grand thing to feel that you are the advocate of truth. Is it not?"

Mrs. Winthrop trembled. She felt so guilty that she could not at first find any words of reply, and just as she was beginning to stammer out something the door opened and a footman appeared, looking very much astonished and full of curiosity.

"If you please, ma'am." he said, "Mrs. Jameson is below and says she must see you. I told her you were engaged, but she——"

Before he could say more the parasite appeared at the door with a feeble tread. The widow uttered a slight cry and Reginald Ormethwaite sprang to his feet.

"A confession!" he said half aloud, and then stood waiting with an ardent interest in what was to come.

'Twas what playwrights would call a strong situation. There was a moment's pause.

Plump Mrs. Winthrop sat in her chair, nerveless, and as white as death. In the background, slightly in the shadow, was Ormethwaite, his keen eyes ablaze with excitement and a certain foiled disappointment. For he knew that a confession would take away once and for all the chance of distinguishing himself, for which he had waited so long. And between them, weakly weeping, and incoherently explaining, was poor Mrs. Jameson in a terrible flutter, quite broken down as it appeared, and almost tragic in her utter agony of mind.

At last, controlling herself a little, she groped for Mrs. Winthrop's hand, and exclaimed in a breathless sort of way:

"Darling, darling, it is no use. I can't bear it any more. Oh ! I can't, I can't. You know I will let you walk over me, anything—" (then she gave a loud sob and choked momentarily)—"But to be pointed at by butcher boys for what I haven't done, and to have John appealing to heaven to know why he ever married me, and all the family—his, I mean—groaning about it, saying they knew always how it would be, is too much. I can't go into court. I won't.

"I cannot face those awful barristers, and have that dreadfully clever Mr. Ormethwaite asking me fearful questions about all I've done since I was a baby. No, I can't. You don't want me to die, do you? Well, I shall die if it isn't stopped, and I'm sure Mr. Ormethwaite will make his name without us. If he is clever, he must. It will tell in the end. Let us speak the truth, and write to the papers and say you have found the watch where you hid it. Mr. Ormethwaite need never know you got it all up to benefit him, and——"

"Stop!" said a cold, grave voice. "What does this mean ? This is not the confession I expected. Mrs. Winthrop, tell me the truth. I have a right to know it."

Ormethwaite's face was rather pale, and his eyes glowed. But his hands did not tremble. He was master of himself and of those two women. Mrs. Jameson, who had not noticed him in her agitation, ceased to babble, and gazed at him silently. Mrs. Winthrop sat like a stone, her fat hands hanging helplessly at her sides.

"What does this mean ?" he repeated.

And then at last the widow found a voice, a shaky one enough. Her green eyes stared at the ceiling as she said slowly:

"It is my doing. You can never forgive me. But it was done for you."

"What was done for me?"

"The watch was never stolen. I arranged it all, I wanted you to get a chance. You were so clever. I felt that you only needed your opportunity. Oh, Mr. Ormethwaite, have I been so very wicked because I tried to give it to you?"

He turned to Mrs. Jameson.

"You never stole the watch?" he asked.

"Never, never," she murmured, sobbing weakly.

Mrs. Winthrop drew her fat little form up suddenly with a kind of dignity.

"Catherine," she said. "go home. You will never need to come to court now. I will see that your reputation is restored. But now you must go. I will come and see you to-morrow."

She led her friend to the door, and Mrs. Jameson, easily awed, trembled down the stairs and went into the street. Then the widow came back. She was on the verge of hysterics, but her plump features had the appearance of being carved in stone. She came back, shut the door, and stood with her hands resting on the arm of a chair.

There was a long and ghastly silence.

At length Ormeihwaite said in a dry voice:

"I must thank you for your desire to get an incompetent person on. It was well meant, I am sure. I ought to be grateful to you."

The widow cleared her throat with a hoarse gulp, and felt near to choking.

"I think I am grateful," he continued, "if I am not yet, I shall be. It is only a question of time."

He moved toward the door.

"Good night," he said, as he opened it.

Then he glanced at Mrs. Winthrop and his face changed. For he saw big tears falling slowly over her fat cheeks. The green eyes were quite dim with them. Her bosom was heaving silently. All her features were distorted in a frightful, piteous expression. She looked rather like some droll figure carved by a sculptor of a wild imagination. Yet she looked intensely humiliated.

Ormethwaite stopped with his hand on the door. And then—then he came back, quite up to her.

"Oh, why did you do it?" he said. "Why did you do it? And I love truth so, and so hate trickery."

Poor Mrs. Winthrop drooped lower and trembled more.

"Don't forgive me," she said, "I can't bear it."

He half stretched out his hand.

"I think I understand," he said. "I am going now, but some day when I have won a big case, I shall come back to you and ask you if you did it because you loved me."

And then he went away.

**   **   **

He has made his name now at last, and he has married the little **widow,** who adores him as few husbands were ever adored.   Mrs. Jameson's reputation has been righted, for the widow found her watch and made due and public apology.   And so, out of disconcerted trickery has sprung a happy love.

A man said in a club the other day: "It's a most extraordinary thing, a most unaccountable thing, but 'pon my soul, I believe Ormethwaite loves that absurd-looking little woman he has made his wife."

Perhaps it is most extraordinary, but the man is right.   He does.—[*Vanity.*

The time has come when men with hearts and brains
Must rise and take the misdirected reins
Of government, too long left in the hands
Of tricksters and of thieves.   He who stands
And sees the mighty vehicle of State
Hauled thro' the mire to some ignoble fate
And makes no such bold protest as he can
Is no American.

—*Ella Wheeler Wilcox.*

A Lesson In Married Life.

M. EARL DUNHAM.

JOHN SMITH—a very common name—was well educated, of fine personal appearance, pleasing in manners, willing to work, but lacking in the faculty of getting on in the world. He was handy at any ordinary kind of business, well liked by his employers, and judged by outward appearances, ought to have succeeded in almost any business enterprise; but success eluded him, for reasons which neither he nor his friends could fathom. Leaving the high school with a medal for scholarship and the reputation of standing in the first rank among his classmates, he entered upon a clerkship in a grocery store, threw himself willingly and cheerfully into the work in hand, won the approbation of his employer, was soon promoted with higher wages; then thought himself in a condition to get married, courted and won an estimable young lady, and set up housekeeping. All his friends and acquaintances approved, and his outlook for the future was in every respect promising.

The girl he married was a thoughtful and sensible young woman, with no stilted ideas of social life, no high-flying notions in her head, no disposition to hide limited pecuniary means under unwarranted display, content to appear as she really was, by living as their income would justify. She began housekeeping accordingly; was economical, saving, doing her own work, and yet found it difficult to make her husbaad's salary cover all their necessary expenses. What could she do to remedy this? She had no thought of laying heavier burdens of toil upon her husband, but rather to find if there was not some way in which she could assist him in providing for the home expenses. Married life is a matter of mutual obligation, and, to her, it seemed not only right but befitting that she should bear a part of the burdens. True, she did the work of housekeeping, but considerable leisure was left her. Why not use this for earning money? Before her marriage she had learned dressmaking; in fact, had gained a fair reputation for skill and taste in fitting and making dresses; why not utilize this now? She would speak to John about it; and she did.

John heard her suggestion with open-eyed astonishment. What! his wife take in work to help support the family! What would folks think about it? Nay, what would folks *say* about it? Certainly it would lower their social standing; it would be derogatory to his ability as a man; it was not to be seriously considered—not for a moment; he did not marry a wife to make a drudge of her; he would provide for the home, and, after a little, through increase of wages or by striking out into business for himself, he would be enabled to provide bountifully. All this and more went trooping through his thoughts, and he said: "No, no, don't think of such a thing. It's entirely out of the question. I'll supply the money, and you may spend it. It's enough for you to care for the home work."

John Smith had peculiar ideas as to the sphere of wifehood. He thought her place was in the home exclusively, looking after household cares. Work, of course, she could in housewifery, but not to earn money. That prerogative belongs to the husband, he thought. And he regarded himself as quite a fair provider. Of course, his salary was not large enough to warrant much indulgence in luxuries, but it was sufficient for all necessary wants. He had no idea how his wife was compelled to economize, to make a little go a great way, to hide scantiness of material under the skill of cookery, or how she deprived herself of many things which would have added greatly to her comfort; and hence he felt somewhat hurt that his wife should reflect upon his ability to provide by hinting that he needed her assistance.

Mrs. Smith saw the state of his feelings, and sought to heal any wound her proposition had made, by saying: "Certainly, John, I shall attempt nothing of the kind unless you heartily approve of it. I only thought this; I am strong and healthy, and could help you carry the burden of support—if you think it wise. That's all."

"You're very kind," replied John, somewhat mollified, "but I don't think it wise. Besides, there is no need of it. If the time ever comes when I need your help in this way, I will accept it as willingly as you offer it."

"Thanks, dear. I will keep that promise in mind;" and her hand quietly slipped into his hand, their lips met, and a sharp, short, loving, caressing report floated out upon the air.

Mrs. Smith was no more satisfied with the state of home finances than before. All this talk did not enlarge the contents of the home purse. But what could she do? To push her own ideas against the opinion of her husband would not be productive of domestic felicity. She could wait, and abide the coming of events.

In the meantime, matters in the Smith household did not improve. Mr. Smith's wages did not increase. The expenses of the family did increase. A young Smith appeared on the scene, and must be provided for. Debts began to accumulate. The outlook was decidedly discouraging. Mrs. Smith resolved to renew her suggestion of supplementing their resources by utilizing her spare hours in dressmaking.

"Spare hours!" repeated John. "I should like to know where the spare hours come in between caring for the housework and the baby?"

"O, I find a few when baby is asleep."

"Then you ought to be asleep, too."

"We must take things as they are, and not as we would like them to be."

"That's true."

"Now, John, we're running behindhand, notwithstanding I try to economize in every way possible, and I see no way out but that of my resuming my trade. I cannot earn much, but every little will help."

"You're a jewel," said John, "but there is no need of your making a slave of yourself. For once we have struck luck; that is, Aunt Lucy, who died recently left me two thousand dollars, which I am to receive in a few days; at least, so her attorney has written me. When it comes I will set up in business for myself, and that will end all our troubles."

Of course Mrs. Smith was pleased at the announcement of this good fortune, but she was not certain about the business project. By close observation of John's business calculations, she had come to the conclusion that he was not always considerate of his ability to pay before purchasing, and she considered this a very serious defect in a business man. Hence she questioned the wisdom of his starting out into business for himself, and thought it safer to put their little inheritance at interest, and seek to increase it by their united earnings. She so stated the case to her husband, and was laughed at for her lack of business knowledge, and assured that the way to increase money is to invest it in profitable business enterprise.

"No, no, my dear," said Mr. Smith, "the way to raise a brood of chickens is to put the eggs through the process of incubation."

"That is true," replied Mrs. Smith, "but it is not safe to count the chickens before hatched. Eggs often spoil during the period of incubation; rats, cats and the pip sometimes decimate the brood; and it is only when the chickens are sufficiently grown to be profitably fricasseed that the success of chicken-raising can be positively estimated."

"I'll risk our eggs," said Mr. Smith. "I've been selling goods long enough to know all the ins and outs of the grocery business, and that's what I purpose to start in. Don't you worry; our two thousand dollar legacy will give us a competency for our old age."

"I hope it will," replied Mrs. Smith, "but somehow I fear."

> "Away with doubts, away with fears;
> Our day of fortune now appears;
> We'll spread our sails to fav'ring breeze,
> And catch our fortune ere it flees."

Of course Mr. Smith had his own way. His wife had not as yet asserted herself. In fact, she had not yet outgrown the old idea that the wife should "obey" the husband, or, at least, yield to his opinion where there is difference of opinion. Hence, though not convinced, she acquiesced.

When the legacy came into possession—as it did a few weeks after—Mr. Smith stocked a small grocery store, and set up in business for himself. He was widely known, was well liked, had hosts of friends who gave him their patronage, and his sales started off briskly. His goods were new and fresh, his treatment of customers was kind and obliging, his trade increased rapidly; a larger stock was needed, and he launched out as the demand seemed to require. Congratulations came in from all quarters, and John Smith was looked upon as the coming groceryman of the place.

At the end of the year Mr. Smith took account of stock, struck a balance of loss and gain, and found to his utter amazement, that he was helplessly and hopelessly in debt. He had given a large amount of uncollectable, in fact, worthless credits; he had purchased lavishly on time; there had been unaccountable leakages; the demands against him could not be met; an assignment was inevitable. He found himself a bankrupt at the end of the first year—not through lack of hard work; but through lack of shrewd business management. He failed just where his wife feared he might—in not considering in the present how he would be able to meet the demands of the future. He bought lavishly on credit, paid little attention to colllecting, good-naturedly trusted everybody who asked credit, and in the loseness of his business methods he came to grief.

So John Smith was stranded on the tidal wave of a two-thousand legacy. Nor was there another tidal wave to set him afloat again. He was out of work and out of money. Everybody knew this. Hence his credit was gone. He had no means of supplying the daily wants of his family. He was willing to work, to do anything that would bring wages, but no work was at hand or prospectively near.

Mrs. Smith again made the suggestion that she try her hand at wage-earning, and, this time, she made it with self-assertion. What could her husband say against the proposition now? Nothing; absolutely nothing; for he was stranded, helplessly, hopelessly, without money, without work, without credit, without any glimmering prospect of relief from any other quarter.

Mr. Smith sat, for a time, in deep meditation, and then said slowly, "It will be necessary for you to hire a girl to do the work and care for baby."

"Oh, no, it won't," she replied.

"Why, you can't do the housework, care for baby and dress-make, too."

"I am fully aware of that."

"Who, then, will do the housework?"

"You."

"I!"

"Yes, you."

"Never!"

"Why not?"

"What would people say? I should be the laughing-stock of the whole communnity."

"Better be that than starve, or beg, or struggle on in poverty. You have tried and failed, and now I purpose to make one brave effort for home and food and raiment—in spite of what people may think or say. We are too poor to start off by hiring help; we must begin alone. I ask you to help me in the only way you can. If we succeed, people will respect us; if we fail—well, it will be time enough to settle that when failure comes. If we sit down, do nothing but drift on the tide of misfortune, they will despise us and let us drift."

Mr. Smith could make no reply, but did not take kindly to the proposed plan. He would think about it; and he did think about it for a week, while his wife was quietly engaging work. He sought for work for himself, sought diligently, but sought in vain. No work for him was to be had, partly because work was scarce, and partly because the grocerymen owed him no good-will, in that he had set himself up in opposition to them, and thereby alienated a part of their trade. But something must be done, and done soon, for starvation was already at the door. His wife's scheme was practicable; that he could see. She was skilled in dressmaking and would find no difficulty in obtaining work; but the disgrace of living on the product of his wife's labor rose up before him as a thing unbearable. John, however, was not a fool, and saw that pride was no offset for want, and an exceedingly poor substitute for food. He knew he could do the housework —that is; he could learn to do it—for he had often assisted his mother in the days of his youth. Why not, then, accept his wife's proposition? If she could succeed in business better than he, why not let her take the business end of home life? That would be sensible and business-like, whatever remarks people might make about it. Why, then, hesitate to do it? He resolved to hesitate no longer. He would pocket his pride, do what seemed for the best, and trust Providence for the result.

With this resolve John went home, feeling more like a man than he had for weeks. As he entered the house he laid aside his coat, walked up to his wife and kissed her, saying, smilingly, "I am ready for work. Install me in the kitchen. Teach me how to cook and care for the house and baby, and I will see what we can do."

"Thank you, John," she replied, with a kiss which sealed the arrangement.

They were to begin on Monday morning; and when the morning came

John was early up, prepared the breakfast, ate heartily of the plain food, then got out the tubs and set about doing Monday's washing. He was no man to do half-way what he had agreed to do, nor do it whiningly. He had set himself to do the housework, and purposed to do it to the best of his ability.

Mrs. Smith went out and soon returned with the work she had already engaged. Thus the new arrangement commenced. It worked capitally. Mrs. Smith's reputation and skill brought in more work than her own hands could possibly do. Help was engaged—at first one girl, then two, then four, then half a dozen; and so in a few months Mrs. Smith found herself at the head of a large and profitable dressmaking establishment. Her success was marvelous. Her business capacity was of the highest order. Her bank account grew rapidly. The question of support for the home was solved. John was convinced that his wife was a wiser woman than he had formerly taken her to be. He was satisfied.

How did John succeed in housekeeping? Admirably. His house was a model of neatness and good order. This kind of work fitted him to perfection. Nor was he ashamed of it, either. When his neighbors attempted to joke him about his domestic arrangements, he never winced, but hurled back the truth, too well known to be disputed: "It would be better for a good many of you to do likewise."

And wouldn't it?—[*Woman's Journal.*

AT SEAFOAM LODGE.

HELEN FORREST GRAVES.

"THERE must be no other boarders taken," said Mr. McCorkindale. "I stipulate for that."

"Oh, there will be none!" said Mr. Dewey, the boarding and real estate agent, nibbling the end of his pen. "I know Mrs. Sweetclover very well— a most respectable widow, in reduced circumstances—and I know all about Seafoam Lodge, a delightful place, on the edge of the ocean, where a man can't help being healthy."

"Very well," said Mr. McCorkindale. "Let her know that I consider the thing a bargain. I will send my trunks on Monday of next week."

Mr. McCorkindale had been summering at the Adirondacks, and had found that mountain breezes, black flies and dried pine-needles didn't agree with him. He was now resolved to try the seaside. And he went home, well pleased with the bargain he had made.

Now Mr. Dewey was in a partnership—Dewey & Salter—and so neatly dovetailed together were the arrangements of the firm, that Mr. Salter, who dined at half-past twelve o'clock, came to "keep office" exactly at the hour in which Mr. Dewey, who dined at half-past one, took up his hat and cane to depart. And scarcely had Mr. Salter lighted his cigar, and settled his chair back at exactly the right angle of the wall, then in came Miss Mattie Milfoil, a blooming young old-maid, who gave lessons in swimming at the Aqua Pura Academy.

"I want board at the seaside for a month," said she. "At a place, please, where there are no other boarders. Prices must be moderate, and surf-bathing is a necessity."

"Ah." said Mr. Salter, bringing his chair down on its four legs at once, "the very place! Mrs. Sweetclover, a client of ours, has taken Seafoam Lodge, on the New Jersey coast, and has a clean, light, airy room to let, with good board, no mosquitoes—"

"Yes, I know," said Miss Milfoil. "Just let me look at her references."

The references proved satisfactory. Miss Milfoil struck a bargain at once.

"Let Mrs. Sweetclover expect me on Monday," she said; and Mr. Salter pocketed his commission with inward glee.

"Anything doing?" Mr. Dewey asked, when he came back from dinner, with a pleasant oleaginous flavor of roast pork and applesauce about him.

"I've let Mrs. Sweetclover's room for her," said Salter.

"Hello!" cried Dewey; "I let it, this morning, to old McCorkindale!"

"And I've just disposed of it to Miss Milfoil," spluttered Salter. "Why the deuce didn't you enter it on the books?"

"A man can't think of everything," said Mr. Dewey; "and I was going to enter it when I came back."

"But what are we to do now?" said Salter.

"Nothing," said Dewey. "Ten to one; one of the parties won't keep the contract. We're not to blame, that I can see."

And Mr. Dewey, a philosopher after his way, arranged his bulletin-board anew, and sat down, a human spider, to await the coming of any flies who might be disposed for business.

Mrs. Sweetclover, in the meantime, had swept and garnished Seafoam Lodge, until it was fresher than a cowslip and sweeter than roses.

She had decorated her up-stairs room with China matting, fresh muslin curtains, and dimity covers to the bureau and dressing-table.

"I do hope I shall be able to let it!" said Mrs. Sweetclover, with a sigh. "But there are so many seaside lodgings this year that—Dear me! here comes a gentleman and a valise up the beach-road, and as true as I live, he's making straight for my house!"

"Have my trunks arrived?" said the gentleman—"name of McCorkindale."

"Sir!" said Mrs. Sweetclover.

"I engaged the room through Dewey & Salter," said Mr. McCorkindale, "last week."

"It's the first I've heard of it," said Mrs. Sweetclover, all in a flurry. But you're kindly welcome, sir, and the room is quite ready, if you'll be so good as to step up stairs."

"Humph! humph! said Mr. McCorkindale, gazing around him with the eye of an elderly eagle. "Very clean—tolerably airy—superb view from the windows. Upon my word I like the look of things."

"Do you think the apartment will suit?" said the widow, timidly.

"Of course it will suit!" said Mr. McCorkindale. "Here is a month's board in advance—ten dollars a week, the agent said. You may serve dinner at one o'clock. Blue-fish, roast clams, lobster-salad—any sort of sea food you may happen to have. I don't eat desserts. And now I'm going out to walk on the seashore."

Mrs. Sweetclover looked after him with eyes of rapture.

"The boarde of all others that I would have preferred," said she. "I am in luck! I thought yesterday, when I saw the new moon over my right shoulder, that something fortunate was going to happen."

But Mrs. Sweetclover had not stuffed the blue-fish for baking, when a light, firm foot-step crossed the threshold, and Miss Milfoil stood before her, in a dark-blue serge dress, and a sailor hat of black straw, while across her shapely shoulders was slung a flat black satchel, traveler-wise.

"Mrs. Sweetclover, I suppose?" said she.

The widow courtesied an affirmative.

"I am Mattie Milfoil," said the lady. "I rented your room, last week, of Dewey & Salter."

"Dear me!" thought the widow. "Am I dreaming?"

"I like the situation very much," continued Miss Milfoil, looking at the curling edges of foam that crept up the beach at the left, and then at a murmuring grove of maple trees at the north. "I shall probably remain here until Christmas, if I am suited!"

"But the room is let already!" faltered Mrs. Sweetclover, at last recovering her voice.

"Taken already!" repeated Miss Milfoil. "But that is impossible. I have taken it."

There's some mistake at the Boarding Agency," said Mrs. Sweetclover, almost ready to cry. "It's been let twice; and I never knew of it until this moment. Oh, dear! oh, dear! It never rains but it pours!"

"But what am I to do? said Miss Milfoil.

Mrs. Sweetclover's faded eyes lighted up with a faint gleam of hope.

"I've only the eligible apartment on the second floor," said she; "but if you don't mind the garret, there's a nice, airy room finished off there, with two dormer windows overlooking the ocean——"

"I'll look at it," said Miss Milfoil.

She looked at it, and she liked it, and she straightway sent to the village for her trunks, unpacked her books, her work-basket, her writing-desk and her portable easel, arranged some sea-weed over the mantle and made herself at home.

Mr. McCorkindale, going upstairs from the dinner table that very day, heard a sweet, clear voice, singing the refrain of some popular ballad, from the upper story.

"Eh!" said Mr. McCorkindale. "Is that your daughter?"

"It's my lady boarder, sir," said Mrs. Sweetclover.

"Look here," said Mr. McCorkindale, stopping short—"this won't go own!"

"What won't go down, sir?" said the bewildered landlady.

"No other boarders taken, you know," said Mr. McCordindale. "That was my express stipulation."

"I'm very sorry, sir," said Mrs. Sweetclover, "but"

"And I'm not going to be trifled with!" said Mr. McCorkindale. "Either she or I must go!"

"Couldn't it be managed, sir?" said the landlady, half terrified out of her senses.

"No, it couldn't" said Mr. McCorkindale.

At this moment, however, Miss Milfoil herself made her appearance on the scene, tripping down the stairs in a quiet, determined sort of way, and facing the indignant elderly gentleman as he stood there.

"What's the matter?" said Miss Milfoil.

"The matter,'" said Mr. McCorkindale, "is simply this. I have engaged my board here, on the express understanding that I am to be the only boarder."

"I see," said Miss Milfoil. "And I am in the way."

Mr. McCorkindale was ominously silent.

"But," said Mattie, with an engaging smile, "if I promise to be very quiet, and to refrain from annoying you in any manner whatsoever—"

"It would make no difference," said Mr. McCorkindale. "I object to young women."

"But," cried indignant Mattie, "suppose I were to object to middle-aged gentlemen on no better pretext?"

"You are perfectly welcome to do so," said Mr. McCorkindale, stiffly, "You see, I am an old bachelor."

"And I am an old maid!" pleaded Mattie.

"It makes no difference—no difference at all!" said Mr. McCorkindale. "I am sorry to disappoint you, Mrs. Sweetclover, but——"

"Stop!" said Mattie, resolutely. "Mrs. Sweetclover, if either of your boarders leaves you, it is I. I came last, and I occupy the least remunerative room. I will take my departure on the noon-train to-morrow."

And Mattie went to her room and cried a little; for she had become very fond of her pretty little room already.

"At all events," said Mattie to herself, "I will get up before daylight to-morrow morning, and have one good swim in the surf."

She supposed, when she came out the next day, in her dark-blue bathing-suit and the coarse straw hat tied down over her eyes, that she would have the coast clear. But she was mistaken. Mr. McCorkindale was paddling, like a giant porpoise, in a suit of scarlet and gray, among the waves. He had always wanted to learn to swim, and here was a eligible opportunity.

He don't see me," said Mattie, to herself, as she crept cautiously down in the shadow of the rocks. "If he did, I suppose he would issue a proclamation that the whole seashore belonged to him. But I hope there is room enough for us both in the Atlantic Ocean."

And Miss Milfoil struck out scientifically, gliding through the waves like a new variety of fish, with dark-blue scales, and straightway forgot all about the troublesome old bachelor.

"It's very strange," said Mr. McCorkindale, revolving around and around, like a steam paddle-wheel. "A log floats, but I can't seem to manage it without the help of my arms and legs. I've always understood that swimming was a very easy business, but—Puf—ah-h—whust—sh—sh! Help! help! Pouf-f-f! I'm drowning! The undertow is carrying me out, and I can't help myself! Whush-sh! Oh! ah! help! he-e-e-elp!"

And Mr. McCorkindale's voice lost itself in a bubbling cry, while the deaf old fisherman upon the shore went on whistling and mending his net, and the solitary individual, who was picking up shells with his back toward the surf, never dreamed but that the stout gentleman was diving for his own amusement.

But Mattie Milfoil, cleaving her way steadily through the waves, perceived in a moment that something was wrong.

Mrs. Sweetclover fainted away when they laid the boarder on a pile of blankets on her kitchen floor.

She was one of those nervous ladies who always faint away at the least provocation.

But Mattie had all her senses about her; and, thanks to her courage and presence of mind, Mr. McCorkindale's life was saved.

"What is that rattling on the stairs?" he feebly inquired, as he sat up, the next day, in an easy-chair, with a curious sensation, as if a gigantic bumble-bee were buzzing in his head, and cataracts pouring through his ears.

"It's Miss Milfoil's trunk going away," said Mrs. Sweetclover, with a sniff of regret.

"Tell her not to go," said Mr. McCorkindale.

"Sir!" said Mrs. Sweetclover.

"Do you think I'm going to turn the woman who saved my life out of doors?" puffed Mr. McCorkindale.

"But I thought you objected to women," said Mattie's cheerful voice outside the door.

"I've changed my mind," said Mr. McCorkindale, with a fluttering semblance of a smile. "A man is never too old to learn. And I mean to learn to swim next week, if you will teach me."

He did learn. Miss Milfoil taught him. And the old bachelor and the old maid spent their month at the seaside, to use Mrs. Sweetclover's expression, "as quiet as two lambs."

"I declare," Mr. McCorkindale pensively observed, on the afternoon before his term was up, "I shall be very lonely after I leave here!"

"You'll be going back to the city, you know," cheerfully observed Miss Milfoil.

"But I shall miss you !" said the bachelor.

"Nonsense !" said Mattie.

"I wonder if you will miss me?" said Mr. McCorkindale.

"Well—a little," owned Miss Milfoil.

"Did you never think of marrying, Mattie?" abruptly demanded Mr. McCorkindale.

"Very often," she answered, calmly.

"And how is it that you never have married?"

Mattie laughed.

"Because I never found the right one," she said.

"Just my reason, exactly !" said Mr. McCorkindale. "But I think I have found her at last—and it's you, Mattie !"

"Is it ?" said Miss Milford, coloring and smiling.

"Don't you think, if you were to try me, I might suit you—as a husband?" he asked, persuasively.

"I don't know," whispered Mattie.

"Try me !" said Mr. McCorkindale, taking her hand in his; and she did not draw it away.

How brief a time will sometimes suffice to turn the current of a lifetime! That month at Seafoam Lodge made all the difference in the world to Mr. and Mrs. McCorkindale.—[*Saturday Night.*

A Plea for Dumb Things.

ELIZABETH AKERS ALLEN.

"**M**AMMA," says the average little girl to her mother, as, suddenly reminded of a great moral question she pauses in the loving squeeze which she is administering to the feline pet in her arms—"mamma, do all good people go to heaven?"

"Certainly, my child," responds the average mother, with cheerful confidence; although all the time conscious of a little dread as to what question may come next.

"But what if they can't read, mamma? and can't study Sunday School lessons, and read good books? Will they go to heaven just the same, if they are good?"

"Surely," replies mamma, a little reassured; "some poor people never have a chance to learn, as you do—they cannot go to school, or learn to read perhaps; but if they do as well as they know how to do, and are never unkind or wicked, the Lord loves them just the same. He is no respecter of persons; he does not love the wisest man in the world any better than the poor, ignorant little child, so they both alike try to live an innocent life, and are as good as they know how to be."

The child's face brightens, and she finishes the interrupted squeeze with—

"Good! then my white kitty can go to heaven, can't she?"

"A kitty go to heaven? No, indeed! Kitties and puppies and chickens do not go to heaven."

"But why?" with sudden disappointment clouding the puzzled face. "I am sure, my kitty does as well as she knows how to do; she never steals nor scratches, and is just as good as she can be. You said it was no matter about reading and being wise; and every other way, my kitty is as good as anybody can be."

"But kittens have no souls, and it is the soul that goes to heaven."

"What *is* the soul?"

This is deep water. But the mother makes another plunge.

"The soul, dear, is the part of you that loves and knows and remembers.—the part that does not die when the body dies—the immortal——"

"But. mamma, my kitty has something to love with, too; and she loved me, and knows me from all the other girls, and remembers where her milk-saucer is, and has learned lots of things; and why isn't that *her* soul just as it is mine? And why must she *all* die when her body does, if I don't?"

Alas, why? and many a little child never gets a satisfactory answer to this question. The mother generally finishes by alluding in a vague way to the Bible; but she cannot, for the life of her, think of a passage therein which would prove her position; and though adroitly changing the subject to the present, she inwardly determines to have a little private consultation with Cruden at her first convenience. She is much disappointed and disquieted, afterwards, at the unsatisfactory result of the conference.

The prevailing belief that animals have no souls; and consequently no existence after this, is supposed to be founded, like many other one-sided theories, on the Bible; two passages of which are invariably flung at the head of the "irreverent" party who dares hint, not that he himself will have no hereafter, but that his winged and four-footed friends are eligible to share it with him. The first of these passages, in the Psalms—"Man being in honor, abideth not; he is like the beasts that perish,"—although often quoted, does not seem, certainly, to strengthen the human side of the question much, since it openly likens man to the beasts, whatever may be the destination of the latter. The other stock quotation is in Ecclesiastes, and speaks of "the spirit of the beast that goeth downward to the earth." This, too, has a hole in it, when brought forward to prove that animals have no souls, since it expressly credits beasts with a "spirit." But even supposing that either of these arguments would hold water, they are a dozen times overborne by the number of Scripture passages wherein the immortality of man is either disputed or despaired of. What hope is there in the cry of Job: "As the waters fail from the sea, and the flood decayeth and dryeth up, so man lieth down, *and riseth not?*" And in the very book wherein occurs the passage supposed to disprove the immortality of the beasts, what do we find better for the sons of men? "For *that which befalleth the sons of men, befalleth beasts;* even one thing befalleth them; *as the one dieth, so dieth the other;* yea, they have all one breath, so that *a man has no pre-eminence over a beast;* for all is vanity. *All go unto one place;* all are of the dust, and *all turn to dust again.*" Now no language can be plainer than this; and it certainly comes much nearer proving that there is no immortality for any of us, than that human beings have a monopoly thereof, to the exclusion of their four-footed friends. The latter theory seems built on precisely the same substructure of ineffable self-conceit which also supports the opinion that this little insignificant point which we call our earth is the only spot in the universe of stars and suns which is peopled by conscious and personal intelligences. It surely cannot be said that the Bible denies immortality to beasts. That it does not distinctly *assert* it, may be met with the fact that neither does it distinctly assert the immortality of human beings. "*The dead know not anything.*"

The common remark that animals do not think, is disproved a hundred times a day in the very sight of those who advance the opinion. True, animals do many things from instinct, or without thought; but there can be no *acquirement* without thought, observation, comparison and memory. None of these attributes belong to instinct. The canary-bird at home builds its first nest just as perfectly as it would build its thousandth, should it live to need it. But confine him in a cage, and he does not all at once know how to draw up the little bucket which contains his food; he does that much better after a little practice.

That animals have reason, must be admitted by every one who ever drove a horse, milked a cow, petted a cat, or owned a dog. That they do not possess it in human measure is admitted; and that all animals are not gifted *alike* with reasoning powers, is evident to all observers. Even children see this difference in their pets, and understand it. A little girl owned a number of kittens, one of which she always specially protected and provided for, although it was quite as large and healthy as the others. When questioned as to why she was so partial, she replied: "Because this kitty is an idiot; the others have common sense." It appeared that "this kitty" really could not take care of itself, and was even unable to secure sufficient food, unless assisted. But the human race, which comprises all the extremes of mentality, from the most enlightened and comprehensive intellectuality, to the dull perceptions of the Esquimaux, the stupidity of the Digger Indian, and the scarcely human degradation of the Bushman, can hardly afford to find fault with the "lower animals" because all of them do not reach the height of mental capacity attained by the comparatively few.

Certainly the disciples of Descartes, who believe, as he did, that animals are mere machines, without thought, or sensibility, or feeling, like a wheelbarrow or a coffee-mill, and are doomed to insensate annihilation when they are worn out or destroyed, must look elsewhere than in the Bible for their authority. The theory of Descartes, revolting and monstrously cruel though it be, is still more consistent with itself than the ordinary "Christian" theory; since, as a wheelbarrow has no conscious life in this world, it is only reasonable to deny it a conscious life in the next. But the asserton that the very qualities and attributes which are supposed to be the immortal part of man, the attributes of thought, reason, memory, love, constancy, faithfulness and unselfishness, are simply earthly and perishable in other animals, and doomed to utter extinction when the body is resolved to dust, seems shockingly inconsistent and unreasonable, as well as insufferably selfish and arrogant.

Nor are these the most mischievous features of the popular belief. Upon this presumption is founded, if the real truth were ferreted out, the almost universal notion that dumb beasts have no rights which human beings are bound to respect. Hence arises much of the abuse and bitter cruelty to which animals are subjected, even in the midst of the highest Christian civilization. The boy who tortures a dog, the man who overloads or abuses his horse, have been taught to believe that these poor tormented things have no souls; that they are mere automata, to be dealt with precisely as their masters choose. "He's *my* horse," said a savage teamster, pausing in the wicked work of beating his poor overworked horse, to answer the remonstrance of a humane woman at an overlooking window; "he's mine; I bought him, and I'll pound him to death by inches, if I choose to, it's no murder to kill a horse. He can't speak nor think, and he hain't no sense and no soul."

There is the argument and its consequence. "He cannot speak." Neither can the ten thousand deaf mutes now within our borders; but who denies them the possession of souls? "He cannot think." He can, but even if he could not, neither does the day-old infant of the wisest parents in the land; yet who disputes the babe's immortality? "He has no sense." Neither have the fifteen thousand idiots which are included in the population of the country, nor the equal number of insane persons. Yet where is the school of theology which denies immortality to idiots and insane people?

Ah, friends, you who may believe that the idea of a beast's immortality is all a mistake, remember that we are all alike liable to mistakes; let us, at least, be sure to err on the side of kindness and mercy. While no believer in the after life of the lower animals will feel it necessary to establish and endow a church for them, there is very much yet to be done in the way of mitigating their sufferings and bettering their condition, even in the most enlightened districts. Let us no longer teach our children that animals have no souls, and were meant by the Almighty to be simply the unrewarded drudges of men, their duty being to accept meekly whatever treatment the freak of the moment may lead him to give them. Let us rather teach the rising generation that these poor dependants have rights, not only given them by the Creator, but earned faithfully by their various service of waiting, of laboring, of amusing, of protecting, of loving, and helping and saving. There is no danger that the present and coming generation will be too gentle-hearted toward their inferiors; on this side they are scarcely liable to err. The evil wrought by want of feeling for dumb things is on every hand an apparent and crying evil. In contra-distinction thereto, how pleasantly shows even the extreme example of the tender-hearted old saint Francis, who wrought from his literal interpretation of the Bible a far more merciful belief than do many modern theologians, and went out into the fields and forests, preaching earnestly and faithfully to the birds and squirrels, in obedience to the scriptural command: "Go ye into all the world. and preach the Gospel to *every creature.—[Sunday Afternoon.*

SUCCESSFUL BLIND MEN.

IN this department, which is dedicated to the cause for the advancement of which this periodical is published, we hope to serve a double purpose. We wish first to call the attention of the seeing world to what it is possible for blind persons to accomplish.

Second, to have this knowledge, by means of the thoughtful kindness of our subscribers, reach the sightless everywhere and stimulate them to make the most of their lives.

Every blind man or woman, young or vigorous, with a favorable opportunity may become self-sustaining. The right amount of perseverance will command the opportunity. All who wish to know what is being accomplished to increase the methods by which blind people may become independent are invited to open correspondence with the American Association to Promote the Education and Employment of the Blind, 3024 Fourteenth St. N. W., Washington, D. C., enclosing stamp for reply.

An uncultured lad, loses his sight by a bullet wound while fighting as a common soldier, under the stars and stripes. While being carried from the battle field by his comrades, he hears one of them say, "Poor fellow he will never see again, he might as well be dead."

The spirit that animated this young man would not allow such a conclusion to go unchallenged and he replied: "Do not be so sure of that, you may hear from me again, yet."

The people of the United States have heard from him again, for he is now a doctor of divinity, and chaplain of the popular branch of the Congress of the United States.

In reaching this position, he encountered and overcame obstacles and difficulties that are encountered by every blind man who attempts to make his life a success.

His capital was energy and perseverance, step by step he advanced; at one time he was supporting himself as a broom maker. Determined to acquire an education, he pushed on through college and theological seminary and became a preacher of the gospel.

Conscious of his ability and strength, he was compelled as is every blind man, to hear his limitation discussed, as the saddest of misfortunes and himself referred to in terms which left no room for doubt, that he was regarded as of little or no account in the world by men, who though in the full enjoyment of their five senses, were pigmies in comparison to him; it is the mind which distinguish man from the brute creation, and knowledge that distinguishes one man from another. He found that everywhere among the seeing, the notion prevailed, that in some way, the loss of sight had coupled with it the loss of mental vigor. Although underestimated in advance he was always able to demonstrate the error of this conception. With a generous nature, a warm heart, and occupying the position before the American people which he does, no man is better qualified to command the attention of the public, and we therefore quote with great pleasure from a letter, which the writer received from him only a short time since. We refer to the Rev. Henry M. Conden, D. D., who writes as follows:

HON. F. E. CLEAVELAND.;

"*My Dear Sir:*—Your most interesting letter at hand this A. M., and it affords me more pleasure than I can express to know that you with others in the great State of Connecticut, have espoused the cause so long neglected: viz., That of widening the sphere of opportunities of the blind, which has for its object the elevation of this class to a larger sphere of usefulness and greater self-respect, by rendering them like their seeing brothers and sisters, independent and self-sustaining; the field is a wide one and hitherto, for the most part, unexplored.

"One of the first duties of the State is to utilize all its resources to the uplift of humanity, by giving to each citizen or child, the best education and equipment for life, and the struggles incident thereto for maintenance through honest endeavor and industry, whatever the calling may be. It is true that the blind are handicapped in the struggle for existence, but the time has come when those blessed with the five senses, should realize that there are latent forces, which by education and practice may be brought into use, enabling the unfortunate to compete successfully with their more fortunate fellows. In this age of mechanism, when the forces of nature are made to do the work of brawn, the difficulties would seem well nigh insurmountable, especially to those who are unacquainted with the resources of the blind, but give them the opportunity and they will solve the problem beyond peradventure. If time permitted, cases might be cited which would afford the strongest evidence in proof of our assertion."

Enoch Spencer Simmons, who became blind eleven years ago, is a successful and prominent lawyer in Washington, North Carolina. He has also won distinction as an author. A recent publication of a work entitled "The Solution of the Race Problem in the South," is from his pen.

Speaking of this work, many of the leading papers in the country have given it serious attention as a valuable contribution of earnest thought, on the one living and burning question throughout the South.

From the many notices of this work we select the following from the Washington Post and the Chicago Inter Ocean.

The Washington Post, speaking of the "Race Problem," says:—"Mr. Simmons, who is totally blind, is a prominent lawyer in North Carolina. He believes that the race problem in the South may be solved by separating the two races and colonizing the negro in the southern part of the United States. There is no evidence of a disposition to do the negro an injustice, on the contrary, Mr. Simmons is entirely equitable and just, but he firmly believes that to expect the two races so materially differing from each other, as does the negro and the Caucasian, to live together on the same soil in peace and harmony, would be in violation of all natural laws, and therefore impossible.

Assuming colonization to be the only solution of this intricate and perplexing question, he undertakes to prove its practicability and the danger sure to come to posterity if neglected."

The Inter Ocean, of Chicago, says:—"A Solution of the Race Problem in the South"—By Enoch Spencer Simmons of the North Carolina bar. (Raleigh, Edwards & Broughton.) Mr. Simmons writes earnestly, and unquestionably with a desire to solve a hitherto unsolved problem. Briefly, his idea is the colonization of the negroes in states wherein they shall be so strongly a majority of the whole as to give to their best men free access to political honors and emoluments, from those of Governor and Senator down to constable. The plan is not new, but Mr. Simmons supports it by new and ingenious arguments. The book is a timely presentation of the views of a gentleman who is certainly not unfriendly to the negro, who knows the Southern situation, and who tell what he knows in a very agreeable manner."

Speaking of his own experience in a recent letter to the writer, Mr. Simmons says, "I am like yourself, a lawyer and blind. When I was thirty I lost my eyesight, and since that time I have been totally blind.

"At first like yourself, I was much discouraged by my friends who thought it impossible for me to practice law, nothing daunted, with a determination to succeed against any odds, I have remained at my post, and while I cannot boast of a large practice, I do a fair share, losing no cases I ought to win and often 'winning others.'

"I fully appreciate all you have said and that has been said of you in the *Washington Post*. I at one time thought I would travel over the country delivering a lecture for the betterment of the blind, begging the world to give them an opportunity, insisting that they had all the feelings, ambitions and desires of other people with eyesight, anxious to help themselves instead of being dependants, and in many instances possessing marvelous capacity if given an opportunity. I did not undertake the lecture for several reasons. First, I am a poor man with a large family and unable to give my time for any work, other than for the support of my family. Second, It is so discouraging to see how little we are appreciated, I abandoned the idea. I will here add, however, I am to-day ready and willing to do anything within my power to better the condition of the blind and if at any time my co-operation with you will serve a good purpose, call upon me."

The parents of Mr. Simmons were prosperous planters and slave owners prior to the war. His work is written from the standpoint of our Southern brothers and he throws a flood of light upon the present conditions.

Men of the North are very far from appreciating the true character of this situation. The writer confesses to having obtained a great deal of information from this book and he is convinced that the white people of the South are sincere and unselfish in their attitude towards the negro.

We can serve our readers no better than to quote the language of Mr. Simmons, somewhat at length on this point.

After referring to the writings of Bishop Bascomb and Harriet Beecher Stowe, to show that his idea of colonizing the negro was held in common by the most noteworthy writers on the subject, Mr. Simmons proceeds to show his own feeling towards the negro. He says:

"The author here desires to say for himself, he has always entertained a kindly feeling for the colored race of people. That among them there are those for whom he has the most sincere and affectionate regard. An old colored woman, now living at Pantego, North Carolina, more than eighty-five years of age, always known in my family as 'Aunt Hester,' remarkable in many ways, is trusty, faithful and true, devoted to the memory of my mother and father, always speaking of them as tenderly and affectionately as if they had been of her own flesh and blood. It is not often we see the old woman; it affords us as much pleasure to have her visit us as if she was one of our own family. The other old favorites of my father's family have long since passed away, among them my old nurse; we have a tender and affectionate regard for their memories and like their children. Only recently we had a letter from Prince, a boy about my own age. We had not seen each other, nor heard from each other since we parted on the plantation after Lee's surrender. Indeed, he writes, he did not know where we were. In this we were alike: we had not heard from him. Among other things, he says: 'The last time I saw you was in Hyde county. I thought the world of you. One thing you did was to take up for me if I got in a quarrel. I have heard recently from a white friend who knows all about you of late years, and it makes my poor heart leap with joy to hear from my young master. I suppose my old massa and missus are dead and gone long ago. May God bless them. I hope you will at least think enough of me to write and tell me all about them in their latter days, as I often think of how much service I might have been to them. Give my regards to your brother and sister and all of the family—you I remember best of all.'

"Of course we answered the letter. We were indeed glad to hear from Prince. Many were the days we spent in childhood together."

Speaking of the attempt of the white people of the South, to manfully meet the conditions imposed by the freedom of the slaves and their enfranchisement, the author proceeds as follows:

"With generous hand taxes were gathered, our Constitution rewritten, distributing the tax revenues for public school purposes equally between the two races in proportion to number, school houses built, schools taught; all this alone, too, with taxes raised upon the property of the white people, except the small parts raised upon the poll, for the negro then had no property and has but little now. To say that our southern people did this grudgingly, as some are wont to do, would not be borne out by the facts; rather the people of the South, both with mind and heart wished to give their old slaves and their children a fair chance in the race of life; they were not forgetful of the fidelity with which he stood guard, protecting our mothers and sisters, wives and children at home, while his master was upon the battlefield, fighting to perpetuate the institution of his slavery; the happy memories of plantation life, baby and childhood, with the lullabies of black mammies, the cabin with banjo and songs of Uncle Tom; the development of our Southland in other days by the use of his strong arm, lingered in the minds of our people.

"Whatever may be said to the contrary, it was true, indeed as many of the old slaves will testify, that their masters had a kindly regard for them and wished them to do well. The younger generation, children of slave owning parents, including many young men who wore the grey at the close of the war, had been tenderly nursed by black mammies, who loved their nurslings with the devotion of mothers: then, too, there were many 'Uncle Tom's' who watched the interests and affairs of their masters, with a devotion and fidelity never surpassed. The pride of their lives was the success of their master's children.

"These sentiments and sincere regard for black mammies and Uncle Toms, caused our lawmakers, who were principally ex-slave holders or the children of such, without stint, not grudgingly, but generously, earnestly desiring their success and the success of their descendants, to do all in their power to make provisions for the education and happiness of this race. After we had become accustomed to these new conditions, for a time things went well, the leavening influence of black mammy and Uncle Tom did much for the good of their race, these old ones, tenderly regarded by their old masters and the younger generation, whom they had nursed and helped to raise, stood a barrier, a rock of safety, between the heat and passion of the younger ones who were fast coming up. The writer wants to say with sincerity that the old slaves made good citizens; most of them, indeed well nigh all, have passed into the shades of forgetfulness.

"The wisdom of their advice, we regret to say, is no longer cherished in the memories of their descendants. A generation has come and another gone since the beginning of these conditions, and instead of a realization of our cherished hopes, disappointment is seen everywhere. Thirty-two years of generous education has for its reward in this race a growing dislike for the people that gave it; education seems only to have educated well in teaching the recipients of this bounty, better ways of disliking, cheating and defrauding its giver.

"Of the generation of negroes now coming on it may be said truly, their best thoughts, purpose and action are bestowed upon ways to get the white race within their grasp and control. A foolish idea, it is true—one in which their dream of hope will only be a dream, but too true withal, of course those of the white race disposed to help them are discouraged; despair has taken the place of hope; while the thousands who have never entertained any feeling but dislike for this race, are made to dislike the negro more because of his ingratitude for the good which has been done him.

"You hear it on every side that the white people of the South owning the property and paying the taxes, have tired of educating this propertyless race, who, in turn for thanks and gratitude, give them all the dislike and animosity common to their nature. There is no doubt, the sentiment of opposition to the education of the negro by the white man is growing; there is no doubt the negro is responsible for this sentiment. For the generosity of his white friends he has given them, whenever and wherever the opportunity presented with but few exceptions, bad government, by imposing upon us characterless white men of the baser sort, whose chief ambition, pride and pleasure is to so administer the affairs of government as to disgrace society, insult the honor and dignity of our commonwealth and degrade the patriotic people of the South, who themselves and their ancestry can boast of noble citizenship, and whose only wish and desire is for the prosperity, success and upbuilding of our beautiful Southland, the peace and happiness of our Union."

The book is exceedingly interesting throughout, and we trust that many of our readers will see fit to send an order to Mr. Simmons for a copy. Price in cloth postpaid, 50 cents, in paper 35 cents. Address, Enoch Spencer Simmons, Washington, North Carolina.

SELECTED MATTER.

Proverbs Up To Date.

G. D. B.

The world's a cycle, and the folks
Are nothing but the cycle's spokes.

One man may seat a cyclist fair,
But ten men can not keep her there.

She rises brightly with the dawn,
While yet the dew is on the lawn,

And ere 'tis dried from hill and plain,
She rises many a time again.

A novice and her wheel soon part,
And pride is humbled at the start.

The upright rider winneth praise,
But who can mend the humped one's
    ways?

Behold the woman riding down
Swift as the lightning through the
    town.

She scorcheth through the outer gate
And goeth far and stayeth late.

Her husband, in the market place
The elders mock unto his face.

"Thou buttonless!" they cry; "all
    hail,
Go clasp thy raiment with a nail!"

He plucks his beard and saith a
    swear,
But he doth not his garment tear.

For no one bides at home to darn
(Save orally) his suit of yarn.

The latest application of electricity to automatic devices is the automatic blind raising and lowering apparatus placed on the market by a Berlin firm. This little device lowers the curtain when the sun shines and raises it when it is obscured. The essential feature of the mechanism is a V-shaped glass vessel, placed outside the window, which carries at its extremities two hollow glass bulbs. One is coated inside with lampblack and the other is not. In the connecting arm of the tube, which is of capillary proportions, is a column of mercury. When the sun shines on the glass balls the air contained in the lampblacked ball is caused to expand more than the other one, thus driving the mercury column higher in the opposite arm. This completes an electrical contact, which starts a motor in operation, lowering the curtain. When the curtain is all the way down another contact is completed, and the motor reversed, ready to raise the curtain as soon as the sun allows the air to contract to its original volume.

The seeds of the laughing plant of Arabia produce the same effect upon persons as laughing gas. The plant attains a height of from two to four feet; with woolly stems, wide-spreading branches, and bright green foliage. Its fruits are produced in clusters and are of a yellow color. The seed pods are soft and woolly in texture, and contain two or three black seeds of the size of a Brazilian bean. The flavor is a little like opium, and their taste is sweet; the odor from them produces a sickening sensation and is slightly offensive. The seeds, when pulverized and taken in small quantities, have a peculiar effect upon man. He begins to laugh loudly, boisterously, then he sings, dances, and cuts all manner of fantastic capers. Such extravagance of gait and manners was never produced by any other kind of dosing.

————— ❧ —————

So finely are the scales of nature adjusted that it is probable every defect has its compensation near at hand. Man's part is to find it. In Kansas and Nebraska the rainfall is insufficient to supply the needs of agricultural vegetation. Nevertheless, it has recently been ascertained that an inexhaustible deposit of water lies directly below all the arid region; while the wind, nature's agent to lift the water, blows during the whole summer. It was from air registering one hundred degrees below zero that Nansen, by means of a windmill wrested the power to light and heat his ice-bound Fram. The Kansas farmers should not be slow to conquer nature as Nansen did.

————— ❧ —————

DR. CLIFTON F. HODGE of Clark University is endeavoring to introduce nature study into the public schools. In preparing subjects that would teach children to observe, he has learned some very interesting facts. He has found that the little garden toad, with proper encouragement, will keep a home free from flies. He made a small pen in his garden and put in a pan of water and a pair of toads. To attract the flies to them he threw in bits of meat. The toads spent most of their time sitting near the bait and killing the flies that came to it. The female toad laid her eggs in the water, and in due time the little black tadpoles made their appearance; these ate up the young mosquitoes, and so both flies and mosquitoes were scarce around that neighborhood.

————— ❧ —————

WHEN the brain is at work marshaling ideas, producing mental pictures, and calling into action stored-up memories and impressions, the cells of its mysteriously potent "gray matter" undergo a change of form. Cavities are formed in them, which, as the brain becomes wearied by long continued action, fill with a watery fluid. Part of the substance of the cells appears to have been consumed in the process of thinking, but in the hours of sleep the exhausted cells regain their original form from the supply of recuperative material coming from the blood, and on awakening, the mind finds its nutriment restored and prepared again for action.

————— ❧ —————

AN aerial bicycle for driving a balloon was tried at the Crystal Palace, London. The machine is fitted to the car of an ordinary balloon, over the front of which a big fan, something like the screw of a steamer, projects. It is worked from the inside exactly as a bicycle is, while between the balloon and the car are two more such fans, which are to drive the balloon up or down. These fans are worked by the driver turning a handle just on a level with his face.

————— ❧ —————

THE report of the Suez Canal Company, dated May 6, shows total receipts for the fiscal year to the amount of $16,500,000, an increase of $145,000 over the previous year. The number of vessels that passed through is 3,503. A marked increase is to be noted in the passage of American vessels bound for Asiatic ports, their number reaching 3 per cent of the total for the year.

————— ❧ —————

GLOWWORMS are much more brilliant when a storm is coming than at other seasons. Like many other mysteries of nature, this curious circumstance has never been explained.

LOCAL Unions of the Woman's Christian Temperance Union in many of the States are celebrating their 25th anniversaries as a great number have already reached their quarter mile post. The next National convention to be held at Seattle, Washington, will be held on October 20-25, the commemoration also of twenty-five years as a National organization.

THE despatches say that the Baroness Suttner is the only woman admitted to the gallery as a spectator of the proceedings of the Peace Conference. This is a recognition of the writings of the Baroness which have aroused Europe more than anything else has done on the subject of peace, and is credited with having inspired the Czar to call the conference.

OF the thirty-three large firms in Manila, only five are Spanish and four of these have little to do with foreign trade. Of the rest, fourteen are German, twelve British, one Dutch, one Belgian. From February 16 to March 11, seventy ships arrived at Manila. Only four of these were Spanish.

FROM a quarry of soft redstone in southern Minnesota, the only stone probably of its kind in the world, the Indians for centuries obtained materials for their pipes, which were probably articles of commerce, as they are found in Indian graves from the Mexican gulf to Canada.

IT has been reckoned that if the whole ocean were dried up, all the water passing away as vapor, the amount of salt remaining would be enough to cover 5,000,000 square miles with a layer one mile thick.

ONLY one-third of the world's population use bread as a daily food. One-half subsist chiefly on rice.

MRS. CHARLOTTE PERKINS STETSON scored a good point the other day, when referring to the fact that purity of the city's milk supply is governed by politics. She said: "This matter of politics is not 'outside the home,' it is inside the baby!"

DR. JULIA MORTON PLUMMER and Dr. Caroline E. Hastings, of Boston, expect to sail next fall for Poona, India, to take charge of a Bible training school in connection with the work of Pundita Ramabai.

SWITZERLAND although she spends only $500,000 yearly on her army, can turn out 100,000 trained men in two days in case of need, and has a reserve of 100,000 more, as well as a militia of 270,000.

THERE are 800 deaconesses in the M. E. church. Of these about 600 are in this country, 150 in Germany and fifty in other foreign lands.

MORE than 500,000 sewing machines are made in this country annually, which is ninety per cent of the production of the world.

A HOSPITAL for women has been established in Penyang, Corea. It is called a "hospital of extended grace.'

TWELVE million acres of land have been made fruitful by irrigation of artesian wells in the Sahara desert.

THE late Sir Andrew Clark, physician to Queen Victoria, was in favor of non-alcoholic medication.

THERE is more exertion used in running two hundred yards than in riding a bicycle four miles.

THE Ohio penitentiary contains 2,339 inmates. Of these 33 are women and 2,306 are men.

Don't.

I might have jest the
  mostest fun
If 'twasn't for a word,
I think the very worstest
  one
'At ever I have heard,

I wish 'At it 'u'd go
away,
  But I'm afraid it won't;
I s'pose 'at it'll always stay—
  That awful word of "don't."

It's "don't you make a bit of noise,"
  And "don't go out-of-door;"
And don't you spread your stock of
  toys
Abont the parlor floor;

And "don't you dare play in the
  dust,"
And "don't you tease the cat,"
And "don't you get your clothing
  mussed;"
And "don't" do this and that.

It seems to me I've never found
  A thing I'd like to do
But that there's some one else around
  'At's got a "don't" or two.

And Sunday—'at's the day 'at "don't,'
  Is worst of all the seven.
Oh, goodness! but I hope there won't
  Be any don'ts in heaven.

A MATINEE AT HOME.

EMMA FRANCES GEROME.

"NOW, Pussy Willow," said little
Ruthie, as she held her kitten
over the set tub in the laundry. "If
you're going to the beach with us,
you must get used to the water.
You're only a kitty, and you can't
climb to the life-line. When we go
in bathing, I shall have to cling with
one hand and hold you with the other,
so I'm going to give you a lesson."

"Ruthie, don't be cruel to your
kitten," called Hannah, from the
back yard where she was hanging out
clothes.

"No," said Ruthie, "I'll only dip
her feet in this time;" and down
went kitty's four paws into the tub of
blueing-water.

"Kitty, dear" Hannah heard her
say, "you've been very good, and I
really must give you another lesson.
Now, then, there's a big wave just
ready to break over your blessed little head. Take care!"

"Ruthie!" shouted Hannah, as she
threw down the basket of clothes-
pins, and rushed toward the laundry;
"Ruthie, stop! You wicked child!"

"Stop!" cried Polly, from the perch
up in fhe wistaria vines. "Stop!
stop! stop!"

But the command came all too late,
for at that moment there was a splash
and splurge, a flying leap to the
laundry floor. There stood Pussy
Willow, a poor little drenched cat,
who seemed suddenly to have shrunk-
en to about one-third her former size.
She looked fearfully about her, as
she shook her wet fur, and scattered
blueing-watter like rain.

"Oh! oh!" shrieked Ruthie, "I
didn't think it could be as bad as
this. I did it for her good, and now
she is afraid of me. My own little
Pussy Willow, now she hates me! I

know by the way she glares at me." Here Ruthie threw her wet apron over her face, and wept afresh.

"Stop!" cried Polly. "Stop, you wicked child!"

"Oh, yes, Polly, I'd do that way, if I were you," sobbed Ruth. "The chocolate creams are all gone now, so you don't care whether you keep friends with me or not. I know one thing, parrots are a good deal like folks. Always on the strongest side."

"Hear that!" screamed Polly. "Hear that!"

"Well Miss Ruthie Wayne," broke in Hannah, angrily, "all I've got to say is this: It's a pity your ma took the trouble to go to the matinee when she might have had one right at home. But if she should happen in now, you'd get a punishment, you naughty child!"

"Don't!" wailed Ruthie. It's worse than punishment — this is. It's a lesson."

"Very well," said Hannah, lowering her voice, "if that's the way you look at it, you can go up stairs and ask Mary to take off your wet clothes, and get them dried before your ma comes. I'll put kitty out in the sun, and she'll soon forget all about her fright."

"Thank you, Hannah, you're very kind not to let mamma know; but I shall tell her myself when she comes home. I'm going to be good now," Ruth said, as she started up the stairs.

"Ha! ha!" laughed Polly, derisively "Hear that! Going to be good! Ha! ha! ha!"

THE ESKIMO BOY'S STORY.

I am a little Eskimo boy. I live far north. It is always cold there so I must wear warm clothes. My clothes are made of bear skin. I think they look very pretty.

I live in a queer house. It is made of snow. It looks like half a ball. It has only one room. The doorway is very low. I go in on my hands and knees.

I have a little sister. Her clothes are just like mine. We both have black hair and black eyes. Our skin is dark.

We play in the snow. We do not mind the cold. Sometimes we go for a ride. We do not have horses. We have dogs to draw us.

They will draw us swiftly over the snow. Will you come to see us ride sometime? We want to give you a ride on our sled.—[Colo. Index.

A MOTHER describes in the *Interior* how she came to look upon the rubbish in her boy's drawer as his unwritten diary and the basis of his autobiography. She said to him one day:

"My son, your bureau drawer is full of rubbish. You had better clear it out."

Yes, that would be his great delight: so we began.

"This horseshoe is of no use—"

"Oh, yes, it is; I found it under grandpa's corn crib, and he let me have it."

"These clam-shells you'd better break up for the hens—"

"Why, mamma, I got them on the beach, you know, last summer!"

"Here is that old flute yet! Why do you heap up such trash?"

"That is a nice flute that Willie gave me two Christmases ago. Didn't we have a splendid time that day?"

"Well, this bottle is good for nothing—"

"Oh. yes, it is! That is the bottle I used for a bobber when we went fishing at Green's lake. A black bass pulled that bottle away under the water!"

Then the mother thought that to destroy these historical relics would be to obliterate pleasant memories.

WISE AND OTHERWISE.

"Gallagher is bound to find a wife."
"What has he done?"
"Started a chain-letter proposal."

"Well," said the war board examiner, "what have you to say about the beef?" "Oh, it satisfied me," replied the high private. "I am a vegetarian, you know."

"Mamma, honest, it wasn't me eat up all that cake—it was Bobby."
"Well, Dick, bring me the cathodal kodak and I'll see at once which of you is guilty."

Mr. Grownes—"In addition to this painful boil I believe I am in for an attack of the toothache."
Mrs. Grownes—"Oh, how nice to have your troubles all at once!"

"So," said Mr. Donegad, "they's been printing the funeral notices av a man that wasn't dead yit. It's a nice fix he'd be in if he had been wan o' these people that believe iverything in the newspapers!"

"Statisticians say that married men live longer than single men," she suggested.
"Of course they do," he replied. "They're tougher, you know, for they're kept in training all the time."

"This can't be an expensive present which Mr. Dinsmore has sent me, mamma," remarked the fair young girl.
"How do you know?"
"He has taken off the price mark."

A four years old little boy recently complained that his teeth had "trod on his tongue."

Dora (to grandpa, in a distributed predicament after a fall on the sidewalk)—"There, grandpa dear, pray don't move till Nora takes a snap shot at you with her camera!"

Old Gentleman (dictating an indignant letter)—Sir: My stenographer, being a lady, cannot take down what I think of you. I, being a gentleman, cannot think it; but you being neither, can easily guess my thoughts.

The German Fire Department—"I have the honor to announce, captain that the fire is in the fourth story, and our ladders and hose will reach only to the second."
"Indeed! Then we'll have to wait till the fire gets down to the second!"

As a brick fell from a carrier's hod it knocked down a Spanish flag displayed from a store front below. "That must have been a American brick," said a passer-by. "Yis," said the hod-carrier above; "but it was of Orish descint."

Old Gentleman (putting a few questions)—"Now, boys—ah—can you tell me what commandment Adam broke when he took the forbidden fruit?"
Small Scholar (like a shot)—"Please, sir, th' warn't no commandments then, sir!"

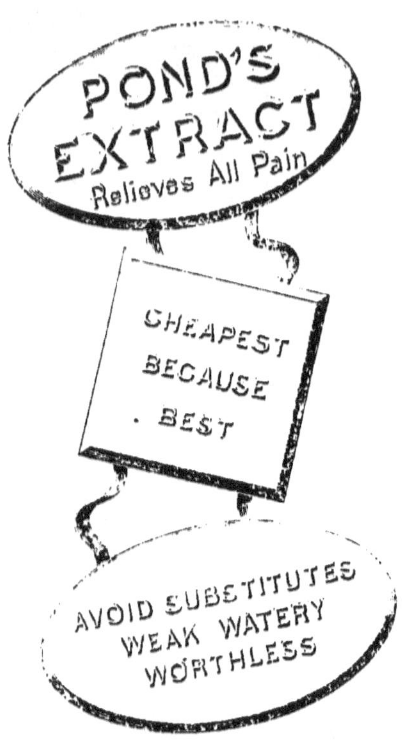

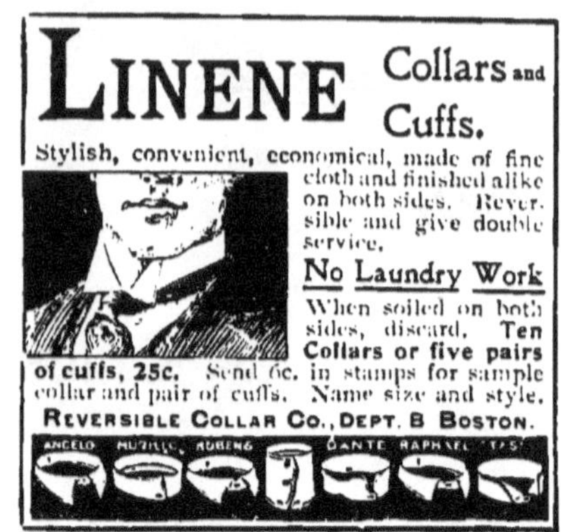

SUMMER HOMES

IN the Southern Berkshire and Litchfield Hills, along the Central New England Railway.

If you are going to the country don't fail to procure our handsomely illustrated guide-book of 240 pages, free at Jacobs' ticket office, 815 Main St., Gridley's ticket office, 18 State St., or will be mailed upon receipt of 7 cents postage to W. J. MARTIN, General Passenger Agent, Hartford, Conn.

TALKS AND TALES.

A MAGAZINE

—PUBLISHED BY—

The Conn. Institute and Industrial Home for the Blind,

Nos. 334 and 336 Wethersfield Ave.,

HARTFORD, CONN.

F. E. CLEAVELAND, President.

Edited by Mrs. ELLA B. KENDRICK.

One Dollar a Year,   -   -   Ten Cents a Copy

PRESS OF
THE CONN. INSTITUTE AND INDUSTRIAL HOME
FOR THE BLIND.

Table of Contents.

The Connecticut Mutual

Life Insurance Company
1846--1899.

To those who desire to do fully, at its least cost and to the utmost of their financial ability, their duty to their families, and to use life insurance for their protection and not for a speculation for themselves, THE CONNECTICUT MUTUAL offers the utmost that life insurance can accomplish, in its simplest, clearest forms, of perfect equity and perfect mutuality, on the soundest basis of any, and at a lower cost than has been achieved by any other company. Greater service can no life insurance company render.

BUTTERMILK FALLS, NORFOLK, CONN.

VIRGINIA D. YOUNG.

ONE day we passed from Italy into Switzerland, and spent a whole day journeying among the lakes and mountains; a day I never shall forget for the visions of beauty and gradeur it left stored in the picture galleries of memory. We had been to Milan, and studied that poem in stone, its grand cathedral. From the dizzy height of its pinnacled towers we had looked down on the rich Lombard plain, and seen the Apennines and Alps; and fancied we had singled out the rugged face of the Matterhorn, his frosty prow glittering in the sunbeams. Descending to the crypts a priest had shown the mummy of St. Carlo Borromeo, the Cardinal who gave his life and fortune to the plague-stricken sufferers of his native city. We had promenaded in the superb arcade built by Victor Immanuel; been introduced to the American consul, and driven out to the cemetery with its cremation temple, where the practice of incinerating the dead is slowly coming into fashion. And now, in the fresh and fragrant morning, we were enroute for Lucerne, to reach which we must penetrate the Italian lakes and the Swiss Alps.

The Doctor and I were fortunate in getting seated in a small compartment at the front, which by its crescent shape and windows all round enabled us to observe the scenery to right and left, and ahead of us. Thus we saw the sweet lake of Como, a bit of the sky set in the green earth of the Piedmontese hills. Lake Orta next, and then the lake of Iseo, with its serpentine windings among groves of mulberries and figs and garden of roses. Next the lakes of Maggiore and Lugano dimpled under the laughing skies, their shores alive with quaint old villages and modern hotels to accommodate the new world of tourists, and still the crumbling old castles, occasionally appeared on the heights. In this lake region we saw extensive vineyards, the vines being trained to tall poles and much resembling our seewee beans in the manner of growing. We seemed to play hide and seek with the lovely lakes, flashing upon one round a mountain curve, losing it in a tunnel, coming in sight of it again as we crossed a valley, or looking down on it from another height. And then we got among the mountains in earnest, great upheavals of earth and stone, vast and rising skyward, till we could scarce tell the snowy summits from the white wisps of clouds with which they mingled.

And now we no longer saw the lakes, but the mountain streams that fed them. These appeared sometimes as slender streaks of silver where they tumbled down the seamy sides of the mountains, or fell headlong, with the white smoke of vapor; then we would be in raptures with the rainbows of a cascade, glittering over the black rocks, or our track lay beside shallow mountain brooks, easily changing to dangerous floods in the thawing season. Among these glorious shapes of earth, which most do demonstrate the mighty mouldings of the master hand, the habitations of men are few and far between but here and there in the valleys, or on some jutting shelf of the mountains, we would see the stone cottage of a peasant and however rude it was, it showed the features of the gambrell roof, projecting over the eaves of the house, and the covered gallery that mark the abodes of the Swiss.

At last we were in the St. Gothard Pass, and our railway lamps shone out as we passed into the blackness of the tunnel; up still we crept to the Ober-alp, and then we came into a sweet table-land-like country of gentle rolling hills, and, set amidst the growing wheat, Swiss farm houses, with rows of beehives beside the currant bushes, tall poplar trees and little plats of homely blossoms, stock gilly flowers, sweet peas, hollyhocks and honeysuckles. It was restful after the exaltation of the mountains, this calm and peaceful thrift of country homes, with many browsing cattle of a smoky mole color. These cows had small heads and evidently yielded much milk, and I never saw a poor one among them, which accounted for the excellence of the Swiss butter. As for the Swiss honey, there is "none like it anywhere in the world," was the verdict of our party. It even excels the "poplar honey" of Mississippi.

I was getting tired as the afternoon waned and hoped Lucerne might be a simple village and our hostelry a place like some of those attractive farmhouses where the daughters would wait upon us after the manner of pretty Anneite Vedchen of "Anne of Geirstein memory;" but as we drew near and the lordly Arsenal appeared, crowning a hill, I perceived the indications of a city, though they call it a small town, of 17,000 inhabitants. The beauty of the place, however, swiftly swallowed up every other impression, and, as for me, I could not keep my eyes off Mount Pilatus, that great eminence of the huge congregation of mountains assembled about Lucerne. You remember

Sir Walter Scott's legend concerning it? That here Pontius Pilate terminated his wicked life, in his despair plunging into the lake at the summit, whence to this day his vexed spirit can be seen to emerge and go through the action of washing his hands? For us no premonitions of "storm in thick mists" appeared, but instead the brightness of sunset illumined the outline of the great lavender-tinted Pilatus, at the foot 'of which the Alpine flower of a city unfolds its beauteous shape.

Turning our backs on this Old World "Stone Mountain," we could see the Righi and its railway, like a little black bug might look to a person in the street, who faintly discerns the minute creature creeping up the white altitude of the Washington monument. But in the nearer foreground spreads out Lake Lúcerne bedight with pleasure boats and gay steamers. The natives call it "Vierwaldstatter sea," or Lake of the Four Forest Cantons. Strolling toward the pier we followed the crowd till we came to the Schweizerhof Quay; which is a most delightful promenade, constructed by the company owning the hotel of that name, said to be the finest in Europe. Beautiful shade trees, with seats underneath, a band of music and an outlook on the lake and Pilatus attract thousands of pleasure seekers to this delicious spot. Here it seemed a cornucopia of delights had been emptied—the God-built mountains encircling the town, the heaven-reflecting lake at its feet, its quaint old curios in the shape of the oddest of bridges. Not once but many times the Doctor and I walked over the Muhleroruche bridge, studying the singular old paintings on the triangular boards of its roof, representing the Dance of Death. Here the court of the king, the castle of the noble, the hut of the peasant were alike haunted by the inevitable figure of Death, with his reap hook, ready to cut down. And then there was the other and longer bridges, the Kapellbruche, with pictures of incidents in the lives of Saints. Joined to this bridge is the ancient Water Tower, or light house, from which "Lucerne," is said to have been named. As we reached the end of this bridge we stopped to look at a great cartoon painted on the outer wall of the Stiftskirche representing the Good Shepherd with the recovered lamb in his arms. This oddity of painting pictures on outer walls we also observed on the town Hall, up in the old part of Lucerne. We liked to stroll by the banks of the river Reuss and feed the swans, pets of the town council, I suppose, and we enjoyed getting fresh fruit from the market women in the early morning. Such cherries they brought in and red currants and small pale-green grapes, that were very refreshing.

We rested a Sabbath over in Lucerne, and I recall the solemn beauty of the worship in our own familiar tongue, (conducted in one of the parlors of the Hotel D 'Angleterre), after our experiences of Catholic service in the Italian cathedrals. There is nothing, I think, the people of Lucerne value more than their "Lion Monument." In going to see it we walked a considerable distance into a kind of park, and there we beheld on a great rock which forms the inner face of a cliff, the form of a dying lion, carved in the stone by Thorweldsen, the sculptor. The lion, stretched in the death agony, has a look of appealing pain, but heroic endurance in his eyes. You see the broken hilt of the bayonet in his side, but in expiring his mighty paw still holds fast to the lilies—the Fleur de Lis of France—on the shield. The magnificent sculpture commemorates the massacre of the Swiss Guards in defending Queen Marie Antoinette at the Tuilleries in 1792. In the basin or lakelet at the foot of the rock, large black and white swans, with scarlet beaks, sail round and dive for the bits of bread thrown them by visitors.

Returning to our hotel by the Kapellbruche, we stopped to buy souvenirs of the old woman who kept a shop near the entrance. I think we saw women at work in all the trades and avocations we are accustomed to consider peculiar to men at home　I recollect seeing one in charge of the gate on revolving bars by which people are kept off the railroad track when trains are in motion anywhere near. It would be easy enough to skip across one would think, but even the possibilities of danger are guarded against in Europe with a care for human life which we would do well to emulate in America. As I afterwards did in Scotland, so here in Lucerne, I conceived an admiration for the noble dogs, which looked as deeply immersed in business cares as women and men. Indeed I saw one walking beside a woman the two drawing a baker's cart, and repeatedly I noticed the dogs traveling along with baskets suspended to their necks, evidently on their way to or from market.

We left Lucerne to "go up the Righi" on a sunny afternoon, boarding one of the elegant steamers, which conveyed us in an hour to Vitznau. Very charming were the green shores with their velvet swarded terraces and ribbon beds of scarlet geraniums, purple, orange and crimson flowers. For the first time in our tour our royal courier failed to get all our party off together, three of the girls, loitering over the selection of sealskin capes, being left in Lucerne without a chaperon. The ladies in charge of these wandering maidens were too exercised by the absence of their proteges to enjoy the beauties of the lake; but the errant damsels put in an appearance that night at the "Kulm," apparently none the worse for their escapade. We disembarked at Vitznau, and went aboard the queerest little train we ever saw. It was drawn by an engine that looked like a cripple, but was really supplied with a cog wheel fitting a cog track laid in the mountain railway. But ascending that immense perpendicular in a jaunting car was by no means a laughing matter.

As we rose between heaven and earth, I held my breath and could not restrain a tension of the nerves such as one feels in holding on to keep one's self from falling. And yet the glory of the outlook was something to efface all thought of self; first, the lake spread forth in all its sky-like loveliness, the little hamlet of Vitznau was a mere bird's nest among the trees on the bank, then as we rose, other lakes and the great panorama of mountains spread before us, like a mighty scroll, and presently the villages and towns became only white specks, and Lake Lucerne but a tiny silver kerchief laid on the ample lap of mother earth. But oh! we kept going higher, and as we got among the clouds I found it was best to look up if I would not be overcome with dizziness. Presently the whistle of our odd little engine evoked ten thousand echoes, and we stopped on this straight up and down line of road at a veritable station. There were three on the route, named respectively the Kurhaus, Staffel and Screeber. The final fourth was our destination, the renowned Righi Koulon. At Screeber, a Swiss maiden, who could give the "Yodel" in full strength of lung offered us sprays of Edelweiss from a basket full, gentlemen and ladies alike putting these pretty souvenirs in their caps. The maidens called her snow flowers "Idilwice." At 4:30 p. m. we landed at the foot of the long flight of steps leading to the Kulm and arriving at this palatial inn were speedily given rooms, handsomely furnished with all the most modern conveniences. We had plenty of time to walk about the beautiful terraces, gather blue bells and get views from all points of the compass before summoned to the elaborate table d'hote dinner.

Not until the shades of night descended did chilling mists and fierce blasts, sweeping about the balconies, warn us that we had invaded the realm of King Winter.

It was so cold up there that we were quite willing to leave the haunts of the "Children of the Mist" and trust ourselves again to be conveyed by our "broken-kneed engine," as Johnnie Allen called it, to a lower and softer atmosphere. We parted company with the "Cog" railway at Arth, took steamer to Zug, thence by mail to Zurich, of which fine, lively, thriving Swiss city we saw only those disappointing and provoking glimpses one gets from a car window, though we waited long enough in the station house to refresh ourselves with plates of soup. Some of us did venture to skip across the street into a big store, where we invested a few marks in small silk shawls.

We arrived at Schaffhausen in a pouring rain; entered the close carriages awaiting us, so could see very little of this quaint old town. The rain soon ceased, however, and, with carriage curtains rolled up, our eyes were gladdened with the sight of the "Blue Rhine," moving majestically to precipitate itself in those magnificent "falls" we had come so far to behold. How cool and sweet was the air, how quaint the houses fronting on the country road we passed over going from Schaffhausen to Nienhausen, where we were to be lodged at the splendid "Schweizerhoff." This fine hostelry, as well as the "Bellevue," faced the far-famed river, but our road turned off and approached the grounds on the other side. Everything here was on a scale of grandeur. We skirted high brick walls, and at length passed through a castellated gateway, then through an enclosure, whose trees, shrubbery and flower beds were evidently selected and arranged by a landscape gardener of first-class talent.

A new feature in our experience was our being taken in charge by a group of Swiss waitresses and shown to our rooms. These wore the national costume, short black skirts, showing the neat buskined feet. The apron of silk or velvet or woolen cloth, is an invariable part of this costume and is trimmed with lace, braid or embroidery as the wearer can afford. Above the laced bodice appears the white linen chemisette, and stiffly-starched white linen sleeves are fastened at the shoulders by pins or buttons, but the sleeves are not sewed in. Every Swiss maid wears the national ornament, consisting of a long silver or imitation silver chain, which passes over each shoulder and hangs down in a point at the back, and two ends in front. Some of these chains were in the shape of coins interlinked, some of a white metal, probably aluminum, shaped like roses. These shining ornaments on the black bodice were decidedly picturesque.

We were much pleased with our pretty attendants, whose agreeable tones gave music to the foreign tongue and whose Swiss independence imparted to their manners an attitude of obligingness, not servility. What a need would be supplied in our part of the country if a similar class of intelligent, self-respecting white girls would consent to enter domestic service instead of resorting to other ways of support, which do not pay near such good wages or furnish such healthful employment as housework.

It began to rain again soon after our arrival, so we could not go out in boats on the river or adopt that apparently perilous mode of getting up to the falls. A great rock divides the falls, and some tourists venture to it in a boat and climb the rock amid the spray and war of the great whirlpool. The "Illumination of the Falls of the Rhine" was down on the programme of our itinerary, but I was too sleepy to sit up till nearly midnight to see it. Those of our party who had seen Niagara instituted laughing comparisons between the insignificance of the German cataract and the mighty marvel of our Western hemisphere; but say what we will of the greater grandeur of our's, the European wonders have a back ground of history, which imparts a fascination wanting in the magnificent phenomena of the New World. Next morning sitting in the hotel terrace inhaling the fragrance of tube roses we "realized" the sublimity of the leaping, rushing, foaming waters to our heart's content.

This region had always had a witchery for my imagination; perhaps from its connection with German stories and legends I had read. To be actually in the midst of it, therefore, was a delight as keen as breathing the air of Scotch lakes or Alpine heights, or basking on the waterways of Venice. My eyes presently told me the origin of the name, for the mighty mountains that rose on all sides wore armor of black rock and the tremendous forests that shut out its sun were of firs, spruces, and hemlocks, short-leaved pines and funereal cedars, whose dark greens so near approach to black as to give rise readily enough to the name Black Forest.

Our first stoppage was for the engine to get water, and our coach was on a shelf of a mountain shoulder, from which we looked down on a primitive village. Oh, how quaintly beautiful the cluster of houses in the hollow, with long slanting roofs; the walls a strange interlacing of crossbeams, filled in with stucco, a species of building material hard as stone. The steeple of the church in the centre of the village was covered with blue tiles, pieced like mosaic. "Peterzell Konigfelder," as the place was called, had a clock tower, which might have done duty in Faust's day. Looking down from my window a stone's throw beneath the garden of a cottager in which an old peasant woman in a blue skirt, with a red handkerchief over her head, was at work among the Irish potatoes. She merely glanced up at the train and its strange faces, and continued her hoeing as placidly as if a thought of America had never entered her brain. As we went on we noticed fields of scarlet summer beans trained to tall stakes. It was hay time and everywhere we saw the women at work, scarcely ever any men, sometimes boys. But Oh, the women! How they toiled, mowed, raked, pitched hay; loaded and unloaded the hay and drove the oxen. The ladies of our party marked this and were much stirred up by it. We interviewed Mr. Dosse, our courier, who, though a naturalized Englishman, now gave us to understand that he had "been a subject of the German Emperor, served in his armies and was a son of Faderland."

Mr. Dosse explained that "the army took away all the men. They are enlisted at seventeen and serve till forty-five. This time is divided between service in the ranks and in the landsturm, which latter is subject especially to imperial orders. No man is exempt from military duty, except he is physically incapable of bearing arms, which, of course, would keep him from laboring in the field." Said Mr. Dosse, "they get so addicted to idling and drinking in the army that when they come out they won't work any more."

Thus the women, sadly submissive, hard handed, go on with the ploughing and harrowing and harvesting and hauling, and the backs are bent and the forms and features aged by unintermitting labor. The people were religious, for all along our route through the Black Forest we saw crosses at intervals set up among the black rocks, bearing the figure of Christ in stucco. Each shrine had its shelter, reminding me of one of Hans Christian Andersen's stories.

We passed through fifty tunnels, twenty of them in rapid succession, emerging from the black abysses to catch glimpses of bright peaks, tremendous gorges, gloomy hemlock thickets and occasional vivid green cultivated spots. A strange sight in these primeval fastnesses was the smoke of a factory; but we saw it work converting the iron of the hills into tools for subduing nature.

I remember noticing on the white, perfect roadway of the country several wagons drawn by milk cows, driven by women, conveying a singular kind of black brick, or coal pressed into the shape of brick, to the railroad depot.

In the Black Forest are many ruins of former baronial strongholds, round the mouldering towers of which the ivy luxuriates, drawing its life from decay. "Marbach Villengen" had for us the spectacle of a Medieval cathedral, so close to our track we could see the color of the eyes of the black-robed sisters as they walked in procession towards it. This is a region rich in legendary lore. There is the story of its dead lake, the "Mummelsee," the Wildsee, whose water nympth drives him to madness who looks upon her beauty.

Ebersteinberg is a great rock overlooking Baden-Baben, whence the Knight of Eberstein made a fearful leap, which, however, led to safety.

And there is the Fromersberg, where the hermits of old days lived their life of abstinence, descending to the lower world to succor the perishing.

After the most exciting wizardry of a romance writer one can descend to the commonplaceness of eating; so we, after the stirring sublimities of that glorious journeying were glad to get to Baden-Baden, and refresh ourselves with lunch, corresponding in time to our dinner hour at home.

The name comes from the German bad, or bath, and is not at all a bad place on the surface, which was all we saw of it. I suppose the gambling goes on, but it was an invisible evil to us. We found it a pretty city and enjoyed the open-air-concert in the Casino garden. There were crowds of people there promenading or sitting listening to the band play.

In our before-breakfast peregrinations we came by accident in the "Trink Halle, Conversation House and Bath House," where the medicinal waters of Baden are dispensed by the glass and all kinds of baths are furnished at stated prices.

Baden abounds in beautiful walks and drives and has a large floating population of health and pleasure-seekers. They say "if you will only stay long enough you can see every celebrity in Europe." It is claimed that 40,000 foreigners come here yearly to "lounge, to gamble, to enjoy the mild climate, and lastly to drink the mineral waters."

The next stage of our journey brought us to the great university town, the flocking point of pilgrims to the shrine of Pallas from all over Europe and America. It was only necessary to walk across the street from the station where we disembarked to the Grand Hotel, where as usual were found rooms reserved for us in obedience to the telegrams of our courier.

Far back to the twelfth century the people named their city the "Pearl of the Palatinate," which their favorite "Otto" added to his heredity dynasty of the Rhine, and made it his permanent residence. The castle of Heidelberg, whose extensive and magnificent views so fascinate the traveler, was built on the "Gaisberg," not so high up as the original castle or fort, the site of which is shown in the Koenigstuhl (2,coo feet above the sea.) Right on top is the lookout tower. A wire rope railway enables one to ascend. Frederick, "the victorious," enlarged the castle and beautified it for his spouse, Clara Tott, a humble maiden whom he had married. This building was destroyed by lightning in 1537. The most beautiful part of the castle was built by Otto Henry, whose name it still bears, a liberal, noble monarch, who introduced the reformation.

Louis XIV, of France, entered the Palatinate in 1688 and on being forced to evacuate had all objects of value taken from the castle and the thick tower blasted by mines. We saw the enormous mass that was thus overthrown, now filling a great ravine. That part of the castle called the "Elizabeth building" was erected by the Elector Frederick V; as the residence of his consort, Elizabeth of England, daughter of James I, or as the Germans called him, Jacob I. She is called Elizabeth, Queen of Bohemia, and it is through her the house of Hanover and Queen Victoria claimed heirship to the throne of England. Of course we went first to the castle, our party filling quite a long procession of carriages. The ascent by pleasant gradations was full of interest. We left our carriages at the outer gateway and entered the beautiful court. It looked here as if the castle were quite fit for habitation and indeed, a portion is occupied by the keeper's family.

Mr. Dosse delivered us to a lady guide, the first woman who had filled that office for us, but she proved most painstaking and satisfactory. For hours she was showing us over the immense buildings. Some parts of the castle are in wonderful good repair. About a hundred years ago the people aroused to the value of their ruins and since then much money and care have been expended in their preservation.

From the ".Gluckru Thrum," or great tower, we enjoyed a view of perfect and peaceful beauty—the town of Heidelberg, lying along its silver river, the Neckar, and the heights of the Black Forest in the distance. The renaissance part of the castle is built of red sandstone and the carvings and adornments are very profuse. We were shown the "Great Tun" or wine cask of the old guzzling electors, who exacted tribute from their subjects to fill this vast receptacle, 40,000 gallons being the quantity. The orgies of those days gave rise to the hereditary appetite of the present subjects of

Emperor William for beer drinking, which have reached such lengths as to force upon him the need of some kind of prohibitory enactments.

We found the royal banqueting hall odorous with cedar boughs and gay with banners, mute testimony to a recent festival of students. Students indeed enter into all the life of Heidelberg, and you encounter their schlager-slashed faces at every turn. For alas! these poor fellows labor under the hallucination that duelling is a test of manhood, honor, and are always slashing one another, we are told. Our next point of interest was the university.

It is built on the site of the Augustine monastery, where Luther defended his doctrines before priests, students and people. The exterior is quite plain, but it is artistically ornamented in its great hall with paintings and sculptures. There are portraits of Ruprecht I; the founder of the University, and "Karl Freidrich," who restored it after its almost complete destruction by the French and Austrians. At that time it took the name of the "Ruperta Cavola," in honor of its benefactors, Ruprecht and Karl.

In 1485 the first book was printed at Heidelburg, which may account for the manifest leaning to learning of this city of schools. Its university library contains 380,000 volumes, 165,000 pamphlets in print and besides this in handwriting 3,334 codices, 2,495 deeds and 2,512 charters. Among its precious things are tenth century manuscripts, a splendid missal, with costly miniatures, and its latest most valued relic is the manuscript of Manesse, bought by Emperor Frederick III of France for 360,000 marks and presented by him to the University of Heidelburg. We enjoyed some lovely walks and drives while in the town. One of the latter was crossing the Neckar. We drove through the Hauptstrasse under the triumphal arch called "Karlsthor," or Charles's gate, in honor of the elector, Karl Theodor, whose statue we also were shown on the old bridge with nine arches. At the other end is a statue of Minerou. We returned by way of the new bridge.

The "Peters Church," as they singularly call it, is the oldest in Heidel-burg; said to have been built by Charlemagne in the eighth century—that is, the original Peters Church, but the one we now see is a work of the year 1485. Behind the old Church we walked down the Grabengasse to the old nunnery now a public school for girls. Near the market place we saw the "Haus Zum Ritter," the only private dwellings that escaped when the French burned the town in 1693. Just opposite is the Holy Ghost Church, a beautiful gothic building. It has wonderful glass paintings, and its groups of red sandstone columns are very handsome and unique. In the centre of the market platz is a fountain with a "Mary column" and the following inscription: "Non statuam aut saxum sad quam designat honore." Translated into English this means: "We do not honor the stone, nor the image, nor the column, but the mother with her child."—[*Sunday News.*

ALVIRA'S LOVE STORY.

DOROTHY E. NELSON.

IT was two o'clock on a hot summer afternoon. Little languid breezes touched the tops of the grasses that fringed the roadside, or moved a few leaves here and there on the maples, but that was all. The sun, beating down on the white picket fence, seemed to draw dazzling lines out into the air. The flowers in the narrow garden beds on each side of the path were dull and drooping. The shrill, ceaseless whirring of the cicadæ seemed like the voice of the heat.

A woman walked down the path; she was large and stout, and her skirts brushed the drooping flowers all the way. She pushed open the door, and stood on the threshold a moment till her eyes could become accustomed to the change from the quivering brightness outside.

"For the land's sake, Alvirey !" she exclaimed, "I sh'd think you might as well be sewing in a cellar—all that black stuff, too !"

Two women were at the windows sewing. A table covered with a mass of alpaca stood in the space between the windows, and both the women had pieces of the work in their hands. Miss Alvirey was pulling out bastings and rolling them into a little wad of thread which she put into her mouth. Her pronunciation was somewhat less distinct than usual, but her dignity was unimpaired by such trifles.

"I guess my eyes is good for some time to come, Mis' Corbin," she answered stiffly. "Set down, an' I'll have this ready to try on. There's a fan on the stand."

Mrs. Corbin found the fan and plied it vigorously, her rosy face seeming to come and go in flashes behind the big palm-leaf.

"Lor', Alvirey, you needn't be so touchy," she said, good-naturedly. "It's powerful warm to-day, and I ain't in any sech a hurry. Lay it by till it's cooler. Jessie, there, is lookin' as white as a ghost."

The girl at the window cast a half-frightened glance at Miss Alvirey.

"Oh, I'm all right," she said slowly,

"I guess she is," snapped Miss Alvirey, pulling out the bastings with a jerk. "She ain't worked hard enough to hurt a fly to-day. Young folks didn't used to think themselves so dredful delicate."

"Sho' now," said Mrs. Corbin, comfortably, "you ain't no need to get in sech a stew, Alvirey. I said it was too hot for both of you; but land, you never was one to give up."

Miss Alvirey worked harder than ever. Her whole figure, with its patient, pathetic droop, made one think of the drooping flowers outside.

Miss Alvirey rose and shook the threads off her dress.

"Now, Mis' Corbin," she said, briefly.

Mrs. Corbin rose stiffly, and put on the black skirt. Miss Alvirey eyed it critically.

"Turn 'round slowly," she said, "There, no, a little farther to the right! I thought so. You are getting to lean to the right, Mis' Corbin."

But Mrs. Corbin's good humor was untouched.

"Mercy sakes, Alvirey!" she said, with a loud, cheery laugh, "when a body gets as old as I be she's bound to lean somewhere. Might as well be to the right as anywhere else."

Miss Alvira had her mouth full of pins, and was kneeling on the floor, pinning up the hem.

"There," she said, presently, "I guess that will do. I'll have it done Thursday, Mis' Corbin."

"Now, don't hurry," begged Mrs. Corbin. "I'd a sight rather wait than have you and Jessie work yourselves to death over it this weather. I ain't in a mite of a hurry."

"When I say a thing will be done I calculate to have it done," replied Miss Alvira, severely. "Weather don't make no difference. I hope you won't get het up going home, Mis' Corbin. Take the fan along if you've a mind to."

"I dunno's I'm so warm as all that," she said, with an attempt at dignity. "Be sure you don't get that dress binding across the shoulders, Alvirey. The last one was. I always felt if 'twas hitching up somewhere. Good-by, Jessie," and she closed the door with mild emphasis.

Miss Alvira had scarcely noticed her. She waited until she was out of hearing, and then went over to Jessie and took the work out of her hands.

"Why didn't you tell me you wa'n't feeling well?" she said. "You're as white as a sheet. I'll do this, and you go lie down. Better stay to supper, and then you can go home in the cool of the evening."

"I ain't so tired," she said, "and I must go home at five o'clock."

"Must? There ain't no 'must' about it. You've got to stay."

"I can't, Miss Alvirey. It's real kind of you, but I can't," the girl repeated with a kind of helpless obstinacy.

"I'd like to know why not."

A faint rose color crept into the pale cheeks and the long lashes drooped over the gray eyes.

"I promised George I'd be ready at five, and he was going to stop for me," she said, slowly.

Miss Alvira stood and looked at her a moment in silence, and a fierce pain seemed to beat through her breast. The girl was so beautiful! She had always envied her her beauty, and now she had a lover—young and beautiful, and had a lover. To the little, thin, plain dressmaker with only a bare, hard girlhood behind her, and only years of bare, lonely life before her, this girl seemed the embodiment of all that should have been hers and never was. She felt for one fierce moment as if she almost hated her. A strange, frightened look came into her eyes as she recognized the feeling. She forced herself to speak quietly.

"You go lie down," she said; "I'll wake you in time."

"If you really can spare me," she said in a bewildered way.

"Spare you," said Miss Alvira, scornfully. "I could do in an hour all you've done to-day. You do as I tell you."

The girl obeyed without a word. She lay down on the old haircloth sofa on the other side of the room. Miss Alvira brought a pillow from the bedroom and awkwardly tried to fix it under her head; and then she sat down by the window and began sewing. She sat very stiff and straight, and her stitches were firm and even. Jeesie, lying passively on the sofa and watching the prim little figure with its uncompromising, almost defiant air, closed her eyes wearily. It tired her to watch her. In a few minutes the girl was fast asleep.

Miss Alvira put aside her sewing, quilting her needle neatly in the work. and then went over to the sofa and stood looking down at the girl. She was more beautiful than ever in her sleep, for one saw only the witchery of the exquisite curves of lashes and cheeks and chin, and the delicate beauty of her coloring, and did not feel the lack of expression. Miss Alvira stood for a long time studying it all. Then she turned away with a sort of a groan.

She went back to her place by the window, but she did not take up her sewing. Then the sun had slipped farther to the west, and a cool, gray shadow was creeping over the tiny yard. The fence was no longer dazzling white. A tiny breeze had sprung up, and was lifting the head of a flower here and there. Miss Alvira folded her hands and sat up straighter than ever. She was going to fight this thing out.

"It's George Harkins she means," she said. "He's a likely young fellow; he'll be real good to her, I guess, and she'll have an easy life of it and grow prettier and happier every day. And here's me, jest living here in this little box of a place, making the covering for other folks' lives and havin' no life of my own. It's all so narrow and scrimpy; I allus did hate working in a pint pot. My very name sounds like snippings—nothing new and fresh." Suddenly she sat up straighter and spoke louder, as if to some invisible opponent. "Look here, Alvirey Simpkins—what are you going to do about it? Do you suppose moping around and wishing you were young again, and had other people's big eyes and black hair, is going to make things any better? And what would you do with a man tagging round all the time, I'd like to know? 'Twould fret you to death, and you know it. Ain't you a heap better off earning your own living in your own way and not being beholden to nobody? You know you are." Her voice changed from its fierce contempt, and there was a pleading tone in it no one had ever heard; she would not have recognized it herself. "But it's the loneliness of it," she said, "nights and rainy days, and times when the wind is howling across the sward, and not a soul comes in, and there's nothing but the clock ticking, till it seems as if I should go wild. And I can't stop it, neither. I tried it once, and it was so still it scared me. I never could bear to have a cat under foot, even if it would be company. I wanted suthin' human and understanding. It doesn't seem's if that was so wicked."

The wistfulness in her tone crept into her figure; there was something humble and pleading in her whole attitude. It was only for a second, however; then she straightened up and spoke in her old quick, scornful manner.

"Well. I didn't think you was such a poor, meeching thing as that, Alvirey Simpkins. Ain't people ever lived alone before you, I want to know? And besides," changing to a grave seriousness, "I s'pose, someways; there isn't love enough to go round. Can't you stand it better than a pretty, useless little thing like that?"

The summer days passed as if in a dream after that. There was an unreality about them that confused and abashed Miss Alvira, who had been used to dealing with plain facts, and facts alone; but she had never in her life been so happy as she was in that summer romance. Her very face changed under its touch. The neighbors could not understand, but they all spoke of it, and said how well Alvirey was looking.

After that night Jessie told her everything. The girl was scarcely more than a child, and had to tell some one, and she could have had no better or safer confidant.

It was a strange friendship, truly, but night after night Miss Alvira would watch the two walk away together, and then would sit through the dusk and far into the dark, thinking over all Jessie had told her during the day, and living the love-life she had never had, in the life of this girl.

She thought and worried about it far more than Jessie. If George was late she was the anxious one; if any quarrel had happened between the lovers she would have suffered twice as intensely as Jessie. But nothing did happen, and the summer deepened and deepened, and one day Jessie said she was to be married in September.

Then a tidal wave of excitement swept over Miss Alvira. The wedding must be nice, and there was so much to do. Nobody but she should put a stitch in the wedding dress. She lay awake a whole night planning it out. She knew well that Jessie would make no objections. The girl was an orphan with only one little sister; there was no one to care for her or plan for her, and she was to impassive to plan for herself.

"There's the money I was laying by for a black silk," thought Miss Alvira; "that will jest do it. But land sakes, I shall want the silk to go to the wedding in! Well—" after a sharp thought, "I can't pay for both, and I rather guess the wedding dress is more important. I can fix over my old silk again, and Jessie's shall be the prettiest I can get."

She told the girl the next morning, and Jessie received the gift in her usual quiet way. It never occurred to her to wonder where Miss Alvira got the money; she was only placidly happy that she could have a pretty dress, and roused into rather unusual animation when the work on it was fairly begun.

One day Jessie brought her little sister—a grave little thing, with big, serious black eyes. She took a strong fancy to Miss Alvira, and it grew to be the habit for her to come every day with Jessie and sit quietly on a stool between the two, fashioning tiny doll dresses from the pieces Miss Alvira gave her, while they worked on Jessie's wedding clothes.

And so the summer slipped away and September came, and in two weeks Jessie was to be married. One morning Miss Alvira heard her knock at the door earlier than usual. She hurried to open it; she was anxious to tell Jessie about the trimming for the bottom of the skirt; she had decided in the night that rose quilling would be the best; she had a scrap of the wedding dress in her hand as she opened the door.

Jessie was leaning against the house, looking down the garden path. The childish lips were quivering, and the pretty gray eyes red and swollen. She had evidently been crying all the way over.

"Jessie, what is the matter?" she cried, quite sharply.

"It's all over." she said, mechanically.

"Jessie Parker, what do you mean? Come in and tell me about it."

"It's all over." she repeated, in the same dull fashion.

"Jessie, look at me!" she commanded, sternly.

'Now tell me what is the matter."

Jessie began to cry hopelessly.

"George says he isn't going to be bothered with Dolly, and I can't leave her alone, and there isn't any one to take her."

"Make you leave your own sister!" she cried.

"Oh, she isn't my own sister!" said Jessie, wearily. "She's only my step-sister. I'd leave her if I could, but I can't."

A sudden thought came to Miss Alvira. Was it—could it be possible that there was love in the world that nobody wanted? Love that she could take and have for her own, with no other claim upon it? She was fairly trembling, and had to cling to a chair before she could speak.

"Jessie, are you sure you would be willing to give her up?"

The girl looked at her in surprise.

"Why, I'd give her to anybody, if I could," she answered. The possibility of caring for the child's love never entered her mind.

Miss Alvira's cheeks were flushing and then paling, and she spoke with a strange effort.

"Jessie, will you give her to me?"

Even Jessie was roused then to a faint protest.

"Why, Miss Alvirey, you don't want her—she'll be such a care!"

But there was an undertone of hope in the girl's voice, and Miss Alvira drew a long breath and sat down in one of the hard, cane-seated chairs as if she were very tired. She picked up a piece of Jessie wedding dress.

"I thought we'd make this with the rose quilling, after all," she said,

.   .   .   .   .   .

Jessie's wedding day was clear and bright. Miss Alvira went over very early in the morning for her and Dolly. All Dolly's clothes had been brought over the day before, and it had given the little dressmaker exquisite pleasure to see how few and poor they were. She dressed the child herself and then dressed Jessie, and the three went over to the little church together.

Miss Alvira had looked forward to that day for months, and yet when it came—Jessie and George, the old minister, and the familiar faces of the neighbors—all seemed like a dream. The reality was the little warm, clinging hand clasped in hers.

In the cool of the afternoon they came back and had tea at Miss Alvira's. Jessie, usually so indifferent, had insisted on that. Then at dusk she kissed the little sister good-by, and she and George walked away together, as they had done before so many times; but they all felt the difference, and knew that now she could never turn back again.

Miss Alvira and Dolly stood at the gate watching them, and then walked hand in hand down the path and back into the little room. The child was tired by the excitement of the day; she climbed up into Miss Alvira's lap, and sat looking into the twilight with her grave, dark eyes. Once she nestled sleepily and said something to herself. Miss Alvira bent down to catch the words.

"Dolly loves Miss 'Virey,' she whispered drowsily, and then the long lashes drooped on the round cheeks and she was fast asleep.

Miss Alvira sat there stiff and straight. Her arms and back ached, but she never moved. The new moon was shining overhead; there were sweet, soft whisperings in the trees, and little plays of light and shadow across the grass and in the tiny garden. The sweetness and graciousness seemed to sweep through her lonely heart and fill it full to overflowing. And then Miss Alvira knew her love-life had begun.—[*Waverly Magazine.*

"THE WORDS OF MY MOUTH."

ELLA WHEELER WILCOX.

Talk happiness. The world is sad enough
Without your woes. No path is wholly rough;
Look for the places that are smooth and clear,
And speak of those to rest the weary ear
Of earth, so hurt by one continuous strain
Of human discontent and grief and pain.

Talk faith. The world is better off without
Your uttered ignorance and morbid doubt.
If you have faith in God, or man, or self,
Say so; if not, push back upon the shelf
Of silence all your thoughts till faith shall come;
No one will grieve because your lips are dumb.

Talk health. The dreary, never-changing tale
Of mortal maladies is worn and stale.
You cannot charm, or interest, or please,
By harping on that minor chord, disease.
Say you are well, or all is well with you,
And God shall hear your words and make them true.

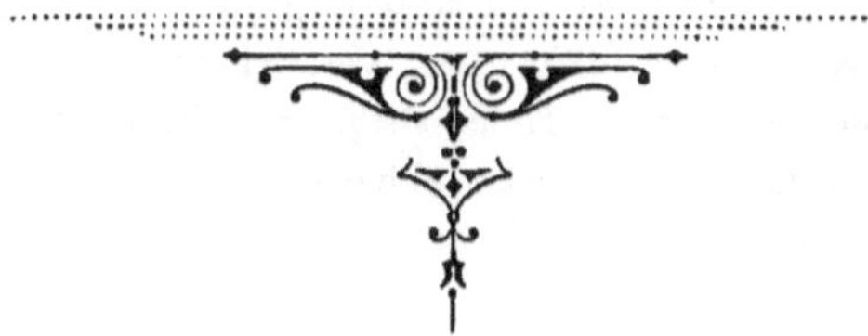

MEADOW FARM.

HELEN FORREST GRAVES.

MARY MILLER came home from the factory upon that April evening, with a light, quick step.

The sky was all jonquil glow; the frogs were croaking in the swamp; the maples were crimsoned with their earliest banners of blossom; and, as she tripped along, Mary found a tuft of violets, half hidden under a drirt of dead leaves—pale purple, scentless blooms.

"The first violets always bring good luck with them," she whispered to herself, as she pinned them into the bosom of her blue flannel gown.

"Home" was scarcely the ideal realization of that poetic word to the factory-girl. She and her mother lived in the upper half of a shabby, unpainted wooden house, with the blacksmith's scolding wife and seven riotous children down stairs, and one-half of a trampled-down back yard by way of garden, where nothing ever grew but burdocks, nettles and Mrs. Muggs' long-legged fowls.

But Mrs. Miller, who had been a school-teacher once, and still retained somewhat of the refinement of her early education, had the tea ready, with a shaded lamp and bunch of maple blossoms on the table, ready for Mary to come home.

"Good news, mother!" the girl cried, lightly. "The Meadow farm is to let! Mother, we must take it."

Mrs. Miller looked dubiously at the bright, eager face, with its blue-gray eyes and fringes of yellow hair.

"Can we afford it, daughter?" she said, slowly. "A whole house, and a farm of forty-three acres?"

"It isn't such a very large house, mother!" pleaded Mary, as she laid the bunch of violets in her mother's lap—"not so many more rooms than we have here. And we could keep two cows, and I could sell milk and butter, and spring chickens and eggs; and I am almost sure that Will Davidge would work the farm on shares. And only think, mother, how delightful it would be to have a home all to ourselves, where we couldn't hear Mrs. Muggs boxing Bobby's ears, or Helen shrieking with the toothache! And a little garden, mother, where we could have peonies and hollyhocks, and all those lovely, old-fashioned flowers that your soul delights in!"

Mrs. Miller's pale face softened. "It would be a great temptation, Molly," she said.

"It is a month now since old Mrs. Dabney died," said Mary. "And they say that her daughter in the city and her son out in California despise the old farm, with its one-story house and its old red barn. So it is to let. And so cheap, too! Only a hundred and fifty dollars a year. Mother, we must take it! I'll leave the factory and turn dairy maid. I've saved enough, you know, to buy two cows and some real Plymouth Rock fowls to begin with; and, oh, it will be such a happiness! Say yes, mother—do say yes!"

When Mary Miller pleaded like this, the gentle widow never knew how to refuse; and the upshot of it was that they leased the old Dabney house, and became co-sovereigns of the realm of Meadow farm.

It was their first night there. Overhead the young May moon shone through a veil of purple mist. A solitary owl hooted in the chestnut-wood back of the house, for Meadow farm was situated on a lonely mountain-side where no one ever came except on special business.

The Plymouth Rock chickens were safely shut up where foxes could not reach them nor minks steal in to bleed their young lives away; the cows— two fine young Alderneys—were chewing their cud back of the old red barn, and Mary Miller had flung a handful of cedar-sticks on the hearth, where their scented blaze illuminated the old kitchen with a leaping brightness beautiful to see.

"Because it's just possible that the house may be damp," she said, "after being uninhabited so long. There, mother, isn't that cheerful? And isn't it nice that our old rag-carpet should fit this floor so exactly?" with a satisfied downward glance. "And do you see those tiger-lilies? I found them down by the garden-wall—oh, such a red wilderness of them! Old Mrs. Dabney set them out herself, they say. It seems only yesterday," she added thoughtfully, "that I came past here and saw old Mrs. Dabney sitting in the big chair by the fire, just where—"

Mrs. Miller uttered a little shriek and grasped her daughter's arm. Mary stopped short, pallor overspreading her cheek. For, as she spoke, the door opposite had opened, and a very little old woman, silver-haired, and shriveled like a mummy, came in, and, walking across the floor, seated herself in Mrs. Dabney's very corner—an old woman dressed in the snuff-colored gown which Mrs. Dabney had always worn, and wearing a snuff-silk cap, while a bag depended from her arm.

"It's cold, ladies," she said, looking around with a deprecating air. "Cold for the season of the year. And they don't keep fires at Tewkstown."

"Mother," said Mary, recovering herself with an hysterical gasp of relief, "it isn't old Mrs. Dabney's ghost at all. It's old Miss Abby, come back from the Tewkstown poorhouse."

"You don't mean—" began the mild widow.

"That Mrs. Daniel Dabney and Mrs. Everard Elberson let their old aunt go to the poorhouse?" said Mary Miller. "Yes, it is quite true. Mrs. Daniel leads society in San Francisco, I am told, and Mrs. Elberson is a great lady in Bridgeport, with a reception day and servants in livery. What could they do with a half-crazy old aunt, who takes snuff and talks uncertain grammar? Poor Miss Abby! She has wandered back to her old home. She was eighty last birthday, and things are all misty and vague to her."

"But what shall we do?" said Mrs. Miller, in accents of perplexity. "A crazy woman here—it doesn't seem just right, Molly, does it?"

"I'll take her back, after she has rested a little, and had a cup of tea," said Mary, cheerily.

"But perhaps she won't go."

"Oh, yes. she will," said Mary. "Poor Miss Abby! She is as gentle as a child."

Her words proved to be correct. Miss Abby Dabney suffered herself to be led unremonstratingly back to Tewkstown poorhouse, where the matron read her a shrill-voiced lecture, and declared she should not be allowed another grain of snuff if she couldn't behave better. Old Miss Abby smiled deprecatingly.

"They are peculiar people here," she said. "I think, my dear," to Mary Miiler, "they forget sometimes I am a lady. But it takes all sorts, don't you see, to make a world."

The next night. however, just as Mary and her mother were sitting down to tea, Miss Abby once more appeared, in the midst of a gentle shower of rain.

"I hope I don't inconvenience anybody," she said, meekly. "But that woman at Tewkstown has cut off my allowance of snuff; and, after all, there's no place like home."

And once more Mary Miller patiently walked back with the poor old crone to the poorhouse. The matron was infuriated this time.

"It ain't in human natur' to stand this," she declared. "I'll put her in the jug!"

"The jug?" repeated Mary, in surprise.

"It's a room down cellar, where we shut up the troublesome cases," said the matron. "I can't stand this running-away business, and I won't!"

The jug, perhaps, proved efficacious, for old Miss Abby Dabney did not appear again for a week. At the expiration of that period, however, she crept noiselessly in, just at dusk, and seated herself like a silent shadow in the chimney corner.

"It is so good to be at home again," said she, rubbing her wrinkled hands. "I somehow seem to get lost of late. Elnathan is gone, and Betsey is gone, and I'm left here all alone. Yes, a cup of tea, please—sugar and no milk. They never remember how I like my tea at Tewkstown. This is good; and butter on my bread, too! We don't get butter to Tewkstown."

Mary burst into tears.

"Mother," said she, "Miss Abby shall not go back to Tewkstown—she shall stay here! Mother, how should I feel if you were wandering friendless and alone through the world?"

"But my dear—"

"She shall sleep in her own old room, out of the kitchen," persisted Mary. "She'll be no more care than a canary-bird. Oh, mother, do say yes! She will think then that she is still in her own home. Oh, if you knew how dreary it is at that poorhouse, with the grass all tramped out, and piles of clam-shells lying around the door, and not so much as a dandelion or a daisy to be seen!"

And Mrs. Miller yielded to Mary's tearful solicitations.

The Tewkstown authorities were but too glad to be rid of the poor old incubus; and Miss Abby Dabney settled down into her old home, as contentedly and unquestioningly as if she had never left it. She ate and drank but little; she talked still less, and seemed to regard Mrs. Miller and Mary as guests, who had come to visit the old farm.

"The Widow Miller and her darter must be rich folks, to undertake to support old Miss Abby," sneered one neighbor.

"She was well enough provided for at the poorhouse," said another.

"I never saw a farm succeed yet that was worked by women folks," jeered a third.

"There'll be the biggest kind of a smashup presently," observed number four. "And an auction sale of everything; and I'll be on hand—for I don t deny that them little Alderney cows is the cunningest creatures I ever set eyes on, and good milkers into the bargain."

But time wore on, and there was no flutter of any red flag over the porch. On the contrary, matters throve, and Mary Miller declared, joyously, that farming was a great deal more profitable business than working in the factory, and she only wished she had found it out before.

One gray, autumnal evening, Mary and her mother came back from a brisk walk to the village, and found a stalwart, sun-browned man sitting opposite to Miss Abby, by the red glow of the fire.

The old woman rose up, in an odd, uncertain way.

"Ladies," she said, fumbling in her old snuff-box, "this is my nephew, Cyrus Dubrey—he as ran away from home twenty-nine years ago come Michaelmas Day, and we all supposed was dead. Cyrus, these are the ladies who are so good as to visit me here. I don't quite recollect their names;

but then, my memory ain't as good as it used to be; and after all, it don't matter much. Nothing matters much nowadays."

And Miss Abby sat down and fell into a "daze" again, as if all necessity for conversational effort were over.

Cyrus Dubrey stood up—a bronzed, bearded giant, with dark eyes and superb stature.

"Ladies, I beg your pardon," he said, "but I s'posed when I came here I was coming home! I knew nothing of all these changes. I never could have dreamed that my cousins would let this old creature go to—the town poorhouse. I don't know who you are, ladies," with a husky sound in his throat, "but I thank you, from the very bottom of my heart, for giving her a shelter in her old age. And if money will pay you for it—"

"It will not!" said Mary, sharply, as if the words conveyed a slur.

"No, I s'posed not," said Cyrus, with a sigh. "But I've plenty of money now. The dear old aunty shall live like a queen all the rest of her days, for she was good to me when all the rest set me down for a black sheep. I've made my fortune out in Panama, and I've come home to redeem myself."

"I have heard of Cyrus Dubrey," said Mrs. Miller, gently.

"And I'll venture, ma'am, you heard no good of me," said the young giant, with a short laugh. "I'll not deny that I was a wild boy enough, but there wasn't any actual evil in me, let folks say what they would. And now I've come back a rich man, and there's nobody to bid me welcome home, except old Aunt Abby, out of the poorhouse."

He could not long have made this statement, however. All the town was up to bid the rich government contractor welcome to Tewkstown within twenty-four hours. Human nature is human nature everywhere. But Cyrus Dubrey cared little for the friendly overtures of the old neighbors.

Aunt Abby was the only person for whom he seemed to care, and his greatest grief was that the old woman refused to leave the old Dubrey farmhouse to live in the stately brick mansion which he built on Prospect Hill. And then he asked permission to deck her little bedroom with the curiosities he had brought her from the Isthmus, and in tacking up draperies and arranging shells and old silver coins he and Mary unconsciously became friends.

Friends. She never knew that it was anything else, until one day old Aunt Abby took a strange idea into her head. And Mary, holding a rich Oriental cord for Cyrus Dubrey to loop into knots for picture frames, heard her introduce Mrs. Miller to a neighbor as "my guest, Mrs. Miller, the mother of the young lady that Nephew Cyrus is going to marry."

Cyrus looked at Mary. Mary dropped the ball of cord and turned crimson.

"Mary," he whispered, piteously, "say that it shall be so. For I love you ! And—and you were good to old Aunt Abby when all the world turned against her. I sometimes think, Mary, that you must be like one of heaven's angels !"

This was how they became engaged.

They still live in the old farmhouse, the happiest of married lovers, and Aunt Abby firmly believes that they are all her guests; for to her the world stands eternally still—the world that is so full of bloom and beauty to Cyrus and Mary.—[*Selected*.

KIPLING ON THE FUTURE.

RUDYARD KIPLING.

When Earth's last picture is painted, and the tubes are twisted and dried,
When the oldest colors have faded, and the youngest critic has died,
We shall rest, and, faith, we shall need it—lie down for an aeon or two,
Till the Master of all Good Workmen shall set us to work anew !

And those that were good shall be happy: they shall sit in a golden chair;
They shall splash at a ten-league canvas with brushes of comets' hair;
They shall find real saints to draw from—Magdalene, Peter and Paul;
They shall work for an age at a sitting and never be tired at all !

And only the Master shall praise us, and only the Master shall blame;
And no one shall work for money, and no one shall work for fame;
But each for the joy of the working, and each, in his separate star,
 Shall draw the Thing as he sees it for the God of Things as They Are !

Miss Bascomb's Vacation.

ELIZABETH L. GOULD.

ONE spring, when Berryville had recovered from an epidemic of scarlet-fever, which had taken young and old impartially to bed, Hannah Bascomb decided to make a long-deferred visit to a cousin in Boston.

"I don't know as there'll ever be a better chance," said Miss Bascomb to the mother of her last patient, little Maggie Rogers. "In fact, I don't know as there'll ever be another chance, any way. 'Long about a month from now Cyrus Hobbs will begin to have his miserable spells, and I shall have to go there and 'tend right to him. Mary means well, but I'd just as soon have a three-year-old to rub me as her, and Cyrus has to be rubbed morning and night, or I don't know but he'd stiffen up into a bow-knot.

"Then I shouldn't know what to make of a spring without some of the children cut themselves in the sawmill when it get's a-going, and doctor always relies on me to be here to help him ou you know, with his surgica cases. June, or the last of May, they generally come on; so I've got to go now and get back.

"Here 'tis the first of April, and I'm about tired out. I calculate to go next Monday and come back Saturday night. Jennie says there's to be a grand parade of military on Wednesday, and I intend to put nursing right out of my mind for a good six days, any way."

"You've earned your holiday, if ever anybody did, Hannah," said Mrs. Rogers, warmly. "I only hope nobody in Berryville will be laid up or struck down whilst you're gone, for what they'd do without you to nurse 'em, I don't know!"

Miss Bascomb set out for her visit on the appointed day, but she failed to return to Berryville on the following Saturday. She gave no account of herself save by means of a postal, which announced to Mrs. Rogers, "Will be home last of next week."

That motherly person, being Miss Bascomb's nearest neighbor, watched for her coming with interest, and was at the door with Miss Hannah's key in her hand almost as soon as the rumbling old coach, which held the returned traveler, late on Friday afternoon.

Miss Hannah was laden with bundles, and was persuaded by Mrs. Rogers to "step over" and take a cup of tea with her before entering again on life in her own house.

"I don't know's I call you much rested in looks, Hannah," said the hospitable neighbor, as the two friends sat together for a sociable talk, while tea was in process of construction; "but I don't know as it's to be expected I would, for, of course, gadding about in the city is real tiresome work, though pleasant."

"I haven't gadded overly much," said Miss Bascomb, smoothing out her silk gloves, thoughtfully. "You see, I haven't had time."

"Time!" gasped her hostess "Don't you call most two weeks time?"

"I'll tell you how 'twas," said Miss Hannah, calmly. "You see, on the way down, I was real interested watching a little boy, that was with a kind of heedless woman, playing with one of those old, blunt, one-bladed knives. Near as I could make out, he was trying to carve his name on the window-ledge. Thinks I, 'If that blunt thing does happen to slip and cut him, it'll be the worst kind of a cut.'

"Sure enough, it did slip pretty soon, and jabbed his other thumb full force. I saw his mother turning kind of pale, so I stepped over and 'tended to the child. Lucky I had some old cloth and string in my bag; I always take such things, just in case of need. Well, we'd got most to Boston before I got him hushed up, and his mother over her feeling that he was going to die.

"Jennie met me at the station, and I saw in a minute she'd got an awful cold, one of the kind that had to be looked after, and she said. 'Mine ain't anything to George's, Cousin Hannah; he's sick in bed; I put him there just before I started to meet you.' So I saw I was right in the nick of time!

"Well, George's turned out to be tonsilitis—kind of a light attack, but the doctor said 'twas lucky I was on hand, and knew what to do. By Tuesday night we got him so he began to feel like himself, and nothing would do but I must go to see the parade with George's brother's folks, whilst Jennie took care of George for the next afternoon.

"George's brother had hired a first-rate window for himself and his wife and two boys, right where the parade would pass, Jennie said. They were real friendly folks, and they came the next morning, and overpersuaded me, and I went.

"Well, when we'd got our seats, and begun to watch the crowd I spied a big covered wagon drawn up right in front of the building, and I asked George's brother what that was. 'Why,' he says, 'it's an ambulance, in case there are any accidents.'

"Well, we hadn't been there long when a boy got under the feet of the policeman's horses, some way or another, and he was picked up insensible. There was another child, a girl, not much bigger'n he, that had been with him, and she began to bawl and scream. The men folks that stood round couldn't seem to quiet her, so I stepped down, and it ended in my going first to the hospital, and then home with the child to tell their grand-mother about the accident.

"I told George's brother I'd take a cab and ride back to 'em, but I didn't get there till the parade was over, so I went right on home to Jennie's. I found George's brother's folks there, and the wife says to me, 'Don't those boys look kind of feverish to you, Miss Bascomb? I suppose it's excitement; this is the first big parade they've ever seen"

"I looked at them pretty sharp, and I says, 'I believe they're coming down with the measles; you'd better take them home, and have the doctor come.'

"'Oh, dear!' says she. 'I don't know how I shall get along, for my nurse leaves to-morrow, and baby's just getting some teeth!'

"'Well, here I am,' said I. 'George don't really need me now, and I'll pack my bag, and go right over to your house.'

"And so I did. The measles came out beautifully; the boys and I were shut off in the back part of the house, and I played games with 'em, and read to 'em, and nursed 'em, what little they needed. They're going to be out in a few days, and their mother got a new nurse yesterday.

"So here I am safe and sound. My, how good that tea tastes, Mrs. Rogers!" said Miss Hannah, as she took her first sip from a steaming cup placed before her.

"I thought you were going to get away from nursing and everything of the kind when you went to Boston," said Mrs. Rogers, with a strong note of indignation in her voice.

"Lauzee! Was I foolish enough to expect that?" said Miss Hannah, easily. "Well, I guess I shan't ever get away from my duty long as I live in this world, particularly when I go a-visiting on purpose!"—[*Youth's Companion*.

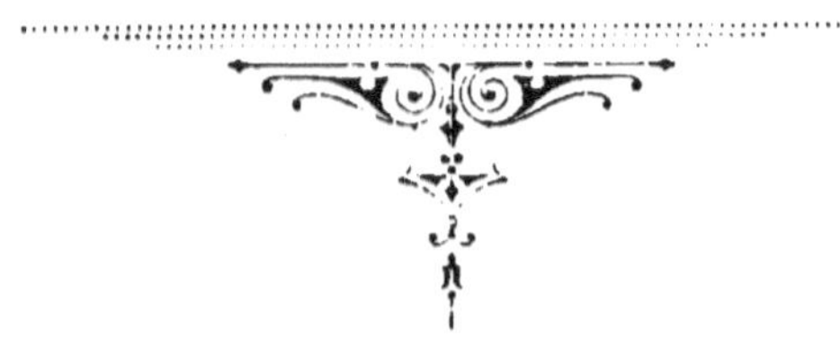

Learn to write English.

IT would be a fine thing if all our young people understoood the importance of knowing how to write good, plain, acceptable English, free
from blemishes of bad grammar and improper phraseology. There is not a
walk in life where this accomplishment does not come in good play, says
an exchange.

It is not necessary to be a rhetorician and have at one's pen all of the
metaphors, similes and synecoches of the fine writer. What is most wanted
by the ordinary person is such a command of plain, pure, direct speech that
he can write a letter without effort, setting forth what he wants to say in
such a manner that it may at once be understood by whoever reads.

It is not such a mountainous task to learn to do this, if only one goes
about it right. Some of the best letter writers are people of very ordinary
scholarship. They simply write as they talk—know what they want to say,
and say it in the plainest and simplest way.

Most weak and unsatisfactory writing results from trying to construct
long and "bookish" sentences, altogether different from those that occur in
the ordinary speech of the writer.

Some people, when they "take their pens in hand," seem to think that
the more "big words" they use the more effective they are, and that there
is great literary merit in long and involved sentences, just as stones and
brick bats are more effective missiles than pillows.

Everyone who wishes to learn to write good English should take a
course of grammar and composition under a teacher.

One might as well try to become a good musician without learning the
notes as to try to learn to write an acceptable composition without learning
the elementary facts of grammar. There is a certain tribe of "smart" people who are fond of sneering at grammar. They usually boast that they
"always did hate grammar," and seem to feel that they are getting along
very nicely without it. These are people who say "hadn't ought,"
"between you and I," "he writes good," "I haven't got no money," etc.
When they write, they usually manage to say what they do not mean; their
punctuation marks are confined to the period, and they do not always use
that; while their verbs are unmatched with the subject and capital letters
are apt to turn up anywhere. These people usually look upon their own
grammatical sins with entire indifference.

SUCCESSFUL BLIND PEOPLE.

In this department, which is dedicated to the cause for the advancement of which this periodical is published, we hope to serve a double purpose. We wish first to call the attention of the seeing world to what it is possible for blind persons to accomplish.

Second, to have this knowledge, by means of the thoughtful kindness of our subscribers, reach the sightless everywhere and stimulate them to make the most of their lives.

Every blind man or woman, young or vigorous, with a favorable opportunity may become self-sustaining. The right amount of perseverance will command the opportunity. All who wish to know what is being accomplished to increase the methods by which blind people may become independent are invited to open correspondence with the American Association to Promote the Education and Employment of the Blind, 3124 Fourteenth St. N. W., Washington, D. C., enclosing stamp for reply.

A BIOGRAPHY BY FRANCES MARTIN, EPITOMIZED BY F. E. CLEAVELAND.

NOT more closely was the birth of a great and free nation interwoven with the life and labors of George Washington, than has the upbuilding of the cause of the dependent blind, been associated with the life and labors of Elizabeth Gilbert, who became blind when only three years of age.

She was the daughter of the Rev. Ashurst Turner Gilbert, who was principal of Bracenose College, Oxford and afterwards Bishop of Chichester. A volume by Frances Martin, published by MacMillan and Co., New York, 1887, will prove most interesting reading to many who may desire to know how a delicate and frail blind woman became the founder of an "Association for Promoting the General Welfare of the Blind." An association which up to the time when her failing health compelled her to relinquish the burden of responsibility connected with its management, was furnishing employment to about one hundred and seventy adult blind people, many of whom were previously begging in the streets, at which time, (1866) the year's receipts of this Association amounted to $38,160.

In 1831 when Elizabeth was five years old, a Mr. Gall of Edinburgh, was enthusiastically advocating the scheme of teaching the blind to read by means of raised characters, and the account of the manner in which the idea was received by those in charge of an Asylum for the Blind, in London, will give our readers, some idea of the skepticism which the seeing world has always manifested, about the ability of the blind to overcome obstacles imposed by this limitation.

"Mrs. Wood, wife of the Rev. Peter Wood, Broadwater Rectory, Worthington, was interested in the condition of the blind. She had visited institutions in Zurich and Paris, had heard of work being done in their behalf in Edinburgh. She was also acquainted with the condition of the School for the Blind at St. George's Field, London.

"She wrote in 1831 to Mr. Henry Vynes, Mr. Gaussen, Mr. Dodd, Mr. Pigou, Mr. Capelcure and other members of the committee of the St. George's Field School, begging them to inquire into the method of teaching the blind to read, recently discovered and at that time attracting attention. With her letter, she sent specimens of books and other data to be submitted to the committee. Mr. Gaussen, writing from the Temple, 12th of March 1831, replies that he will have much pleasure in forwarding her excellent views and that Mr. Vynes has secured the reference of her plan to the committee; that it will be well considered, but for his own part he is bound to express the greatest doubt as to the results. He suggests that instead of teaching the blind to read there should be more reading aloud to them 'so as to stimulate their minds to more exertion, which in many cases is the source of the kind treatment they meet with.'

"A brother of the Secretary, Mr. Dodd, writes that he also will do what he can, although he has heard that the benefit of the plan 'is so limited that quite as much good is accomplished by teaching the pupils to commit portions of Scripture to memory as by teaching them to read.'

"Mr. Vynes informs Mrs. Wood that he has at her request attended the meeting of the committee, that only two of the other gentlemen she had written to were present, Mr. Pigou and Mr. Gaussen. 'The latter is not favorable to the plan, neither is Mr. Dodd, the Secretary.' The gentlemen present who spoke were all 'well satisfied with the amount of religious knowledge which their blind pupils already possess, so that I must fear they will take little trouble to increase it.' He refers to a rumor that the 'art of reading' has been introduced into the Edinburgh School for the Blind, but adds that the 'meeting did not seem inclined to give any credit to it,' and suggests that if it is true, Mrs. Wood might let them hear more about it, as he had secured a reference of the whole matter to the consideration of the House committee."

Now Mrs. Wood was nothing daunted by these successive dashes of cold water. She wrote afresh to members of the committee. She obtained facts from Edinburgh and she wisely limited her appeal, to a petition that the blind should be enabled to read the Scriptures for themselves. But whether at that time, she recognized the fact or not, there can be no doubt that the whole question of what the blind could themselves do would be opened by this step and must be decided.

Mr. Vynes writes to her again on the 29th of March, and it is interesting to observe, that a committee in 1831, was very much the same sort of thing that it is now.

"Among the seven or eight gentlemen present, I found Mr. Jackman, the chaplain of the institution, being the first time I had ever the pleasure of meeting him. Both Mr. Jackman and Mr. Dodd (the Secretary,) affirm that these poor blind pupils are already as well instructed as it is possible they should be under their afflicting circumstances. They are correctly moral in their general conduct, influenced by religious feelings and principles, with contented and pious minds. Mr. Jackman mentioned as a proof, that they do think beyond the present moment, the average number who now participate at every celebration of the Lord's Supper, is one or two and twenty, though formerly there had been but three or four. They can repeat a large portion of the Psalms, not merely the singing of Psalms, but take the alternate verse of the reading vession without requiring any prompting. And all the pupils have a variety of the most important texts strongly impressed upon their memories. Their memories are generally good and they assure me that they are fully exercised upon strong truths. These gentlemen are of the opinion that more is to be learned by the ear than can ever be acquired by the fingers and therefore see no advantage attending the new plan, which can at all compensate the trouble and expense of introducing it."

This is most amusing to educated blind people of to-day, but it is only an example illustrating what may be expected from the skepticism of the seeing world, whenever any advanced step, or progressive measure is undertaken in behalf of the sightless.

However, the door had been opened by Mr. Gall and could not be closed.

"Two years later the parents of 'Bessie,' as she was then called, were able to procure from Edinburgh an outfit which is listed as follows:

"1. Galls' First Book; Three other Books and the Gospel of St. John.

"2. Hay's Alphabet and Lessons; (Mr. Lang's Friend,) with Outline sketch of Map.

"3. The String Alphabet, with a printed statement of its invention and use.

"4. Seven brass types, constructed on principles of the alphabet.

"5. Several packets of metalic pieces representing the notes in music.

"Bessie's first contribution to philanthropy was made before she was twelve years old. 'Mary Howitts' Sea Gull,' set to music by her, was sold for twenty pounds, which went to the Irish Famine Fund.

"In 1853, Bessie heard from a friend much of the poor in London, of their troubles and their poverty.   Her own sympathies naturally led her to consider the condition of the blind poor.   She began to make inquiry as to their number, the places they lived in, the work they did, their homes and social condition.   Note books full of facts, dates and numbers testify to the activity of this time, and then once again, her attention was directed to the blind teacher in the Avenue Road school.

"In the autumn of that year she wrote to ask Mr. W. Hanks Levy, the blind teacher above mentioned to call upon her.   She said she had been told, he could give her the information she wanted as to the condition and requirements of the blind.

"This interview was one of the most important events in her life.

"Her feeble health, her limited opportunities of ascertaining the condition of the poor, her imperfect knowledge of their requirements and their powers, made it imperative that she should find an ally with health and energy, with experience that might supplement her own and with equal devotion to the cause she had at heart.

"W. Hanks Levy, who called at her request to tell her about the blind poor, was one about whom she had often heard and with whom she had already corresponded. He was an assistant teacher in the school at Avenue Road, married to the matron of the girls' department.

"Levy was of humble origin and blind from early youth.   His education, such as it was, had been received at the Avenue Road school, but he was essentially self taught.   Outside of the narrow routine of the school, he had worked and striven to obtain knowledge, to find help for himself and others.

"Levy was a man of eager intelligence and generous heart.   He earnestly desired the amelioration of the condition of the blind.   Their disabilities had pressed upon him, from his youth upward and upon all around him.

"Although taught by experience, not to be swerved from his purpose by the incredulity or misgivings of the sighted, and while he would not have suffered interference from them, he submitted to the blind lady; her nurture, training and delicate sense of the fitness of things, gave her a strong hold over him.   He accepted her judgment when it was opposed to his own will, and faithfully carried out her wishes and views.

"During this first interview, he told her of the various institutions in Great Britain, and their work and especially of the work done in London. At her request he investigated carefully and obtained dates, facts and figures, that were reliable.   Bessie found that the institutions for the blind provided instruction for the young and for them only.   Statistics showed however that by far the greater number of blind persons lose their sight as adults, from such causes as fever, small pox and accidental injury.   They lose sight, when others are dependent upon them and when blindness means either the life of a beggar, or the poor house; and again learned, tha tthe existing institutions dismiss young men and women who have been fairly well educated and taught a trade, on the assumption that, as adults they can practice their trade and earn a living. This conjecture tells cruelly upon the blind. They leave many of the institutions with an adequate stock of clothes and with either tools or money to purchase tools and then begins a hopeless struggle. Private friends diminish in numbers and are gradually lost. The blind men and women can not go about from place to place in search of work, cannot work without special contrivances, which are not to be found in ordinary workshops, and have no market for their goods if they work at home.

"But do the blind people wish to work, or would they not rather beg? asked many to whom Bessie spoke upon this subject. To this she replied that she did not know, must try to find this out. For some months at her request, Levy went into the streets and accosted every blind beggar whom he met, asking him or her to tell the story of a life to a blind man. 'Which would you rather, work or beg?' he would ask when the speaker had finished and in almost every case the answer was, 'Work! why I would rather work, but how can I get work, or if I get it how can I do it? and where can I sell it if I do it at home without orders?'

"These were the difficulties that experience brought to light and after many months of close and patient investigation, Bessie at length saw a way open before her. 'Don't work yourself to death, a friend said to her at this time. 'Work to death,' she said with a happy laugh., 'I am working to life.'

"She saw that some one must come forward to befriend the blind poor, some one who could supply material, give employment, or dispose of the articles manufactured.

"Why should she not do this? Her parents warmly approved of the course she proposed to take and brothers, sisters, and friends encouraged her. They saw that it would bring occupation and interest which she sorely needed. They could not foresee how the little rill was to widen into a broad stream and what far-reaching results it would have.

"In May 1854, Bessie's scheme was started. Seven blind men were employed at their own homes. Material was purchased for and supplied to them at cost price; the articles manufactured were to be disposed of on their account and they were to receive the full selling price, minus the cost of material.

"A cellar was rented in New Turnstile, Holborn, at the cost of eighteen pence a week, and Levy was engaged as manager with a salary of half a crown a week and a percentage upon the sales. The cellar was to be a store room for materials and goods and as the basket makers could not bleach their baskets at home, a binn was fixed so that this part of the work could be done in the cellar. Levy recommended a young man named Farrow to put up the bleaching binn. Farrow had lost his sight when eleven years old in consequence of a gun accident. He had been educated in the St. John's Wood School, was a very good carpenter and cabinet maker, a man who could readily turn his hand to anything. But like many others who had left the school, he was without work or prospect of work.

"He fixed the bleaching binn and arranged the cellar as a storeroom, without any assistance and from that time on has been employed by the institution which sprang from that small dark cellar in Holborn.

"So many were the applications for employment from the blind and so rapidly did the school develop, that twice within the year they were compelled to move into larger and more commodious quarters, and later the undertaking became so extensive in its operations, that Bessie's father, now a Bishop of the Established Church, urged that a committee be appointed to share her responsibilities.

"Being the daughter of a Bishop and acquainted with many noted and influential personages, she readily obtained their co-operation and assistance.

"An association was formed styled 'The British Association for Promoting the General Wellfare of the Blind.'

"It was conceded from the start that while the members would do all in their power to assist, the knowledge, experience and judgment of Bessie should be relied upon in carrying on the work.

"Bessie and her manager, Mr. Levy, had both started in with the idea that it would be better that blind people should do all the work and that nothing should be undertaken that the blind people could not accomplish unaided by the seeing.

"They argued that if seeing people were employed for any purpose whatever, the seeing and not the blind would receive credit for what was accomplished. This idea was however subsequently abandoned. The change not only made their work less difficult, but the blind people themselves were thus enabled to accomplish much more."

In the closing years of Miss Bessie's life, her health became so impaired that she was confined to her room, but her mind was active and her heart was still in the work. But from the room of the invalid continued to go forth directions and suggestions that were implicitly followed.

During her life her strength and her means were at the service of the blind, and at her death was found as her last will and testament, a written document, which embodied rules and suggestions for those who should succeed her in the work to which she had devoted her life, and nothing that the writer has observed or experienced during twenty-five years of blindness, seven years of which have been devoted to similar work for the blind, would induce him to add to, or take away from, the counsel here given.

The suggestions and rules referred to, are as follows:

"In the endeavor to promote the welfare of the blind, it is essential that some important facts should be borne in mind, viz.

"1st. That many blind persons, although instructed in some trade, are either reduced to begging or are driven to the poor house, not through their own fault, but simply for the want of any regular employment in their trade.

"2d. That children constitute but a small proportion of the blind, as about nine-tenths of the thirty thousand blind in the United Kingdom, become so above the age of twenty-one.

"3d. That about half the sightless population live in rural districts.

"4th. That the health of persons without sight is, as a general rule, below that of others.

"5th. That this cause operates, in addition to loss of sight, to bring about the slow rate at which the blind work, as compared with the sighted.

"6th. That social ties are even more essential to the blind than to others."

OBJECTS TO BE AIMED AT.

"1st. To foster self-reliance and to enable the blind to help themselves.

"2d. To eradicate the habit of suspicion, by promoting friendly intercourse between the blind and the sighted.

"3d. To develop the faculties of the blind in every direction.

"4th. To improve their physical condition.

"5th. In industrial training, to endeavor to lessen, as far as possible, the difference in speed in the work between the work of the blind and that of the sighted, while making it the first object to secure good and efficient work.

"6th. To do everything to reduce the dependence of the blind as far as possible, while endeavoring, by Christian instruction, to enable them to accept the unavoidable dependence of their condition in a spirit of humility and thankfulness which will soften and sweeten it to them and will turn this dependence into one of their greatest blessings, as it will be the means of uniting them more closely to their fellow creatures."

MEANS TOWARDS THESE ENDS.

"1st. Endeavor to enable the blind to earn their own living and with this view seek out and send children to existing blind schools.

"2d. Promote establishments for providing the blind on leaving the schools, with regular employment and for teaching trades to persons ineligible for admission to the schools, which is the case, as a rule, with those above twenty-one years of age.

"3d. When practicable supply blind persons with regular employment at their own homes and encourage them to do anything they can on their own account independently of any institution.

"4th. Try to introduce trades hitherto not carried on by the blind, giving the precedence to such as can be practiced without sighted aid.

"5th. Cultivate habits of method and precision in the blind, which will all tend to improve the rate at which they work.

"6th. Make the training of efficient blind teachers a special object.

"7th. Encourage residence in the country rather then in the towns by giving employment at home, thus cementing family ties and promoting health.

"8th. Form lending libraries of embossed books in all the various systems in use and establish classes for religious and other instruction."

There can not be a more suitable ending to this article, than the prayer formulated by Bessie's father, the Bishop of Chichester, for use at the meetings of the association.

BISHOP GILBERT'S PRAYER.

"O Lord Jesus Christ, Who in Thy ministry upon earth, didst make the blind to see, the lame to walk, the deaf to hear, the dead to be raised up, (Matt. xi. 5, Luke vii. 22), and by Thy holy apostle has commanded Thy followers, that we should bear one another's burdens (Gal. vi. 2), regard with Thy favor we beseech Thee and with Thy blessing, our humble endeavor to remove stumbling blocks from before the feet of the blind, to smooth their difficulties and to strengthen their steps.

"Prosper our efforts, we humbly beseech Thee, O Father, to their worldly relief and sanctify them, by Thy Spirit to the increase in us of humility, faith, thankfulness and charity and to the growth in our afflicted brethren and sisters, of patience and resignation, of good will to those around them, and of love to all, with all other graces that adorn the Christian life. Of Thy mercy, O Father, Son, and Holy Ghost, one ever blessed Trinity in Unity, hear our prayer and accept and bless the work of our hands. O prosper Thou our handiwork. Amen."

In the March number of TALKS AND TALES, among other statements made by the former pupils of this Industrial Home for the Blind, we published the following:

"I learned the trade of broom making at the Industrial Home for the Blind at Hartford, Conn., and now consider myself competent to earn my own living as soon as I can get a start in the way of broom machinery tools and broom material.

"I am working for the Institution now and have been for the past few months, earning from two to three dollars a week. The Institution has been of great assistance to me and I am very grateful for the help I have received, as I have not been able myself to make any return to it for what it has done for me, except by my labor. I am not totally blind, but so nearly so that I am compelled to work as blind people do, and what sight I now have is gradually failing."

M. J. GILMORE.

In April Mr. Gilmore with his savings and money raised for him by the Institution, aggregating about $75.00, determined to start in business for himself.   He chose as his location, the town of North Adams, Mass., near which he formerly lived.

He expended his capital in the purchase of machinery and with some borrowed money bought a small quantity of broom material.

Just at this time, when he greatly felt the need of a little more capital, he received a check for $100, from Miss Annie E. Tucker of Philadelphia, Jefferson County, New York, who had read the foregoing statement in our magazine.   This amount put him right upon his feet, and at this writing, July 4th, 1899, Mr. Gilmore reports that he is making an average of $9.00 a week, has all he can do, and already has besides his outfit fully paid for, the sum of $50.00 to his credit in the Savings Bank.

The writer joins with Mr. Gilmore in expressing his thanks for, and appreciation of, the generous gift from Miss Tucker, at the same time feeling assured, that the consciousness of having extended a helping hand to this young man just at the time when it was of the utmost service to him, will amply reward one who must, as we believe, experience joy in the happiness of others.   F. E. CLEAVELAND.

JUST BETWEEN OURSELVES.

Hot weather has come, and all too early. The rain has withdrawn its frown and the voice of the complaining farmer is heard in the land. It is a curious illustration of the way in which we are dissatisfied by almost any kind of weather, that a year ago we were whimpering because there was too much rain. But our present lament seems well founded as we look out and see the lawn turning to a sere and "jaundicy" complexion in the middle of June.

* * * *

And because of these sultry conditions, those who are so fortunate as to be able to do it, are turning with longing eyes to the country and the sea-shore. The stream of travel has set from the city outward. It is unfortunate that a good many people who need the change most cannot have it, and must swelter on in the city home.

* * * *

But some people affect to say that they prefer to remain at home. There they are sure of congenial company and comfortable beds and food to their liking. There are two errors of judgment here: (1) a change does not necessarily imply dissatisfaction; (2) it always does physical and mental good. We may be perfectly happy in our homes; I hope all the readers of TALKS AND TALES are. But we want to get out of the rut in which our life is prone to run. And if in the country we find disagreeable companions, hard beds and poor food, it will do one thing, at least, —it will make us glad to get home again and doubly appreciate it. And that is something all of us need at times.

* * * *

What are we going to do when we get into the country? First of all, I hope we may all open our lungs and take in copious draughts of the free air. For my own part, that is the best thing about the country. I do not find it so much cooler, sometimes it is dreadfully hot. But there is always plenty of air. I am not cooped up in a house, with no place to get the air save the window and the street. I can go out on the hill top and planting myself under the shade of a hospitable tree, cast my gaze twenty miles across the beautiful valley to where Wachusett reigns in solitary grandeur. And it must be hot indeed when that view does not refresh and invigorate.

* * * *

Then I hope every denizen of the artificial town will "get near to nature's heart." I do not mean by that study botany or rave over sunsets, or go into ecstacies over a waving field of wheat (which later on you find is barley, and not wheat at all). Keep foolishness out of it; sober sense is the prime quality. Just look around and see some of God's handiwork, unspoiled by man. Watch plants grow. I have a bit of a garden patch, and it is the joy of my life. It is a revelation to spy out the bashful first sprout crowding up, pushing aside the earth, and confident that no one is watching, come slowly out into the light of day. I have just now come from "paris-green-ing" the potato vines. Even that prosaic and unlovely task had its lesson. I thought of George Herbert's familiar lines, beginning:

"A servant with this clause,"
and really found "drudgery divine."

*   *   *   *

But most people go on a vacation to loaf, just pure, simple, undisguised loafing. Most of us busy, nervous Americans need to loaf once in a while. It keeps us from early graves. And people who loaf usually read—when they are not asleep. At these times some folks wish the Sunday paper came daily. They would like to keep the piazza and lawn strewn with its billious pages seven days of the week instead of only one. Failing in this ambition, they resort to one but little better,—they read cheap books: cheap in paper, print, manners and morals. If nothing worse comes of it, they develop literary dyspepsia. Their justification is that these things " kill time."

"Dearly beloved bratheran" (as Archbishop Trench used to say,) there are better things than these for killing time There are books which please and elevate, though they neither drool nor preaclf. Read again the old standard novels; the kind you were not ashamed to show your mother when you read them as boy or girl. Keep your head clear by letting only clean things pass through. Read a romance like "The Duke of Linden," by J. F. Charles, if you must have something new. *That* is clean and sweet. Read Mr. Jennings' story of his life as "A Texas Ranger," from which I append an extract. Stimulate your sense of humor by laughing at Mr. Dooley. Broaden your knowledge of your native empire by reading Lucien Young's "The Real Hawaii," There is enough and to spare of good books. If you read any other kind it is your own fault. It is because you are bound to degrade your mind, to stunt and dwarf your growing soul.   ELLIS WORTH.

THE HEART OF THINGS.

THE BEGINNING OF THE END. From "A Texas Ranger," by N. A. Jennings. Charles Scribner's Sons. $1.25.

It was about this time that Hall, of the Rangers, first met Judge Henry Clay Pleasants, the district judge whose district took in De Witt County.

"You do your part," said the old judge to Hall, "and I will see that the courts deal justice. Together we can bring order out of chaos."

We brought in members of the Sutton gang in December, 1873. Habeas corpus proceedings were begun in their behalf in a few days, and the court sat for a week hearing them. Every day the court-room was crowded with members of both the Taylor and Sutton parties, but as we were careful to disarm every man who entered the building, there was no clash.

As the proceedings drew to a close, we received information that the members of the Sutton gang were determined that their seven comrades, under no circumstances should be sent to jail. Judge Pleasants received several anonymous letters in which the threat was made that he would be shot and killed if he decided against the accused murderers. Hall decided to run no chances, and accordingly sent for more Rangers. They arrived the night before the day Judge Pleasants was to render his decision. With the reinforcements, we had thirty Rangers, enough to take care of every "bad man" in the country, if need be.

When court was called to order the room was crowded with men, and everywhere it was whispered that Judge Pleasants would be shot if he decided against the prisoners and sent them to prison to await trial, instead of admitting them to bail.

The old judge took his seat on the bench amid a profound silence. One could feel the suppressed excitement in the court-room and see it reflected in the faces of the spectators. Just before the Judge arose to give his decision, six of the Rangers stepped up to the bench and stood on either side of the Judge. I was one of the three on his right and was next to his side. Like the other five men, I had my carbine in my hand and, like the others, I threw a cartridge into the breech and cocked the gun in plain sight of all in the court-room. Then we stood at "ready" while Judge Pleasants addressed the crowd of men in the room. With supreme dignity he stood and looked at them for a full minute before he spoke. Then he said, in a calm, distinct voice whose every tone carried conviction:

"The time has arrived for me to announce my decision in this case. I shall do so without fear or favor, solely upon the evidence as it has been presented. This county is and has been for years a reproach to the fair name of the state of Texas. Over it have roamed bands of lawless men, committing awful outrages, murdering whom they pleased, shooting down men from ambush in the most cowardly manner possible.

Here in this very room, listening to me now, are murderers who long ago should have been hanged. I do not speak of the prisoners at the bar, but of you who yet are free. You are murderers, bushwhackers, midnight assassins.

"Some of you have dared to threaten me with cowardly anonymous letters, and I have had to bring state soldiers into this court of justice. I learn that you have blamed the Sheriff of this county for calling upon the Rangers to assist in restoring order. No, it was not the sheriff who had the Rangers sent here; it was I. I called for them and I am going to see that they remain in this county until it is as peaceful and law-abiding as any in the State—as quiet and orderly as any in the Union. I tell you now, beware! The day of reckoning is surely coming. It is close at hand. When you deal with the Texas Rangers, you deal with men who are fearless in the discharge of their duty, and who will surely conquer you.

"I shall send these men at the bar to jail to await trial for as wicked and cowardly a murder as ever disgraced this state. It is but the beginning. Others will soon follow them. The reign of the lawless in DeWitt County is at an end!"

Never shall I forget how the gray haired old Judge's eyes flashed and his fine voice rang as he pronounced these words. Angry looks came into the faces of scores of men in the court-room, but they knew better than to make any demonstration.

"Lieutenant Hall, clear the room, sir," ordered Judge Pleasants, when he concluded. In a very few minutes the order was obeyed, and men who had come to Clinton determined to create trouble were leaving the town thoroughly cowed.

It was the beginning of the end of their power in the county, and they knew it.

———

Any communication for this department may be addressed to Ellis Worth, Waltham, Mass

CURRENT EVENTS.

GRACE A. CHILD.

THE TRANSVAAL.—The republic of the Boers in South Africa is again causing the English government no little trouble. Large mining interests in the Transvaal are owned and operated by the English who with other foreigners are said to make up about four-fifths of the entire population. The foreign element has almost no voice in the government and is heavily taxed in addition. A demand has been made that these grievances be remedied and President Krüger has made slight concessions in regard to the franchise, requiring but seven years' residence in the country necessary to full rights of citizenship, where twelve are now required. He has also decided to break the dynamite monopoly which is one of the chief causes of trouble. Mr. Joseph Chamberlain, British Secretary for the Colonies, says these proposals do not constitute a fair measure of reform and insists that the just claims of the Outlanders be respected; while President Krüger stubbornly declines concessions to further demands which if yielded to would result in the ultimate extinction of the Dutch republic. Meanwhile troops have embarked from England for Cape Town, and soldiers in Cape Colony are ready for immediate service in the Transvaal. Trade is said to be paralyzed in both Johannesburg and Cape Town.

THE DREYFUS CASE.—The cause of justice to the individual has had a triumph in France, in the shape of a retrial granted to Alfred Dreyfus, by the Court of Cassation. In 1894 Dreyfus was sentenced to imprisonment for life on the Ile du Diable, on the charge of having sold military secrets to a foreign government. New facts have come to light since his conviction which make it appear that he is the victim of a monstrous conspiracy of either his enemies or those who wished to shield themselves from their own crimes. Dreyfus has been brought back to France and awaits his trial at Rennes. This affair has brought to the front several characters of heroic mould of which any nation might be proud. Foremost among these is the wife of Dreyfus, who has worked persistently and courageously for the vindication of her husband, and Colonel Picquart of the French army. In his connection with the intelligence bureau of the general staff Picquart found documents which led him to believe in the innocence of the victim. Since then he has been strenuous in his efforts that justice should be rendered even in the face of firm and malignant opposition which ended in his imprisonment for nearly a year. The novelist Zola must also be mentioned as one of the most active in the cause of justice.

VENEZUELAN COMMISSION. — An example of the workings of international arbitration is even now being furnished at Paris, where the Venezuelan Arbitration Commission is holding its sessions. The meetings are held in the rooms recently occupied by the Spanish-American conference and at a previous time by the Behring Sea Conference. Chief Justice Fuller and Associate Justice Brewer are members of the tribunal for Venezuela and ex-President Harrison and ex-Secretary Benjamin F. Tracy the leading members of the counsel, while on the British side, Sir Richard Webster is the leading counsel and other eminent English judges are on the bench. The umpire is Professor Martens, a Russian authority on international law, who is also a delegate to the Conference at The Hague. The importance of this Commission is measured more by the principles involved than by the territory under dispute. It means that the United States will not suffer South America to be divided by European nations as Africa has been, but will resist any encroachment on the republics of its neighbor.

AUSTRALIAN FEDERATION. — The federation of the Australian colonies is now practically assured. New South Wales has hitherto held aloof because the remaining colonies raise a portion of their taxes by duties on imports while she pursues a free-trade policy, but her vote has at last been cast for the establishment of a federal government. The assent of Queensland to the union, has not yet been secured, but enough of the colonies are in favor of it to make her co-operation unnecessary. The size of the United colonies will be about that of the United States exclusive of Alaska, while the population differs but little from our own at the time of Washington's inauguration. Great interest will be felt in watching the working out of the problems of republican government in these states where experiments in political and industrial reform have already been carried so much farther than in the conservative mother-country or our own republic.

THE PHILIPPINES.—The rainy season is now on in the Philippines and although operations are greatly hindered by the great rainfall our forces are surprising the Filipinos by their activity while they in their turn are surprising our generals by their stubborn and well-organized resistance. Owing to the departure of volunteer regiments for America, General Lawton is left with a force of but 10,000 which necessitates the sending of 7,000 regulars to fill their places; in addition the President has issued a call for ten regiments of volunteers. He is quoted as saying that he thinks it will be necessary to send no larger force than this to the Philippines, but others who are familiar with the conditions there say that an army of no less than 100,000 is needed to properly subdue and hold the islands.

SAMOA.—Despatches from Samoa state that peace has been restored in the island. The Commission after examination of the claims of the contending factions, sustained the decision of Chief Justice Chambers, that Malietoa was the rightful king; he then resigned his office and the natives laid down their arms. The new government which is to be a provisional one, will include a Governor, a Council of three to be named by the Treaty Powers, Germany, England, and the United States, and a native House of some kind.

THE ALASKAN BOUNDARY.—The trouble over the boundary of Alaska in the Klondike region, which threatened to put a stop to the negotiations of the joint High Commission of the United States and Great Britain, bids fair to be settled peaceably. Arrangements have been made by which the respective rights of American and Canadian authorities may be determined for the next two years, the permanent settlement of the boundary to be determined later. When the United States bought Alaska of Russia it was specifically stated that the boundary line should follow the windings of the coast about fifty miles inland. Now that gold has been discovered in the Klondike, Canada wants a port on the Lynn Canal, which is the easiest approach to the passes of the gold region. By the temporary adjustment Canada is given a port on a tributary of the Canal which can be reached by canoes but not by steamers.

INTERNATIONAL PEACE CONFERENCE. — The International Peace Congress at the Hague bids fair to play a larger part in the movement of the world toward universal peace than even its most earnest advocates had dared hope. In addition to resolutions favoring greater humanity in warfare, the nations represented have agreed upon the establishment of a permanent tribunal of arbitration, which will undertake the settlement of international difficulties. On July 10, the Conference adjourned for ten days, that the delgates might consult their respective governments and receive final instructions.

ON June 24 the Queen-Regent of Spain signed the bill which added to Germany almost the last remnant of Spain's once large colonial empire. By this act Germany becomes the owner of the Caroline, Peleu, and Ladrone Islands, with the exception of Guam which belongs to the United States, and Spain's treasury receives an addition of about 5,000,000 dollars.

IT is reported that General Leonard Wood, now Governor of Santiago, has refused an offer from a Washington corporation to become its president on a salary of something like $30,000 a year and has decided to remain in Cuba. His government needs him and Cuba needs him, considerations which carry greater weight with him than money.

DAVID B. HENDERSON of Iowa has practically been chosen to succeed Mr. Reed as Speaker of the House of Representatives. His close connection with Mr. Reed on the Committee of Rules, has given him the experience which, with his natural ability, has led his party to look on him as the man for the office.

THE estimate has been made that 35,000 traveling men alone have been thrown out of employment by the rapidity with which trusts have been formed in the last few months. The change in the methods of selling goods under the new conditions of trade is the cause.

SELECTED MATTER.

It Pays.

It pays to wear a smiling face
  And laugh our troubles down,
For all our little trials wait
  Our laughter or our frown,
Beneath the magic of a smile
  Our doubts will fade away,
As melts the frost in early spring
  Beneath the sunny ray.

It pays to make a worthy cause,
  By helping it, our own;
To give the current of our lives
  A true and noble tone.
It pays to comfort heavy hearts
  Oppressed with dull despair,
And leave in sorrow-darkened lives
  A gleam of brightness there.

It pays to give a helping hand
  To eager, earnest youth,
To note, with all their waywardness,
  Their courage and their truth;
To strive with sympathy and love
  Their confidence to win;
It pays to open wide the heart
  And "let the sunshine in."

A MILLION bobolinks killed last year! Four million other birds slaughtered in the same year—and for what? That their torn and distorted bodies might be flaunted in the headgear of American womankind! These are no guesswork figures, but the official report of the Audubon Society of Massachusetts. And what does it mean? It means five million voices stilled in nature's avian choir. Five million flashes of cheeriness and gladness taken from human life, and millions of other young lives doomed to starvation or prey in order that the plumaged corpse of the murdered mother-bird may be rent by a milliner, and jammed in hideous shapelessness in my lady's hat!

THE Bayeaux tapestry is a web of canvas or linen cloth upon which is embroidered in woolen threads of various colors a representation of the invasion and conquest of England by the Normans. The canvas is 214 feet long by twenty inches broad and is preserved in the public library at Bayeaux. Tradition asserts that it is the work of Matilda, wife of William the Conqueror, and it is believed that if she did not actually stitch the whole of it, she at least took part in it and directed the execution of it by her maids.

A SUBSCRIBER to a rural Pennsylvania paper recently wrote to the editor of that journal to ask whether he would take his pay in chickens. The editor replied: "Yes—and wood and meal, meat and corn, and potatoes and peaches, and billy goats, and pigs, and horses, and hay, and land, and mules, and cows, and calves, and rabbits, and wheat, and turnips, and any old thing you've got. We have on rare occasion even taken in money on subscriptions."

IT is said that John Bunyan, seeing a drunkard staggering along the street exclaimed, "There, but for the grace of God, goes John Bunyan!"

SENATOR BAYARD started in life as a clerk in a Philadelphia hardware store, Senator Beck began as a farm hand, Conger as a lumber hand, Davis, of West Virginia, as a brakeman, Dawes as a school-teacher, Fair as a bartender, Farley as a coach-driver, Gorman as a Senate page, Jones, of Florida, as a carpenter, McDill as a department clerk, Morrill as a country store-keeper, Plumb as a printer's devil, Sawyer as a laborer, Sherman as a surveyor, and West as a reporter.

———— ♦ ————

WHEELMEN should be interested in an English decision rendered by Judge Lushington of the Surry County Courts. A bicycler ran into a cow straying on the highway, and he claimed damages from the owner. The latter contended that there was no evidence of negligence on his part, but his Honor said the mere fact of the cow straying was sufficient evidence of negligence, and he gave judgment for the amount claimed with costs.

———— ♦ ————

WASHINGTON IRVING, speaking of system in making notes for his histories, said: "I never had any. I have my little budget of notes, it is true—some tied this way and some another—which I think I come upon in my pigeon-holes by a sort of instinct."

———— ♦ ————

CARLYLE talked best directly after supper when under the influence of his half dozen cups of strong tea; with pipe in mouth, an additional stimulant, he would pour forth a continuous stream of rich thought nigh equal to his writings.

———— ♦ ————

HENRY WARD BEECHER once said that the past belongs to gratitude and regret; the present to contentment and work; the future to hope and trust.

A BIT of genuine enthusiasm is sometimes very refreshing. Lafayette on parting kissed Josiah Quincy on both cheeks. A lady to whom Quincy related his experience declared: "Had it been me, I would never have washed my face as long as I lived."

———— ♦ ————

"AULD LANG SYNE" is popularly supposed to be the composition of Burns; but, in fact, he wrote only the second and third verses of the ballad as commonly sung, retouching the other from an older and less familiar song.

———— ♦ ————

A BIG black dog of uncertain breed seizes the mailbag when it is thrown off the train at a certain rural town in Georgia and scampers away with it to the postoffice. It is said he seems to know the time when the train is due, and is always punctually at his post.

———— ♦ ————

MRS. FRANCES HODGSON BURNETT, the successful novelist, gives the following directions how to write a novel: "You must have pen, ink, and paper. Use the first with brains, the second with imagination, and the third with generosity."

———— ♦ ————

A MONUMENT to the mother of Abraham Lincoln is to be erected by the old soldiers of the 2d Iowa brigade, three regiments from Illinois, the 14th, 15th, and 16th, and two from Indiana, the 26th and 53d.

———— ♦ ————

IN Maine there are seventeen spool factories, and the white birch trees of that State annually supply the material for 300,000,000 spools, on which are subsequently wound about 50,000,000,000 yards of thread.

———— ♦ ————

HIAWATHA reached a sale of 50,000 in less than two years after its publication.

Beautiful Things.

Beautiful lips are those whose words
Leap from the heart like songs of
   birds,
Yet whose utterance prudence girds.

     *   *   *   *   *

Beautiful feet are those that go
On kindly ministries to and fro—
Down lowliest ways, if God wills it so.

THE POTATO BABIES AND HOW THEY GREW.

GRACE BROWNELL PECK.

ONE day last fall, when the children were at grandma's, it began to rain. Grandma always had something laid away for a rainy day. After breakfast, the twins, Tommy and Daisy, got hold of grandma's hands and led her to the cupboard. She laughed, and said she was Old Mother Hubbard, going to the cupboard to get six little doggies a bone. She reached up to the top shelf and took down two boxes, one large and one small.

What do you think was in the large one? Little tiny potatoes. And in the small one? Burnt matches, with the ends rubbed on sand-paper to make a point. Grandpa had thought of the children when he dug his potatoes, and had saved all the little ones—the "pig potatoes" —for them, and grandma had thought of them, too, and saved all her burnt matches.

The children gathered around her now and watched her make a potato baby. First the head must be fastened on. This was done by sticking one end of a match into a small potato, and the other end into a larger one—for the body.

After that she stuck two matches in for legs, and two for arms; and there was a man all done. Then, when she had shown them how to make a horse and a cow, grandma went back to her work and left them.

They had a good time, making men and horses and cats and dogs. The rain got all through raining, the sun came out, and the grass was dry before they thought of stopping. At last the dinner-bell rang, and they laid the potato babies away for another rainy day.

Now comes the funny part of the story. The potato dollies lay quietly in their dark box for three long months; then the children were all there again, and wanted them to play with. Grandma brought the box down—opened it—and what do you think they saw? The potato babies had begun to grow. Their bodies were dry and shrunken. Out of every one came long white roots that looked like horns and arms and tongues and tails. The father potato had a trunk like an elephant. The fat boy had turned into some strange bird. The mamma, on horseback, had a real face, with nose, eyes and a tongue coming out of her mouth, as well as long hair. The cat and the camel were both turned into reindeer, and one man had two horns and a tail.

They looked so funny that the children laughed and laughed till all the mammas and aunts and uncles came in to see what was the matter. Auntie May made a picture of them the very next day, just as they came out of the box.—[*Union Signal.*

THE NEW GEOGRAPHY OF THE UNITED STATES.

The recent war with Spain means more to the map makers and students of geography than we are at first inclined to think. Much has already been written on the subject, but some facts given by the Philadelphia Press, are of special interest. Until 1898 the empire of the United States has taken its course westward, mainly. But now, the changes have been so great that we look northward, southward, eastward as well. Our domain extends through 174 degrees of longitude, from the outlying islands of Porto Rico, 65 degrees west of Greenwich, westward to Manila, 121 degrees east of Greenwich—10,000 miles on a straight line. Northward it has pushed to 71 degrees to Point Barrow, Alaska, and extends southward to 13 degrees north of the equator, the latitude of Guam in the Ladrone Islands; or if the coaling station at Pago Pago, Samoa, be counted we stretch below the equator 12 degrees, into the South Sea. By degrees merely, north and south, it is about 4,000 miles from Point Barrow to Guam, or 6,000 to Pago Pago, so that 10,000 miles one way and 6,000 the other represents the sphere of the influence of the United States one hundred and twenty-two years after it was a confederation of colonies, clinging close to the Atlantic coast and looking upon the Alleghenies as barriers.— *The Palmetto Leaf.*

COMPOSITION CURIOSITIES.

Mark Twain tells of a pupil with the words zoölogical, geological and theological, which he was required to use in the construction of sentences. He got mixed on the words and in two of his sentences he let out a couple of secrets that ought never to have been divulged. Here they are:

Some of the best fossils are found in theological cabinets.

There are a good many donkeys in theological gardens.

The following definitions were given in an examination in mathematics:

Parallel lines are lines that can never meet until they come together.

Things that are equal to each other are equal to anything else.

To find the number of square feet in a room, multiply the room by the number of feet, and the product will be the result.

A circle is a round straight line with a hole in the middle.

Here are some answers given by the class in geography:

Ireland is called "Emigrant Isle" because it is so beautiful and green.

The principal occupation of the people of Austria is gathering ostrich feathers.

The two most famous volcanoes of Europe are Sodom and Gomorrah.

Here are some written answers to questions in civil government:

The first conscientious congress met in Philadelphia.

The constitution of the United States was adopted in order to secure domestic hostility.—[*American Journal of Education.*

WISE AND OTHERWISE.

He entertained an idea, and his friends said that he had given an intellectual feast.

———

Clara—"What a terrible noise that wagon makes!" George—"Yes, it's dreadful, isn't it?" Clara—"What makes it groan so, George?" George—"Why, it is filled with green apples."

———

Teacher—"John, illustrate the difference between sit and set."

Bright and Patriotic Boy—"The United States is a country on which the sun never sets and the rest of the world never sits."

———

Gadzooks—"Does your minister believe in the policy of expansion?" Zounds—"I should say he does! His text yesterday consisted of two words, and he made an hour's sermon out of it!"

———

Fuller—"Dr. Nomad told Tibby that drugs would not help his complaint, and recommended outdoor exercise on a wheel as being the best thing for him." Butler—"The Doc is simple to throw business away like that." Fuller—"Oh, I don't know; he charges double rates for surgical visits."

———

A pert miss of eight summers, while visiting in the family of a country cousin, wanted them to understand that she must not be thought far behind in the matters of country life, and noticing a quantity of honey on the tea-table, exclaimed —"O, I see you keep a bee."

Mamma—"I'm surprised at you, Johnny!" Johnny (thoughtfully)—"I wonder if you'll ever get used to me, mamma? You're always surprised at me."

———

Tommy—"Come, Bridget, play with us. We're playing soldier."

Bridget—"G'way, yez little imp. Oi ain't no soldier."

Tommy—"No, Bridget, but you're a red cross nurse."

———

He (telling a hairbreadth adventure)—"And in the bright moonlight we could see the dark muzzles of the wolves." She (breathlessly)—"Oh, how glad you must have been that they had the muzzles on!"

———

Teacher—"Billy, can you tell me the difference between caution and cowardice?" Billy—"Yes, ma'am. When you're afraid yourself, then that's caution. But when the other fellow's afraid, that's cowardice."

———

"Lowfer—I notice you have put an orchestra in your restaurant. Did you do it on the theory that music aids digestion?" Mr. Eatonhouse—"No; the music sets the boarders' teeth on edge, and they bite the toughest steak with the greatest ease."

———

A little boy observed, when asked why he remained on his knees after he had finished his prayers, "Well, mother, you know it says in the hymn, 'Satan trembles when he sees the weakest saint upon his knees;' so I thought I'd make him shake a little longer."

Talks . . .

. . . . . . and . . . . . .

. . . Tales

$1,00 per year in advance.

Every subscription helps furnish employment for the Blind, as the work is largely done by them.

Columbia Bevel-Gear Chainless
$60 to $75.

Ask riders of the Columbia Bevel-Gear Chainless their experience with the wheel. We have yet to hear of one who does not say that the Chainless is easier to take care of than the chain wheel; that it has a longer life; that every ounce of power applied to the pedals is made effective; that it seems to possess an activity and life of its own and that you will notice this in starting, stopping, back-pedaling, riding on levels and especially in ascending grades.

CHAIN WHEELS.
Columbias, Hartfords and Vedettes
Prices $25 to $50.

POPE MFG. Co., Hartford, Conn.

Cures while you sleep

Whooping Cough,

Croup, Colds, Coughs,

Asthma, Catarrh,

Bronchitis and Hay Fever

Hundreds of thousands of mothers use Vapo-Cresolene. Do you? CRESOLENE cures WHOOPING COUGH every time; stops CROUP almost immediately, and if used at once will cure a COLD before any complications can arise. I. N. Love, M. D., of St. Louis, says: "I have instructed every family under my direction to secure it." Mrs. Ballington Booth, says: "I recommend that no family where there are young children should be without it." W. R. Chichester, M. D. of New York says: "As a vehicle for disinfecting purposes CRESOLENE is immediately successful." Anthony Comstock, says: "MALIGNANT DIPHTHERIA in my house; Cresolene used; cases recovered in two weeks; no others were affected."

Descriptive booklet with testimonials free. Sold by all druggists.

VAPO-CRESOLENE CO., 69 Wall St., New York.
Schieffelin & Co. New York, U. S. Agents.

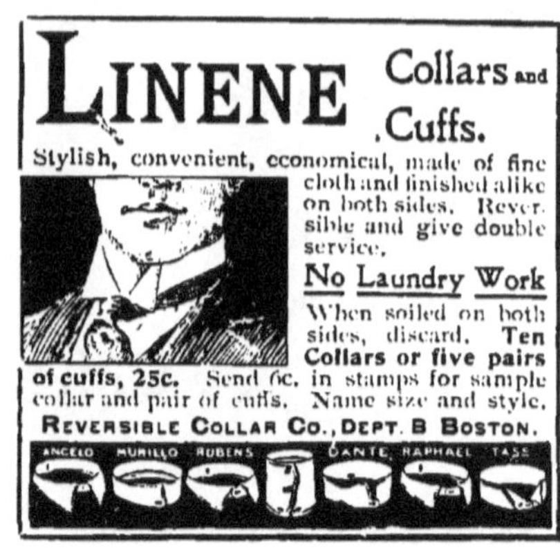

SUMMER HOMES

IN the Southern Berkshire and Litchfield Hills, along the Central New England Railway.

If you are going to the country don't fail to procure our handsomely illustrated guide-book of 240 pages, free at Jacobs' ticket office, 815 Main St., Gridley's ticket office, 18 State St., or will be mailed upon receipt of 7 cents postage to W. J. MARTIN, General Passenger Agent, Hartford, Conn.

TALKS AND TALES.

A MAGAZINE

——PUBLISHED BY——

The Conn. Institute and Industrial Home for the Blind,

Nos. 334 and 336 Wethersfield Ave.,

HARTFORD, CONN.

F. E. CLEAVELAND, President.

Edited by Mrs. ELLA B. KENDRICK.

One Dollar a Year,   -   -   Ten Cents a Copy.

PRESS OF
THE CONN. INSTITUTE AND INDUSTRIAL HOME
FOR THE BLIND.

Table of Contents.

The Connecticut Mutual

Life Insurance Company
1846--1899.

ALONG THE FARMINGTON RIVER CONN.

TALKS AND TALES.

Vol. II. Hartford, Conn., Aug. & Sept., 1899. Nos. 11 & 12.

CLARA BEWICK COLBY.

A TEN days' trip on the water is interesting written up by Mrs. Colby and published in her paper, The Woman's Tribune. As we know our friends will find it pleasant reading, we reprint it herewith.

It is over ten days since we left the shores of America, and we shall not reach until too late this evening to land. We have just put off the passengers for Londonderry which took more than half of those on board. The day is cold and rainy, and they set off for their fifteen-mile in a tender with no protection from the elements but a torn sail cloth awning. In the United States people would not be ferried across a river with so slight a protection. The dinner was hurried and served first to "Derry" people. There was much excitement, singing of "Auld Lang Syne," hurrahs, hand-shakings, and waving of farewells as long as the boat was in sight, and so they went off with as much good cheer as if the acquaintanceship had been lifelong instead of covering but little over a week. I remained on deck in the rain watching Moville and Greencastle, with their churches and their long, white houses with very high, sloping roofs of gray, which in the distance blend with the landscape so as to be invisible, giving the effect that the row of windows was all there was to the house. Lights and signal stations are always of interest and there are many of these along this rocky coast of Ireland. At Greencastle there is a fort with a ruined castle, overgrown with ivy, near by. The soft tints of the verdure on the bank are very pleasing to the eye. Some of the fields are even under this gray sky of so bright a green that it would seem impossible in a picture. The high, sloping banks give a good opportunity for one to see how the little farms are divided into fields by green hedges. Some of the enclosures are square, but many are triangular for no reason that one can detect from the character of the soil. It is too wet and cold to remain out, so with an occasional run up to see some rock or island of interest, this gives a little time to write this letter, to be mailed on arrival in Glasgow.

We have had a pleasant trip, but as we have seen several ships and several times "shipped a sea," it has not been monotonous. The days have not been long enough to watch the ever varying waves, and I have not heard anyone complain of the length of the voyage. The ocean has fulfilled all my expectations and satisfied the longings I have felt for it for a quarter of a century.

My own immediate party includes Mrs. Fray, who is a delightful traveling companion. We have read aloud together H. Emilie Cady's "Lessons on Truth," and they seemed to fit admirably into the setting of the ocean in whose presence all things petty and trivial or transitory seem wholly out of place. Magazines that I took along remained unread, as also the New York papers I bought before sailing. It is a strange sensation to be absolutely ignorant of what has taken place in the world for more than ten days. The only other reading I have been able to do is that of the beautiful poems of "Evangeline" and "Hiawatha," with which I have beguiled Zintka to rest in the cabin, and which I am sure she will always remember as a part of the new and wonderful pleasures of the voyage. Not one of us had even a qualm of sea sickness. Whether this was because we did not expect it, or because we so persistently stayed on deck, I do not know. Some of the travelers having been told by their physicians to stay in their berths one whole day, found themselves unable to leave for several. One day there were few who could venture to the table, but we came in from our mad dance on the waves in our chairs lashed to the boat, with appetites sharper for each meal than for the previous one. After a royal day, never to be forgotten by the few who ventured to stay out, we were kept awake by a hubbub in the lower part of the cabin. A Swede assured all within the sound of his voice that the ship would go down within two hours, and then he fell on his knees and began praying. Others prayed, cried and swore, according to sex and temperament. Many, however, laughed immoderately, and all this, with the breaking of glasses and the rolling from side to side of everything movable, made a din that banished sleep.

While we learned to appreciate many of our intelligent and genial companions in the second cabin, we became very good friends with a few. There was a gentleman from Washington, whose father was in the saloon, and as we usually occupied the same seats in a quiet part of the boat, next the walk of the saloon passengers, we made some pleasant acquaintances across the line. One of these was the Rev. Mr. Grubb, who gave us an excellent discourse the first Sunday on board and who always had a friendly word for everyone as he passed by. Another confessed that he thought the second cabin passengers enjoyed themselves much more than the saloon passengers, and really it seemed as if the latter were a rather melancholy lot. The second cabin people had two concerts with recitations and all the old Irish and Scotch ballads, sung with various degrees of excellence. "Auld Lang Syne" was always the finish, and it was wonderful with what spirit and good feeling this was always sung. At the last dinner, just before the passengers were put off for Londonderry, they sang it with fervor standing clasping hands across the table. We went down into the steerage to see what was the state of mind there, but there was no hilarity or expression of friendliness. It was the silence of despairing endurance or an open outcry at their discomforts. The steerage accommodations were abominable, considering that they paid within a few dollars of as much as the second cabin which had a fairly good table, comfortable berths and excellent attendance from the cheerful and obliging stewards. The head steward was quite a character, and did the old maid and the Irish schoolmaster to perfection in the concerts. The last night a vote of thanks was proposed to him and to his assistants. The latter certainly deserved appreciation, for they were always hard at work. In addition to waiting at table from early morn to the close of the day that seems to have no end on ship board, they were busy scrubbing or taking a hand at the ropes. However, the way the vote of thanks was worded gave me an opportunity to show my colors by moving to amend by adding the stewardess. This amendment was endorsed most heartily. This stewardess, a refined, business-like Scotch woman, is educating a son at the University with the proceeds of her work, and at the same time, making her ever changing, and by no means unimportant world, happier for her faithful ministrations.

We were particularly fortunate in seeing an iceberg, a rather small and upside-down one to be sure, but as one of the deck hands said he had been six years on the water and had seen but one, we felt very proud of even this. We saw, also, porpoises and whales, and there were but few days when we were not followed by the graceful sea gull. But time fails to tell of the interesting incidents of the voyage, which would seem trivial to the reader, but which were the whole world for the time to the traveler.

We reached Glasgow at midnight and remained on board until after an early breakfast. We are a little astounded to find that baggage is inspected on entering this free trade country, but certain articles, such as liquors and cigars are dutiable. One glance at our traps is sufficient for the customs inspector, and then we are free to step on the soil of Great Britain.

During our three days in Glasgow, we remained at the North British Hotel on St. George's Square. Opposite our window is the splendid post-

office building, and to the left of the square, the municipal building. In
the square are statues of Watts, Burns, Peel, Livingstone, and others. There
are also fine equestrian statues of Queen Victoria and the Prince Consort,
while towering above prince and statesmen in the centre is a very high
monument to Sir Walter Scott typifying that the power of the romancer
surpasses that of all others.

SOME TIME.

Some time, when all life's lessons have been learned,
  And sun and stars forevermore have set,
The things which our weak judgment here has spurned—
  The things o'er which we grieved with lashes wet—
Will flash before us out of life's dark night,
  As stars shine most in deeper tints of blue:
And we shall see how all God's plans were right,
  And how what seemed reproof was love most true.

     *   *   *   *   *   *   *

But not to-day. Then be content, poor heart:
  God's plans, like lilies, pure and white, unfold;
We must not tear the close-shut leaves apart:
  Time will reveal the calyxes of gold.
And if through patient toil we reach the land
  Where tired feet, with sandals loose, may rest,
When we shall clearly know and understand,
  I think that we shall say that "God knew best."

—*Selected.*

A Week Without the Women.

KATE WHITING PATCH.

"COME Esther, where is breakfast, I must be at college in less than an hour. Why can't you be on time?"

"Oh, dear!" sighed Esther as she set the coffee-pot on the table, "I wish you would not be so impatient, Ned. You know it is washing day, so Bridget is busy, and I had to help her get the breakfast, besides sewing half a dozen buttons on Jack's coat."

"I wish we had some one who could do her own work," replied the young collegian as he sat down to his hot muffins and coffee. "It seems to me Bridget has a pretty easy time of it. You do too much for her, Esther."

"Yes," piped up Jack, from the other end of the table, "she's awful lazy!"

"Hush, Jack!" said Esther, "she will hear you. Bridget is faithful and works hard. I do not know what a certain little boy would do without her griddle cakes. Will you have more coffee, Uncle Elisha?"

Jack bolted his oatmeal, and then left the table. "Do you know where I put my spelling book, Esther?" he asked, rummaging among books and papers.

"Why, Jack, haven't you learned your spelling lesson yet? I thought you studied last night," sighed Esther.

"Oh, I meant to," replied the small boy, indifferently, "but you know what it is to get into an awfully interesting book. The first thing I knew it was bed-time, and I had lost my speller."

"Well," said Esther, as she handed him the missing book, "sit right down and study now, Jack, and do not read another night before you know your lesson."

"No, my son," said Ned, shaking his head wisely as he arose from the table, "you will never reach college at that rate."

"Who cares?" retorted Jack "I wouldn't be as proud as you are, any way, just 'cause you're a Harvard sophomore."

Ned laughed, and threw a sofa pillow at his young brother, and then went for his coat and hat. Esther began gathering the dishes together.

Soon Ned appeared again, exclaiming, impatiently, as he tossed Esther one of his gloves, "There, put a button on that, will you, please? It just snapped off—when I was in such a hurry, too!"

"Say, won't you hear my spelling?" asked Jack, as his sister flew to her work basket.

"Wait a moment, Jack. Oh, dear! I've dropped the button; never mind, here is another."

In a few minutes Ned had his gloves and was striding off collegeward, and Esther was hearing Jack recite a very poor lesson. Half-past eight came and she had started the restless little boy off to school, and Uncle Elisha had gone out for a walk.

Then Esther washed the glasses and silver, and carried her little dishpan to the kitchen. Here she encountered a new trouble. Bridget was sitting among the soiled clothes, her wet apron flung over her head, and from this dismal retreat, loud sobs and moans proceeded.

"Why, what is the matter?" asked Esther, as she put down her pan in alarm. "Are you ill, Bridget?"

"No, Miss Esther," answered the tearful Bridget, "but the pennypost just brung me a letter as sez that me sister is sick ter die, an' what iver shall I do?"

Esther seized the letter and glanced hurriedly through it.

"No, Bridget," she said, "this only tells you that your sister is not well, and probably wants a good nurse like yourself to take care of her. Hurry with your washing, and I will have Mrs. Flanagan come and do the ironing, and you can go to-night and stay a day or two with your sister if she needs you."

At this Bridget murmured tearful words of gratitude and returned to her washtubs, and Esther opened her own mail—a letter from her Aunt Margaret inviting her to spend a week in Milton.

"I should like to go," the girl said to herself, "but as Bridget is to be away, of course I cannot think of it."

Esther Desmond's mother had died when Jack was a baby, and her father, whose health had never been perfect, was now obliged to spend his winters in the South. That he might do this, many luxuries had to be sacrificed, and among them, as Esther had finished school, the old housekeeper.

For two years now Mr. Desmond had spent a large part of his time in Florida, and his daughter had kept house in Cambridge for her brothers and their great uncle.

Uncle Elisha was not an easy person to live with. He was a crabbed old man, and a miserly one. Ned's going to college and Esther's keeping a servant he regarded as useless and expensive; and although he always made way with his share of Esther's dainty dishes, he considered it necessary to shake his head over them. Esther had difficulties to encounter, but she was a plucky little woman and did not often grow discouraged.

To-day she was so busy the morning passed quickly, and before she had realized that it was noon, Jack was at home again.

When he heard that Bridget was going away for a while, Jack was very repentant of his hasty words at breakfast, so after dinner he went out in the kitchen and offered her some chocolate creams.

"I'm awful sorry you've got to go, Bridget!" he said, taking a seat on the kitchen table. "I shall miss your griddle cakes very much." Then, feeling that he had made proper amends, he trudged off to school again.

Bridget departed not long after. Esther made some biscuit and prepared the supper, and everything looked as bright as usual when they sat down at the table, but it had been a hard day for the girl; her head ached, and she was tired and nervous when she took her accustomed place behind the tea urn.

"Bridget's gone," announced Jack, with the important air of one imparting information.

"Great Scott!" exclaimed Ned, "you don't say so? Well, I think we can do better. I could do in a couple of hours the work that girl takes a day over."

Esther sighed. "She has only gone for a day or two, Ned, to take care of a sick sister. I am sorry you do not like Bridget; she is very good, I think."

"Oh, the old story of a sick or dying relative, is it?" laughed Ned, provokingly.

"Well," put in Uncle Elisha, as he munched his toast, "I don't think she'd better come back. When your ma was your age she used to do all the housework at home, and there was a sight more to do."

"Yes," replied Esther, her usually composed manner ruffled by this speech; "yes, and she killed herself working. If my mother had kept help instead of slaving so before she was married, she might have been alive still."

Uncle Elisha was not prepared for this answer, and even Ned was surprised, Esther was usually so quiet and gentle. The remainder of the meal was eaten in silence.

It did not take Esther long to clear away the tea things; and she sat down to her sewing, while Jack went faithfully to work at his spelling.

In half an hour, Ned looked up from his book. "Did you mend the lining of my black coat?" he asked.

"Oh, Ned, I forgot! I was so busy to-day."

"Forgot it!" exclaimed her brother, impatiently; "why, I told you I must wear the coat to-morrow. What is there about this house that keeps you so busy, I would like to know?"

Ned spoke thoughtlessly; but he had wounded his sister. Esther laid down her work and rose before him with flashing eyes.

"Ned Desmond;" she said, "you are cruel. You know I have to work all day to keep you comfortable—and this is the thanks I receive!"

Her voice faltered, and she hastily left the room. Ned was dumb in his surprise; Jack did not know what to make of his sister, and Uncle Elisha stared in open-mouthed wonder to see that "Esty" had so much spirit.

Once in her own room, Esther threw herself upon the bed and had a good cry, but as soon as she grew quieter, she sat up and thought, in wonder, of what she had done. Yes, she, Esther Desmond, had actually lost her temper, and spoken to her brother and uncle in a manner before unknown to her. What could it mean? "I can't be well," she said, putting her hand to her throbbing head. Then she arose and bathed her forehead, and let her hair fall over her shoulders.

"I am sorry I spoke out so," she thought, "but then, Ned had no business to say what he did, nor Uncle Elisha, either. They both think because I stay at home I have nothing to do."

She knew that her brother had spoken thoughtlessly, but Ned had been growing into the habit of petty fault-finding, and Jack sometimes considered it well to echo his elder brother; complaining was nothing new to Uncle Elisha. Heretofore Esther had borne it quietly, but the long strain of care and worry was beginning to tell upon the girl. At nineteen these things are not easy to bear—if they are easy at any time.

"I cannot stand it any longer," she said to herself, "unless I have a change. I must take some way of showing them that my patience is exhausted."

Just then her eyes fell upon Aunt Margaret's letter. She took it from the desk and read it again; then she sat thinking a moment, and at last said, half aloud:

"Yes, that is just what I will do. There is nowhere that I can rest better than at Aunt Margaret's and it will teach them all a lesson." Just then there came a little tap at her door.

"Please, Esther, may I come in?" and she opened the door to admit Jack. "Please, can I do anything for you, sister? what is the matter?" and he looked at her with wondering eyes. She drew the little boy to her side and kissed him, but he felt the hot tears fall on his cheek.

"Why, what is it, Esther?" he asked again.

"Nothing, dear, only I do not feel well. Tell Ned I will not come down again, I am going to bed."

Sympathetic little Jack kissed his sister and stroked her cheek, soothingly, and then went down to give Ned her message.

Ned had been industriously abusing himself. "What a fool I was!" he exclaimed, at Jack's words; and throwing aside his book, he went up-stairs.

Esther opened the door, her long, brown hair falling about her, the traces of tears still upon her cheeks.

"Why, what is the matter, sister?" he asked, as he drew her to him, "I did not mean to hurt you, Esther. I spoke before I thought. I did not mean half I said. Can't you forgive me, little sister?"

"Oh, Ned, I was so tired!" and the brown head went down on his shoulder, and Esther was crying again.

Ned brushed the hair aside and kissed her cheek. "There, there! you are tired. Go to bed now, and to-morrow you will be all right;" and feeling his conscience lighter, Ned went back to his book.

Esther waited until he had gone, and then she softly glided across the hall to his room and took from its place in the closet Ned's black coat. The lining was badly torn, but in spite of a blinding headache and trembling fingers, she mended it carefully and laid it across a chair in his room. Two hours later Ned found it there. He looked at the neatly mended lining and then said aloud, with disgust, "Ned Desmond, you're a brute!"

The next morning at breakfast Esther surprised the household by remarking carelessly that she was going to Aunt Margaret's for a week.

"What, while Bridget is away?" exclaimed Ned.

"Yes," she answered, "I am tired and need the change. You all say that there is very little to do about a house like this, and I shall make enough food to last you for some days. If the bread gives out you can go to the baker's. Uncle Elisha says that servants are a useless expense, so you won't miss Bridget, and Ned can do her whole day's work in two hours, anyway. He has more than that free from college duties each day. I shall go to-morrow afternoon. If everything does not run smoothly, you can hire Mrs. Flanagan; or, if worse comes to worse, telegraph for me. It will be something like camping out, as you are not used to the work, but you know there is not much to do about a house."

By the time this speech was finished, Uncle Elisha and Ned looked rather grave, but Jack's face was radiant. "Oh, it will be bully fun!" he cried, jumping from his chair to perform a sort of Indian war-dance.

Ned glanced at his sister to see if she was in earnest, and satisfying himself that she was, he said, with an indifferent air. "Oh, I fancy we will do very well."

"It'll be splendid!" exclaimed Jack, "it'll be most like Robinson Crusoe. Oh, I wish we lived on a desert island!"

"You would not wish so long," laughed Ned.

"Yes, I would," replied the small boy. "Say, Ned, let's play we do! You can be Robinson, 'cause you're the biggest. I'll be Man Friday, and—and we'll let Uncle Elisha be one of the savages. Say, that will be fine; will you?"

Ned laughed heartily. "All right," he replied, "on one condition; you, as my Man Friday, must do just as I tell you. Esther, you need not worry about us, we shall do beautifully, I assure you. Why, when you return, everything will be so lovely you will forget that you have ever been away."

"O Esther!" cried Jack, going through his war-dance again, "I'm so glad you're going away! No, I don't mean that; I mean I'm glad we're going to play Robinson Crusoe."

Esther smiled. "I'm pleased that you like my plan," she said, but added to herself, "I wonder how it will be when the week is over."

That morning Jack trotted off to school the happiest of boys, and Esther went about her work. She made a quantity of bread, cake and cookies, and baked some apples. When all was done she surveyed her pantry shelves with some pride. "They won't starve for several days, any way," she thought. Then she wrote a note to Aunt Margaret accepting her invitation, and sent another to Bridget telling her that she might stay with her sister until she was sent for.

After dinner Esther packed her trunk and then ran across the street to tell her friend, Dora Harte, of her proposed visit. "Now, Dora," she said, as they were parting, "I want you to keep an eye on the boys, and if they break all the china and turn everything upside down, or seem on the point of starvation, just let me know."

Jack was a little homesick next day at the idea of his sister's going away, but the thought of Man Friday kept him up until Esther had departed in the afternoon, leaving a tempting supper ready for them. When Ned reached home he found Uncle Elisha sitting by the fire and Jack in a rather quiet mood, but at the sight of his brother, the latter jumped up with a bright face. "Halloa, Robinson!" he said, "Esther left us a bully tea; come along." They all sat down, and though it seemed strange not to have Esther there, this did not prevent them from enjoying their supper exceedingly. Soon Jack looked at Uncle Elisha's plate and observed: "The savage wants his toast; he always has it, you know. I'll make some."

He slid out of his chair and went into the kitchen. Ten minutes later he returned with a very long face, and something black in his hand.

"What is that?" asked Ned.

"The—the toast," gasped Jack. "It fell into the fire, and this is all I could fish out. You needn't laugh—" for Ned was leaning back in his chair with his napkin to his face.

"Never mind, Friday," he said, "I guess the savage will have to go without his toast to-night. I will show you how to make some to-morrow."

After tea they cleared the table, but Ned said they would not bother about washing the dishes then, so they were piled up by the kitchen sink.

The next morning Jack awoke very early. He bounded out of bed, dressed as quickly as possible and stole down stairs to the kitchen. The fire was out; they had not thought to "keep it over night," as Bridget did, so the kitchen was cold. Man Friday was not to be daunted by such a trifle. He went to the closet where Esther kept all the old papers and magazines, and seized upon some *Harper's Weeklys* and *Youths' Companions*. Jack did not like to burn these, but then, there were no newspapers within his reach; so after carefully looking at the pictures, he crammed the Weeklies into the stove and lighted a match. There was a beautiful blaze for a few minutes, but he had forgotten to put on any sticks, so it soon went out, and there was nothing left but a heap of charred paper. Then he tried again, and this time added wood, but it was too hard, and he had no kindlings; so after a brief struggle for existence that fire followed the other, and after two more vain attempts, Jack gave it up and sat down on a cracker can to rest and eat a slice of gingerbread.

It then flashed across Jack's mind that Robinson ought to be down, so he stole quietly upstairs again and paused at the door of his brother's room. Not a sound. Ned was still asleep. Jack opened the door and went in. "Oh, dear!" he ejaculated, as he sat down on the edge of a chair, "I wonder if he knows how pretty he looks with his mouth open." Then the spirit of mischief entered into him and twinkled about the corners of his mouth and in his eyes. There was a sponge on the washstand. Jack tiptoed across the room. It did not take long to wet that sponge, and it did not take much longer to creep over to the bedside and squeeze it, just a little—just a little; but a cool stream trickled down Ned's throat. In an instant he jumped up, choking and sputtering; in an instant more he had seen Jack with the sponge in his hand, and in another instant a pillow was flying at Jack's head. He dodged it and then threw it back again. A lively skirmish ensued; chairs were overturned; bed-clothes scattered about, and it ended by Jack's sliding down the balusters with a pillow flying after him, while Ned locked his door and hunted under the *debris* for his missing clothing.

Breakfast was not a very cheerful affair. Ned succeeded in making the fire and some very bad coffee, and they ate on a corner of the kitchen table, to save the trouble of carrying the things into the dining-room.

After breakfast Jack hunted for his spelling book, and at last found it under the kitchen stove. Then he trotted off to school with no collar and a very dirty face, but he did not care, for his pockets were full of cookies.

Uncle Elisha looked at the pile of dishes and said to Ned, as that young man prepared to leave, "What about them?"

"Oh, I don't know!" was the careless answer, "I must go now."

And he did; but the old man still looked doubtfully around him. He supposed that, some time or other, he must have had experience in dish-washing, but he had forgotten it. These must be done, however, so he set resolutely about it.   He did not go far, for he broke a cup to begin with and that discouraged him; but after carefully sweeping up the pieces, he carried them out to the stable and emptied them in a rat hole.   "Make 'em useful that way," he muttered to himself.

When Ned came home at noon he found Jack in great distress.   "Why, what is the matter, Friday?" he asked, in surprise.

"Oh, dear!" replied Friday, in miserable tones, "I was climbing Smith's fence, and I caught on a picket and tore my pants! Oh, dear! oh, dear!"

"Jupiter! what will you do?"

"I don't know; I 'spect I'll have to stay home from school."

"No, sir!" replied Ned, dashing the small boy's hopes at once.   "You can put on another pair."

"Haven't any but my best ones, and Esther don't let me wear those to school."

"I can't help it; you will have to now.   I don't know how to mend the things."

Dinner was not more cheerful than breakfast had been; the afternoon was dull, and when the supper hour arrived, they found the stock of clean dishes greatly diminished.

While Jack was studying his lesson that evening and Ned was writing a "sophomore theme," Uncle Elisha ventured to remark that he thought they had better send for "Esty."

"No sir!" exclaimed Ned, throwing down his pen; "We said we could do without her, and I tell you we will.   Come, Jack, it is time for you to go to bed."

"Aren't you coming soon?" asked the little boy. putting down his book.

"Yes, you run along.   Good.night."   Ned turned to his writing again, and Jack went upstairs; yes, he went upstairs, but he did not go to bed.   He opened his door and lighted the gas, then he stopped where he was and exclaimed. 'Gracious Peter!"

Next he opened Ned's door; before him lay the wreck of that morning's battle.   Then, with a grin, Jack leaned over the baluster, "Say, Ned!"

"What's the matter?"

"The beds ain't made."

"Thunder!"

Jack heard that, and then the light went out, and Ned bounded up the stairs, with Uncle Elisha creeping behind him.   As they passed Esther's room Jack paused.   "How nice it looks!" he said.   "Let's sleep there!" but Ned went on resolutely.

"No, sir!" he replied.   "Not a thing of the little sister's shall be disturbed."

They tussled with Jack's bed first, but that was nothing compared with what they encountered in Ned's apartment. The bedclothes were scattered to the four winds of heaven, or to speak more literally, the four corners of the room, while chairs and pillows were in a state of wild confusion; and when the beds were made, after long and silent labor, what wretched affairs they looked ! how different from Esther's !

"Well, Jacky, they will have to do !" said Ned, mopping his head with his handkerchief, "now get to bed as quickly as possible."

Jack obeyed, but, although he was very tired, he could not sleep.

Ned's bed was not more comfortable, but he made the best of it, and had been asleep about two hours when he was awakened by the sound of half-stifled sobs just outside the door. He jumped up and hastily lighted the gas, to discover poor Jack curled up in a woeful heap on the rug.

"Halloa, Friday ! what's up now !" asked Ned, as he surveyed his tearful brother.

"Oh, dear ! Oh, dear !" sobbed Jack. "My bed's uncomfortable, and I don't feel well, and I want Esther—and—and Bridget !"

"I shouldn't wonder if we all did," groaned Ned; and then he added-laughing, "Come, cheer up, Friday; it will never do for you to give in. Get into bed with me, and remember there are only five days more."

Five days more ! only five days more ! Ned sighed heavily as he turned out the light. What a wretched day this has been, and there were five more like it to come ! He was filled with remorse and chagrin. What would Esther say, after all his bragging? He had really been hard and ungrateful for all the work his sister and Bridget—yes, Bridget—had done every day to make him comfortable.

And thus, amid the ruins of his fallen pride, Ned fell aslep.

Some days later Esther was reclining in an easy-chair in Aunt Margaret's cosey sitting-room, a book that she was not reading lying open upon her lap. She was certainly having the rest that she needed, but it would not be strictly true to say that she was happy. The three at home weighed heavily upon her mind. She had pictured them many time; but, in spite of their boasts, never a cheerful picture could she make of it.

"Oh, I was very wrong to leave them ! I ought to go home !" she said to herself that morning. She had said it many times before, but Aunt Margaret would not listen to her. She saw no reason why her niece should go before the week was over, and Esther did not care to tell her the real reason. Aunt Margaret would be severe if she suspected that any one had been criticising her favorite niece. But while Esther was thinking this over, the morning mail arrived and brought her two letters and a postal card. The latter was from Ned, on which he sated briefly that they were "all well and happy," but the "happy" did not look quite truthful.

The first letter she opened was in Jack's scrawly handwriting. "Oh, dear!" sighed Esther, as she glanced over it, "I am afraid he has lost his spelling book!"

Dear Esther: she read. I havent writen you a leter since you went away but I spose you know we're gettin on al rite. We've eatin up most every thing that you left, so Ned tried to mak some pan cakes but they wer not as good as Bridgets. They was kind of sticky inside. Uncle Elisha broke one of your cups with the roses on it and put the peaces down the rat hole in the barn, he didn't tell me, but I fonnd em there and I think it was awfol mean of him to do it, for that rat was getting real tame and I used to feed him with corn every morning. I fished out all the peaces I could, but I don't bleve he'll ever come up that whole again.

I tore my pants the other day so I had to put on my best ones, for Ned sed I must go to school. Its packs of fun to see Uncle Elisha wash dishes. He got tired of seeing so many round I spose, so he tride to wash em to-day. He did it ones befor I gess, and broke that cup. there wasn't any fire so he took cold water, which is not right, is it? We could not find any towels so he wiped them on one of your apens. I tell you Esther, when you come home, I am going to lern how to wash dishes and make beds so I'll know how when I'm an old Bachelor like uncle.

The savage is getting tired of it and wanted to send for you but Robinson wood not let him. We had a pillow fite the morning after you went away, but it was hard to fix up after it, so we didn't have another. The beds aint very nice the way Ned makes em and some times we don't make em at al. I will be glad when you come home. It aint as much fun playing Robinson Cruso as I thote it wood be. Good by. I have ben a long time writing this letter. Does ant Margaret like to have little boys visit her? and dose her Bridget make gridle cakes?

Your loving Jack.

Esther folded the letter with a little smile playing about her lips, "Mercy!" she exclaimed, "it is surely time for me to go home when Uncle Elisha uses my hand-painted cups to stop up rat holes, and Jack sits on the kitchen table in his Sunday trousers."

Then she opened the second letter, which was addressed in Dora's familiar hand. It began:

My Dear Esther: You asked me to let you know when it was necessary for you to return, and I think that the necessary hour has come. I do believe that those three across the way are as penitent and miserable a set of mortals as ever existed.

Jack made us a short call this morning, and quite opened his heart to me. Mary was frying doughnuts, and his eyes and nose turned so wistfully towards the kitchen door that I went in and brought in two hot ones for him. Then he told me his troubles.

Oh, Esther! that house looks as though a hurricane had swept through it. I did not quite dare offer my services in putting things to rights, for I was afraid Ned would not like it. Poor fellow! I gave him a loaf of bread last night, and he thanked me as fervently as though I had presented him with a small gold mine. Little Jack is miserably homesick, and Uncle Elisha has grown wonderfully meek.

Now, dear Esther, do not be hard-hearted any longer, but come home at once, and I can assure you that you will find a warm welcome awaiting you. I hope you are well rested by this time.

Yours, as ever, Dora.

That settled the question. A note was posted to Bridget, and at last Aunt Margaret gave her consent to Esther's leaving next day.

About two o'clock on the following afternoon, Bridget arrived at the house in Cambridge. Uncle Elisha was the only one at home, and he disappeared as speedily as possible.

"Och! what a mess!" exclaimed the good-natured Irish girl; but she was soon at work, and the kitchen looked as orderly as usual when Esther arrived an hour later.

"What, no one at home, Bridget?" she asked, "that is good! we can surprise them. Ah, you have been at work I see."

"Och, yis, Miss Esther! sich a clutter as it was! but I'm done wid the kitchen now, and I'm about to sweep the dinin'-room."

At that moment there was a light tap at the door, and Dora came in. "Ah, Esther, my dear! I saw you arrive, and now I want to help you and Bridget, so that all will be in order before the boys come."

"Thank you, Dora. We will go upstairs, Bridget, let us have a very nice supper, and you can light a fire in the dining-room grate."

Upstairs all looked very hopeless, but the girls set to work and an hour made great changes. Then Dora went home, and Esther came down in her pretty gray gown with a spray of heliotrope fastened at the throat, and took her accustomed seat by the low work-table in the corner of the dining-room. A wood fire crackled in the grate, the table was laid for tea, and everything looked bright and cheerful. It was not long before Uncle Elisha came in.

"Well, Esty," he said, as cordially as he knew how, "we're right glad to have ye home again!"

"I hope you are, uncle," answered Esther, drawing his arm-chair up to the fire for him, "and I am glad to be at home."

Just then the door flew open, and Jack, with a delighted scream, rushed into Bridget's arms. "Oh, are you really home? Are you going to stay? Has *she* come? has Esther?" but Esther was before him, and Jack clung to her, sobbing for very joy.

"Why, Jack, what are you crying for? aren't you glad to see me?" she asked, laughingly; but he only clung the closer and said in a whisper:

"It's 'cause I'm so awful glad you've come back. It seems as if you'd been gone a hundred years!"

"O Jacky! Jacky!" exclaimed Esther, as she kissed him, "you have on no collar—and such a dirty face!"

"You come up and fix me," he said, pulling her toward the stairs, When he looked quite neat again and they started to go down, Jack said, as he glanced at the inviting-looking beds, "My! won't it be nice to sleep in a home-made bed again!"

As they entered the dining-room Ned's step was heard on the piazza; Esther slipped behind the door and put her finger to her lips, "Don't say a word, Jack!" she whispered.

Ned came in, tired and cross, but at the door he stopped in amazement. "What!" he cried, as the cheerful and orderly room broke upon his view. But Jack's eyes could not keep away from the door, and throwing it back, Ned caught his sister in his arms. "We are glad to have you home again, little woman, we are indeed!" he said, with a hearty kiss, and he looked quite like another being as the anxiety vanished from his face.

They had a pleasant supper and a very happy evening, and little was said, then or afterwards, of the days that had just passed; but by a hundred thoughtful actions and patient words, Esther could see that her lesson, though severe, had not been in vain. Jack did indeed learn to wash dishes and make beds, and was a real help to his sister, and Uncle Elisha was never heard to grumble about "servant gals" again. If any of them did venture an ungrateful remark, however, Esther had only to look up with a mischievous twinkle in her eyes. To their dying day Uncle Elisha or Ned or little Jack, will never forget that week they spent without the women.—|*Household.*

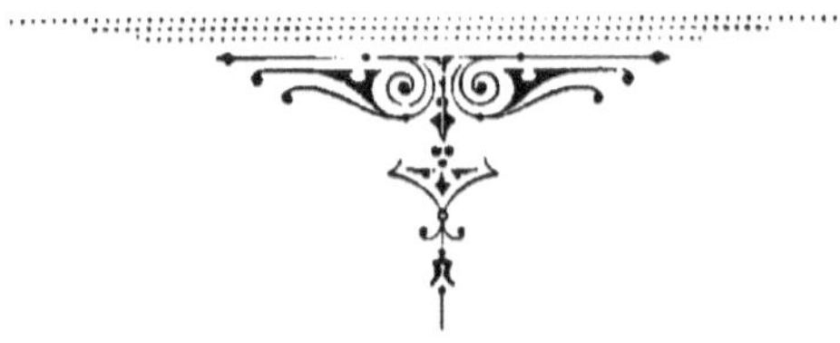

Mail Carrier of Pelham's Point.

SALLIE PATE STEEN.

"**S**EEMS kind of hard Martha couldn't have been a boy." A note of complaint sharpened the soft Southern drawl of Mrs. Bixler's voice. "We've had mighty hard luck ever since she was born. We somehow appeared to get in a moving way on down-hill road, as pap used to say. From Arkansas to Kansas, and from Kansas to the Strip, was jumping from the frying-pan into the fire, according to my mind. And just as we'd got this claim, and a sod house put up, pap he took sick and died. You don't know what trouble is, Mrs. Perkins, till you're left a widow, with a lot of girls to bring up. You've got a lot to be thankful for, with your husband living and three big boys to work for you."

The visitor stirred uneasily in her chair. Of a far different type from her hostess, she was thin and wiry, with a strong-featured, New England face, and a quiet, undemonstrative manner. The hot winds of the prairie seemed to have seared her, mentally and physically, and the hard life of a farmer's wife had knotted her lean hands and twisted her shoulders. There was no weak self-pity in the firm mouth and the steady gray eye, but as she listened, a strange sense of loneliness tugged at her heartstrings.

In their struggle with mortgage and drought, her three big boys had grown away from her. She had failed to keep them close to her, as other mothers could keep their daughters. She thought of the day she had laid away her own baby girl, buried from a camper's wagon, upon the wide-stretching plains, as mariners commit the bodies of their dead to the limitless ocean. In all this barren land she would see forever that lonely, sun-scorched little grave—and the baby, had she lived, would have been just Martha's age.

"I should think you'd take a sight of comfort in Martha, though," she said, in a hard, dry voice, twisting and untwisting her bonnet strings. "She must be lots of company, and she's smart too. There isn't a better butter-maker in the Strip than Martha is, and you told me yourself that she kept up the table, about, with her chickens and the garden. I don't see why you should wish she was a boy, unless 'twas for her own sake."

"And that's just what I'm coming to, Mrs. Perkins." Mrs. Bixler settled herself comfortably in her splint-bottomed chair. "Here's Scott Landis, over on the next claim, with that mail contract to sublet, and if Martha was a boy, she could take it easy as winking. It would bring in about twenty-five dollars a month, and it's just a matter of ten miles from Pelham's Point to Luella.

"Martha's just wild to earn a little money, so she can go into town to Normal School this summer, She's harped on that string till she's set me pretty near crazy. She allows if she could go to Normal, she could get the school here next fall, and then she could teach a while and go to school a while. She's a great notion of landing in college one of these days, Martha has. I tell her," Mrs. Bixler chuckled, "that she'll turn goose like her mother, and get married before—"

"Ma!"

There was a rustle in the morning-glory vines outside, and a girl's flushed, indignant face framed itself in the low window.

"Well, and what are you nosing around listening for, Martha Bixler? Eavesdroppers—"

"I wasn't eavesdropping. I came up to the house for the picket-pin, to put Moll out on the rope, and here you—"

The hot words stuck in the girl's throat. She turned away, the mare following, while Mrs. Bixler's high, good-natured laugh rang out.

Martha bit her lip at the sound. To think of all her secret hopes and plans being confided to Mrs. Perkins!—hopes which the girl herself had scarcely dared to cherish, plans which she had tried to form through many a busy day and wakeful night!

Her love of books was an instinct, a passion, and her slumbering ambition had been aroused by the only good teacher she had ever had. He was a college-bred man who had drifted to the Strip, and in stress of need had applied for the Spring Valley school for a term. His teaching had opened up a new world to Martha's eager vision.

"You have it in you to be a great woman, Martha," he had said, kindly, on the last day of school. "Don't give up: Don't wait for opportunities; make them." And his words, carelessly uttered, and soon forgotten by himself, had been Martha's inspiration.

She brooded over them as she sat in the saddle through long days of herding, with no human creature near, the great, stainless sky stretched out above, and the flower-decked prairie, with its grazing cattle, spread beneath. They haunted her as she guided her horses from the seat of a sulky plow, the sod curling up in brown waves behind her.

And to think that all this bitterness of longing should be laid bare to a woman who was almost a stranger, and who, in Matha's judgment, could feel no sympathy with such aspirations! A lump rose in her throat as she bent over the picket-pin. Her pink sunbonnet hid her indignant tears, but the woman who had quietly followed divined them. She laid her hand gently upon the girl's shoulder.

"I've come out to see the filly, Martha," she said. "Your ma's been telling me how you raised her from a colt when her mother died. She's a picture now, isn't she? If there's anything I do like, it's a good horse; and the bucking broncos these Westerners ride seem like a different sort of animal to me."

"She's a thoroughbred, you know, Mrs. Perkins," Martha explained, eagerly. It was impossible to feel resentful toward a woman who could appreciate the mare's good points. "Pap brought her mother from Kentucky before I was born, and she died in the big blizzard up in Kansas three years ago. I wish you could have seen Moll when he first gave her to me. She was the pitifulest little thing, all scraggy and big-jointed. You wouldn't think it now, would you? And she'll follow me anywhere. She's as rope-wise as a cow-pony, and she goes like a rocking-chair." Mrs. Perkins glanced from the girl's flushed cheek and brightening eye to the mare's arched neck and impatient forefoot.

"She's just the one to carry the mail. Martha," she said slowly, "and I do not know but I'd trust you with the mail-bag as soon as I would any boy around."

"Why, Mrs. Perkins! Why, you don't mean—"

"I mean to say that Scott Landis isn't the man to stand in the way of a girl that wants to help herself, and I believe he'll think you're just as able to ride twenty miles three times a week as anybody. You picked castor-beans for him last fall, and kept up with his men hands, too, didn't you? You've herded every season since the Strip opened, and you've run a sulky-plow all the spring. I haven't heard anybody complain about your doing those things because you were a girl. It seems to me Martha Bixler, that if I wanted an easier job, with bigger pay, I'd pretty near ask for it, and I'm no strong-minded woman, neither."

So from this unexpected source Martha gained courage to make her first opportunity. Fortunately, Scott Landis was not a difficult man to approach. He was a good-natured old bachelor, with a shrewd, dry humor of his own, and "the girl's nerve," as he expressed it, appealed to him.

"I don't know but you might as well be knocking out twenty-five dollars a month by riding over these prairies as to take to bloomers and a bicycle, Martha" he said, slowly, "and they tell me that's what girls are coming to.

"But there's another side to it," he went on. "It ain't a regular thing, you know. The place has never been held by a woman, and I don't know how the neighborhood might take it. I hold myself responsible for anything I do, but if I give you a trial you must back me up. I shall want you to be the best mail-carrier we've ever had. The last one got drunk; the one before him robbed the bag. We've never had punctual deliveries. The fact is, you must show folks what you can do."

Martha promised that no one should ever have cause to complain of her.

It was well for her peace of mind that she never guessed the feeling which her appointment aroused. The salary, although small, was enough to excite envy. Almost any man could muster the necessary equipment of a cow-pony and a saddle, and the chance of earning twenty-five dollars a month by an effort involving little or no muscular exertion was one not to be despised.

But Scott Landis was an able champion. He had caused it to be generally understood that if there was "any kick coming," to use his own words, it was ¡to be directed to him as the responsible party; and he had an easy way of encouraging comment, and a silent patience in listening to objections, calculated to lure a talker on to his own undoing.

"There's one or two things that really disqualify a mail-carrier, in the opinion of some folks," he drawled, one afternoon, as he stood the centre of a group of disapproving loafers. "For a government employe to ride up to an office, leave the mail on time, and ride off again about her business, is a thing anybody's got a right to complain of. I don't believe Martha's spent an hour yet whittling a goods box and gassing, with her horse tied out in the sun yonder for the sand-flies to devour. She doesn't patronize any saloon that ever I've heard of, nor treat the crowd on Saturdays. And if that isn't a gross neglect of duty, I don't know what is. I can't say whether Uncle Sam would consider it sufficient cause for removal or not, but you might make out your complaint, boys, and send it in. When you get your papers fixed up, hand them over, and I'll sign them."

But Martha herself was gaining ground. She had had to pay the penalty of establishing a precedent, but little by little the neighborhood was reconciled to the new order of things. Indeed, through her bravery, her cheerfulness, her willingness to oblige, there was every indication that she might be regarded as a public benefactor.

Numberless little commissions were entrusted to her. She did errands in the small town which was the end of her route. She carried messages, she shopped for the women. And once, at midnight, Mollie thundered along a lonely road, urged to her utmost speed by her fearless young rider, to bring a doctor's aid and comfort to a dying child and its distracted mother.

People learned to welcome the sight of the bonny brown mare and the brave young figure that she bore. It came to be a matter of pride that even the appearance of their mail-carrier reflected credit upon the neighborhood. Comparisons, damaging to the other man of the postal territory upon another route, were freely indulged in.

"It's kind of funny to watch Griggs crawling in from Luella," commented an observant loafer, "humped up on that old go-cart of his, a-driving a one-eyed cow-pony with rope lines, and then to see Martha skipping in on that slim-legged thoroughbred, the mare's coat as shiny as the girl's hair. Strikes me they're an institution Uncle Sam might be proud of." And he spoke the sentiments of the entire community.

But the time limited by Martha's contract was drawing to an end. It had been pleasant to earn the money. It had been pleasanter still to win the good-will and friendship of her neighbors. She had taken an honest pride in her work, and she had rejoiced in pleasing her employer. He had expressed his entire satisfaction with the way in which she had acquitted herself. She therefore felt vaguely surprised and alarmed at the unwonted gravity of his manner when he met her, one evening, on her homeward way.

"I've been wondering if you wouldn't like a little lay-off, for a day or two, Martha," he began, stooping as if to examine the saddle-girth.

"So near the—the end of the time, Mr. Landis?" Martha faltered. "Why, I believe I'd like to keep on—to—to finish, if I'm pleasing you."

"Oh, bless your heart, yes you're all right. It's just this, Martha. I don't want to make you uneasy, but we've got it about straight that Zip Wyatt is prowling around in the neighborhood somewhere, cut off from his gang since that hold-up down at Chandler, and trying to get back to the Glass Mountains. He's a regular cattle-lifting, train-robbing, murdering desperado, and the boys are hot on his trail. There were two big rewards out for him, and the Rock Island Railroad has offered another.

"We're bound to get him, dead or alive," Landis went on, "for he's been up to all kinds of devilment, single-handed as he is. He's already stolen three or four of the best horses around and ridden them down, trying to get out. I've no idea you'll ever catch a sight of him, but I presume all girls are kind of nervous, and I thought I'd better tell you than have somebody else scare you to death. So, if you'd rather lay off, as I said, for a day or two, till we've caught him, I could have somebody take your place."

"Will the other carriers lay off, too, Mr. Landis?" Martha interrupted.

"Well, now, I don't suppose they will, but—"

"And I won't, either, if you please, sir. I'm much obliged to you, but I'm not a bit afraid, and I reckon I'll just finish up, if you'll let me," and Martha cantered off, leaving Mr. Landis in the road, staring after her.

She had spoken the simple truth when she said she was not afraid. She felt that desperadoes, like cyclones or tarantulas, are to be avoided, not worried about. Despite her warning, Martha carried the mail, as usual.

For the first few days, indeed, she felt a thrill creep over her at every lonely turn in the road. The leap of a jack-rabbit, the swishing roll of tumbleweed, would bring her heart to her throat. The swirl of any passing cloud of dust might reveal the figure made so familiar to her by repeated description.

She knew all its characteristic features—the easy seat of the practised horseman, the wide, slouched hat, the cowboy saddle with its pistol holsters, and the deadly Winchester slung from the horn.

When the shadow of this dreaded figure did really fall across her way, one sunny morning, she felt no more surprise than if, in turning the pages of a book, she had chanced upon a picture which she already knew was there. Indeed, as the man rode out from behind a high bluff to the right of the road, she was conscious of a vague disappointment. There was certainly nothing of the gaily adventurous in his appearance.

He was haggard, worn, and weather-stained, his horse dark with sweat and flecked with foam, his bridle arm hanging limp in a bloody sling; but the Winchester was in evidence, and the glint of a pistol-barrel emphasized his hoarse "Hands-up!" The girl's arms went above her head at his command, and Mollie swerved as the man flung himself from his horse.

"Get off and change the saddles, and be quick about it!" he ordered. His voice was a husky whisper, and he reeled as he stood.

Martha slipped to the ground with a sob, but the sob was for Mollie. She unsaddled the mare without a word, letting the mail-bag drop softly in the dust beside her. By the time she had dragged the heavy cowboy saddle from the man's bronco she had forgotten the mare, and was thinking, with a throbbing brain, of her trust.

"I've got something to say," she panted, "and I can say it while I'm buckling." The man stared at her with bloodshot eyes.

"You can take the mare, but before you get the mail you'll have to shoot me—and the shot will be heard. The whole country's out after you. They went twenty different ways this morning. If they find me—dead—they won't wait to give you a trial."

"Curse the mail!" he said. "So they're after me, are they?—the blood-hounds! I'll give them the slip yet, if this hole in my side don't let the life out. Lend a hand here, girl!" and almost before Martha could spring aside, his spurred heel had gashed Mollie's quivering flank, and the mare was off.

With knees that trembled and hands that shook, Martha picked up the mail-bag and stepped out into the road. The bronco had fallen, and lay gasping its last. There was but one thing to be done. The mail must be taken to the nearest farm-house, and sent on thence to its destination. It should never be said that, girl-like, she had given up at the first difficulty.

She set her teeth, and lifted the bag to her shoulder. With every step it grew heavier. The heat was intolerable, the dust stifled her. Oh, for poor Mollie's fleet stride!

She turned at the sound of hoof-beats upon the road behind her, and her heart ceased beating. The outlaw was coming back. He had determined, then, to rob the mail! Well, she would never give it up. She stood still and waited, while the mare stopped beside her.

The man leaned toward her from the saddle. He was deadly pale, and the blood dripped from his bandaged arm.

"It's no use!" he said, hoarsely. "I'm played out. Lead the mare down into that corn-field behind the bluff, and help me off."

She obeyed him without a word. He sank down, heavily, upon the cool, moist earth between the corn rows.

"And now,,' he said, as a tinge of color crept back to his face, "take your horse and ride to town,—for a man's life,—do you understand? Go straight to the sheriff, and tell him that Zip Wyatt is lying wounded in a corn-field on the old Sun City Trail.

"Stop!" For Martha's hand was already in Mollie's mane. "You've got to swear that until you see the sheriff you'll stop nowhere, speak to nobody. I'm not such a fool as to risk being butchered by these hayseeds when I can live behind the bars."

Martha repeated the oath he dictated.

People stared at her as she flew past them that morning. Her oath bound her, and a feeling of pity, in no wise akin to morbid sympathy for a criminal, awoke in her heart. It was one thing to fall into the just hands of the law, and another to be butchered outright.

And Martha understood her neighbors. They were relentless when aroused. She knew which one of those two conditions of the offered rewards, "dead or alive," they would prefer; and the man was dying already, his life ebbing out in those rustling corn rows, while the blackbirds chattered in the draw.

The postmaster gasped when the Pelham Point mail-carrier, bareheaded, breathless, dashed up to the door, and, tossing him the bag without a word, rode off in the direction of the sheriff's office. Nor was that official less astonished at her appearance and information.

The buggy already awaited him, and a mounted deputy was speedily summoned; but there was doubt in the sheriff's face, as he turned to the excited girl.

"I must ask you to go back with us as guide," he said, sternly, and Martha suddenly realized that the outlaw's possible escape would give the lie to all her statements.

But such apprehensions were groundless. They found him lying just as she had left him. He had fallen asleep from sheer exhaustion, and he awoke as the sheriff bent over him. When they had shaken hands, and he had been refreshed from that official's flask, after the friendly Western manner of administering justice, the outlaw turned his heavy eyes upon Martha, as she stood close to Mollie's drooping head.

"I guess you'll have to give the girl the credit this time, sheriff," he said, with a grin; and the sheriff, with some apparent discomfiture, agreed that he would. But Martha was glad enough to be dismissed upon any terms. She rode home in a state of limp reaction, utterly unprepared to be received as a heroine.

' There was nothing else to do," she explained, over and over, to persistent admirers; and Scott Landis, with all his diplomacy, had a hard task in persuading her to accept the modest purse which friends and neighbors, far and near, made up for her.

"It's no reward, and no blood-money," he declared, "but the folks appreciate the girl, and I'm proud of it. Although I wouldn't let her know it, I took a lawyer and a Rock Island agent in to see Zip, and he did the square thing. He told the agent, with that grin of his, that if it hadn't been for Martha he wouldn't be behind the bars to-day; and, although I can't say whether the Rock Island fellow took it all in or not, his road has sent her a very handsome acknowledgement."

So Martha's dream of college was realized, and Mrs. Perkins delights in saying to her mother that a girl may be quite as good as a boy.—[*Youth's Companion*.

Four things a man must learn to do,
If he would make his record true;
To think without confusion clearly,
To love his fellow-man sincerely,
To act from honest motives purely,
To trust in God and heaven securely.
    —*The Rev. Dr. Henry Van Dyke.*

HOUSATONIC RIVER, NORTH OF CANAAN, CONN.

AN OLD GUITAR.

ALICE D. LE PLONGEON.

(Written for "Talks and Tales.")

"THIS is the place!" Jessie announced, stopping before a small shop window in Oxford Street.

It was a hazy summer's afternoon in old London; and my services had been enlisted to help in the choice of a guitar. Miss Jessie already had two, but neither of these quite suited her fancy; one was a little too hard for her small fingers to play on with ease; the other lacked volume of sound.

Decidedly, this was the smallest shop in Londontown. It contained one upright piano, one slender chair, a counter five feet long, and various instruments in cases against the walls. A fashionably dressed man was purchasing theater tickets; in making way for him to pass out, we found ourselves in contact with the piano.

"You wrote to me that you had a Spanish guitar," Jessie explained to the proprietor of the establishment, "and I have come without delay to judge of its qualities."

"Ah! yes, here is the instrument. It is cheap at ten guineas, but a reduction may be made for a professional."

"Of course" sweet Jessica promptly acquiesced. "It's shabby enough, too; never was a beauty, in fact. This dark stain suggests blood, and here on the rosette is a charred spot that smells of a conflagration; altogether it looks positively tragic! I don't believe I care for it—please show us some others."

But I took hold of the guitar, sat on the solitary chair, screwed up the old-fashioned pegs and struck a few chords. Full and sweet came the responding tones.

In quick succession we tried several instruments, but finally chose the one first offered, and agreed upon a price to be paid C. O. D.

On the following day we welcomed the guitar, made under the sunny skies of Seville more than half a century ago, as attested by a grimy label beneath the rosette.

Jessie, quite enthusiastic now, over her latest acquisition which was, bye the bye, a present from her brother Tom, counted the shining guineas into the hand of the boy who had brought the instrument, gave him a sixpence for himself, rushed to the nearest seat, and drew her fingers across the strings—somewhat out of tune.

"O, you dear old thing!" she exclaimed, "I do like you! I shall call you Carmen; that must have been the name of your owner, and besides, Carmen (red) is appropriate for a guitar that seems to have had blood spilled over it."

The demonstrative creature rattled off a lot more nonsense, but was checked by the postman's sharp rat-tat.

A maid brought in three letters for sweet Jessica; two requested that she would sing, to swell certain philanthropic funds; the third asked her to get up an entire entertainment at Marchmont Hall, 94 Marchmont Street, Burton Crescent, W. C., for the education of the "great unwashed" of that neighborhood. It was not the first time Jessie had undertaken such affairs in the slums, to give pleasure to those upon whom Fortune frowned.

Within an hour three affirmative replies were sent out, and I was invited to contribute a guitar solo and a song. Three professional acquaintances generously consented to lend their services, and a very attractive programme was drawn up and printed for distribution among the audience. Therein it was stated that the entertainment was kindly arranged by Miss Jessie Dixon, that the entrance was free, but that no babies would be admitted, nor children unaccompanied by elders.

A wet night was Saturday, October 24th, 1896, but at eight o'clock Marchmont Hall was packed with a sorry-looking lot of men and women, young and old.

We made our way to a big room back of the hall. A cheerful fire blazed in an open grate, and two large tables occupied the middle of the floor. Here we deposited our wraps, a cornet, and "Carmen." In this room the women of the neighborhood were, on certain evenings, taught, free of charge, how to cut out, and make, garments. Here too, were shelves of books, and all kinds of games, including a box of chessmen, for the recreation of the poor of both sexes.

Our entertainment was a success from its beginning, the performance being good, and the audience appreciative. When I stepped on the platform my heart swelled with sympathy and pity, quickly checked as I desired rather to convey a thought of joy and courage. So with a few cheery words to the people before me I gave them the English meaning of the merry foreign song they were about to hear. The little talk quite won their hearts and, in response to an encore, I sang a second melody; but in the interval two things occurred. First, a young woman looked behind her, moved by curiosity to see which man was so vigorously shouting encore. Her eye was then attracted to a man who stood, supported on crutches, at the further end of the room. Instantly she arose, approached him with

silent swiftness, and after a little persuasion, induced him to go and occupy
the seat she had left. Heaven bless the girl! my heart went out to her!
Life evidently did not handle her gently, but she at least knew the joy of
unselfish impulse.

The second incident was in connection with the "Carmen." At one
instant the light had fallen upon it in such a way that I had clearly distinguished a faint pencil scrawl upon its upper surface; the name "Paquita"
had sprung to my vision. Once having seen this I easily found it again
after retiring from the platform; but I waited till the next day to say to
Jessie:

"You had better change the name of this guitar." "No indeed! Why
should I?" she objected. Thrusting the instrument before her I pointed
out the pencilmarks and boldly asserted: "This must have been the name
of its owner."

Jessie's blue eyes danced, and she at once began to unscrew the pegs.
"What do you intend to do?" I inquired.

"Unstring it and clear the rosette to look inside for other marks. How
nice and romantic this is!"

But no, much twisting and turning of the instrument and of our necks,
under various lights, revealed nothing further. True, we could not see the
inner face of the wall at the broadest part of the guitar, nor did this matter
for, as we sagely observed, no one could write there.

"Emma, lend me your duster," Jessie requested, turning to a maid,
adding "I'll wipe the dust from inside before stringing this up again."

I left the room and was ascending the stairs when arrested by the excla-
mation, "Well, I never!"

Returning, I found Jessie with her right arm out of sight in the guitar,
her face flushed with excitement, and on the sofa by her, lay a fragment of
discolored paper.

"Just think of it!" she ejaculated, "there's something stuck inside down
here; perhaps it's a great secret!"

"Nonsense!" I retorted, "you are always full of imagination! There
is not a line on this scrap."

"Wait!" she expostulated, still more excitedly, and fumbling in the
body of Carmen-Paquita. "There is something soft here. I am tearing off
one thickness that is fastened at its edges, and there is more under it—Ah!
Now what do you say?" she concluded, triumphantly drawing forth two or
three folded sheets of paper covered with faint pencil marks. Thoroughly
interested I seized upon these and found them covered with Spanish writing, indistinct and very faulty.

"What is it?" Jessie impetuously demanded, "Give it to me!"

She held the sheets a moment, turning them round and round, then a blank look overspread her face; as she handed them back to me saying: "I can't read a word!"

I laughed at her discomfiture and wanted to know if she had expected to find an English document in a guitar from Seville. Then I congratulated myself on having lived long enough in Mexico to become very familiar with the Castillian tongue.

"Please read it quickly!" urged Jessie.

"Look here!" I replied, "every one in the house, as well as each caller, will, for the next few days, want to hear the story. You don't expect me to carry around this almost unreadable scrawl and translate it a dozen times a day, do you?" Jessie pouted.

"I'll tell you what," I added, "I'll translate this into good clear English, that each can read for himself."

"But, can't you tell me what is it about?"

"Why yes, these big letters at the beginning say *My Confession*. Now, have patience, and let me go to work."

At the four o'clock tea I read aloud the result of my afternoon's labor, here reproduced.

MY CONFESSION.

Alas for me! In a few days I shall die, alone! and must perish without confession or absolution: This is why I will write what I ought to tell. Some day a pious soul may read it and be moved by holy compassion to order masses for the salvation of my soul. Santa Maria! What will become of me. I was not a wicked lad, and yet I am now a murderer! Yes, this is my dreadful secret, and I am hiding in this miserable hut, this lonely place, beyond the sound of a church bell. How shall I begin? It was on the day of Saint Iago that I first saw Paquita, as I passed the house where she lived —lived! May the Blessed Virgin now hold her in Her arms! for there, too, I killed the light of my soul! But I must tell it all. Paquita was singing and drying her hair in the sun. She thought no one could see her, but when I heard her voice I peeped through a crack in the wall. Her hair was lighter than that of the other girls I knew, and her soft eyes were so large and kind! While I looked an old woman slapped me on the back, saying, "Go away!" I did so, but looked over my shoulder and saw her enter through the great wooden portal.

After that I used to watch for a sight of the girl. I had found out that her name was Paquita, that she lived with her grandmother, and had one brother, absent, in a foreign land.

One Sunday afternoon when I was in the bull ring, for I have always been a toreador, I saw Paquita, her face half hidden by a fan, and wearing white flowers in her hair. Afterward, I waited by the exit she would have to go through, and she passed close by me. I soon found out where she heard the Holy Mass, and went to that church every day, till at last the beautiful girl saw I watched her; then I slipped into her little hand a folded paper on which I had written:

"Be not cruel! Let me see thee—I will enter thy garden and whisper my hope.—Amando Benoits."

Every day I looked, but could find no way to get in; till at last, when I had not 'seen my idol for a long while, the great wooden door stood ajar and I peeped through. The old dame was there, but did not see me, for she was stooping to pluck flowers, and I saw a tear fall from her eye. I pushed the door a little wider open and, as an excuse, took off my hat and begged for a flower. Then, as she did not try to hide her tears I asked if I could serve her.

"No," she responded, "I weep because my granddaughter is ill."

Ah! What a pain shot through me.

"Ill! Paquita!" I cried.

The Señora stared at me. I had betrayed myself.

"Who are you?" she demanded. "Does Paquita know you?"

"I am Amando Benites. Oh, no! Paquita does not know me; but for weeks past my happiest moments have been those when I have watched her."

"Ah! You were the one I caught looking through the wall!" the grandmother exclaimed.

I did not deny this. Hat in hand, I begged, most humbly, to be allowed to inquire, each day, how Paquita was; and finally obtained permission.

Horrible was my anguish until my adored one was said to be recovering; and now a happier time drew near. I did everything to win the heart of the old Señora, and after a while she let me see Paquita now and then, so that, finally, the dear girl promised to be my bride some day; at which I was over-joyed.

Those were blessed evenings when the Señora let me sit at Paquita's feet while we both sang to the accompaniment of her guitar—O yes! the happiest moments of my life! And then, before saying good-night we enjoyed the little cigarettes; and one night my Paquita, absorbed in a bull-fight story I was telling, let her lighted cigarette rest on the guitar that lay in her lap and it scorched a spot in the wood—there it is before me, now.

God have mercy on me! I write so slowly, and I grow weaker—I must at once go on to the dreadful thing that happened. It was a Sunday after-noon, and on my way to the bull-ring, I glanced through the crack in the garden wall, not expecting to see Paquita, but there she was, seated on a bench under the big tree, and by her side sat a man against whose shoulder her head reclined. Jesus-Maria! I reeled, I became blind and deaf, I was suffocating! Presently I looked again, then walked away—to the bullfight.

I do not know anything that happened that afternoon. In the evening I went to Paquita, for I said to myself, "she has a brother, if he has returned home she will tell me and all may be well explained."

Alas for her! Alas for me! No brother did she mention; and then I knew I wanted to kill Paquita. I was mad, mad, as God is my witness, with jealousy that I cunningly concealed—for the silky hair had never rested on my shoulder.

They thought I had gone home, but I went only to the gate, and crept back in the dark, for sometimes Paquita lingered in the garden after the old Señora went in. She did so now, and took up her guitar. Satan was with me, and I glided behind her . . . I cannot tell how my awful crime was accomplished; the dagger did it, and Paquita made no sound. Scarce knowing what I did, I seized the guitar as it slipped from her, and fled—out of the city. All night long I wandered and the first thing I saw at daylight, was a great blood stain on the guitar. I sat down by the highroad and rubbed the stain with earth; then I saw a piece of paper in the guitar. I pulled this out and read:

Dear Little Sister:

. "In a few hours you will have me by your side for a short time, but there are grave reasons why no one should learn that I am in Seville, Therefore, say not a word to anyone except grandmother, and caution her as I caution you.   Your loving brother,
   June 9th, 1842.   Felipe Trufills.

And Sunday was June 11th! Too late! too late! I knew the truth now, but she lay dead and cold, and I was accursed!

This is my confession. I do not know how long ago it happened, nor what I have done since that day, nor where I am. I found this tumble-down shed. I do not want to see anyone. I am glad I had this pencil and paper that I carried to try to write verses for Paquita; I have wax too, and with it will fasten my confession inside her blood-stained guitar. I will wander till I come to some abode, place this at the door and creep away to die—like a dog! May the heart of the Christian who reads this, be moved to pity for a mad wretch, and not grudge a few coins for masses to redeem his soul!   Amando Benites.

There was a moment's silence, then my hearers ejaculated in chorus: "Well!"

"Now Jessie, you know all about the stain and the burn" I observed.

"Yes, and it just shows what horrible deeds may result from judging hastily!" some one remarked.

"How about that poor fellow's request?" asked another.

Opinions were divided.

"Meanwhile," Jessie concluded, "the guitar shall be called Paquita. Now play some jolly tune to banish the doleful tale! I would not be a bit surprised if Amando only wounded Paquita and that she is now a grand-mother!"

THE HOLY CITY.

REV. DR. GEORGE M. STONE.

AT BETHEL.

BY horse from Peter's lake to Jordan plain,
 We met the dawn at Bethel, to behold
Another morn, when rose the Moslem fane
 Where erst Jehovah's temple shone in gold.

 At Jacob's Bethel, sacred trysting-place,
The house of God and gate elysian;
Age-long, footsore, have pilgrims of his race
 Felt high and tearful rapture o'er this vision.

ON OLIVET.

DAYS pass, until at eventide we stand,
 With Olivet beneath our weary feet.
Here once, the center of a little band,
 He gazed on temple, tower and street.

We looked below on brook and garden wall,
 While holy Bethany behind us lay,
And oh, how sad, before us, over all,
 Rose hall and temple site, and Calvary.

FROM JAFFA GATE.

LAST solemn gate of all, from that thronged gate,
 That westward looks toward the classic sea.
O Salem! fadeless glories yet await
 Thy resurrection and thy jubilee!

Though Gentile dust defile the great King's throne,
 Rock founded still is its eternal base,
And his lost tribes, recalled from every zone,
 Shall here behold unveiled the King of grace.

The Discipline of Life.

ENRY DRUMMOND says, "Sooner or later we find out that life is not a holiday but a discipline. Earlier or later we all discover that the world is not a playground. It is quite clear God means it for a school. The moment we forget that the puzzle of life begins. We try to play in school; the master does not mind that so much for its own sake, for He likes to see His children happy, but in our playing we neglect our lessons. We do not see how much there is to learn and we do not care. But our master cares. He has a perfectly overpowering and inexplicable solicitude for our education; and because he loves us He comes into the school sometimes and speaks to us. He may speak very softly and gently or very loudly. Sometimes a look is enough and we understand it, like Peter and go out at once and weep bitterly. Sometimes the voice is like a thunder clap startling a summer night. But one thing we may be sure of—the task He sets us to is never measured by our delinquency. The discipline may seem far less than our desert or even to our eye ten times more. But it is not measured by these; it is measured by God's solicitude for our progress; measured solely by God's love; measured solely that the scholar may be better educated when he arrives at his father's. The discipline of life is a preparation for meeting the Father. When we arrive there to become so pure in heart—and it needs much practice—then we shall see God. That explains life—why God puts man in the crucible and makes him pure by fire."

Oliver Wendell Holmes has told us of the debt of gratitude he owed to the nurse of his childhood who taught him to ignore unpleasant incidents. He says to her teachings is due largely the sunshine of a long life. The lesson is easily learned in early life, but we are never too old to realize that "whatever is, is right" and that whatever comes to us belongs to us, our lives are rounded out by our trials and if we care so to do, we can use circumstances for our spiritual growth as well as for our material comfort.

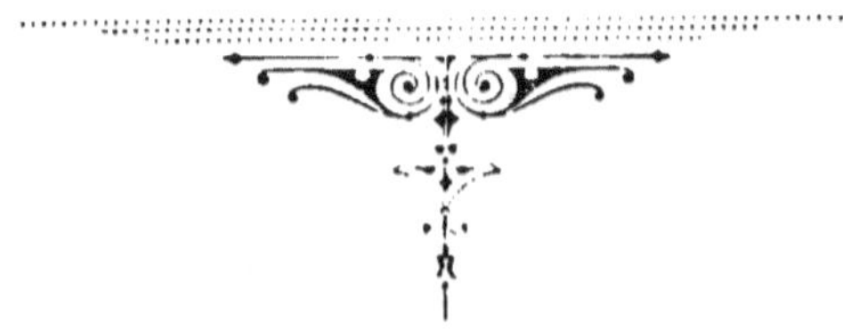

OUR EYES.

ND yet how careless we are about the use of our eyes. Here is an organ whose adjustments are more delicate than those of a chronometer, one that is in constant action from the moment we awake until we close our eyes in sleep. Its demands upon the nervous system for continued healthy action are enormous. It uses up enough nervous energy in a short time to supply us for digging a good many hills of potatoes, or walking several miles; and where there is a defect, either in the focus or the muscular adjustment, this energy is so wasted that strong men have headaches, become irritable, sleepless, dyspeptic; women become nervous, good for nothing, languid, and impatient; and children seem stupid, indifferent, and slow to learn.

It is a mistake to think that the function of seeing is a purely passive one. It is intensely active. It requires an expenditure of nerve force to simply see an object. What is the eye in sleep? Cautiously pull up the lids of a sleeping child, and you will find the eyes turned upward and inward. That is their muscles are relaxed. Now does it not require constant nervous force and muscular action to draw those eyes down and direct them hither and thither?

Perhaps one of the little muscles on the outer side of one of the eyes is weak. The great strong muscle on the inner side next the nose tries to pull the eye inward. The weak muscle exerts its utmost force and pulls against the stronger muscle, and maintains the eye in its proper position, looking straight forward. The eyes therefore look all right; but it is only by a great waste of nervous force that this is done. The child has headache, and does not feel well. Now relieve this strain by glasses, or by an operation, and, behold, a miracle is done! The headache disappears, the child becomes bright and joyous.

Many a time a stupid child is made happy and active by just this proper attention to the eyes. Yes, it requires energy to see. Go to a picture gallery, you whose eyes are strong and normal. Walk around for half an hour, and admire the works of art. By the time you are through you will feel as if you had sawed half a cord of wood, and perhaps you may have a headache, or at least an uncomfortable feeling in the head. What is the matter? Those muscles which lift the eyes are not so strong as those which depress them; and as you looked up and craned your neck to see those particularly fine gems of art that had been "skied" almost out of sight, you simply overworked a certain set of muscles. After such an experience you will be inclined to admit that seeing is not such a passive and easy function as it appears to be.

It is almost a daily experience to see children that have become either partially or totally blind from ignorance or neglect. Ignorance is perhaps responsible for the greatest amount of blindness. Only lately I saw a boy of fifteen years who had only one-third of the normal amount of vision, and he was anxious to study evenings and work in the daytime, for an education. He had a certain amount of astigmatism, which simply means that the eye was not perfectly round in all its diameters, but was flattened in a certain direction. This made all objects partially blurred to his sight. The retina of the eye had received blurred images since he was born, and had become satisfied with this condition so that it could not be made to see all lines perfectly clear. If he had put on glasses at five years of age, or even earlier, his sight might have been saved.

Every child's eyes should be examined before he goes to school for the first time. It is not necessary with improved methods of examination for the child to know a single letter in order to have glasses prescribed. Even after he begins to go to school his eyes should be looked after every two or three years.

Children too often put their noses down into the copy-book, and after a time become near-sighted. Sixty-seven per cent. of all educated Germans have defective eyesight. Our eyes seem to have been intended for long distance seeing; like that of the savage on the plains. Close work at the desk is an artificial condition imposed on the eye. We were intended to till the soil, if one can judge by the shape of the eye. A defective eyesight rules out many occupations, and seriously handicaps a child who is brought up in the midst of our intricate and exacting civilization. The occupations of weaving, jewelry making, designing, bookkeeping, and many others, require healthy eyes. Many a young man undertakes work of this sort and fails because of weak eyes. All this could have been foreseen by an oculist. Hence when about to take up an occupation requiring a close use of the eyes, much may be gained by a careful examination, and a breakdown may be thus warded off.

Much as I respect some opticians I am positive in saying that a child should never be taken to an optician, but to a competent oculist. After middle life it is easier to fit glasses; but even then the optician too often fails to see a cataract beginning, or a nerve or brain disease, or even the evidence of disease in the kidneys. All this and much more can be detected by the expert oculist, and the skill of the family physician can be brought to bear to ward off the fatal termination. An optician spends a few weeks studying refraction and thinks he is competent to adjust glasses. The oculist spends four years in studying the body, and a year or two abroad in the hospitals studying eyes, and it should not require much reasoning to determine who is the amateur and who the expert.

See that the child does not let the sun fall across the book. Never let him face the light while reading. Let it be a rule that the book must be closed at sundown. Reading in the twilight is particularly injurious.

·See that the lamp gives a clear, steady light. Shade it from the eyes, or else put on the lamp a glass shade that is green outside and white inside. Don't let the head be so near the light as to become heated. Stop using the eyes when they ache or when the letters become blurred. Blurring is a pretty certain sign of weak eye- muscles. Look up and off the book every few moments. Don't let the child read much while recovering from any illness. This is exceedingly injurious. Remember that glasses which at first fitted perfectly may need to be changed after fevers or after la grippe. Don't use eye washes unless prescribed for you. Don't fly to colored glasses. Smoked glasses which bulge out like tiny saucers strain the eye unless the child is nearsighted. Don't let the sunlight shine on the face before awaking in the morning. Do not burn a lamp to have a light in the room at night. The retina needs rest and does not want to be bombarded with particles, molecules, or atoms of light day and night.—[*Mt. Airy World.*

SUCCESSFUL BLIND PEOPLE.

F. E. CLEAVELAND.

In this department, which is dedicated to the cause for the advancement of which this periodical is published, we hope to serve a double purpose. We wish first to call the attention of the seeing world to what it is possible for blind persons to accomplish.

Second, to have this knowledge, by means of the thoughtful kindness of our subscribers, reach the sightless everywhere and stimulate them to make the most of their lives.

Every blind man or woman, young or vigorous, with a favorable opportunity may become self-sustaining. The right amount of perseverance will command the opportunity. All who wish to know what is being accomplished to increase the methods by which blind people may become independent are invited to open correspondence with the American Association to Promote the Education and Employment of the Blind, 3124 Fourteenth St. N. W., Washington, D. C., enclosing stamp for reply.

IN our July number, we gave our readers some idea of what wsa accomplished by Elizabeth Gilbert, the blind daughter of the Bishop of Chichester.

The impetus, given by the pioneer work of Miss Gilbert, was not lost. The many persons interested by her in the work of her life, became valuable assistants to those who subsequently took the responsible positions of leaders and advocates of progressive measures.

The history of the progressive work for the blind in England after the death of Miss Gilbert, is so connected with the labors of two men, both blind, one an Englishman, and the other an American, that an account of what these men have wrought, and what has been accomplished by their example and suggestions, will place before the reader the most exact information pertaining to the subject.

Thomas Rhodes Armitage was born at Tillgate, Sussex, in 1824. The greater part of his early education was received in Germany.

He became a medical student in King's College, and afterwards pursued his studies in Paris and Vienna. After completing his studies he returned to England, and began the practice of medicine in London.

His sight, which had never been perfect, soon became so seriously impaired that he retired from his profession, and thence forward devoted himself to the improvement of the condition of the blind.

He organized the Indigent Blind Visiting Society, and established the principles which now govern its action in visiting blind people at their homes, stopping street begging, teaching reading and writing, and assisting them to become self-supporting.

He afterwards founded a pension fund for those no longer able to work, and a Samaritan fund for temporary aid to the deserving. He was founder of the British and Foreign Blind Association, of which we shall have more to say hereafter.

The work of Dr. Armitage however, though of great importance, did not take on the character of a decided uplift and progressive movement, until the arrival on the scene of a blind man from the United States; whose wisdom, foresight, and enthusiasm, backed by an indomitable will and unconquerable perseverance, reminds us of that Genoese, who, baffled in his own country, labored on until his genius obtained recognition in a foreign land, to which and for which, this same genius opened up the treasures of a new world. And what this new world has been to the seeing, the higher, broader, and more exalted plane of life; this Blind Columbus points out and would make possible for those who live in a sunless world.

F. J. Campbell, L. L. D., was born in Franklin County, Tennessee, on October 9th, 1834, and was rendered blind as a child of three and a half years old in 1838 by the sharp thong of an Acacia tree running into his eye while he was playing in a yard. Inflamation set in, and by bad management the doctors allowed it to continue till the sight of both eyes was utterly gone.

The writer has not at hand the biography of Dr. Campbell, but he recalls two incidents which serve to illustrate the character of the boy and the man before he undertook his great work of establishing the Royal Normal College, of which he has been the head for more than a quarter of a century.

When a boy at school, he had a great desire to become a successful musician. He was told however, by the teacher of music in the institution, that he had no ear for music, and that it would be no use for him to attempt to take up that study.

Although he was thus debarred from instruction in music, he never faltered in his purpose. Making use of every opportunity of gaining the information he desired, from the pupils, and practicing clandestinely when he was supposed to be at play, he made such progress that when at length he was discovered, all further opposition was withdrawn, and he was suffered to demonstrate by his subsequent success, the fallacy of the proposition, that none can excel in music, but those who are styled "born musicians"

It was the habit of Dr. Campbell during vacation season, to search out and bring into the school, all blind children entitled to be received. And it was on one of these expeditions to locate the blind child of a mountaineer, the rumor of whose existence had reached him, that Dr. Campbell illustrated the ability of the blind, under certain circumstances to make themselves useful, if not indispensable, to the seeing.

If the reader is familiar with Bulwer Lytton's "Last Days of Pompeii," he will remember a wonderful rescue by blind Nydid, and will see in the following incident, a parallel occurrence in real life.

In ascending the mountain, the party which accompanied young Campbell, was compelled to ford many small streams, and to travel over places which demanded the exercise of considerable caution even on the part of those who could see.

When the party was well up into the mountain, night overtook them, and a hurricane, accompanied by a great downfall of rain, made further progress out of the question.

The danger of the situation made it apparent to all, that the sooner they retraced their steps, the greater would be their chance of safety. The darkness was so intense that all the seeing members of the party were helpless, and young Campbell took command. Tying a rope about his waist, and dealing it out to the other members of the party; he, with staff in hand, safely piloted them down the mountain, across the swollen streams, and out of danger.

At this point, we can do no better than to refer the reader to an article by Cannon Farrar running through November and December numbers of "The Mentor" of 1892, entitled "The Education of the Blind."

This brings us at once to the varied work of the Royal Normal College for the Blind at Norwood; of which I wish to describe the methods and the success.

Let us begin with its strange history. It mainly owes its existence to two men, Dr. Armitage, the friend of the blind, who devoted to it so much of his time, energies, and fortune; and Dr. Campbell, who blind himself, has made it the aim and the poetry of his life, and the daily effort of his undaunted purpose to raise the status of those similarly afflicted with himself. He has so largely succeeded, that though the number of blind children and youths under his charge rarely exceeds one hundred and sixty, the College is a "beacon on a hill," showing the way the blind should be educated, and enabling them at other places to undertake education in a like way.

Continuing his reference to Dr. Campbell, the writer says he was himself a noble specimen of the power of a blind man "to take up arms against a sea of troubles, and by opposing end them." He has been a man

> "Who breaks his birth's invidious bar,
> And grasps the skirts of happy chance,
> And breasts the blows of circumstance,
> And grapples with his evil star;
> And makes by force his merit known."

But, if it was a "happy chance" which marked out his career for him, it was something much more. Chance, after all, is but "God's incognito," "God's unseen providence," which we call by a nickname.

Dr. Campbell had just finished a tour of inspection into the condition of the blind in Germany. His ticket for the return journey to the United States was taken January 23d. On the evening of the 21st he went to a tea-meeting for some hundreds of the blind in London. The meeting decided his fate. The blind guests had a good meal provided for them, seemed happy and contented, and made grateful speeches; but, on moving about among them, he found all this contentment and gratitude were superficial. Almost all of them were charity pensioners. They had come to this meeting, guided by wives or children or friends or, shocking to say, in some instances by dogs. Most of them were charity pensioners, hopelessly degraded by the sense that they were so; and many of them feeling with bitter dissatis-faction, that if a fair chance had been given them, they need not have been thus pauperized. He found, that out of 3,150 blind persons in London, nearly 2,300 depended on charitable relief. Struck and depressed by these facts, he deferred his voyage, sought out Dr. Armitage, and entered into earnest discussion with him about the whole subject of the education of the blind.

He told Dr. Armitage that at the Perkins Institute for the Blind at Boston he had induced Dr. Howe to let him see what could be done in musical training for a class of twenty pupils. These pupils, to the general astonish-ment, he selected not for any musical gifts or attainments, but solely for mental qualifications. Of those twenty pupils, nineteen are now self-sup-porting men and women. With Dr. Armitage he visited all the chief insti-tutions for the blind in London; and, seeing how greatly needed was a total reformation in the training of the blind, he offered to remain a year in Eng-land to organize new methods of instruction. (The one year has become thirty years.) In 1872 the school was opened near the Crystal Palace, with *two* pupils. In 1873 the present beautiful free hold site, on which stood an Italian villa of the late Sir T. Sinclair, was purchased, and, by the noble liberality of the Duke of Westminster, Dr. Armitage and others, has grad-ually been fitted up with a library, a gymnasium, a swimming bath, all kinds of athletic apparatus,—said to be the best in England,—and every requisite for a first-class training. But it must not be supposed that things wore from the first what may be called their present roseate aspect. New efforts are always met by suspicion, keen jealousy, hostile criticism, and angry opposition, which are forgotten and denied when once perseverance has been crowned with success. Those that return in joy, bringing their sheaves with them, have often sown in tears and overwhelming disappoint-ment.

"As late as September, 1871," says Dr. Campbell, "the discouragements were so great, the movement had been practically given up. On a certain Saturday afternoon Dr. Armitage and I had, as we supposed, our last walk in the park. I returned to Richmond, and on Sunday spent several hours in a quiet nook in Kew Gardens. The long meditation did not show even a faint path, and early Monday morning, packing was commenced. During breakfast the morning letters were brought; and the first opened was from William Mather, Esq., Member of Parliament for Groton. It was to this effect: 'Since your visit to Manchester, I have thought much of what you said about the higher education and training of the blind. I wish to do my share, and enclose a check for the purpose. If more help is needed, write to me..' Mr. Mather's letter gave a new inspiration. I immediately returned to London, and the result is well known.

"Let us now walk round the beautiful gardens of the college.

"We shall be surprised at first to see that, though it contains many paths and turnings and, what looks still more fatal, many terraces and flights of steps, yet boys and girls and youth and maidens are enjoying it, walking, running, driving tricycles, using the great swings, rowing boats on the piece of water, and moving about in every direction with the utmost independence. We soon learn the secret of this. There is not a tree on the lawns themselves, or in the adjoining fields, so that there the blind can run about with perfect safety. On the walks, whenever there is a turn or a flight of steps, they are instantly warned of this by a gentle rising in the asphalt pavement. This teaches them at first the exact position of everything, and soon familiarity becomes second habit; and they would find their way safely over every foot of the grounds without this aid.

"They can dash about unhesitatingly and unerringly and so the garden becomes a daily delight and source of health. If it is Summer time, a blind boy or girl will act as *cicerone* to the visitor, and to his astonishment will tell him about the beds of flowers and their colors and their varieties. Visitors who see the children act their Christmas plays, and go on and off the stage as freely as though they enjoyed their sight, are justly amazed. The secret is that *they are warned by the touch of the feet.* The position of every chair and carpet is so arranged as to make them know exactly where they are. Besides this, the recuperative and compensative beneficence of nature gives to the intelligent blind an acuteness of hearing so preternatural, as it seems to us who do not need it, that they can *hear* hedges and even lamp-posts."

Before drawing this article to a close a few words from Dr. Campbell himself will serve to give the reader a better idea of what the American Association to promote the education and employment of the blind, is endeavoring to accomplish. "When the Royal Normal College was established," says Dr. Campbell, "as a practical result, the old pupils of the College during a given year, earned about $80,000.

"The young blind, even a majority of those in early manhood, can be made active and useful members of the community by suitable training; and it is clearly the duty of society to give the blind such educational privileges and business training as will enable them to earn their own support.

"In the public mind, blindness has been so long and closely associated with dependence and pauperism, that schools for the blind, even the most progressive, have been regarded hitherto as asylums rather than educational establishments.

"The fact of being classed among dependents and considered subjects of special charity, is not only a mortification, but a serious disadvantage, it leads to the workhouse. A sad mistake in the training of the blind, is the lack of an earnest effort to improve their social condition. Whenever pupils in institutions are treated and habitually spoken of as poor indigent blind children, a feeling of semi-pauperism is fostered: and when the blind leave such institutions, they become paupers in reality. In most countries, free education has been provided for seeing children; but when instruction is given to the blind, it is still considered a charity. In the United States, free education is regarded as the cornerstone of the republic: the public school system provides a good education alike for rich and poor, the seeing and the blind. But even in America, the schools for the seeing are placed under the management of State Boards of Education; while corresponding schools for the blind, in common with asylums for the imbecile and insane, with workhouses and reformatories, are placed under Boards of State Charities."

In view of recent events we desire to refer with special emphasis to the words of Dr. Campbell which follow:

I rejoice that a more enlightened public opinion is working an important change, and already a few of the States have transferred the management of the schools for the blind from the Board of Charities, to the Board of Education.

Dr. Campbell still lives to battle manfully and valliantly against the popular prejudice and ignorance which adds so much to the burdens of the blind. Dr. Armitage has passed over to the silent majority. During his lifetime he is said to have expended from his private fortune more than $200,000 to improve the condition and chances in life of the blind. May we not hope that the great need of the blind in America, may in a measure be understood by some of its wealthy and philanthropic citizens, and that friends may be raised up, not only willing, but glad to assist in rescuing the hundreds and thousands of blind people in the United States, from wasting their lives in idleness and dependence.

That "Spare Room."

WE all like to feel that our guests, even the chance visitor of a night and a day, enjoy themselves. It gives us a thrill of pleasure to hear, at breakfast, "I've had the most delightful rest," or on departure, "I don't know when I have enjoyed a visit so much." On the contrary, nothing so discourages a hostess as to feel that her guests are tired and cross—a state of affairs hard to conceal utterly by the most honeyed speeches—and glad when the time comes to leave her hospitable roof, even though she has studied their wishes in all possible ways. If she will put herself in their place for one night occupying her own "spare room," she will be pretty sure to receive some light on the whys and wherefores of this unpleasant condition of things.

For it is true that the average guest-chamber is often about the most drearily uncomfortable corner of an otherwise pretty country home. As above suggested, if the mistress doubts this statement, just let her pack her handbag with the things she needs for a one night's visit, desert her own cozy nest and go across the hall to pass twenty-four hours in that cage of gilded misery to which her long-suffering guests are consigned. That's the only way to truly find out what uneasy nights and unsettled days your friends endure for your dear sake in the spare bedroom.

You will learn all about it by lying awake half the night, rising stiff and rather tired in the morning, fuming over your toilet and coming down to breakfast a sadder and a wiser woman. This being the case, it is the duty of every individual who has entertaining to do this summer to dismiss all that rubbishy poetry talked and written about flowers and dainty devices in the guest-chamber and find out first if the bed is a truly downy couch of ease.

Don't make it a habit, when a guest leaves, to have it redressed immediately in clean sheets, ready for the next visitor, who may not come along for a month.

A bed grows chill and dampish and must if left long in the folds, so to speak. The old-fashioned plan of airing fresh sheets and putting them on only the day a guest arrives is the proper rule, for then the bed is somewhere near the temperature of the body. Don't forget to keep, even in summer, an extra pair of blankets in the closet of this room, and always have one pillow hard-stuffed and one quite soft, for you never know just what may be the little notions and vagaries of a friend.

All season through keep your spare-room windows as open to sun and air as your own room, for nothing is more destructive to sleep than the dead atmosphere behind blinds always closed up.

When a friend leaves, order all the water poured out of jugs and tins and don't let the maids fill them until an hour before the new comer is expected, for how often, oh ! how often, has a weary traveler been shut into his or her apartment to battle with water a week old, on top of which floats a heavy coat of dust, also to dry off on dank towels and lay away belongings in drawers and cupboards reeking with the smell of moth-balls !

Also how often have timid individuals been shown into a room where some essential, such as soap or a pitcher of warm water, was lacking, and for want of any means of communicating with a servant been driven to desperate measures !

If your guest chamber does not communicate with a bath-room, then be heedful of abundant dry towels, a perfectly fresh cake of soap, and never forget the pitcher of hot water. Also, strain a point to provide a bell in this room that will communicate with the servants, and let your visitor understand its workings.

Don't fail to provide plenty of rack-room for towels and wash-cloths, sponges and brushes. See carefully to it that, if you have outside green shutters, they are in perfect working order; if you have them not, then show the guest that there are perfectly opaque dark-green shades, which will keep out the morning light. Simply because you can sleep with the sun's glare full in your eyes, don't for mercy's sake think all the world can do the same; and as you are a considerate human being, don't fill up the guest-chamber with flowers.

Few persons sleep with flowers in their bedroom, and sometimes a bowlful of sweet-scented roses will keep a delicate individual wide-awake.

Stop to think a moment, and you will refrain from loading the dressing-table with toilet articles. If silver trifles, they are usually the cast-offs from your own bureau, and of no genuine service to any guest, since women carry about their own precious little instruments with them, and men cordially detest these feminine playthings. Leave the cushion bare, and the shelf of the bureau free for the guest's own pins, brushes, combs, etc., and then try to provide a waste-basket where a woman can throw her combings and a man his shaving-papers.

Provide the room with a stand or table that can be placed by the bed to hold a candle, matches and a pitcher of water, and then take thought beforehand as to the placing of the furniture. Put the bureau where a good light will fall day and night on the individual before the mirror, not on the mirror itself; set the little escritoire in front of a window and furnish one easy chair, at least.

Every guest-room ought to have a lounge, not a divan, at the foot of the bed, and a light coverlet folded at one end of it, an ample shoe-bag on the inside of the closet-door, a few wooden or wire coat-racks in the closet, and thus given the essential of true comfort, the hostess can be sure that her visitors are not eduring more for her sake than true friendship demands.

A very well fitted guest-chamber is always provided nowadays with two single beds, in place of the double couch, a hostess ought never to ask two young women who are not related, or in the habit of sleeping together, or two men, even if they are brothers, to occupy one bed. Health and comfort now demand the separate beds, and a hostess is simply outraging the laws of hospitality if she invites strangers, or even sisters, to her home and condemns them to share one mattress.

When you lure a friend in to stop over a few days try to call to mind all the peculiarities and pander to the little weaknesses as far as possible.

If Miss Jones, for instance, is a timid old maid, be sure to tell her, on retiring how near her room is to those occupied by the family; assure her as to the nature of any probable noises she may hear during the night, and offer to have your own door ajar, to put her room into communication with your daughter's, or the nurse maid's, in order that her faintest alarm may be soothed.

She will call down blessings on your head for this. So also will Bachelor Brown if you keep the children out of the upper hall and from under his windows in the morning, and give him a chance to get his six-o'clock snooze in peace. All these are mere mole-hills of precaution that can grow into mountains of unpleasantness to your guests if you unkindly ignore or stupidly forget them.

Among these hints will be found those which may be wisely adopted by the mistress of a pretty cottage where but one servant, or none at all, is kept, as well as by the hostess in a more pretentious home. Most frequently it is here that the less comfort is to be had, after all.—[*The American Woman.*

Miss Ella on the Farm.

To the Editor: Noticin' in your columns quite recent a paragraph to the followin':

"Miss Ella Witchazel, a charming young school teacher of Villisca, Iowa, finding the close confinement and arduous duties of the schoolroom injuring her health, tried the outdoor cure. Instead of spending her Winter's salary and Summer vacation in a crowded hotel at the seashore, she went on a farm, cut twenty acres of prairie hay, harvested forty acres of wheat, gained twenty pounds in weight, a coat of tan for her hands and face and a rugged health that cannot be equalled anywhere off a farm. There's the girl you are looking for, young man."

Now, what I want to say: I am well acquainted with this young school marm. Fact, as it was my farm she spent the Summer on. Nice girl, Ella is, as ever ran wild in the sun. We was glad, wife an' me, to have her come. I'd often read in the papers 'bout these young women that taught school in the Winter, an' farmed in the Summer, but I never had any experiences of 'em before.

Well, sir, she farmed. First day, nothin'd do but she must drive the hoss-rake. Well, every man and woman that comes from town wants to drive the hoss-rake, an' they call that gittin' in the hay. My little Janey, eleven year old next May, usually drives the rake for us, but she ain't been feelin' overly peart this Summer an' I kinder kept her out of the sun. So Miss Ella gits herself boosted up on the hoss-rake—my boy Joe he boosted her—an' then she screamed an' fell off. Then she got on again, hit the hoss a crack an' away she went on a dead jump out o' the field into the road, hoss a goin', dust a flyin', an' Miss Ella screechin'. Some of the men headed her off an' stopped the horse. Then she tried it again. This time she struck right through the standin' grass, where it was the tallest an' thickest an' tangledest; hoss a balkin' an' tuggin' away by turns, grass holdin' on or comin' up by the roots, rake teeth a snappin'. We got her out of that, an' lost a whole day on the rake gettin' it mended.

Then she tried drivin' a load into the big barn. Had to send to the house for a ladder, an' then all the men had to go clear out of the field while she climbed up on the load. Drivin' in she got the wagon caught in a hedge gap as wide as the Missouri River, run over two stands of bees, upset the load and buried herself under 300 pounds of hay. It was the safest place for her under the excitin' circumstances; so we jest left her ther ontil the bees got cammed down an' we got some work done. Next load she went in on, an' then turned all the men out of the barn while she climbed up into the mow, an' then she wandered around ontil she stepped in a chute and shot out about twenty-eight feet into the cow-barn an' lit right on the back of a Jersey calf that was worth $250 of any man's money an hour before. Miss Ella wan't killed, but she was that jammed up that she lay in bed two days, an' but for that providence we'd hev ben workin' at that hay yet. An' anybody that wants a broken back calf can hev one at his figgers.

Well, come wheat harvest, she must drive the self-binder. That was a little too risky, but she had her own way. But she couldn't be trusted up above the knives, so somebody had to set up there an' hold her on. My boy Joe, held her on—I told Joe she was makin' a fool of him—an' if she didn't make him drive around every poppy an' every blossomin' weed she seen in that field to save it. Never mind the wheat; but save the blamed weeds. There was only one stump on that 320 acres of prairie land, just one stump, an' I hope I may go to seed before Thanksgivin' if that girl didn't run into it an' break the reaper. Lost all the rest of that day a mendin' of it.

And yet, we all liked the girl. But the idea of her farmin'—Why, do you know sir, one day in hayin,' she went to town—took one of my best work horses an' was gone all day, an' came home with 'bout 20 yards of blue and white ribbons, and tied 'em on the men's hats and the rake handles, and wanted us all to wear biled shirts, with the sleeves looped up with blue ribbon, go marchin' out to the hay field, me at the head with the most and longest ribbons, a singin,' "We merry hay-makers, tra, la, la, la, la!" She saw it done that way once in a concert or theater, an' thought that was the way hayin' was always done. An' she was so vexed that she cried when we wouldn't wear 'em. Law, when I put on that hat, ma laid back and laughed till the tears ran down her dear old cheeks. "Job Thistlepod," she said, "if you'll go out an' work in that rig, you'll scare away the grasshoppers." My boy, Joe, he did wear his hat out, but he hid it under the hedge when he got out of sight of the house. I told Joe he was the biggest fool I ever see.

Well, Miss Ella got along fairly well after wheat harvest. Gathered some graceful sprays, she called 'em of poison ivy one day, and couldn't see out of one eye for nigh a week. One day she took a tin pail to go out after berries, and when she went through the cow pasture the cows thought there was salt in the pail and chased her till she was nigh ready to drop. And she went to the barn once an' tried to harness a young Tuckahoe colt that had never had a halter on him, an' how she got out of that stable alive's more'n I can tell. But what I wanted to say is, that's about the way the young woman who farm so graceful in the newspapers usually farm on the farm. But we liked her. An' we hated to see her go. An' she will make a splendid wife for some man, if she can't run a farm, but I don't know about your young men comin' out to look after her, for when she said good-by to me to go back to town, she throwed her arms around my neck an' gin me a kiss that I says to my boy Joe, standin' by the wagon to take her to town, he was always somewhere around, "Joe," I says, "you'd give your share in the farm for that;" an' Joe he didn't seem to care for anything of the kind, ah' Miss Ella, she up an' give me another squeeze an' a kiss, an' I saw her looking over my shoulder at my boy Joe and—haw! haw! haw!—ANON.

FRIENDLY WORDS.

As one who, walking in the twilight gloom,
   Hears round him voices as it darkens,
And, seeing not the forms from which they come,
   Pauses from time to time and turns and hearkens;

So, walking here in twilight, O my friends!
   I hear your voices softed by the distance,
And pause, and turn to listen, as each sends
   His words of friendship, comfort and assistance.
                —*Longfellow.*

JUST BETWEEN OURSELVES.

I am writing this in a quiet little room, under the rafters. The one window gives me a soul-refreshing vista of waving corn against a background of woodland. On the shingles I hear the "blithe down-patter of the summer shower." It is such a place and such a scene as ought to convince one that all the world's at peace.

* * * *

But in this peaceful place I am not at peace. I do not think we quite appreciate the extent to which we are the creatures of conditions. We are not subject to habits more than to states of mind. And just now my own mind is troubled and spent by a work of fiction. I have read the last word and laid the book down. I was glad to see the end, and the closing of the cover was much like the sound of closing a coffin.

* * * *

It was the story of two unhappy marriages:—one man, two wives. Not that he was a bigamist, for he waited for the first wife to grow decently cold before he took unto himself the second. Indeed, Anthony Musgrave was a religious man of the intense type usually referred to as "pious." He was the representative of a certain religious faith of the Calvinistic order, of which the less said the better, since the author portrays him as cold, unloving, and, to the reader's mind, unlovable. Two women, however, loved him; one an eccentric heiress, the other his pretty cousin. Both women are reduced to the humiliating extremity of doing the love-making. Anthony never felt the moving power of the tender passion. When the heiress proposed to him he resolutely declined, but was at last won by the promise of a new chapel in which to preach the caricature of religion that he professed.

* * * *

The heiress had bad blood of the insane order flowing in her veins, but the author had small cause to introduce *that* as the cause of her insanity. Living with such a creature as Anthony Musgrave would make any woman crazy without any hereditary assistance. At any rate, she died in the mad-house. Then the pretty cousin, now middle-aged, came as housekeeper and guardian to the three small children. If we remember aright she came before the death of Number One and thereby created, as might be expected, a distressing scandal in the quiet, orthodox neighborhood.

* * * *

We have read many stories whose plain intent was the conversion of the erring and unrepentant. Here we have a story whose undisguised purpose is the alienation of the reader from the cold, hard, selfish tenets of the Christian religion. And were it true that Anthony Musgrave was a possible type of the kind of man Christianity produced; were it true that Musgrave's home was representative of the kind of home Christian training was capable of producing, we should certainly agree with the author that the sooner the world forsook it the better. The gospel of science, barren as it is, would be an improving substitute. But as a matter of fact the Christian religion never produced any such man as the aforementioned Musgrave. If any such character ever professed the Christian faith, as doubtless some have done, it is a long stretch of logic to make Christianity responsible. The kind of religion portrayed as existing in the Musgrave household has no part or lot in the present century. Christian homes have not been uniformly unhappy, nor has the Christian idea of marriage been uniformly void of successful practice.

*   *   *   *

The truth is, this dismal book (I do not mention its title, for I would not lead anyone to read the unhealthy rubbish) is a creation of the author's brain. So are most "purpose novels," even the good ones.

They postulate something that does not and never did exist, or they caricature a real difficulty that a theoretical solution may be offered and pictured as in successful operation. I do not believe the trend in modern fiction is altogether for the best. The simple love story of other days left something to be desired. It was unreal, sentimental, uninstructive. But it left no bad taste in the mouth. It sometimes caused real tears to flow for imaginary woes, but it did not upset our faith in men and women. Too many of the modern works of fiction do just that. Nor can we believe that they are inspired by any sincere desire to help and encourage the reading public. Rather is it because it is the fad, the thing of the hour. Let us leave all such alone. The world is full of difficulties pressing for solution; we shall add to the list none that exist in no other place than the novelist's fertile brain.

ELLIS WORTH.

SELECTED MATTER.

A Sermon In Rhyme.

If you have a friend worth loving,
  Love him. Yes, and let him know
That you love him, ere life's evening
  Tinge his brow with sunset glow.
Why should good words ne'er be said
Of a friend, till he is dead?

If you hear a song that thrills you
  Sung by any child of song,
Praise it. Do not let the singer
  Wait deserved praises long.
Why should one who thrills your
    heart
Lack the joy you may impart?

If you hear a prayer that moves you
  By its humble, pleading tone,
Join it. Do not let the seeker
  Bow before his God alone.
Why should not your brother share
The strength of "two or three" in
    prayer?

If you see the hot tears falling
  From a brother's weeping eyes,
Stop them, and by kindly sharing
  Own your kinship with the skies.
Why should any one be glad
When a brother's heart is sad?

If a silvery laugh goes rippling
  Through the sunshine on his face,
Share it. 'Tis the wise man's say-
    ing—
  "For both grief and joy a place."
There's health and goodness in the
    mirth
In which an honest laugh has birth.

If your work is made more easy
  By a friendly helping hand,
Say so. Speak out brave and truly,
  Ere the darkness veils the land.
Should a brother workman dear
Falter for a word of cheer?

Scatter thus your seeds of kindness,
  All enriching as you go;
Leave them. Trust the Harvest Giver.
  He will make each seed to grow.
So, until its happy end,
Your life shall never lack a friend.

———————

CLIFTON M. NICHOLS the life-
long friend of the poet Coates
Kinney, tells in the Woman's Home
Companion how the well-known song-
poem "Rain on the Roof" came to
be written. "Whoever has known
the luxury of being lulled to sleep
by the drowsy rhythm of raindrops
pelting upon a cottage or attic roof
has wished that he could translate
into words the rain's dream-song.
Such a longing for expression of
these thought-fancies came to one
Coates Kinney, a young lawyer in
Ohio, forty-eight years ago, after a
pleasant June rain had cast a spell
over him. Acting upon the inspiration of the passing shower he wrote
the little song-poem "Rain on the
Roof," which has passed perma-
nently into literature as one of our
choicest classics of lyric verse. Printed in a country newspaper, and subsequently in the school readers, it
at once sprang into universal favor,
principally with schoolchildren, who
loved to recite it and soon knew it

by heart. Afterward, when set to music, like Dr. Smith's immortal hymn, 'America,' it literally sang itself into the hearts of all the classes, being especially appreciated by those reared in village and farm homes, where all know the soothing music of the patter of the rain on the roof."

———— ♦ ————

THE largest sum ever given for a single pearl was $550,000, which was the price paid for the great Tavernier pearl. It was originally owned at Catifa, in Arabia, and M. Tavernier made the trip from Paris, France, to the desert city of Arabia for the express purpose of purchasing the pearl about which so much had been said and written. He went prepared to pay any price, from $5000 to $500,-000. It was thought that he might succeed in closing the bargain for about $125,000, but this proved to be a great mistake. The sum first offered was $50,000, but the deal remained open for some days even after that offer had been increased to $375,000. Finally, the bargain was closed for $350,000. Pearl connoisseurs declare that it is not only the largest, but also the most perfect gem of its kind known, being exactly two inches in length, oval, and of spotless lustre. Among the Crown jewels of England there is a pearl over an inch long, and egg shaped, which cost the government not less than $500,000.

———— ♦ ————

AMONG the notable incidents of the recent commencement season was the action of President Raymond, of the Wesleyan University, at Middletown, Conn. In an address to the students he announced that all applicants for tuition scholarships must sign the following pledge: "On consideration of receiving aid from Wesleyan University in payment of part or all of the charge for tuition in 1899 and 1900, I hereby promise, so long as I hold a tuition scholarship, not to visit a saloon nor to indulge in the use of intoxicating liquors." President Raymond said he would not go around to the various Methodist conferences begging money for students to spend in the saloons of Middletown. This will affect quite a number of the applicants, as over two-thirds of the students receive the whole or part of their tuition gratis.

———— ♦ ————

BRET HARTE'S first poetic effort began this way,

"I sipped the nectar of her lips; I sipped and hovered o'er her,"

and ended thus,

"Her father's hoof flashed on the scene— I'm wiser now, and sorer."

Will Carleton's first attempt at rhyme was a letter to his sister. Of it he says, "I represented her favorite horse as about to die of melancholy, because she was not there to ride him; told her the trees and flowers were all perishing because she was not present to smile upon them, and killed off two very worthy and healthy neighbors because their names happened to rhyme with some word of a mortuary character. The whole letter was wildly sepulchral in its nature and closed with,

I now must end my letter
  And bring it to a close,
Perhaps it will be better
  To make the next in prose."

———— ♦ ————

"BLIND ALEX," who lived in Stirling, Scotland, from 1830 to 1840 had the most wonderful memory of which any account has ever been recorded. He was familiarly known as "Complete Concordance," on account of the fact that he knew the entire Old and New Testaments "by heart,"

He was tested a half dozen or more different times before the "Scottish Society of Advanced Learning," and always succeeded in convincing the professors that he was all that had been claimed for him. If any sentence in the entire Bible was repeated to him he would instantly name chapter and verse, or if the book, chapter and verse were named he could give the exact word of the quotation.

THE lightest known solid is said to be the pith of the sunflower, with a specific gravity of .028, or about one-eighth that of cork. The sunflower is extensively cultivated in central Russia, and various uses are served by its different parts, the recent discovery of the lightness of the pith essentially increasing the commercial value of the plant. For life-saving appliances at sea, cork has a buoyancy of one to five, while with the sunflower pith one to thirty-five is attained. About eight hundred cubic inches of it would weigh as much as one cubic inch of iridium, the heaviest metal.

THE first attempt to manufacture watches or clocks on a large scale in America was made by Eli Terry, a Connecticut Yankee, who invented wooden wheels for clocks in 1792. In 1837 Chauncy Jerome, of Massachusetts, first applied machinery to the making of metal-wheeled clocks, and, as a result, drove the wooden-wheeled clocks out of the market. The manufacture of watches by machinery, which has since become such an important business, was begun at Roxbury, Mass., in 1850, and was continued there until 1854, when the works were removed to Waltham.

COLORADO Springs has been having a tunnel bored through a spur of Pike's Peak, to furnish a larger supply of water for the city's use. The length of the tunnel is over six thousand feet, and work on it is being prosecuted from both ends. The other day a very rich vein gold bearing rock was cut about 2100 feet from the western end.

A WOMAN'S university is to be established at Moscow through the generosity of a wealthy Russian engineer, who recently gave $500,000 toward the foundation of the institution. The university is to comprise a mathematical, a scientific and a medical faculty. The municipal council of Moscow has voted it an annual grant of $1,300.

IN the village of Withersfield, near Newmarket, England, there are two blind men, named George and William Fairbank, who act as letter-carriers. The letters are put into their hands, and they are told whom they are for, and there is seldom, if ever, a case of wrong delivery.

THE American people ought to be supremely happy. The civilizing and Christianizing influences of 400 new saloons in the Philippines and 2,000 in Cuba are among the things accomplished at the point of the humane bayonet!

THE stinging annoyances of life are not much to be feared, nor the hiss of ridicule, the snarl of detraction, even the wolf of poverty; not these who are to be feared, but the serpent we carry with us--the secret sin.

MISS ALCOTT'S books are still in good demand if, as is reported, they produced $12,000 last year in royalties.

CHILDREN'S DEPARTMENT.

The Little Boy's Lament.

A. T. WORDEN.

I'm goin' back down
to gran'pa's.
I won't come back
no more
To hear re-
marks a-
bout my
feet
A-muddyin' up the floor.
They's too much said about my
clothes
The scoldin's never done—
I'm goin' back down to gran'pa's,
Where a boy kin hev some fun.

I dug up half his garden
A-gittin' worms fer bait;
He said he used to like it
When I laid abed so late;
He said that pie was good fer boys,
An' candy made 'em grow.
Ef I cain't go to gran'pa's
I'll turn pirate, fust, you know.

He let me take his shot-gun,
An' loaded it fer me.
The cats they hid out in the barn,
The hens flew up a tree;
I had a circus in the yard
With twenty other boys—
I'm goin' back down to gran'pa's,
Where they ain't afraid of noise.

He didn't make me comb my hair
But once or twice a week;
He wasn't watchin' out fer words
I didn't orter to speak;

He told me stories 'bout the war,
An' Injuns shot out West.
Oh, I'm going down to gran'pa's,
Fer he knows wot boys like best.

He even run a race with me,
But had to stop an' cough;
He rode my bicycle an' laught
Bec'us' he tumbled off;
He knew the early apple trees
Around within a mile,
Oh, gran'pa was a dandy,
An' was "in it" all the while.

I bet you gran'pa lonesome,
I don't care what you say;
I seen him kinder cryin'
When you took me away.
When you talk to me of heaven,
Where all the good folks go,
I guess I'll go to gran'pa's,
An' we'll have good times, I know.
—*Judge.*

HOW LITTLE GRANDMOTHER'S SHOES WERE MADE.

"**B**UT grandmamma," said little May, holding up the tiny pair of calfskins, "were these your very bestest shoes? Didn't you have any shiny black ones, with a tassel on, like mine?

"And where did you buy them, Grandmamma? Did Columbus bring them with him, in his ship?"

"What notions the child does get," laughed grandmamma. "She hears so much about Columbus nowadays, that she thinks he did everything.

"No, dearie; Columbus didn't bring grandmamma's shoes over. He sailed away to England again, many hundreds of years before these little shoes were made.

"Bring your chair and sit down by me and I will tell you all about these little worn-out shoes of mine.

"When I was a little girl," began grandmamma, "people did not wear shoes all the time. They went barefoot in summer, except when they were dressed up. One pair of shoes was expected to last a whole year. When we went to church, we used to go barefoot, carrying our shoes in our hands till we reached the brook at the foot of the hill. Then we washed our feet and put on our shoes. So they did not wear out very fast; and if one of the children lost his shoes, as you did the other day, he had to go barefoot till the shoe man came again."

"Oh, dear!" sighed May, "how dreadful! But who was the shoe man, grandmamma, and when did he come? Tell me all about it, please."

"The shoe man," grandmamma said, "was a very important man in our time; and shoe week was a great week for the children.

"Every family kept an old shoe bench; and I can remember just what a stir there was all over the house when my father came in and said, 'Wife, Jabez Brown will be here to-morrow.'

"The shoe bench was brought down from the attic to a warm corner of the kitchen, the favorite lasts were brought out, and we children talked about the new shoes till we fell asleep.

" Early in the morning the old man would appear, trudging up the road with his bag of tools, lasts and leather on his back; and by nine o'clock he was seated on his bench hard at work.

"We children used to sit on the floor beside him, watching him as he measured and cut out the shoe, just as mamma does a dress.

"After the shoe was cut, the shoe man carefully fitted it on the last. Each of us children had a last of our own, just as you have patterns for your dollie's clothes. And just as mamma has patterns when she cuts out your dresses. Then the shoe man punched holes with his sharp awl, all along the edges of the little leather, and the shoe was ready to sew.

"For his sewing, he used a waxed end. A waxed end is a long linen thread with pig's bristles fastened in at each end for needles. And all day long the shoe man would sit there, thrusting the two needles into the holes, as you would lace a shoe, and drawing them out with a jerk, till the shoe was sewed so firmly that the stitches lasted till the leather wore out.

"When the shoes were finished, he packed his bag and said good-by for another year."

"How nice it must have been, grandmamma," said little May.—*Selected*.

THE STORY OF DISCONTENTED HANS.

FRANCES BENNETT CALLOWAY.

THIS is the story of discontented Hans. His room was too small, his bed was too hard, his porridge too salt. He found fault with his mother because she called him so early in the morning, and with his shoes because they were clumsy, and with his work because it was always hard. He was always unhappy.

"What do you want?" asked the Spirit of the Field, meeting him at his work one day. Hans knew it was the Spirit of the Field by the rustle of her light garments over the clover leaves and the touch of her perfumed gossamer veil in his face. "What do you want?" repeated the Spirit of the Field.

"Oh, I want everything!" cried Hans impetuously.

"If you could only find the little blue flower," said the Spirit of the Field, "you would have love, riches, happiness, everything," and she passed on her way.

Hans left his tools in the field that day and started out in search of this wonderful blue flower which was to give him love, riches, happiness, everything. He traveled over mountains and valleys, past woods and streams; he searched through the little villages on the way, and hunted over deserts and in great cities. He was often cold and tired and hungry; his heart ached with loneliness, and many a night he had no roof to shelter him but the stars, no blanket to dream under but the low-hanging clouds; and the little blue flower was nowhere to be found.

After a long, weary while, when he had traveled clear round the world, he came back in sight of his own little cottage. His mother opened the door.

"Hans, my dear child!" she cried, with tears of gladness in her eyes. Then Hans was in her arms.

"Where is the little blue flower?" the mother asked, when she could speak for crying. "Have you found it yet?"

"Yes, mother," answered Hans, also in tears, "I have found it in your eyes."

———— ✦ ————

A LITTLE Boston girl, out walking with her nurse on the occasion of President McKinley's visit to that city, happened to espy that gentleman as he went in to the breakfast of the Algonquin Club. Turning to the nurse, our small friend exclaimed with great satisfaction; "Well, I'm thankful I can tell my great-grandchildren I've seen George Washington."

———— ✦ ————

THE committee-man of a western town visited the village school, one day, and was invited by the teacher to ask the scholars some questions. "I'll try 'em on spellin'," said he. "John, spell egg-wiped!" John, astonished, after an instant's hesitation, gave it up; so did everybody else, and the pretty teacher found it hard work to keep the class in order when, the committee-man triumphantly spelled the word out himself: "E-g-y-p-t!"

Summer.   Winter.   Sunshine.   Shadow.

WISE AND OTHERWISE.

"Tommy, who was Joan of Arc?" asked the teacher. "Noah's wife," was Tommy's guess.

———

At every picnic every guest secretly believes that every other guest didn't bring her share.

———

"Name the four seasons, Nellie," said the teacher one day. "Pepper, salt, mustard and vinegar," answered Nellie, promptly.

———

"Now, you must learn to observe little things and remember what you see every day. Who can tell me how may feathers a hen has?"

———

Wife—"Why are you so angry at the doctor?" Loquacious Man—"When I told him I had a terribly tired feeling, he told me to show him my tongue."

———

"I never heard of but one perfect boy," said Johnny, pensively, as he sat in the corner doing penance. "And who was that?" asked mamma. "Papa—when he was little," was the answer; and silence reigned for the space of five minutes.

———

Mrs. Julia Ward Howe was talking with a dilapidated bachelor, who retained little but his conceit. He said: "It is time now for me to settle down as a married man, but I want so much. I want youth, health, wealth,—of course,—beauty, grace." "Yes," she said sympathetically, "you poor man: you do want them all."

———

"Your husband doesn't smoke, Mrs. Price?" "No; but he sometimes fumes."

———

Tommy—"Mamma, why have you got papa's hair in a locket?" To remind me that he once had some, Tommy."

———

"Oh, mamma," cried a little girl, "there isn't any school to-morrow, because Miss A. is going to the *teachers' convulsions.*"

———

"The Thompsons can't decide what to name their twins." "Well if the twins resemble their other children, they should call one Vesuvius and the other Etna."

———

A little Rochester girl drew a dog and cat on her slate, and said to her mother, "A cat ought'n't to have but four legs; but I drew her with six, so she could run away from the dog."

———

The following epitaph is in Lanesboro, S. C.: "Here lies Jane Smith, wife of Thomas Smith, marble-cutter. This monument was erected by her husband as a tribute to her memory and a specimen of his work. Monuments in this same style, $250."

———

Miss Smithers to Adolphus—"What do you think of this cutting up of cats to serve the purposes of science?" Adolphus—"I can't say that I approve of it. We have had some experience in our back yard, and I cannot say that I approve of cats cutting up for any purpose."

Talks . . .

. . . . . . and . . . . . .

. . . Tales

$1,00 per year in advance.

Every subscription helps furnish employment for the Blind, as the work is largely done by them.

The Columbia Bevel-Gear Chainless.

is pre-eminently the wheel for women. The picture shows its manifest advantages. Nothing to catch or soil the skirt; no unsightly chain guard to work loose and rattle; no sprokets to entangle guard la ings. There is no good reason why a woman as well as a man should not have a bicycle of the highest efficiency — no good reason why most women should not have a Columbia Chainless when we sell Model 51 for $60 and Model 60 for $75.

CHAIN WHEELS: Columbias, Hartfords and Vedettes, $25 to $60.

POPE MFG. Co., Hartford, Conn.

Cures while you sleep

Whooping Cough,

Croup, Colds, Coughs,

Asthma, Catarrh,

Bronchitis and Hay Fever

Hundreds of thousands of mothers use Vapo-Cresolene. Do you? CRESOLENE cures WHOOPING COUGH every time; stops CROUP almost immediately, and if used at once will cure a COLD before any complications can arise. I. N. Love, M. D., of St. Louis, says: "I have instructed every family under my direction to secure it." Mrs. Ballington Booth, says: "I recommend that no family where there are young children should be without it." W. R. Chichester, M. D. of New York says: "As a vehicle for disinfecting purposes CRESOLENE is immediately successful." Anthony Comstock, says: "MALIGNANT DIPHTHERIA in my house; Cresolene used; cases recovered in two weeks; no others were affected."

Descriptive booklet with testimonials free. Sold by all druggists.

VAPO-CRESOLENE CO., 69 Wall St., New York.

Schieffelin & Co. New York, U. S. Agents.

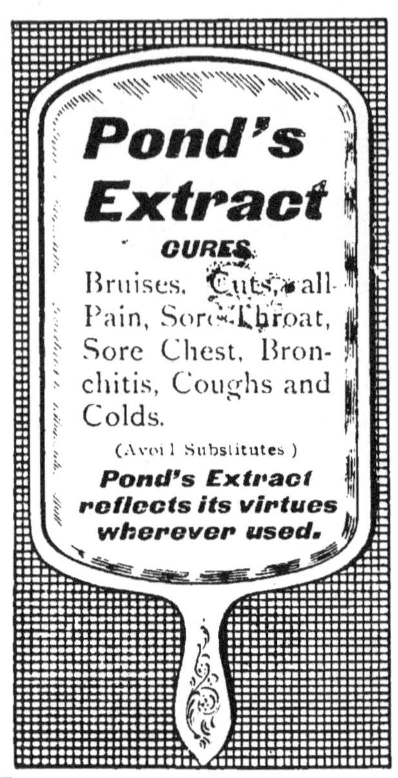

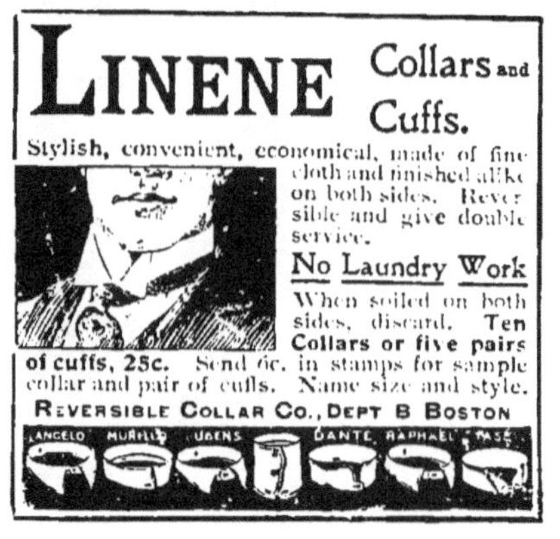

SUMMER HOMES

IN the Southern Berkshire and Litchfield Hills,
along the Central New England Railway.

If you are going to the country don't fail to
procure our handsomely illustrated guide-
book of 240 pages, free at Jacobs' ticket office,
815 Main St., Gridley's ticket office, 18 State
St., or will be mailed upon receipt of 7 cents
postage to W. J. MARTIN, General Passenger
Agent, Hartford, Conn.